SINGAPORE SAPPHIRE

SINGAPORE
SAPPHIRE

* *A Harriet Gordon Mystery* *

A. M. STUART

BERKLEY PRIME CRIME
New York

BERKLEY PRIME CRIME
Published by Berkley
An imprint of Penguin Random House LLC
1745 Broadway, New York, NY 10019

Library of Congress Cataloging-in-Publication Data

[CIP DATA TK]

First Edition: August 2019

Printed in the United States of America
1   3   5   7   9   10   8   6   4   2

Cover art by [TK]
Cover design by [TK]
Book design by [TK]

*To my husband, David, who took me to Singapore
and gave me the space and encouragement to pursue this
mad dream of writing.*

Glossary of Malay Words

Atap: Roof
Bukit: Hill
Dhobi: Laundryman
Gharry: A horse-drawn carriage available for hire
Godown: Warehouse
Hantu: Ghost
Jambatan: Bridge
Kampong: Village
Ricksha: Rickshaw
Sungei: River
Tuan: Sir
Ulu: Unkempt foliage/jungle
Wallah: A person with a particular duty, e.g., *ricksha wallah*—a
man who pulls rickshaws; *dhobi wallah*—a laundryman

Other Words

Amah: A female house servant or nursemaid
Ducks: The white twill tropical uniform of the colonial civil
service
Kapok: A fluffy cotton seed of the kapok tree. Often used to stuff
bedding.

Pith helmet: A lightweight cloth-covered helmet made of pith material (sola topee is a variation)

Sam Browne: A wide belt, usually leather, supported by a narrower strap passing diagonally over the right shoulder

Samfu: A light suit consisting of a plain high-necked jacket and loose trousers, worn by women from China

Walletjes: The red-light district of Amsterdam

CHARACTER LIST

ST. THOMAS CHURCH OF ENGLAND PREPARATORY SCHOOL FOR ENGLISH BOYS

Reverend Julian Edwards: Headmaster. Older brother of Harriet. Unmarried. Passionate about cricket.

George Pearson: Senior master and deputy headmaster.

Ethel Pearson: Wife of George. House mother and matron to the boarders.

Michael Derby: Junior master.

William Lawson: A pupil.

John Lawson: William's father. A rubber planter.

ST. THOMAS HOUSE (THE HEADMASTER'S RESIDENCE)

Harriet Gordon: Widow. Shorthand typist and unpaid assistant at her brother's school. Former suffragette.

Huo Jin: Housekeeper at St. Thomas House. Chinese opera singer.

Lokman: Cook at St. Thomas House.

Aziz: Odd-job boy. Orphan.

STRAITS SETTLEMENTS POLICE FORCE

Inspector General of Police W. A. "Tim" Cuscaden: (Not fictional)
1853–1936. Retired from Straits Settlements Police in 1913.
Introduced innovative policing methods such as fingerprinting.
Has a road in Singapore named for him.

DETECTIVE BRANCH

Inspector Robert Curran: Straits Settlements Police Force
Detective Branch. Former military policeman. Grandson of the
Earl of Alcester. Black sheep of that particular family. Opening
batsman for Singapore Cricket Club.
Sergeant Gursharan Singh: Third generation Sikh policeman.
Curran's right-hand man.
Constable Earnest Greaves: Branch "wonder boy." Newly arrived
from London.
Constable Tan Jian Ju: Excellent undercover detective and lover of
motor vehicles.

FRIENDS AND ACQUAINTANCES

Khoo Li An: Curran's live-in lover. Scarred woman of mystery.
Dr. Euan Mackenzie: Chief surgeon at the Singapore General
Hospital and part-time police surgeon. Old friend of Harriet's
late husband, James Gordon.
Louisa Mackenzie: Wife of Euan. Harriet's best friend.
Griff Maddocks: A gentleman of the press and friend of Harriet's.

THE HOTEL VAN WIJK

Henrik Van Gelder: Hotel manager.
Mrs. Van Gelder: His wife.
Stefan Paar: A clerk.

Hans Visscher: A clerk.
Nils Cornilissen: A guest. Dealer in Asian antiquities.
Gertrude Cornilissen: Nils's wife.

THE EXPLORERS AND GEOGRAPHERS CLUB

Sir Oswald Newbold: President, explorer of northern Burma and
crashing bore.
James Carruthers: Secretary. A paid functionary
Colonel Augustus Foster: A member. Keen on cricket and motor
vehicles.

ANIMALS

Leopold: Curran's horse.
Shashti: Harriet's kitten.
Mr. Carrots: The school's trap pony.

❦ Prologue

Singapore
Friday, 4 March 1910

> *Shorthand and Typewriting. An Englishwoman undertakes casual work as a stenographer and typist. From Monday to Friday after 5:30 P.M. daily. On Saturday after 2 P.M. She guarantees rapid and careful work together with ABSOLUTE SECRECY. Address Mrs. Gordon, Tanglin Post Office 35.*

Sir Oswald Newbold picked up his pencil and circled the small advertisement on the second page of the *Straits Times*, folded the paper and set it down beside his place mat. He crossed one leg over the other and, picking up his teacup, he surveyed his garden.

The early-morning mist rose out of a jungle beyond the boundary of this barely tamed corner of Singapore. The thick, humid air seemed alive with the *boobook* call of the native birds and the screech of macaque monkeys.

The smell of the hearty English breakfast of bacon and eggs that Nyan set before him seemed curiously at odds with the tropical surroundings.

As he ate, Sir Oswald's eyes strayed once more to the *Straits Times*. He set down his fork and dabbed the egg yolk from his moustache.

Folding his napkin, he pushed back his chair and stood up.

"Nyan, I have a letter to write. Be ready to take it into town for me later this morning."

✵ ONE

The day had not begun well for Harriet Gordon. A domestic upset in the kitchen had to be smoothed over before she even arrived at the school to find the unreliable typewriter on her desk refused to work. The decision to retrieve her own little typewriter from the home of Sir Oswald Newbold, had been where it all began.

As the pony trap turned off Bukit Timah Road into the long drive that wound its way through the abandoned rubber trees and thickets of jungle up to Sir Oswald Newbold's home, the hairs on the back of her neck began to prickle.

Not a monkey, a bird or an insect could be heard in the *ulu* that surrounded the house, and a hush, as thick and impenetrable as the humidity of the late morning, settled around Harriet.

The pony flattened his ears and slowed his jaunty pace, as the low silhouette of the old plantation house came into view. Aziz clucked his tongue encouragingly but Mr. Carrots came to a standstill, his ears pressed against his lowered head. The boy shifted in his seat, his gaze darting around the overgrown garden.

"Sorry, mem. We go no further and I think we should not stay. They call this place Bukit Hantu. It is a bad place.'

"Bukit Hantu? What does that mean?" Harriet asked.

Her client had told her that he had named the property *Mandalay*, in memory of his long connection with Burma.

Aziz shook his head. "There are evil spirits here."

Harriet smiled at the boy. "There are no such things as evil spirits, Aziz. You stay here with Carrots and I'll just pop in and collect the typewriter."

Aziz jumped from the trap and helped Harriet down.

She narrowly avoided a puddle, remnant of the morning rainstorms. Lifting her skirts to avoid the cloying red mud, she strode the last fifty yards to the steps of the old house. On her first visit to Mandalay, it had not seemed quite so run-down but now she could see the wood on the verandah supports were rotten and in need of painting, green mildew stained the stone steps and a single shutter somewhere around the side of the house flapped and banged, even though there seemed to be no wind.

And again, the silence . . . no sound of servants chattering, no clanging of pots from the kitchen. Nothing.

Her unease intensified as she set her foot on the lower step leading up the verandah.

Glancing back, she forced a smile and waved at Aziz. The boy stood in the shade of a massive rain tree, holding Mr. Carrots's bridle. As she watched, the pony shook his head, almost sending the slender boy flying. The animal started to back away and it took all Aziz's strength to hold him. Neither boy nor animal wanted to be here, and her unease began to grow.

Bukit Hantu? Harriet's knowledge of Malay was still rudimentary. She knew *bukit* meant "hill," but *hantu?* She would ask Julian when she got home.

The wooden boards on the verandah creaked as she approached the door. Her client would not be expecting her until later in the day, but she needed the typewriter she had left with him. She knocked loudly on the frosted-glass panel and stood back, expecting Sir Oswald's elderly Burmese servant to answer the door as he had done the previous day. The seconds ticked past without any movement from within the house.

She tried the door handle and found the door unlocked. Given the valuables she had seen in the house, she considered Sir Oswald's security a little lax.

"Hello," she called, her voice vanishing into the dark bowels of the house. "Sir Oswald? Are you at home?"

"Damn it," she swore under her breath. She needed the typewriter.

If no one was at home perhaps she could retrieve her property and be gone, leaving a note of apology for her intrusion.

Remembering the name of Sir Oswald's servant, she called out again.

"Nyan? Sir Oswald?"

Only an echoing silence reverberated through the house to the open back door visible from where she stood.

Just collect the typewriter and go. You can leave a note . . .

She stepped over the threshold and as her eyes adjusted to the gloom, she caught her breath. The main living room bore no resemblance to the cluttered room she had admired the day before. Then every space had been filled with oriental rugs, antique furniture and Asian art. This morning nothing remained in place. Furniture had been overturned, cushions torn apart and valuable porcelain lay shattered on the rugs.

A sensible woman would have turned on her heel.

She glanced at the study door. It stood ajar and, drawn by an invisible force, she approached it, her breath held tightly in her throat. Something under her foot crunched and she started, taking a step back. The splintered remains of two port glasses lay scattered across the floor, along with a small silver tray and a broken decanter. Her nose twitched as she caught the scent of the port and something else, sweet and sickly, at odds with the pervading odor of damp and dust.

She skirted the broken port glasses and put her hand out to push the door open, but recoiled at the sight of dark smears on the chipped white paint.

With a single extended finger, she pushed the study door. It opened on protesting hinges and she peered around it, her gaze seeking the familiar solidity of the sturdy black case of the Corona typewriter. It sat where she had left it, on the round table in the center of the room, but as her peripheral vision widened she let out her breath in a gasp.

Every book had been swept from the shelves, papers scattered across the floor, interspersed with copious amounts of broken china, and in the middle of the carnage, between the table and the big desk, Sir Oswald Newbold lay spread-eagled.

Years of assisting her husband's medical practice and his work in the worst slums of India had enured her to death in its many forms but nothing could have prepared her for the sight of the bloodstained corpse lying on the expensive oriental carpet. He stared up at the ceiling with sightless eyes, his face fixed in a grimace of horror, echoed only by the hideous grin of the devilish imp carved on the handle of the antique knife, the *dha* Sir Oswald had called it when he had shown it to her the previous day, that had been thrust into his neck.

The scream stuck in Harriet's throat.

❧ TWO

R unnels of sweat trickled down the back of Inspector Robert
Curran's neck, softening the stiff, starched collar of his uniform. He took off his helmet and wiped his forehead with a
handkerchief, before turning his attention to the old colonial
plantation house. Time and the elements had not been kind to
the once-proud structure that bore a crudely painted sign above
the steps leading up to the veranda. MANDALAY. A name that
conjured up the romance and mystique of Burma, not this neglected building.

Dark-green moss stretched over the weathered timber like the
grasping fingers of the jungle eager to reclaim the building back
into the forest. Several windows were missing shutters and on
others they swung crookedly on rusty hinges. Even from where
he stood he could see the verandah floor had warped from the
constant humidity.

A pony trap, guarded by a young Malay boy, stood in the shade
of a rain tree some distance from the house. Avoiding a large puddle in the rutted driveway, remnant of the morning rainstorms,
Curran approached the boy. The lad bobbed his head, his hand
stroking the nose of the skewbald pony, whose ears twitched un-
happily as a large drop of moisture landed squarely on the white
patch between his eyes.

In his fluent Malay, Curran asked the boy his name.

"Aziz, *tuan*," the boy replied. His gaze darted to the verandah. "I told the mem this was a bad place. Bukit Hantu is a place of bad spirits. Can I take the mem and go home?"

"Not just yet." Curran gave the boy a reassuring smile. "I need to speak to the mem. You just wait here."

He turned toward the house, pacing the distance in easy strides. What had the boy called the place? Bukit Hantu? The haunted hill.

He made a mental note to ask one of the Malay constables how the place had acquired that name. The name on his notes just said *Newbold—Mandalay*.

He approached the steps leading up to the verandah. Beyond the wide expanse of warped and broken boards, the front door stood open but the bulk of his sergeant, Gursharan Singh, loomed out of the gloom, obscuring any view into the house.

"Who found the body?" he asked Singh.

"She did, sir." His sergeant indicated a European woman who sat bolt upright in a rattan armchair on the verandah, her hands clutching a leather handbag. A fall of pink bougainvillea that climbed across the verandah and threatened to engulf the house had hidden her from sight.

The woman looked up at him from beneath a sensible pith helmet swathed in a net and he had an impression of a youngish woman, with brown hair, coiled, as was the fashion, at the nape of her neck. She wore a plain white, high-necked blouse fastened with a brooch at her throat and a skirt of an indeterminate dark color. A thoroughly respectable woman who seemed at odds with the decayed house.

Beneath a complexion far too unfashionably browned to have ever graced his aunt's drawing room, she looked gray and drawn. Although he was yet to view the corpse, Curran knew it would be no sight for the fainthearted. It surprised him the woman had not succumbed to the vapors. Instead she sat waiting for him, pale but perfectly composed.

"What's her name?"

"Gordon. Mrs. Harriet Gordon," Singh said. He leaned toward his superior officer. Curran topped six feet, but Singh had several inches on him.

"You should know, sir. There's not just one body. We found a servant dead in the kitchen."

Curran's lips tightened and he issued curt orders to Singh before crossing the verandah to address Mrs. Gordon.

"Inspector Curran, Detective Branch," he said, holding out his hand. "You are Mrs. Gordon?"

The woman rose to her feet to shake his hand.

"Mrs. Gordon."

"What brought you out here today, Mrs. Gordon?"

She raised her chin, her shoulders straightening. "I did some secretarial work for Sir Oswald yesterday and I came to retrieve my typewriter." Beneath the tight white collar of her blouse, her throat worked as she swallowed, and with a trembling hand she pushed a damp tendril of brown hair back behind her ear. "You don't suppose I could have it back? I need it for work at the school."

"Perhaps later. Are you all right?"

Mrs. Gordon's face had taken on an unhealthy sheen and she swayed slightly. Curran wondered if shock had begun to set in. With two corpses on his hands, he did not need a fainting woman. He gestured at the chair.

"Please take a seat, Mrs. Gordon. Is there anything I can get you?"

A tremulous smile caught the corner of her lips. "A cup of tea would be nice, but failing that, a glass of water?"

"We'll see what we can do." Curran strode across to the verandah rail and gestured to his driver, Constable Tan.

"Tan, fetch some water for Mrs. Gordon."

Mrs. Gordon subsided onto the chair, running a hand over her eyes. He studied her anxiously for signs of imminent vapors, but whatever momentary weakness had afflicted her had passed and she met his gaze with surprisingly cold, hard eyes.

"I would like to return home, Inspector."

His instincts prickled at the obvious animosity in that gaze.

"How well were you acquainted with Sir Oswald?"

"Not at all. I met him for the first time on Saturday and at his request came out here yesterday afternoon to do some work for him."

Curran leaned against the verandah rail, crossing his booted feet at the ankles. "He was not expecting you today?"

"No. We had agreed that I would return on Wednesday afternoon to continue my commission."

"Which was?"

"I was typing his memoirs, Inspector."

Curran cleared his throat. "I apologize for the questions, but can you tell me exactly what you did when you arrived at the house today?"

Her lips tightened and she looked down at her hands, her fingers teasing a leather tassel on her handbag. "The front door was ajar. I knocked and called out but nobody answered. I called out again and concluded that no was at home."

Curran gave her a skeptical glance. "So, you turned your hand to a little breaking and entering, Mrs. Gordon?"

Her head came up, her eyes blazing. "I . . . I didn't see it that way. I intended merely to retrieve my typewriter, leaving a note for Sir Oswald."

"Go on."

"You will see for yourself, the living room has been pulled apart. At the door to the study I trod on some broken glass and that was when I saw the marks on the closed door." She swallowed. "It is blood?"

Curran shook his head. "I haven't been inside yet."

Her shoulders lifted and she blew out a breath. "I thought . . . no . . . I knew something was terribly wrong. I pushed the door open and went in."

Curran wondered how many other women of his acquaintance would have had the courage to open that door.

"And what did you see?" he prompted.

"My typewriter was where I had left it but like the living room there was a terrible mess and of course, Sir Oswald . . ." She trailed off and took a shuddering breath before looking up at Curran. "I assure you I have touched nothing in the room, Inspector."

Curran gave her what he hoped was a reassuring smile. "It makes a refreshing change to meet someone who understands about crime scenes."

Something flickered behind her eyes. Amusement? Irony? "My father is a crown prosecutor in London, Inspector. I understand about the importance of evidence."

"He taught you well, Mrs. Gordon. What did you do after finding the body?"

"I hoped there might be a telephone but I couldn't see one so I sent Aziz to the nearest police post."

"Leaving you alone?" Curran glanced at the house.

Her chin came up. "Sir Oswald had been dead some time. I did not believe the murderer would still be in the house, and the dead couldn't hurt me."

An unusual woman, Curran thought.

Straightening, he caught the eye of Sergeant Singh standing sentinel by the front door. "I will have further questions for you. Do you mind waiting here? Ah, Tan, well done."

Constable Tan, carrying a pitcher of water and a glass, clattered onto the verandah. He poured Mrs. Gordon a glass and handed it to her. She drank without drawing breath and set the glass down on the floor at her feet.

With an audible sigh, she said, "If it is absolutely necessary to detain me, at least let me send my boy home with a message? My brother will be worried."

"Your brother?"

"The Reverend Julian Edwards. He is headmaster of St. Thomas Church of England Preparatory School."

Curran nodded. "I am acquainted with Reverend Edwards. Tell him that I will arrange for you to be returned home in the motor vehicle. Thank you, Mrs. Gordon."

She stood up and, passing him, descended the steps and walked briskly over to the boy holding the pony cart. Curran turned his attention to his sergeant.

"Let's get this over with."

Ten years in the army and the police force had hardened Curran to the sight of death, but his stomach still heaved as he stepped across the threshold. The unmistakable odor of death, sweet, cloying and sickly, overlaid the familiar Singapore murk of heat and mildew. Newbold had not been dead long but in this climate decomposition set in fast.

Nothing in this wretched climate lasted long.

The front door opened onto a large, airy living room furnished for a man with opulent tastes that belied the run-down exterior of the bungalow. Colorful oriental rugs covered the floor but the antique vases, plates and statues, including two fine statues of Buddha in the Siamese style, which may once have been crammed onto the surfaces of the dark, teak furniture, were now scatted across the floor, the fragile china in pieces. There had either been a fight or the intruders had been looking for something.

He let out a long low whistle. "Are all the rooms like this?"

Singh nodded. "All of them, sir."

In the typical flowing design of houses of this vintage, the rooms opened onto each other with no corridor. All the doors stood open through to a back door at the rear of the house.

Singh gestured at a doorway to the right. "The first body is through there, sir. Careful of the broken glass on the floor."

This had been the glass the Gordon woman had mentioned. The shattered remains of what looked to have once been two port glasses lay strewn across the floor by the study door, along with a small silver tray and a broken decanter. Curran touched his finger to a pool of dark liquid, half-dried around the edges, and sniffed. The sweet smell of the spilled port mingled with the other odors.

"Port. Two glasses . . . Sir Oswald had a visitor. Someone he knew? Someone to whom the servant was bringing port." He speculated aloud and pointed at a dark stain on the floor closer to the door. "What's that?"

Singh bent over. "A boot print."

Curran straightened and, skirting the dropped silverware, bent over to inspect the other mark. "A man's boot, I think, and if I'm not mistaken the owner of the boot did not step in the port."

"Blood?" Singh's magnificent, graying eyebrows quirked.

Curran nodded. He turned to the door, noting the dark smears on the chipped white paint.

"There's blood in the doorway and on the door handle," Singh observed. "Mrs. Gordon says she found the door ajar and did not touch the handle."

Curran nodded. "Good. Hopefully Greaves can find a fingerprint. Let's see where these footprints lead."

The gloom of the old house made it difficult to pick out the bloody footprints but once he knew what he was looking for, they were easy enough to spot. Curran paced out the footprints from the study door, through the next room that appeared to be a dining room and another unfurnished room, to the back door.

"Long strides. He was running toward the kitchen."

"Sir. Perhaps we see thecrime scene now?"

Curran glanced at Singh but the sergeant's face remained implacable. Singh had worked with him long enough to know he was delaying the inevitable confrontation with death itself.

Steeling himself he pushed the study door open. The stench of death was stronger inside the room and Curran had to stop himself from raising a hand to his mouth and nose. He could not show weakness in front of his men.

Like the living room, the floors were covered in oriental rugs, and heavy teak bookcases lined the walls. Framed maps and prints were jammed together on the only remaining wall space. Some of these had been pulled off the wall, their glass and frames smashed into pieces. A large, heavy European desk dominated one end of the room facing the door, with a leather chair still visible behind it. A circular table stood in the center of the room, with four chairs, now upended, around it. A neat square black case sat untouched on the table and a quick inspection revealed it to be a portable typewriter. Mrs. Gordon's typewriter, he presumed.

Smashed vases and books with broken spines and torn pages littered the floor. Another exquisite statue of the Buddha, about eighteen inches high, lay on the ground beside Sir Oswald's outstretched hand. A quick glance behind the desk revealed a small safe, the door wide open, and more papers, folders and envelopes spewing out of it. The desk drawers had been upended on the desk and papers fell in drifts around Sir Oswald Newbold's body, some trailing in the pools of blood.

Someone had spent a great deal of time and energy looking for something.

Having scanned the room, Curran forced himself to turn his attention to the mortal remains of Sir Oswald Newbold.

The man lay on what had once been a fine oriental carpet laid in front of the desk, its geometric design rendered in rich reds and blues. He had been neatly dressed in linen trousers and a shirt with the sleeves rolled up. The shirt had now been dyed a dark reddish brown with the victim's own blood. Newbold stared up at the ceiling with sightless eyes, already misting with death, the handle of an antique knife protruding from his throat.

"That killed him?" Even the phlegmatic Singh's lip curled as he contemplated the grinning devil on the knife.

Curran shrugged. "It looks like he was stabbed several times in the torso before that went in." He picked up Newbold's right hand. The cuts on the palm spoke of the man's last desperate attempts to ward off his attacker. His index finger had been almost severed. "But he must have put up quite a fight."

"Dear me. My patient looks far from well."

At the sound of the soft Scottish burr, Curran turned to look at the man by the door.

"And good morning to you, Doctor, or is it afternoon?" Curran rose to his feet as the chief surgeon of the Singapore General Hospital and sometime police surgeon, Euan Mackenzie, advanced into the room and set his bag down on the table.

"Afternoon, I fear, Curran."

Putting his hands on his hips the doctor surveyed the body on the floor at his feet.

Curran broke into the doctor's reverie. "Not sure that you can tell me anything that I can't see for myself. But before you start mucking around with him, I need to get some photographs in situ. Where is that boy with his camera? Greaves?"

"I don't think I know this young man?" Mackenzie commented as a perspiring Constable Greaves hauled his photographic equipment into the room.

Curran affected a cursory introduction adding, "We're lucky to get him. He only arrived a month ago. Cuscaden listened to me and we recruited him from London. Not only is he a natural with languages but he's been specially trained in the new fingerprinting techniques. Talented lad, aren't you, Greaves?"

Greaves's sweaty face appeared from beneath the black curtain of his camera. "Kind of you to say so, sir."

Curran and the doctor moved out of Greaves's way and stood at the doorway watching the young man work.

"Well, well, Sir Oswald Newbold." Mackenzie shook his head. "Man was a crashing bore but I am not sure he deserved to die this way."

"You knew him?"

Mackenzie shrugged. "We met socially on a few occasions and I made the mistake of attending one of his lectures at Victoria Hall." The doctor rolled his eyes. "Three hours of my life wasted listening to the man droning on and on about his explorations in Burma."

"Burma?"

"Oh yes, if he was to be believed, Sir Oswald here is single-handedly responsible for the opening up of the ruby and sapphire mines in northern Burma."

"I would have thought Burma would be an interesting subject."

Mackenzie's moustache twitched. "I believe there is a mountain named after him somewhere in northern Burma. He's most notable for the ruby mines he unearthed nearby. That's how he made his fortune, but you need to ask his colleagues at the Explorers and Geographers Club if you want to know more about his exploits."

"The Explorers and Geographers Club? I've not heard of them," Curran said.

"Very exclusive. You must have a piece of geography named after you to be a member, I believe. You'll find the club up behind the museum."

"Finished, sir." Mopping the sweat from his face, Greaves stood back from the corpse.

"Some general scenes of the room and the other rooms, Greaves, and you'll be done. I want this room dusted for fingerprints first."

He didn't miss the dismay on the young constable's face as he contemplated the task ahead. They hadn't even seen the second crime scene yet.

Curran and the doctor returned for a closer inspection of Sir Oswald. The smell of decay had worsened since Curran had arrived and he took a discreet step backward, ostensibly not to interfere with Mackenzie.

"What's Harriet Gordon doing up here?" Mackenzie crouched down beside Sir Oswald and opened the black bag he carried. Curran tried not to look at the array of shiny, anonymous instruments that glinted at him from its depths.

He gestured at the bloodied corpse. "She found him."

Mackenzie looked up. "Harriet?"

"You know her?"

"Very well. I went through medical school with her late husband, James. Her brother's the headmaster of St. Tom's in River Valley Road. Luckily for you she's a sensible woman. If it had been my wife that had stumbled on this . . ." Mackenzie gestured at the corpse. "But you haven't told me why she was here."

"She tells me she was doing some work for Newbold. Typing." Curran cast a glance at the typewriter. "Do you know anything about her work with Newbold?"

"She and her brother came for supper on Saturday night and she mentioned that she had placed an advertisement in the *Straits Times* and had obtained her first client. I'm not sure she gets any money for the hours of work she does at the school." Mackenzie wiped the instruments he had been using, snapped the bag shut and rose to his feet. "We need to get him out of here and down to the morgue. He's going off pretty damn fast."

"Time of death?"

Mackenzie tilted his head. "I'd say before midnight. That's as good as you'll get, Curran. Have you looked at that knife in his neck? Nasty-looking chap."

The red eyes of the demon sparkled malevolently and it grinned at Curran, its fanglike teeth protruding from its jaw. He could almost believe the hideous creature capable of committing the crime itself. Bukit Hantu indeed . . . there were evil spirits here and this was one of them.

Like most houses in Singapore, the kitchen, laundry and servants' accommodation were detached from the rear of the house and connected only by a covered walkway. Leaving Mac with Sir

Oswald, Curran traced the running, bloodied footsteps to the back door. A Malay constable squatting in the shade outside the kitchen jumped to his feet as Singh and Curran approached.

The smell of death emanating from the kitchen seemed stronger than inside the house and again Curran had to compose his face before entering the kitchen. Like the study, the kitchen showed clear signs of a struggle. Pots, pans and broken crockery littered the floor and the body of an elderly man dressed in *baju malayu*, the traditional loose trousers and smock favored by local men, lay in a crumpled heap half under the kitchen table, a dark pool of congealed blood around him, buzzing with insects.

Curran knelt beside the corpse and waved the flies away. The man stared back at him with clouded eyes from a mottled face. Like his master, the servant showed signs of having tried to defend himself and he had been stabbed multiple times. To judge from the amount of blood, he had probably bled to death on the floor where he lay.

Curran rose to his feet and considered the corpse. "What do we know about him?"

"Mrs. Gordon told me she had met a Burmese servant by the name of Nyan when she came to the house last night. It could be he," Singh said.

"So, for the moment only Mrs. Gordon can identify him?" Curran scratched his chin and wondered if he could ask Mrs. Gordon to formally identify the man. Perhaps after Mackenzie had seen the body and it could be presented in a slightly less appalling manner?

Curran turned to the unwashed plates and cooking utensils that stood piled beside the wash trough.

"Only one set of crockery and cutlery so his visitor arrived after supper. What happened then? Was Nyan summoned to take port to Newbold and his visitor but when he got to the door of the study he walked in on his master being murdered?"

Singh grunted agreement, used to Curran's habit of thinking aloud, adding, "So he was chased down the corridor and cornered in here. There was a struggle and he was stabbed?"

Curran exhaled. "Nasty, but I think this suggests that the knife we found in Newbold's body was not the murder weapon. The murderer would have had to have a knife with him to finish off the servant."

Singh shrugged and looked around the kitchen. "This is a kitchen, sir. No shortage of knives."

"Where's the body, sir?"

Both men turned at the sound of Greaves's voice. The young constable stood in the doorway with Dr. Mackenzie. Curran gestured at the body under the table, and with his finger Greaves pushed his glasses back up his shiny nose and took a breath before entering the room.

Outside Curran lit a cigarette and offered one to the doctor, who accepted. The smell of tobacco did something to alleviate the stench of death.

"This is a bad business, Curran," the doctor said, his face grim. "To think I was only saying to Harriet at supper last night that nothing untoward happened in Singapore."

"Really? Wishing yourself bad luck, were you, Mac? In fairness, I was only complaining to Singh this morning that nothing interesting had crossed my desk for weeks. The most exciting matter troubling me is the theft of two valuable vases. Be careful what we wish for, Mackenzie."

Mackenzie frowned and glanced back at the house. "Here's something for you, Curran. Given the violence of these crimes, the murderer would have been covered in blood."

Curran nodded. "I'm doubtful that will get us anywhere, but it is worth bearing in mind." He glanced back into the kitchen, where Greaves was folding up the legs of his camera. "Now, Mackenzie, the bodies are yours, and I had better see that Mrs. Gordon returns home safely."

"I can take her if you like," Mackenzie said. "I have my motor vehicle with me."

Curran shook his head. "No, I have some questions for her and it may be easier if she is away from here."

Mackenzie glanced at him, his eyes narrowing. "She's not a suspect, is she?"

Curran almost laughed. "I can't rule anyone out for the moment, Mackenzie, but I can't see Mrs. Gordon wielding a knife with such ferocity over a criticism of her typing skills."

Mackenzie shrugged. "Women are capable of feats of incredible strength when enraged, Curran."

Curran shook his head. "I don't consider Mrs. Gordon a suspect. Just a very important witness that I need to be pleasant to."

Mackenzie nodded. "I warn you. She's not that fond of the constabulary."

"I guessed that. Can you tell me why?"

Mackenzie shook his head. "None of my business and, I suggest, none of yours."

That last statement, Curran thought, remained to be seen.

THREE

Curran reentered the house through the back door and took a moment to check Newbold's bedroom. Like the study, it had been ransacked. Clothes had been pulled from the drawers and scattered across the floor. A small bathroom led off the bedchamber and here Curran stopped in the doorway and swore aloud. Two bloodstained towels lay on the floor and even from where he stood he could see the washbasin full almost to overflowing, the water stained red with the blood of Sir Oswald Newbold and his unfortunate servant. The murderer had cleaned himself before he left, possibly, if he had any sense, wearing something of Newbold's and carrying his own bloodstained clothing. They would not be looking for a man covered in blood.

He strode down the corridor to the front door and paused. Harriet Gordon had abandoned the chair and leaned against the verandah rail, looking out at the busy scene in the front garden.

She turned as Curran approached her, his footsteps ringing loud on the wooden boards.

"Have you found anything of interest, Inspector?" she inquired as two of the attendants from the mortuary wagon that had just arrived, hurried up the steps, carrying a stretcher.

"It's all of interest, Mrs. Gordon."

"And those men?" She pointed at the uniformed constables combing the garden.

"Murder weapon, abandoned clothing, signs of a vehicle . . . anything."

"It rained this morning. I doubt you will find anything of use."

"You may be right but it doesn't stop us looking."

She crossed her arms. "I would like to go home, Inspector."

"We will be leaving shortly," he said. "But first I have one last, unpleasant task for you. If you're up to it?" He indicated the stretcher being carried around the corner of the house by two of the mortuary orderlies. The body of the old servant had been covered with a gray, woolen blanket. "I was wondering if you could identify the servant for me."

Her lips tightened and she gave a slight inclination of her head before striding down the steps with purpose in the set of her shoulders. Curran summoned the men across and ordered them to uncover the man's face.

"Is that the servant who you met here?"

Mrs. Gordon swayed back on her heels, her hand going to her throat. "Yes. That's Nyan." She straightened and, to Curran's surprise, she touched the man's cheek. "He seemed a gentle old man. He did not deserve to die in such a violent way."

Something in the tone of her voice gave Curran pause. Why the grief for this man but not for Sir Oswald?

A curt nod from Curran and the orderlies hurried away to stow their burden in the back of the mortuary wagon.

"Thank you," Curran said. "That is never an easy task."

"No worse than what I saw in the study," she said. "I had years of assisting my husband's medical practice and his work in the worst slums of Bombay. Death does not generally unsettle me."

"Did he just have the one servant?" Curran asked.

"I only saw one—Nyan. Newbold told me he had come with him from Burma. There could have been others but as I told you, I only visited here the one time. Excuse me . . ." She opened her handbag and produced a neatly laundered handkerchief, which she pressed to her mouth and nose. "Please take me home. My brother will be worried."

Curran nodded. "My motor vehicle is at your disposal."

She glanced back at the house. "Did you find the manuscript?" she asked.

Curran frowned. "What manuscript?"

"Sir Oswald's memoirs. It was a pile of papers about three inches thick"—she indicated the thickness between thumb and forefinger—"secured with string. I saw him place it in the safe last night but the safe has been ransacked. Silly, I know—"

"Wait here." Curran turned back into the house.

In the study, he found the mortuary orderlies loading Sir Oswald onto the stretcher. Skirting the sweating men and the blood-soaked carpet, he circled the desk and crouched down beside the safe. He began sifting through the spilled contents—share certificates, title deeds, but nothing that matched the description of Sir Oswald Newbold's memoirs.

"It's not there, is it?"

He jumped to his feet, spinning on his heel to face Harriet Gordon. She stood a few feet away, pale but perfectly composed.

"Are you quite sure he put it in the safe?"

"Quite. After I found Sir Oswald I looked to see if there was a telephone and I saw the safe had been opened. I noticed the manuscript missing straight away."

Curran scanned the room with its expensive antiques and valuable books. So, something had been taken. Something of value to the murderer?

"Thank you, Mrs. Gordon. I'll get a full description from you when I take your statement. For now, you shouldn't be in this room."

"I really have no need of a police escort to take me home. If I could send a message to my brother, Aziz can bring the pony trap back for me." An edge of ice had crept into to her tone.

Her evident reluctance to spend any more time with the police than was strictly necessary, only served to intrigue him.

"It would be remiss of me not to ensure you reach home safely, Mrs. Gordon. My motor vehicle is waiting outside and you will be home much quicker if I take you."

He ushered her out of the study and down the steps to the pride of the Singapore Straits Settlements Police Force Detective Branch, the newly acquired 15.9 horsepower, Arrol Johnston motor vehicle that had arrived with Constable Greaves.

"I didn't know the police now had motor vehicles, Inspector," Mrs. Gordon remarked as he opened the rear door of the vehicle to allow her to enter.

"It is, I believe, the first of its kind in Singapore. Inspector General Cuscaden is very keen to embrace modern methods of policing and while I am fully supportive of some, such as finger-printing and photography." He paused. "Personally I consider motor vehicles a noisy, dangerous necessity. Give me my horse any day. Come on, Tan, get a move on, it looks like rain."

Constable Tan grinned and as he cranked the handle to start the mechanical beast, Curran lowered his voice. "He treats this monster like a favorite girl, Mrs. Gordon. Now, where are we going?"

"St. Thomas House . . . next to St. Thomas School in River Valley Road."

With the engine of the vehicle purring smoothly, Tan jumped into the driver's seat and with infinite care navigated the "beast" down the rutted driveway and out into Bukit Timah Road.

As the police motor vehicle turned onto Bukit Timah Road, Harriet heaved a sigh. She had gone past the need for tea. All she wanted now was a stiff whisky and a long bath. Perhaps then she could get the lingering smell of death and the memory of Sir Oswald's bloodstained corpse out of her mind.

"You've been very brave, Mrs. Gordon." Inspector Curran's well-modulated tones interrupted her reverie.

She cast him a sharp, angry glance. "Please don't patronize me, Inspector. I've seen dead bodies before."

Curran cleared his throat and a slight color stained his lean, tanned cheeks. "My apologies, Mrs. Gordon. I did not intend to patronize you." He cast her a rueful smile that softened his face and for a moment almost made him look human. "I am not sure I know how to deal with ladies who admit to seeing dead bodies on a regular basis. Most ladies of my acquaintance would be reaching for the smelling salts."

Harriet didn't carry smelling salts and had little time for the vapid women who did.

"My husband ran a small clinic in the slums of Bombay. Sadly, the deaths I saw there were from neglect and poverty. Never a murder victim." She thought of Sir Oswald Newbold and realized beyond the revulsion and her own shock at the manner of his death, she could summon no feelings of grief or pity. "Sir Oswald . . . Did he suffer?"

He gave her a sharp appraising glance.

"He clearly fought off his attacker and sustained several very bad wounds before the final blow. I expect his assailant got him to the floor before plunging the knife into his throat."

Harriet raised her hand to her mouth as she swallowed back the bile. She hadn't eaten since breakfast, apart from a couple of glasses of tepid water. It was hardly surprising that she felt a little light-headed and nauseous. The fumes and smell of new leather arising from the motor vehicle did not help.

"Are you feeling unwell, Mrs. Gordon?"

Curran's voice brought her back and she took a deep breath. "Quite well, Inspector."

"Why had you left your typewriter at the house?" Curran asked.

"It seemed more convenient to leave it there than to keep

carrying it back and forth but the school typewriter was broken and I have a term's worth of school fees to type up. When can I have it back?"

"I'm sorry, Mrs. Gordon, but the house is a crime scene. I will make sure it is returned to you in due course."

Harriet let out a heavy breath and leaned her elbow on the door of the motor vehicle, pretending an interest in the passing scenery. She hoped her apparent disinterest would deter further questions but the policeman did not take the hint.

"What was in Sir Oswald's memoirs?"

She glanced at him. "If you want to know why the murderer took them, I can't help you. I only did one session with Sir Oswald on Sunday afternoon and I can tell you now that they were hardly likely to excite the literary world. He was quite an exemplary little boy."

"And yet someone thought his memoirs of sufficient interest to steal the manuscript, as you yourself pointed out, Mrs. Gordon," Curran mused.

Harriet shrugged. "He had written the entire thing in shorthand. Even I had trouble interpreting it so I fear the thief may not find them very illuminating."

"How did Sir Oswald contact you?"

"I received a note from him on Friday and on Saturday afternoon I met him at the Hotel Van Wijk. You know it?"

It was a foolish question. Of course he knew it. Everyone knew the Hotel Van Wijk on Stamford Road.

Curran frowned. "Why the Van Wijk?"

She shrugged. "I gained an impression that he stayed there often. All the staff seemed to know him. In fact, one of them paid a call at his home just as I was leaving on Sunday night."

She sensed the policeman stiffen and his unusual light-gray eyes fixed on her with renewed intensity. "A visitor? Why didn't you mention this before?"

His annoyance amused her. "You didn't ask me," she replied.

"Did you recognize him?"

"One of the young clerks from the reception. A nice boy, always very polite," She frowned, trying to recall the name. "Fisher? No, Visscher. Dutch, I think. He had been on duty at the desk of the Van Wijk when I arrived for my meeting with Sir Oswald."

"Why did he visit Sir Oswald's home? Was he expected?"

"Definitely not expected. I must say Sir Oswald did not seem very pleased to see him at all. Visscher said he was returning something that Sir Oswald had left at the hotel but he seemed quite agitated."

Curran's lips tightened and the gray eyes narrowed. "Did he say what the object was?"

Weary of the interrogation, Harriet snapped, "I have no idea. He didn't appear to be carrying anything that I could see."

"What time was that?"

"Six. I checked my watch because I had to be home by six thirty for supper. I took Visscher's arrival as my excuse to leave."

"How did you get home?"

"The servant, Nyan, took me. Sir Oswald had a barouche and pair."

Suddenly desperately tired, she turned away, trying to ignore the growing thud of a headache behind her eyes that had been threatening all day. She thought of Aziz and his apprehension on the drive to the plantation house, to the place he had called Bukit Hantu.

"Inspector Curran, how good is your Malay?"

"Fairly good."

"What does Bukit Hantu mean?"

"'Haunted Hill,'" Curran replied without hesitation.

A shiver ran down her spine. Perhaps she should have heeded Aziz's warning.

Curran continued, "The locals have a large regiment of evil spirits called *hantu*. I suspect they will have added another *hantu daguk* to those already roaming around Sir Oswald's home."

"What's a *hantu daguk*?"

"The ghost of a murdered man, Mrs. Gordon. It appears as a mist or a cloud to lure other men to their death."

Despite the heat, Harriet shivered. "Poor Aziz. No wonder he was terrified, but it did have a bad atmosphere, don't you think?"

Curran shrugged. "I am not superstitious, Mrs. Gordon."

The motor vehicle turned onto River Valley Road and as the two-storied bulk of the school came into view, a wave of relief washed over Harriet. No *hantu* would dare come near St. Tom's and she longed to see her brother and share the horror of the day.

"It's an impressive building," Curran remarked.

"Like Sir Oswald's home, it is an old plantation house that has been converted into a school. Our house is around this corner in St. Thomas Walk."

With a shaking hand, she tucked a loose tendril of hair behind her ear as Constable Tan turned the motor vehicle into the walk.

"Oh dear, I'm afraid I feel a little light-headed."

"Mrs. Gordon, you have gone quite pale," she heard Curran say from a long way away.

"The heat," she murmured. "Just need . . ." She trailed off, wondering if she was about to disgrace herself by fainting or, even worse, being violently sick into the policeman's lap. She took deep breaths of the thick air and thought, for the first time, nostalgically of her parents' respectable home in faraway Wimbledon.

Tan hauled on the brake and jumped from the vehicle, running up to the house.

"How long have you been in Singapore, Mrs. Gordon?"

The world swam before Harriet's eyes and she covered them with a hand, fighting the waves of nausea. "Three months," she said faintly, "but I lived in India for nearly ten years . . . You would think . . ."

"It takes time to acclimatize," Curran said. "You've had a bad shock today and the heat has probably got to you."

"Don't be ridiculous. I told you I am not one of those women who succumb to the vapors."

A smile twitched the corners of his lips. "Of course," he said. "Pardon my impertinence. I blame myself for detaining you so long without food and water. Tan has gone up to the house for help."

"Harriet! My goodness, what's happened?"

At the sound of Julian's voice, she pushed her hair into some semblance of order and managed a watery smile for her brother. "Just the heat," she said. "I'm fine, Julian."

Constable Tan opened the door and Curran slid from the seat, his feet crunching on the gravel.

"I am afraid your sister has had a bad shock today, Reverend," he said, holding out his hand for Harriet.

She took it gratefully and stepped out of the vehicle with as much dignity as she could muster, but her legs seemed to have turned to rubber and only Curran's hand on her elbow stopped her from sinking to the gravel. She thought for one awful moment he would sweep her into his arms and carry her into the house, a mortification she could never have borne, but instead he stood back, allowing Julian to put his arm around her waist and assist her up the stairs into the comparative cool of St. Tom's House, as it was affectionately nicknamed.

Curran followed, stopping in the doorway as Julian allowed Harriet to sink gratefully onto the daybed. Curran stood there, circling his hat in his hand.

"We will need to take a proper statement from you, Mrs. Gordon."

"Not now, surely?" Julian snapped.

Curran shook his head. "Tomorrow will be fine. Good evening to you both."

Harriet lay back on the daybed and closed her eyes. She heard Curran's boots on the verandah, the motor vehicle door slam, the engine fire up and the growl of the engine. The police were out of her life.

Another wave of nausea passed over her and from a long way away Julian issued orders to their *amah*, Huo Jin, that involved fetching a basin, cold compress and tea.

The basin arrived just in time, not that Harriet had anything substantial to throw up but it made her feel a little better and she lay back on the cushions while her brother knelt beside her on the floor, bathing her wrists and temples with cool water.

"Stop fussing, Ju," Harriet grumbled, and seized the compress from him, laying it across her brow. "It's just this stupid heat."

"No, it's not. Aziz had some garbled story about dead bodies and evil spirits."

"Sir Oswald has been murdered, Julian. I found him."

She heard her brother's sharp intake of breath.

"Then, of course, I had to wait for the police and they wouldn't let me take my typewriter. Oh, hang it . . ." She burst into tears.

"I have tea for mem," Huo Jin said, and Julian helped Harriet to sit up. She took a mouthful of Huo Jin's brew of black tea so strong, Julian swore it dissolved teaspoons. Right now the tea tasted like the finest wine.

"The policeman, Curran. Have you met him before, Harri?" Julian asked.

She shook her head.

"He's one of the best cricketers in the Singapore Cricket Club. He's the one who knocked eighteen off me in two overs at the game two weeks ago."

Harriet tried to recall the game but they all merged into a blur of idiots in white flannels trying to pretend they were on gentle English village greens and not the hard buffalo grass, baked clay and blistering heat of the tropics. She glanced at her brother, whose mouth had curved into a blissful smile as it always did when considering one of his favorite topics, cricket.

"Really, Ju, a man is dead and you are thinking about cricket?"

The smile vanished. "Of course. Sorry, old thing. Do you want some more tea?"

"Forget the tea." Harriet lay back with the cold compress pressed to her throbbing temples. "I want a brandy and make it a strong one."

❦ Four

Leaving his principal witness in the care of her brother and servants, Curran returned to Mandalay, just as a tropical thunderstorm broke. He leaned against the rail of the verandah that surrounded three sides of Sir Oswald Newbold's house and watched several damp constables searching the garden for the murder weapon. He doubted they would find anything useful and the heavy rainstorm would quickly obliterate all trace of any evidence.

Looking out into the unnaturally silent, gloomy evening made darker and more ominous by the twisted rubber trees and heavy vines, he thought of the *hantu daguk* that would now haunt this place. He had worked too long in the East not to have developed a respect, if not an understanding, for the beliefs of the people who worked with him. There had already been mutterings among the Malay constabulary and he knew better than to try and detain them here after dark.

His thoughts strayed to Harriet Gordon. He suspected it took a great deal to discompose Mrs. Gordon, but the stressful day, coupled with the shock, would probably have felled a stronger man.

"Sir, sir!" A young constable ran up to the verandah.

"Found something?"

"I think you should see."

Curran pulled his collar up in a pointless gesture against the rain and followed the young man down the driveway. Halfway between the house and the road, the boy pointed to a set of tracks, rapidly dissolving in the rain, running alongside the drive itself.

Curran squatted down to inspect them. A vehicle had sunk into soft mud, deep enough for the tracks not to have been washed away by the rain earlier in the day. Unfortunately, any detail had been lost.

"A motor vehicle?" Curran speculated aloud.

"How do you know, sir?"

Curran swept a hand around the surrounding area. "No evidence of horses." Bless the beasts, their presence was hard to disguise. He stood up, looking up and down the rutted, muddy driveway. "Why halfway? Why not come all the way up to the house?"

The constable stared at him. "A surprise, sir?" he suggested.

"I think you're right. A surprise and not a pleasant one."

Curran did a quick circumnavigation of the house. Doors opened from the bedrooms onto the wide encircling verandah but Singh had assured him that these were all locked when he had arrived at the house. Only the study doors had been open to the outside but the *pintu pagar*, the half doors that allowed ventilation, had been secured. The back and the front doors offered the only viable access to the house and neither bore any sign of forced entry. Anyone could have entered the house from either end. It bore out his suspicion that Newbold's murderer had been invited in.

Pausing at the back door to shake off as much water as he could, he went in search of Greaves, who had been occupied in the study for most of the afternoon.

He paused at the doorway, allowing his senses to adjust. Newbold's body may have been removed but a sour, lingering miasma left by the decaying blood and other body excretions that had soaked into the carpet, still hung over the room.

"Find anything useful?"

Greaves looked up from his painstaking work of fingerprinting every surface of the study and, seeing Curran, straightened, wiping his face on his sleeve. Beneath the perspiration, the young man had a worrying, pasty, complexion. It had been a long, stressful day and Greaves had been in Singapore only a month. As Curran had told Mrs. Gordon, it took time to become accustomed to the energy-sapping humidity.

"Not much, sir. I took the prints off Newbold and his servant before they were taken away and I'm guessing that most of the prints in this room are theirs."

"What about Mrs. Gordon?"

Greaves looked shocked. "She's surely not a suspect, sir?"

"Maybe not but no doubt her prints are in this room and we need to eliminate those from any others. We'll ask her next time we see her."

Curran peered at the bloody marks marring the chipped white paint of the door. It looked to Curran as if the murderer had grabbed the edge of the door and wrenched it open, no doubt in pursuit of the servant.

"What about these marks on the door?"

"Too smeared to be of any use, sir."

Curran stooped to pick up one of the framed maps that lay shattered on the floor, the paper lining on its back ripped apart. He set the fine, hand-tinted map of Burma against the wall and picked up a second map in a smashed frame. This was a smaller-scale survey map labeled MOGOK DISTRICT. A river ran through a valley flanked by steep mountains, the largest of which bore the name MT. NEWBOLD in large block letters. The mountain was inscribed with a height of 12,463 feet. A sizable mountain.

Peering at the fine detail he located the MT. NEWBOLD MINING ENTERPRISE (BURMESE RUBY SYNDICATE) indicated by several small black dots, tucked into the side of Mt. Newbold along a narrow valley branching off from the main river valley.

He traced the waving line of the river with his forefinger. "The Irrawaddy," he said aloud, allowing the consonants to roll off his tongue.

"Sir?"

Curran turned to look at the young constable. "I have always thought the name of the Irrawaddy River had a certain romance to it."

Greaves stared back at him. Romance and Constable Greaves were clearly not well acquainted.

"Take a break and go and find something to drink, Constable. I don't want you passing out with heat exhaustion."

Greaves nodded and set his brush and powder down. "Don't mind if I do, sir."

"In fact, pack it in, Greaves. The light's going."

Alone in the room, he stepped over the dark stain in the rug and picked up the fallen Buddha. Despite the dusting of fingerprint powder and the bloody smears it was a beautiful piece. Carved from stone, and of some antiquity, it sat on a waisted plinth carved with lotus buds. One hand rested across the folded knees while the fingers of the other hand balanced on the edge of the plinth. The head had been carved with snaillike curls and the Buddha gazed down serenely at the hand in his lap. From the beauty of its proportions and the artful simplicity of the carving this would be a piece Curran would have been proud to own.

Curran resisted the urge to wipe the blood off it. It seemed sacrilegious that such a sacred and benign deity should be defiled with the evidence of such violence but it needed to be properly photographed and that could be done tomorrow at South Bridge Road. He carried the statue over to the circular table and set it down beside the typewriter to be taken to Police Headquarters. The little statue surveyed the room from beneath lowered eyelids, its benign smile unaltered by the violence it had witnessed.

He turned his attention to the desk and safe. A copy of the *Straits Times* dated Friday, 4 March, lay folded on the blotter and Curran picked it up, drawn by an advertisement circled in blue pencil on the front page.

Shorthand and Typewriting. An Englishwoman undertakes casual work as a stenographer and typist. From Monday to Friday after 5:30 P.M. daily. On Saturday after 2 P.M. She guarantees rapid and careful work together with ABSOLUTE SECRECY. Address Mrs. Gordon, Tanglin Post Office 35.

The careful wording and the intentional capitalization of *AB-SOLUTE SECRECY* amused him. Mrs. Gordon was proving to be an intriguing woman.

He sat in the sizable leather chair and began a methodical search, setting aside documents to go back to South Bridge Road as he went through them. Most of the papers appeared to be routine correspondence between Newbold, his bank and a publisher in London. In a leather folio, he found the land deeds for the plantation dated 1908. He wondered if that had been the year Newbold came to Singapore.

Aside from a number of share certificates in the Burmese Ruby Syndicate and a letter of appreciation from the board to Newbold dated 1906, acknowledging, with grateful thanks, his years of service, he found nothing else to mark Newbold's time in Burma. Nothing at all.

The sound of raised voices disturbed his reverie and he found a sodden Constable Tan in hot argument with an equally damp Englishman.

"Ah, Curran, tell your constable here who I am," the man appealed to Curran, the soft lilt of a Welsh accent unmistakable.

"A gentleman of the press has arrived," Curran said drily. "It's all right, Tan. I know Mr. Maddocks. Tell the men to finish up and organize a guard to be left on the house tonight."

Tan frowned. "The Malay will not stay here," he said. "They say it is haunted."

In a flash of exasperation, Curran snapped. "I know that. I don't care who stays here but we need a watch kept and any man who disobeys will be dealt with, understood?"

Tan's mouth tightened and he gave a quick salute.

Maddocks removed his pith helmet and mopped his perspiring face with a limp handkerchief. It might have been raining but the rain did nothing but thicken the air with an even damper humidity.

"How long does it take get used to this accursed climate, Curran?"

Curran faced the journalist at the "stand easy" position, his hands clasped behind his back and his feet firmly planted on the verandah, obstructing any view inside the house.

"What are you doing here, Maddocks?"

The journalist shook himself and straightened, his eyes gleaming with what Curran took to be journalistic fervor. "There's been a murder, Inspector. I am here for the story."

Maddocks stepped to one side, craning his head around Curran in an attempt to get a view of the crime scene. Curran took the man by the arm and steered him along the verandah as far away from the study windows as the building allowed.

"The best you'll get from me is a statement, Maddocks," he said.

Maddocks heaved a theatrical sigh and leaned against the verandah rail.

"Very well, a statement," he said, flicking through the pages of a dog-eared notebook. "With any luck, I'll get this through to the *Times* in London before six. Violent murder of famed explorer . . ." he said as he began to write.

Curran tilted his head and peered at the squiggles and dots that covered the pages of the journalist's notebook.

"Is that shorthand?" he inquired.

Maddocks flicked back a few pages. "Yes, why do you ask?"

"Is it hard to learn?"

Maddocks shrugged. "It can be. Damn useful in my business though and worth the effort. Now, Inspector, your statement for the anxious readers."

Maddocks stood with pencil poised and Curran began. "On the evening of Sunday, sixth March, Sir Oswald Newbold and his servant were attacked and killed in his home on Bukit Timah Road, by person or persons unknown. Investigations are being undertaken by the Detective Branch of the Straits Settlements Police."

He turned to walk away. Maddocks looked up. "Wait . . . that's it?"

Curran turned back. "I've nothing else to say."

"Start with how he was killed?"

"Further details will be released after the surgeon has examined the body."

"Who found the body?"

Curran hesitated. "The scene was discovered this morning by an Englishwoman."

Maddocks fixed Curran with an enquiring look. "Who?"

"I'm not revealing the lady's identity."

The blue eyes gleamed. "Was she Sir Oswald's mistress?"

"God, no!" Curran blurted out. "You have a prurient mind, Maddocks. A thoroughly respectable lady who was assisting Sir Oswald with writing his memoirs."

"Not Mrs. Gordon, by any chance?"

Caught by surprise, Curran's hesitation gave Maddocks the answer he sought and he scribbled in his notebook. Curran took a step toward him. "On no account are you to publish her name, Maddocks. How do you know her?"

Maddocks leaned back against the rail as if he thought Curran would hit him. The rotting wood groaned ominously and he held up a hand in a conciliatory gesture. "Harriet and I came out on the same ship three months ago, Inspector, and we have mutual friends. She mentioned she was taking up a bit of shorthand and typing work. I don't think that the school pays her a penny for being the headmaster's assistant. You have my word, I won't mention her name, but surely it will come out at the inquest if not before."

Curran relaxed and Maddocks stepped away from the verandah rail, snapping his notebook shut.

"Any chance I can see the crime scene?"

"None," Curran said. "Now, go and write your story."

Maddocks touched his fingers to his damp hair and hurried down the stairs to jump in the *ricksha* he had arrived in. Curran spared a sympathetic thought for the thin, wet and dispirited *ricksha wallah* who now had to trundle the three miles back into town.

Curran returned to the study, gave orders that the papers and the statue were to be boxed up and taken back to South Bridge Road, where the Detective Branch had their headquarters.

"What about the typewriter?" Greaves inquired.

Curran picked up Harriet Gordon's typewriter. No reason why she should not have it back tomorrow.

He thought of her cool demeanor toward him and decided to make a few discreet inquiries of colleagues in London. In the meantime, the typewriter made a good peace offering.

✒ FIVE

"**S**o much blood," Harriet murmured.

Julian placed his hand over Harriet's. "You should never have gone alone," he said. "I blame myself. I should have gone with you."

She glanced up at him, seeing the loving concern in his eyes but instinctively bridling at the implication that she needed his protection. Not that this gentle man of the cloth would have been any use to her had the murderer been lying in wait for her.

"I only went to collect my typewriter. I wasn't to know that Sir Oswald would be lying in a bloody heap on the floor of his study." She forced a smile and patted his hand. "I saw plenty of dead bodies in India." She paused and took another sip of the brandy, her second since arriving home. "But I must admit what I saw today was horrible."

Julian huffed out a breath, which Harriet recognized as both exasperation and remorse.

"I know you told me Sir Oswald bound you to confidentiality but I think his death releases you from that obligation. Can you tell me now why he had contracted your services?" Julian asked.

She laughed. "I was only typing his memoirs. It was hardly a work of literary merit and in fairness I had not got terribly far. I was still in his nursery reminiscences." She frowned. "Although I find it somewhat disquieting that the only thing I could see that had been taken was the manuscript."

Julian's eyebrows shot up. "Odd thing for an intruder to take?"

Harriet stared at her empty glass. "Julian, what really worries me is that the . . . business in London will come out. What if the school governors find out?"

Julian gripped her hand and gave it a squeeze. "Harriet, my dear Harriet. The bishop knows. He will look after you."

"I have a police record, Ju."

"You were hardly a criminal. There is a world of difference between a suffragette and an out-and-out felon."

She gave his hand an answering squeeze. "I hope you're right."

She drew her bare feet up onto the chair, letting the warmth of the tropical night wrap around her like a cloak. Normally this would be her favorite time of day but now the thick darkness hid a thousand watchful eyes and she couldn't help the feeling that the murderer of Sir Oswald Newbold lurked in the dark, like the bogeyman of her childhood nightmares. Over the repetitive rasp of insects and the distant cries of monkeys, the sharp unmistakable crunch of gravel underfoot cut through the night and she started, her breath catching in her throat as she reached for Julian.

"What was that?" she whispered, her fingers tightening on his as the sound came again.

Julian stood up, peering into the damp darkness. "Who's there?"

A ghostly apparition moved beyond the light thrown by the kerosene lamp and Harriet fought for breath as her heart raced. Not that she believed in ghosts or, what had Curran called them . . . ? *Hantu daguk?*

"Come forward, whoever you are," Julian said in his best headmasterly voice.

The apparition took the solid form of a slight young man in

sodden white clerical ducks, who stood in the rain at the foot of the steps, his arms wrapped around himself.

"Mrs. Gordon? Do you remember me?" he inquired, his accent immediately catching at the corners of Harriet's memory.

"Mr. Visscher, isn't it?" Harriet rose to her feet. "Come up here, out of the rain."

The boy, for he couldn't have been much older than eighteen or nineteen, stood at the top of the stairs, dripping and shivering under the shelter of the wide verandah roof.

"You're soaked, young man. Sit down and I will fetch a towel," Harriet said.

Julian shot his sister a questioning glance.

"Julian, Mr. Visscher is a clerk from the Van Wijk Hotel."

"Can I get you a drink, old chap? You look like you could use one," Julian said.

Visscher shook his head and raised his hand to detain Harriet, who had turned to go into the house.

"No, I cannot stay. I didn't know who else to ask. You seemed like a lady I could trust. Is it true? Is he dead? They said his head had been severed . . ." The young man's voice rose in his agitation.

Harriet placed a hand on his arm. "Was Sir Oswald a friend of yours?"

Visscher looked at her and his eyebrows drew together. "No, but he came to the hotel often. I saw you at his house last night and you were there." The boy blinked. "I . . . I was working on reception today when some people came into the hotel talking about a terrible murder on Bukit Timah Road. When I heard the name Newbold mentioned, I panicked. I went up to his house but there were police at the gate so I dared not go in. I came straight here. Is it true?"

Harriet nodded. "I'm afraid so. Sir Oswald was attacked last night by an intruder and stabbed to death."

The boy flung his head back. "I tried to warn him but he

would not listen." Visscher looked from one to the other. "Did you tell the police I was there on Sunday night?"

"Of course I did. I had to tell them," Harriet said, "and I am sure Inspector Curran will want to speak to you."

Visscher took a step back, nearly falling down the front stairs. He righted himself and ran a shaking hand through his damp hair. "The police? If they know I have talked to the police, then I too will be a dead man."

"Mr. Visscher, really. You have nothing to worry about," Julian said in the sort of soothing tone of voice he used with his students.

"No, you don't understand." Visscher looked from one to the other. "It is the VOC." He pronounced it as *V-O-C*.

"The VOC?" Julian frowned. "What is the VOC and why are you so frightened of it?"

Visscher shook his head. "I cannot say or you will be next. They are dangerous." He straightened and glanced out into the darkness. "I must go."

He gave an odd, stiff little bow and hurried down the stairs to be swallowed up in the darkness before Julian or Harriet could say another word.

Julian shook his head. "What a peculiar young man."

"A very frightened young man." Harriet looked up at Julian. "What do you suppose the VOC could be?"

"I don't know but I am beginning to have a bad feeling about this, Harri."

"So am I. It's inevitable that my name will come out. There will be a coronial inquiry," Harriet pointed out, "and possibly a trial . . ." She reached out for the reassuring solidity of the verandah post. "Oh, Julian. I can't . . ."

Julian laid a brotherly hand on her shoulder. "Harriet Jane," he said fiercely, "you are not the one on trial. All you will have to do is give your evidence and that will be it. No one is sending you back to Holloway."

* * *

Curran returned home late in the evening to the little bungalow off Cantonment Road that he called home.

He knew Li An waited for him on the verandah, as much a part of the night as the monkeys in the trees and the background drone of the myriad of insect life that inhabited the jungle surrounding his house. A creature of the dark, his Broken Bird.

Leaving his horse with the *syce*, Mahmud, Curran approached the bungalow. The scent of the frangipani tree Li An had planted by the front steps filled the air, banishing the pall of death that had surrounded him all day, and he sensed rather than saw her rise from her chair, graceful and silent as a *pontianak*, the spirit of a beautiful woman sent to lure him to his death.

"You are very late, Curran," she said. A statement, not a reproof.

He took her in his arms, twining his fingers in her thick, dark hair that hung loose around her face.

"It's been a long day, Li," he murmured into her hair. "You smell good."

Her shoulders lifted in a silent laugh and she wriggled out from his grasp.

"You must eat," she said, "and you can tell me what it is that keeps you from me."

She took him by the hand and led him into the house, where a single candle burned on the table. Curran poured himself a whisky and collapsed into his favorite armchair, tearing at his constricting collar. He knew the disapproving gossip that circulated the English population about their senior detective. *Curran has gone native*, they whispered, but he paid them no heed.

Mesmerized, he watched Li An as she busied herself around the room, lighting the kerosene lamps that cast a soft glow and filled the room with the scent of the fuel. A visitor to the bungalow during the day would find her in a simple "uniform" of black trousers and a white tunic top, with her hair tied back in a long, simple plait. The picture of a compliant native housekeeper transformed at night.

The flowered cotton *cheongsam* she wore tonight accentuated, rather than disguised, her slim, lithe body and her hair tumbled in dark shining waves almost to her waist. At night she wore it loose, swept up over her right ear with a single frangipani flower. The simple trick of the flower in her hair distracted the eye of the beholder from the long, ugly scar that transected her left cheek from the corner of her eye to her mouth. Her brother's parting gift.

She called herself Broken Bird.

It continually amazed him that Li An stayed. He had told her that she was under no obligation to him and that her life was her own but she would lay her long fingers on his chest and kiss him and tell him she stayed because she chose to stay.

She poured herself a whisky and turned to seat herself in the other armchair, swirling the amber liquid in the crystal glass.

"Tell me about your day, Curran," she said.

And he did. She asked questions, prompting him when he fell silent. Khoo Li An was no stranger to violent death and he knew nothing he said would shock her.

She rose to her feet in one supple movement and crossed to him, taking the glass from his hand.

"This Newbold," she said. "He is a man of many secrets, I think."

Curran grunted his agreement.

"There is something not quite right about him. A *tuan* requiring great respect but he is like the *jing* in Chinese opera. His is a painted face."

Curran smiled and caught her hand, pressing her fingers to his lips.

"So wise and so beautiful," he said.

She laughed and extricated her hand. "Enough of work. You must be hungry. I will cook dinner now."

He smiled up at her, knowing that after they had eaten they would retire to bed and he could lose himself in her arms and the troubles of the day would be swallowed up by the dark night. For whatever reasons she chose to stay with him, he had allowed himself to break the rule of a lifetime.

He loved her.

✦ SIX

Tuesday, 8 March 1910

Curran arrived at South Bridge Road the next morning at seven thirty to find he already had a visitor waiting to see him. The neat, rotund figure of Mr. Clive Strong of Lovett, Strong and Dickens, a reputable legal firm that had offices off Raffles Place, sat on a bench in the outer office, tapping a well-polished shoe on the floor. Curran and Strong had formed a nodding acquaintance over a burglary matter some months previously, and as Curran's staff jumped to their feet, Strong in turn rose, coming forward, hand outstretched to greet Curran. Curran gestured for the man to enter his office and closed the door behind them.

"I beg your pardon, Strong. I hope I haven't kept you waiting. You're an early riser."

Strong shook his head. "I've been in Johor and only got home last night to the terrible news about Sir Oswald. I thought you would want to see his will as soon as possible."

Strong opened the briefcase he carried and laid the neatly folded document on the table. Curran picked it up, slipped off the pink ribbon that encircled it and scanned the contents.

"You're his executor?"

Strong nodded. "Yes, that's why I didn't delay. I will need to make funeral arrangements. Where is his body?"

"At the hospital. Dr. Mackenzie will be performing the autopsy at nine. After that it can be released to you for burial."

Strong pinched the bridge of his nose and closed his eyes as if he could smell the decomposing corpse. "The sooner the better. I suppose I should see to poor Nyan as well."

"That would be appreciated," Curran observed. "I believe he was Burmese. Did he have any family here in Singapore?"

Strong shook his head. "I doubt it. He was only a servant."

Curran flinched inwardly. Only a servant and therefore of no importance? As far as he was concerned Nyan was an innocent bystander who had died a violent and unnecessary death. Servant or not, he deserved respect—and justice.

Strong continued, "As soon as I depart here I shall make immediate arrangements for a funeral."

Curran read through the rest of the document, laid it down and tapped it with a forefinger. "No family?"

"No. Newbold had no close family, Inspector, and his estate is quite considerable. As you can see, there are a few minor bequests, including a generous legacy to his unfortunate servant but the bulk of his estate is divided between the Explorers and Geographers Club here in Singapore and his old school in England. I regret for your sake that there are no obvious murder suspects among the beneficiaries, Curran."

Curran allowed himself to smile. "Not unless his old headmaster is anxious for the bequest." He handed the document back to Strong. "Were you aware Sir Oswald was writing his memoirs?"

"Yes indeed. He had a publisher in London quite anxious to publish them. On which subject, do you have the manuscript?"

Curran shook his head. "The manuscript is missing and interestingly I have been unable to locate any reference material, such as diaries or letters."

"There are none," Strong said. "All his records were destroyed in a house fire in Rangoon not long before he left to come to Singapore."

"He was writing from memory? Hardly reliable," Curran remarked.

Strong shrugged. "I haven't read any of his work so I cannot comment, Inspector. I believe much of it was written before the fire, during his time in Burma. Did you say the manuscript is missing?"

"It appears to be the only thing stolen from the house."

"How extraordinary." Strong said.

"When did Newbold arrive in Singapore?"

"Early '06, I believe. My initial dealings with him were purely professional. I handled the purchase of Mandalay. Did you find the title deeds to the property?"

Curran inclined his head and Strong let out a sigh. "That's a relief. Makes selling it much easier if I'm not struggling to find the paperwork."

"How well did you know Newbold personally?"

Strong sat back in his chair and mopped his face with a large, pristine handkerchief. "He was one of those hail-fellow-well-met kind of chaps. Good company and a generous host. I must admit I enjoyed a couple of pleasant meals at the club. The food there is very good."

From the way the buttons on his linen jacket strained, Strong looked like a man who enjoyed a good curry.

"Did he talk about his time in Burma?"

Strong frowned. "Of course. It was a large part of his life. He talked about it often,"

"What did he have to say about his exploration of northern Burma?"

"He spoke of that at great length." Strong dropped an extra inflection on the words *great length*. The eyes of the two men met in perfect understanding and Strong's moustache twitched in a smile. Mackenzie was not the only person to find Sir Oswald Newbold a crashing bore.

"However, I'm not sure I learned very much beyond the sad fact that most of his companions on that journey perished. Of course, that was when he discovered the famed Newbold Ruby." Strong made a circle between the thumb and forefinger of his left hand.

Curran raised his eyebrows and let out a low whistle. "A stone that size would be worth a fortune."

"And the color of pigeon's blood, apparently."

Curran had often heard this description and wondered about the exact color pigeon's blood that excited the comparison.

"Was it still in his possession?"

"Alas, no. I believe it now graces the regalia of some minor European royalty. You must understand Newbold was in the employ of the Burmese Ruby Syndicate and when the Mogok area was opened up, he returned as the mine manager. He had no legal claim on anything he found, except by virtue of his shareholding."

Curran frowned. "Then, where did his wealth come from?"

Strong blinked. "The returns on the BRS shares were good and I can believe there may have been some inherited wealth. I can give you a full accounting when we have finalized the estate."

Curran waved at the cardboard boxes stacked against one wall of his office. "There are the contents of his desk and safe, Strong. We will let you have them when we have finished with them."

Strong nodded. "Sooner rather than later, Inspector?" He pulled a watch from his waistcoat pocket and glanced at it. "Is there anything else I can help you with?"

Curran shook his head. "Nothing for the time being. Thank you for your assistance."

"Then, I shall see the poor fellow laid to rest. Have the police finished with the house?"

"Not yet. I'll send the keys around when we're done."

Strong shook his head. "It is an ill-fated property. The previous owner committed suicide. Hanged himself from the rain tree in the garden. After two violent deaths, I doubt anyone will want to buy it."

A chill ran down Curran's spine. Little wonder the locals called it Bukit Hantu.

"Three violent deaths," Curran said. "You forget Nyan."

Strong rose to his feet. "Thank you for your cooperation, Inspector. It's greatly appreciated. I shall advise you of the details of the funeral in due course."

After the lawyer had left, Curran found his men standing around a board that had been set up in the main office. Greaves was pinning his crime scene photographs to it.

"Where are we with the Newbold murder?" Curran inquired.

Singh turned at the sound of his voice. "We spoke with the neighbors and their servants but no one heard or saw anything, but the house is very isolated so we would have been fortunate to find such a witness."

Tan chimed in. "It is as if the spirits of the hill have been at work. We did learn that the hill was reputed to be the burial site of a famous prince and his retainers. Their restless spirits still roam the *ulu*."

Curran rolled his eyes. "Don't you start on that superstitious nonsense. Unless the *hantu* come armed with sharp knives, there are no ghosts involved."

Curran moved in for a closer look at the crime scene photographs. Without color or scent, the two-dimensional, cold shades of black and white removed the horror from the scene that had confronted them the previous day.

"Mrs. Gordon says the Visscher boy turned up just as she was leaving. At the moment he is our prime suspect," Curran said.

Singh shook his head. "Ah. Not Visscher. We found a *ricksha wallah* who says a young man of Visscher's description flagged him down in Bukit Timah Road about seven. Newbold had time to eat his evening meal and Nyan could not have served that until he returned from delivering Mrs. Gordon to her home."

Curran swore under his breath and ran his hand through his hair. "If not Visscher, then who? How did he arrive and how did he leave?" He pointed to the photograph of the kitchen. "Newbold ate his evening meal so the visitor could not have arrived until after that had been finished and cleared. So, between eight and nine? Looks like he let his killer in and sent for port."

"Mrs. Gordon said she found the front door open," Singh put in.

"Doesn't mean anything. The murderer probably fled that way or it could have been left open for ventilation."

"We have made enquiries with the *rickshaw wallahs* and except for Visscher, we cannot find a driver or *ricksha wallah* who took anyone to or from Bukit Timah Road, between seven and nine," Singh concluded.

Curran glanced at his sergeant. "Of course we are assuming he took a *richsha* or *gharry* and did not have his own transport. There are the tracks of a motor vehicle in the driveway."

"I have men asking questions." Singh glanced at the clock on the wall. "Are you not expected at the hospital at nine, sir?"

Curran glanced up at the clock. Five to nine. He would be late.

Huo Jin woke Harriet with a cup of tea, the *Straits Times* and the news that the *tuan* had gone up to the school and she was not to hurry. Harriet pushed back the heavy mosquito net and glanced blearily at the little carriage clock on her bedside table. It showed eight o'clock. She had overslept and her mouth felt like it was stuffed with kapok. Hardly surprising as she had taken the precaution of self-administering a sleeping draught on top of several brandies.

She picked up the paper and the lurid headlines glared out at her. *Brutal Attack in Bukit Timah. Famed Explorer Sir Oswald Newbold Dead.*

She forced herself to scan the article, dreading to see her name mentioned but the article simply recorded that the body had been discovered by an "Englishwoman." In fact, the article was decidedly short on fact and heavy on speculation. Intruders had broken in . . . valuable antiques stolen. She tossed it to one side and swung her legs over the edge of the bed, her limbs heavy and unresponsive.

"The *tuan* say that you are to stay at home today. School will manage without you," Huo Jin said without much enthusiasm. The *amah* preferred her days to herself without interfering memsahibs breathing down her neck.

Harriet shook her head. "No, I have work to do at the school. Bring me some warm water and I will have breakfast on the verandah."

Fortified by toast and marmalade, Harriet gulped down two cups of tea and had just poured herself a third cup as a *ricksha* turned into the drive.

Griff Maddocks jumped down, exchanged a few words with the *ricksha wallah* and, waving his hat in greeting, loped up the stairs.

"My dear, Harriet, how are you?" he inquired.

"Griff, while it's always a pleasure to see you, I hardly think this is an appropriate time of day."

Maddocks smiled. He had a sweet, disarming smile, which he no doubt employed to advantage in his chosen profession.

Being much of an age they had spent a great deal of time in each other's company on the long voyage from London, frequently being called on to form a pair for bridge or participate in deck sports. Griff had brought something back into Harriet's life that she had thought long forgotten . . . laughter.

His charm was wasted. Harriet remained unmoved. The journalist glanced meaningfully at the *Straits Times*, open on the table beside her.

"You've read my column this morning? I even managed to get a byline in the *Times* of London."

"Yes, terrible news about Sir Oswald Newbold." Harriet picked at a loose thread on the tablecloth.

"Harriet." Maddocks grinned. "I know it was you who found him."

Harriet met his gaze, her face a study in innocence. "Your report says merely an 'Englishwoman,' Griff."

"Curran requested I not name you," he said.

Curran went up in Harriet's estimation.

"You may as well join me, Griff."

"I don't wish to intrude—" he began.

"Yes, you do," Harriet said. "Please sit."

Huo Jin appeared in the doorway and Harriet sent to her to fetch a fresh pot of tea and a second cup. She waited until Huo Jin had returned before fixing her uninvited guest with a stern eye.

"I am not compelled to talk to you," she said, handing him the cup.

"Of course not." He set the cup down and leaned forward, all humor gone from his face. "I can understand why you'd not wish your name mentioned. That business in London last year."

She took a deep breath. "You know . . . ?"

"I was the court reporter for the *Daily Mail* in June last year, Harriet."

Harriet shivered, despite the warmth of the morning, and her cup rattled in the saucer. She set it down. "You didn't think to mention this before?"

"I assumed if you wanted me to know, you would tell me yourself."

She ran a shaking hand across her eyes. "You must understand that I am in a very precarious situation. The bishop is the only member of the school trustees who knows the full story. If the others find out, Julian could be dismissed."

He raised a hand. "Harriet, I would like to think we're friends and despite my profession, you can trust me. Although I can't guarantee that your name will not come out at some point."

"I'm not afraid of my name being public knowledge, Griff, only my history."

"But you were exonerated."

"Of the assault, not the affray. That remains on my record and for which I spent three long and very miserable months in Holloway."

Maddocks nodded. "I see your dilemma but you have my word that if any of that does come out, it will not be through my agency."

Harriet smiled. "Thank you for your discretion, Griff."

"For a journalist, I am plagued with a basic code of integrity and there is nothing to be gained in my pursuit of the truth in revealing your unfortunate encounter with the law. You're a victim of a political system, not a criminal."

"Integrity? Is that a word one associates with the press?" Harriet wondered aloud, remembering the London Times report. . . . *Also arrested was the widow of the late Dr. James Gordon, daughter of respected crown prosecutor Mr. G. Edwards. She has been charged with assault and hindering a policeman in the execution of his duty . . .*

All humor went from Maddock's eyes and his eyes took on a brilliant intensity. "Mrs. Gordon . . . Harriet . . . I don't for one minute believe that a woman prepared to go to Holloway for a cause she believed in, can dismiss it so easily." He studied her for a moment. "A journalist is supposed to be impartial, but I have a great sympathy for the suffrage cause. There are stories coming out of Holloway of force-feeding and—" He stopped, his eyes widening as Harriet gave an involuntary start, her hand going to her throat.

"You?"

She nodded. "That's one of the reasons I decided to come to Singapore."

Griff Maddocks said nothing, but his gaze didn't move from her face as he took a studied sip from his cup, his silence inviting her confidence.

"I joined the hunger strike," Harriet said in a tight small voice. "Every day for a week the wardress would hold me down while a man forced a tube down my throat. It was intended to break me."

"Did it?" Griff asked.

Harriet looked away, studying the bright purple bougainvillea that curled around the lattice of the verandah.

"They inserted the tube into my lung and I nearly died."

Griff leaned forward, his hands clasped together. "But why on earth did you join them?"

Harriet closed her eyes. "All my life I wanted to be a lawyer, just like my father and his father before him, but even my darling father could see no point in wasting education on a woman when all I was going to do was get married and live, like my parents, in a comfortable house in Wimbledon, dispensing tea and cake and doing good work. That's why I studied shorthand and typing. My mother was appalled when I suggested I work for my father's law firm. Then I met my husband and escaped to India. I spent ten years working with my husband until he died, leaving me with insufficient funds for independence. I found myself back in Wimbledon, taking tea with my mother's friends, facing a life of impecunious widowhood and taking care of my parents as they grew older. I stumbled on a rally in Hyde Park and everything Mrs. Pankhurst said resonated with me. Why shouldn't women have the vote? Why can't they be doctors or lawyers?" She raised her gaze to meet his. "Or journalists?"

Griff smiled. "You'd be a fine journalist, Harriet."

Griff's smile was hard to resist and she allowed herself a low chuckle, remembering her mother's face when she told her she had joined the Women's Social and Political Union. Then came the protest outside the Houses of Parliament and the three months of hell in Holloway. Had that experience broken her?

"Harriet? Maddocks prompted.

She brought her attention back to him and forced a smile. "I am here now, thousands of miles from London, living in a society where women are less than chattels. I hope you can understand why I do not wish my past to follow me here."

He nodded. "You have my word and I've taken up enough of your time." He rose to his feet and collected his hat, giving her the benefit of his disarming smile, once again the charming journalist. "But is there anything you can tell me about Sir Oswald's murder that may be of interest to the readers?"

Harriet shook her head. "Nothing that the police cannot tell you. Thank you for your concern. Good day."

He clapped his hat on his head. "And to you, Mrs. Gordon."

As he turned for the stairs down to the driveway, his hand raised to summon the *ricksha wallah* who squatted in the shade, Harriet rose to her feet. The memory of a frightened boy emerging out of the dark and the rain made her run down the steps and catch him by the sleeve as he mounted the *ricksha*. "Griff. There is something you can do for me."

He turned. "Anything."

"Let me find a book and then come with me to the Van Wijk Hotel."

❧ SEVEN

Curran did not envy Dr. Mackenzie the job of "honorary" police surgeon. He saw nothing honorific in the unpleasant criminal cases he shared with Mac. Autopsies were one aspect of his job he particularly disliked but he felt his presence was necessary both from an evidentiary point of view and as a mark of respect to the deceased.

Even the rudimentary refrigeration rigged up in the hospital morgue using large slabs of ice did little to lessen the rate of decomposition and he knew as he opened the door to the morgue he would be in for an unpleasant morning.

Mac looked up and grinned. "I started without you. I want to get this over with before it gets too hot."

"How do you stand it?" Curran asked, covertly rubbing his nose in a vain attempt to lessen the smell.

"I like a mystery," Mac replied, and with a cocked head regarded the corpse on the cold marble table. "The human body is a wonder."

There didn't appear to be anything to wonder about Sir Oswald Newbold. The corpulent body had sustained fifteen wounds, including the one that had almost severed his finger.

"The attacker got Newbold on the ground and plunged that dagger into his neck." Mac pointed with a scalpel.

"How do you know that?" Curran asked.

"The flow of blood from the wound," Mackenzie said, and a slight smile twitched his moustache. "And the bloody great bruise on his chest from someone's knee holding him down. But the knife in his neck did not inflict the other wounds." Mackenzie looked down at the mutilated body on his dissection table and indicated one of the wounds to the man's torso. "You see how this wound tapers. I suspect a curved blade of some description. Very, very sharp." He glanced at the second table, where the body of Nyan lay covered in a stained sheet. "Same knife was used on the servant."

Curran waved a hand in the direction of Newbold's neck. "Where's the knife that was left in the body?"

Mackenzie jerked his head at a metal bowl. "In there. It's all yours."

Using his handkerchief, Curran grimaced as he picked up the hideous object. The red eyes of the demon winked at him as he carried the knife over to the window.

Several brown smudges indicated that the hand gripping the knife had already been covered in blood. With any luck Greaves would find fingerprints.

Curran ran a thumb experimentally across the stained edge of the stout, pitted blade and shook his head. It was as blunt as a butter knife.

"Which wound killed him?"

Mac gestured at the neck wound. "Probably that one. He would have bled to death in minutes."

Curran dropped the object into a paper bag, washed his face and hands and excused himself. Outside in the fresh air, such as it was, it still felt like the miasma of the autopsy room clung to him as he walked down Outram Road. He needed the exercise and he needed time to think.

*　*　*

Of all the hostelries in Singapore, Harriet particularly liked the Hotel Van Wijk but the lure of its famous ice cream or curry tiffin, was forgotten as she strode into the entrance foyer. The young man on the reception desk looked up as she approached and her heart sank. Unlike the cheerful face of Hans Visscher, the young man on duty had a sharp, pointed face, dark hair, heavily slicked with oil, and a spotty and perspiring visage. The smile of welcome was not reflected in his eyes. She glanced at the name engraved on his brass name badge: PAAR.

"Can I help you, madam?" Paar inquired, his accent betraying a European background similar to Visscher's. Dutch, she presumed.

Harriet forced a smile. "Good morning. I was hoping to find Mr. Visscher on duty."

Paar's smile did not slip. "He is not on duty this morning. Is there anything I can assist you with?"

"No." Harriet thought fast, conscious of Griff Maddocks standing behind her, his journalist's ears pricked. "I was talking to him when I was here on Saturday and had promised to lend him a book. Where might I find him?"

Harriet tapped the volume of improving sermons she had grabbed from Julian's bookshelves.

The tight starched collar of Paar's uniform rose and fell as he swallowed, his eyes darting to the main door, where an Indian *jagar* in uniform stood awaiting the arrival of guests.

"I'm not sure," he said.

"He must lodge somewhere nearby."

"At the manager's house, but . . ." Paar began but Harriet had already turned, pushing her way through the bustling early-lunchtime crowd, with Griff in tow.

"The manager's house?" Griff inquired.

"I think we will find it is one of the bungalows on Victoria Street," Harriet said.

Maddocks fell into stride beside her. "Tell me why we are interested in a hotel clerk?"

"He has a connection with Newbold," Harriet said. "I'm worried about him. Ah, this must be it."

The Van Wijk Hotel included a number of separate bungalows rounding the corner into Victoria Street. She stopped outside the one at the far end of the row, clearly labeled PRIVATE RESIDENCE.

Harriet mounted the steps and rapped on the door. The young Chinese maid who answered it peered up at her with wide eyes.

"I would like to speak with Mr. Visscher," Harriet said.

"Mem!" the girl called without opening the door any wider.

Harriet heard quick steps on the wooden floor and the girl vanished. A short, rather dumpy, fair-haired woman opened the door wider.

"Can I help you?"

Harriet smiled. "I was hoping to speak with Mr. Visscher and I believe he lodges here."

The woman frowned. "Who are you?"

"My name is Mrs. Gordon. I met Mr. Visscher on Saturday at the hotel and I had promised to lend him a book."

The woman glanced at the book in Harriet's hands. "I am afraid he is not here."

"When do you expect him to return?"

The woman shrugged. "I do not know where he has gone. I have not seen him since yesterday evening."

The skin on the back of Harriet's neck prickled. She held out the book. "I am sorry to have missed him," she said. "Perhaps I can leave this for him and you can tell him I called, Mrs. . . . ?"

"Van Gelder." The woman took the volume and glanced at the title on the spine. "Sermons. *Ja*, that is so like Hans. I will see that he gets it. Thank you for taking the trouble to bring it for him."

The door shut in Harriet's face and she took a moment to compose herself before returning to Maddocks, who waited in the shade of a rain tree.

"Well?"

"He's not there," she said. "Now I am really worried. Griff, where would I find Inspector Curran?"

"Curran? We could try South Bridge Road."

Harriet hailed a *ricksha* and as he helped her into it, Maddocks said, "Do you mind if I accompany you?"

She smiled. "Can I stop you?"

But Maddocks had already turned away, waving in a second *ricksha*.

"Where, mem?" the *ricksha wallah* inquired.

"Central Police Station, South Bridge Road," Harriet replied.

Curran was not in his office but the harassed young Malay clerk who greeted them on their arrival at the Detective Branch assured them he would not be long. He indicated a bench and Harriet seated herself.

"You don't have to wait with me," she told Maddocks.

He removed his hat and wiped his face. "Nothing better to do."

They heard Curran before he reached the door. A clatter of boots on the stairs and a yell of "Singh!" brought the clerk to his feet.

"Oh, sir, there is no one here. No one except this good lady and gentleman."

Curran rounded on Harriet and Maddocks. Whatever he had been about to say died on his lips and he whipped off his hat.

"Mrs. Gordon, Maddocks . . . what brings you here?"

Harriet rose to her feet, pushing a stray of lock of hair back behind her ear. "Mr. Maddocks and I are here to report a missing person."

Curran frowned. "A missing person?"

"I mentioned the clerk from the Van Wijk? Visscher. Well, it would appear he has not been seen since last night. I am extremely worried about him."

"And why is that of concern to you?" Curran inquired.

"Because I'm afraid I might have been the last person to see him."

Curran took a deep breath and gestured at the door to a half-glass-partitioned office. "You'd better come in."

Harriet had to pass Curran to enter the office and he gave off a peculiar scent of warm male combined with something sickly mingled with carbolic.

He must have caught her expression. A flush of color darkened his high cheekbones. "I've just come from Newbold's autopsy," he said. "Never a pleasant thing to witness first thing in the morning." He hung his hat on a hook and indicated the two visitors' chairs, taking his own seat behind the desk.

"Tell me what it is that concerns you about Visscher?"

Harriet related Visscher's strange appearance out of the dark and the rain.

"The VOC?" Curran shook his head. "Are you sure those were his words?"

"Both Julian and I thought it quite peculiar."

Curran sat back in his chair and looked up at the dusty beams high above him. "The VOC. I know I've heard it referred to somewhere." He cast a glance at Maddocks. "Do you know?"

"Isn't it the acronym for the old Dutch East India Company? I don't know what it is in Dutch," Maddocks replied.

Curran nodded. "You're right, but hasn't the Dutch East India Company been defunct for years?"

Maddocks shrugged. "A century, if not longer."

"I fail to see what an extinct company of Dutch merchants has to do with the murder of Sir Oswald Newbold," Harriet said.

Curran pushed back from the desk. "I think I need to visit the Hotel Van Wijk and I still need to get a statement from you, Mrs.

Gordon. Can I send Constable Greaves up to see you this afternoon?"

She nodded. "He'll find me at the school." She paused, seeing the frown puckering his eyebrows. "I prefer to keep busy, Inspector."

A smile tugged at the corner of Curran's mouth. "I expect nothing less, Mrs. Gordon. You may take your typewriter." He waved a hand at his bookcase and her heart jumped at the sight of the familiar neat black box.

She smiled in relief. "Thank you, Inspector. I really didn't want to handwrite all those letters."

He lifted the box down and handed it to her.

Maddocks rose to his feet. "Inspector, I have a mind for one of the Van Wijk's ices on such a hot morning. Perhaps I could walk with you?"

Curran held up a warning finger and opened his mouth as if to berate the journalist, but Maddocks only smiled in response.

Curran shook his head. "Choose your friends wisely, Mrs. Gordon. This one is trouble. Unfortunately for you, Maddocks, I intend to take my horse."

Harriet tightened her grip on the handle of her typewriter case. "Inspector, please tell me what you find out about Visscher. I am worried about him. He seemed like a nice boy and he had been badly frightened by something."

"Of course. Maddocks, perhaps you would care to see Mrs. Gordon safely to a *ricksha*?"

Maddocks opened his mouth as if he intended to protest but changed his mind. "Of course. My pleasure. Harriet, I do believe the inspector wishes to be rid of us."

The smell of the fabled curry tiffin drifted into the reception hall of the Hotel Van Wijk. Curran sniffed appreciatively but it still lacked an hour or so until lunchtime and his lunch generally comprised whatever he could find at the nearest street stall. A young European man, dressed in the white ducks that were the uniform of the clerical class, stood behind the reception desk. He looked up and, seeing Curran striding across the foyer, the red blemishes that marred his face went a slightly darker shade as his gaze swept across Curran's khaki uniform and badges of rank.

"Can I help you?"

Curran's gaze dropped to the polished brass name tag on the young man's jacket. "Paar, is it? I wish to speak with the manager. Mr. Van Gelder, I believe."

Paar nodded and vanished into the office behind the reception desk.

Curran knew the hotel manager by sight, a short, stout man with a round face and a halo of wispy white hair. There had been several thefts and disturbances at the hotel in the three years Curran had been in Singapore but none of sufficient gravity to warrant his attention so he made a point of introducing himself.

A momentary disquiet crossed Van Gelder's pleasant features, to be replaced by an unctuous smile as he shook Curran's hand in a two-handed grip.

"It is always a pleasure to help the police, Inspector Curran. What is it I can assist you with?"

Conscious of the studied insouciance of the clerk, Curran gestured at the office. "A private word, Mr. Van Gelder."

"Of course, but excuse me, first I must greet the Cornilissens."

An expensively dressed European couple had entered the hotel and stood waiting as the porter secured their luggage from the carriage in which they had arrived. As they sallied forward, Van Gelder greeted them as if they were royalty. The man was in his early middle age, tall, dressed in a well-cut linen suit, and his wife, a much younger, slender blonde, was dressed in a froufrou of ruffles and lace, set off by glittering jewels. A testimony to the adage that money did not buy taste, Curran thought as he waited patiently as Van Gelder addressed the couple in Dutch.

Curran's years in South Africa had given him a smattering of Dutch and he understood enough to know that the couple were not strangers to Van Gelder. The hotel manager bowed obsequiously with a raised eyebrow and a declaration that he was assisting the police in a trivial matter and would they excuse him while he concluded his business.

"Frequent visitors?" Curran inquired.

"Meneer Cornilissen comes every year at this time," Van Gelder said.

More out of habit than curiosity, Curran inquired, "Why?"

Van Gelder's eyes widened. "You have not heard of Cornilissen? He is an Amsterdam dealer in antiquities. If you are seeking a special gift for Mrs. Curran, I can introduce you—'

"There is no Mrs. Curran," Curran cut in sharply. "And I do not have time to pass in pleasantries."

Van Gelder inclined his head. "Of course. Perhaps if you care to come through to my office, Inspector."

The room behind the reception desk housed two unoccupied clerks' desks and another desk at which a young Chinese girl, barely visible over the enormous machine, sat typing at an impressive speed. Van Gelder did not bother to introduce the girl. He hurried Curran through to a glass-partitioned office and took his place behind a large teak desk, gesturing at a low, uncomfortable seat across from him.

Curran remained standing and came straight to the point.

"I believe you have a young man working for you by the name of Visscher?"

"*Ja*, Hans Visscher." Van Gelder indicated one of the empty desks beyond the window and frowned. "He did not turn up for work today and Paar tells me the boy did not come home last evening."

"Paar . . . the young man on duty?"

"Stefan Paar." Van Gelder rolled his eyes. "He is cross with me because I make him work when really Visscher is the duty clerk."

"And you haven't reported him missing?"

Van Gelder shook his head. "Why should I? He is a young man. I thought perhaps he may have fallen prey to the charms of a pretty young lady in Serangoon Road."

Curran turned back to look at him. "That is a liberal attitude, Mr. Van Gelder."

Van Gelder held his hand up. "I was a young man once myself, Inspector, but do not mistake me. When he returns he will feel my wrath and have his pay docked." He steepled his fingers and considered the policeman. "No, I see no reason to be concerned. I expect he will return by this evening. Probably with a tattoo and a bad hangover."

"He does this often?"

Van Gelder picked up a pen from its stand and twirled it in his fingers, dropping blobs of ink on the blotter. "I must confess, such behavior does seem out of character. He is a steady young man. Now, if it were Paar . . ."

Curran turned to glance at the young clerk whose dark, greased head he could see above the frosted-glass partition and a familiar sense of foreboding tugged at him. His instincts were not often wrong and right now they were telling him that Visscher's disappearance was not attributable to the folly of youth.

"How long has Visscher worked here?"

"He came to me about nine months ago with impeccable references from a colleague in Amsterdam. He told me he was keen to learn the hotel business and he has, until now, been exemplary in his conduct. However, he will be returning to Amsterdam at the end of his contract. There is a young woman but . . . isn't there always a young woman, Inspector?"

"Have you heard of Sir Oswald Newbold?"

Van Gelder tapped a copy of the *Straits Times* that sat folded on his desk. "Terrible business. Sir Oswald was a frequent guest at this establishment. He would stay here if he had meetings of the Explorers and Geographers Club. It is walking distance and the hospitality at the club could be"—he coughed—"quite expansive. Why, he was only just here on Saturday night."

"For a meeting at the club?"

"I believe so. A dinner to welcome a new member or some such." Van Gelder's moustache twitched. "It is, however, a very exclusive club and he was not forthcoming about their business."

"When did he leave?"

"In the morning. His man fetched him after breakfast."

"Did he leave anything behind after his stay?"

Van Gelder frowned and shook his head. "Not that I am aware. Why do you ask?"

"Because Mr. Visscher paid a call on him on Sunday evening, claiming to be returning lost property."

Van Gelder sat back in his chair and his eyes widened in surprise. "Why would he do that?"

Curran shook his head. "I'm asking you."

"Sir Oswald was a genial gentleman and much liked by all the staff at the hotel. I would like to think of him as a personal friend." Van Gelder glanced down at the paper again and his moustache drooped. "I knew him in Rangoon and I have him to thank for introducing me to my lovely wife. She is most upset by his tragic death."

Rangoon? The Burmese connection again.

"When were you both in Rangoon?"

Van Gelder frowned. "I came to Singapore in '07. Mrs. Van Gelder and I were married there just before I took up this post."

Curran filed this bit of information away. Connections were always interesting and often the key to solving crimes but he still had to establish why Hans Visscher had turned up at Mandalay on Sunday night.

"Was it possible that Visscher was doing some sort of private work for Newbold?"

Van Gelder shrugged. "What the boy did in his spare time was up to him. I am not a slave driver, Inspector."

"Where does Visscher live?"

"The young single men lodge with us in our residence on Victoria Street. My wife looks after them." He smiled fondly. "She likes to think of herself as mother to the youngsters. At the moment we have only Paar and Visscher in residence. I am expecting two new clerks on the next steamer from Amsterdam."

"Did he have any particular friends that you were aware of?"

Van Gelder shook his head. "I could not tell you that. Perhaps Paar may be the one to talk to?"

Curran straightened. "I would like to speak with him now, if I may?"

"Of course, whatever we can do to assist the police." Van Gelder gestured at the door.

"And then I would like to talk to your wife."

"My wife, but why?" Van Gelder stiffened.

"I need to speak to everyone who knows Hans Visscher."

"I will, of course, accompany you, but surely there is no reason to be concerned for him?"

"Mr. Visscher was the last person to see Sir Oswald Newbold alive. He has disappeared and I think there is every reason to be concerned for him. Don't you, Mr. Van Gelder?"

Van Gelder rose to his feet. "You are right. Come this way. You shall speak to Mr. Paar and then I will take you to my residence to speak with my wife."

"Stefan Paar?" Curran stood over the desk, forcing the young man to look up at him. "Do you mind if we have a word?"

Sweat beaded the fine, dark hairs on the young man's upper lip. "I am on duty, sir."

"This won't take long, and Mr. Van Gelder has given his consent for me to speak with you." He glanced at Van Gelder. "I would prefer to speak to Mr. Paar alone."

Van Gelder frowned but gave a brusque nod of his head.

"Very well, I will look after the desk while you speak with the inspector."

Curran glanced at the door that led out onto the terrace and the garden of the hotel. "Shall we step outside?"

The boy nodded and Van Gelder took his place behind the desk.

Outside on the terrace, Paar fumbled in his pocket, producing a cigarette case. He flicked it open, offering Curran a cigarette. Curran obliged by taking one.

"Do you have matches?" Paar asked.

Curran rummaged in his pocket for a book of matches and lit the boy's cigarette, noticing that the young man's hand shook as he cupped the flame. Nerves or something else? he wondered.

He lit his own cigarette, tossing the dead match into a clump of bright purple bougainvillea.

"What can I help you with?" Paar asked.

"How long have you been in Singapore?" Curran asked.

"Nearly a year," Paar replied, adding, "I hate it. As soon as my year is up I am going back to Amsterdam."

"Why do you hate it?"

Paar ran a finger around the high, tight collar of his white ducks. "This heat stifles me and it stinks." He pulled a face and gestured at the distant *dhobi wallahs*, or laundrymen, spreading their washing on the bank of the canal. "And I don't speak any of these infernal languages. I was supposed to go to Batavia, where at least they speak Dutch. Instead I end up here." His lip curled in distaste.

"You are a friend of Hans Visscher?" Curran asked.

The boy took a long inhale of his cigarette, blowing the smoke upward, where it seemed to linger in the humid air. "We work together and share the same lodgings but we are not really friends."

"Let us walk a little, Mr. Paar," Curran suggested.

They strolled in silence through the gardens of the hotel to the bank of the Stamford Canal, where a few *dhobis* crouched at the waterside, scrubbing laundry of indeterminate origin. Most *dho-bis* worked farther upstream where the canal was still a river.

"Did you know Hans Visscher back in Amsterdam?"

Paar shook his head. "No. He arrived a few months after me. He is from The Hague, not Amsterdam. He hates it too but we are contracted for two years."

"When did you last see him?"

"Yesterday. He finished work about five and went straight out."

"What sort of mood was he in?"

Paar glanced at him. "We'd heard the news about Sir Oswald Newbold's murder and it seemed to upset him."

"Why?"

"Sir Oswald was a frequent guest and a good tipper. He seemed to favor Visscher."

The careless shrug accompanying those words made Curran's spine prickle. A pretty young boy and an older man?

"Was there anything"—he paused seeking the right words to convey his meaning—"particular about the relationship?"

Paar stared at him and a flush rose to his face as understanding dawned. "No . . . at least I don't think so. Visscher had a girl back in Holland. He was here to earn the money for them to marry."

"How desperate was he for money?"

A sneer twisted Paar's mouth. "Not that desperate, Inspector."

"So, you haven't seen Visscher since late yesterday afternoon?"

Paar shook his head. "I was on duty until ten and when I got back to the lodging, he was not there. Mrs. Van Gelder said he had not returned home at any time that evening. I went to bed. When he had not returned this morning, this meant I had to do his shift. When I see him . . ." Paar fumbled for another cigarette. "Can I have another light?"

Curran obliged but this time Paar did not offer him the cigarette case.

As he took a deep draught on the cigarette, Paar asked, "Are you asking me these questions because you think Visscher's disappearance is connected with Newbold's murder?"

"Have you ever heard Visscher mention the VOC?"

Something flickered behind the young man's eyes and he looked down at the cigarette, toying with it between his fingers before replying. "The old Dutch East India Company? That has been gone for over a century. It is just part of history." Paar puffed on his cigarette, trying to finish it in haste. It only made him cough. He glanced back at the hotel. "I should get back to work."

"Mr. Paar, you seem singularly unconcerned that your colleague is missing," Curran said. "Do you think it is possible he is with a girl in Serangoon Road?"

Paar laughed, a cold, humorless laugh. "He would not know what to do if he did meet one, Inspector. I told you he has a sweet little virgin waiting for him in Rotterdam."

So much for Van Gelder's theory, Curran thought with a mounting sense of disquiet.

Paar turned and began to walk back toward the hotel.

"Wait. I haven't finished," Curran called after him. "Where were you on Sunday night?"

Paar's step faltered and he turned back to face the policeman. "Me?"

Curran fixed Paar with an unblinking stare. The young man's eyes slid sideways. "I was with a girl at Madam Suzi's in Serangoon Road," he said, naming one of the many brothels to be found on that street.

"Her name?"

Paar looked Curran in the eye and grinned. "I didn't bother with a name but ask Madam Suzi. She will vouch for me. I am a regular."

Curran's skin crawled. "I will do just that," he said.

* * *

Curran waited for Paar to return to his post. He lit one of his own cigarettes and stood watching the slow trickle of water in the canal. The next rainstorm would turn it into a raging torrent. That was Singapore, a place of extremes.

He couldn't put a finger on what it was about Paar that irritated him. Perhaps it was just the greasy hair and the callous disregard for a young girl he had paid for sex. He stubbed out his cigarette, grinding it into the dirt with the heel of his boot before returning to Van Gelder. Paar, back on the reception desk, looked up from the guest he was attending to, his hard gaze raking Curran's face as he and Van Gelder passed the desk.

Van Gelder led him through the gardens to a smaller bungalow, tucked away at the back of the property, facing out on to Victoria Street.

"*Mijn vrouw* and I occupy the main rooms," Van Gelder said as they mounted the steps to the verandah. "There is an attic room where the young men lodge. *Mijn vrouw* . . . I apologize . . . my wife looks after them as if they were her own sons."

"A good woman," Curran said, reflecting that it was the second time Van Gelder had expounded on the motherly care Mrs. Van Gelder showed the clerks.

"*Ja.* A very good woman."

He opened the door and called out, "*Mijn lieve?*"

Curran looked around the front room of the bungalow. Van Gelder lived well for the manager of a hotel, Curran thought, his gaze taking in the teak furniture, the antique vases and a handsome statue of the Buddha in the style of the statuary at the Bukit Timah house. Maybe Van Gelder's guest Cornilissen helped in the selection of the pieces.

A small, plump woman emerged from the back of the house to greet them, wiping her hands on her apron.

"*Wat brengt je huis in het midden van de dag?*" she inquired of her husband.

"*Mijn lieve*, this is Inspector Curran of the Straits Settlements Police."

The woman flushed and bobbed her head. "My apologies. You are a policeman. I can see that now. Is there trouble?" She patted the coiled plait of fair hair that circled her head. A few stray wisps clung damply to her forehead and she pushed these back with an impatient gesture. "I apologize for my appearance. I have been trying to teach that useless girl how to cook *poffertjes*."

Curran held up a hand. "Excuse my unannounced visit, Mrs. Van Gelder. I am curious about your clerk Visscher. Has he returned this morning?"

Mrs. Van Gelder glanced at her husband. "There was a woman here asking the same question only an hour or so ago. Mrs. Gordon . . . is it she who has sent you? Is he in trouble, Inspector?"

Curran ignored the reference to Harriet Gordon. "I am anxious to interview Mr. Visscher in relation to the death of Sir Oswald Newbold. Is this prolonged absence in his character?"

Mrs. Van Gelder's already flushed cheeks pinkened further. "I would say not, but surely he is just off on some boyish frolic?"

"Hopefully he is," Curran agreed. "When did you last see him?"

"At breakfast yesterday morning. The boys eat with us."

"How did he seem?"

"He was a very quiet boy, Inspector Curran. A good boy."

"And Sunday night?"

The woman frowned. "Ah *ja*. It was his day off and he went out for the day. He would have attended church and then . . ." She shrugged.

"What time did he get in on Sunday night?"

She thought for a long moment. "I believe it was about eight. I asked if he had eaten and he said he hadn't. I made sure he ate something and he went up to his room shortly after. I did not see him again until the morning." Her lips tightened. "Unlike Paar, who did not come home until nearly eleven reeking of cheap perfume and who knows what else beside. I told him that the good Lord turned his hand against Sodom and Gomorrah and he should have a better care of his soul. It is a rule of my house that they must tell me if they are to miss a meal or have made some other arrangement for the night. The front door is locked at eleven o'clock each night and I do not let them keep a key. If they wish to return after that hour, they must answer to me."

"And pay a fine," Mr. Van Gelder added.

Curran redirected the woman's attention back to Visscher, asking if she had noticed anything unusual about the boy on his return home on Sunday or over breakfast on Monday.

"No." She clasped her hands in front of her apron and drew herself up, every inch the outraged housewife. "He shall get such a scolding when I do see him."

I am sure he will, Curran thought, his sympathy entirely with the wayward young men who had the good fortune to lodge with this woman. He had met too many formidable Dutch ladies of Mrs. Van Gelder's ilk in South Africa.

Mrs. Van Gelder's expression softened. "Don't mistake me, Inspector. I hope no harm has befallen him. He is a nice young man. Never any trouble, always polite. Not like others."

He thanked Mrs. Van Gelder for the inconvenience and handed her his card with a request that she contact him if Visscher should return home. "Of course, Inspector Curran, whatever we can do to assist the police. I just pray the boy is safe and well."

"As do we all," Curran agreed, but as he returned to the motor vehicle, the feeling that all was not right with Mr. Visscher settled on his shoulders.

✣ EIGHT

Nothing distinguished the Explorers and Geographers Club from any other old bungalow of its vintage, except a discreet brass plaque beside the front door. It read simply EGC, NO ADMITTANCE TO NONMEMBERS.

Friendly and welcoming, Curran thought, and rang the bell anyway.

An Indian *jagar* in Punjabi dress answered the door, a man of immense size who would have dwarfed the not-insubstantial Sergeant Singh. It appeared the khaki uniform with its insignia of an officer of the Straits Settlements Police and highly polished Sam Browne were not sufficient to identify Curran as being an official who should be given appropriate deference. Instead the *jagar* filled the doorway with his looming, silent presence and eyed Curran as one would an insect that had strayed across his path.

Curran said loudly, "The name is Curran, Straits Settlements Police. I wish to speak to the secretary."

The *jagar* moved his gaze to the brass plaque.

With rising annoyance, Curran said, "I don't care much for signs of that nature. I am investigating the death of the president of this club. Admit me now."

"What is it?" An English voice came from behind the massive man.

"Inspector Curran, Straits Settlements Police. I wish to speak with the secretary of this club about the death of Sir Oswald Newbold."

"Of course," the unseen man said. "Stand aside and allow the inspector in."

The *jagar* complied, without haste and without removing his inscrutable gaze from Curran, revealing a tall, slender man of middle age, his graying hair balding at the temples.

The man held his hand out. "James Carruthers. I am secretary of the club. Do come in, Inspector Curran. We can speak in my office."

Carruthers led Curran through a large open room, furnished with rattan chairs and plantation furniture. Dusty *punkas* stirred the air, pulled by unseen hands behind the wall. Just like any exclusive gentlemen's club in London, the ubiquitous glasses of whisky stood on tables beside the occupied chairs and newspapers rustled in disapproval at the intruder.

Curran disliked such places. They reminded him of the time his uncle had summoned him to attend his London club and confronted him about the "disgraceful incident" that had led to him being sent down from Cambridge. The injustice of the accusation brought against him had set him forever against the establishment and everything his uncle and these exclusive gentlemen's clubs stood for.

The spicy aroma of curry permeated the building, reminding him it had been a long time since breakfast.

"Smells good," he remarked.

"Next to the Van Wijk, we serve the best curry tiffin in Singapore," Carruthers said, opening a glass-paneled door marked SECRETARY in gold lettering.

The secretary's office was a pleasant room, looking out onto

Fort Canning Hill, wood paneled and furnished with solid, well-polished English furniture. Several hand-tinted maps of Southeast Asia decorated the walls and statuettes of dancing maidens and elegant clay pots jostled with the books on a large bookcase.

Carruthers indicated a chair and asked if Curran would like refreshment. Thinking fondly of a beer to wash down a plate of curry, Curran asked for tea. A white-clad club servant was summoned and dispatched with the order. As they waited for the servant to return, Curran asked how many members the club had.

"At last count, forty-seven," Carruthers said.

"That seems like a lot of exploring," Curran remarked.

"Not all local, you understand. We've members who have done their life's work in Africa, South America and Australia."

"And you?"

Carruthers lowered his eyes and gave a self-deprecating laugh. "Alas, there is nowhere on this planet that bears my name, Inspector. I am but a paid employee of the club."

The downturned mouth made Curran think that some members of the club probably took delight in reminding Carruthers of this status.

The servant returned with a tray bearing a silver teapot and delicate crockery. Curran waited until the tea was poured before he turned to the main purpose of his visit.

"I am enquiring into the murder of Sir Oswald Newbold," he said.

"Of course." Carruthers set his teacup down and took out a handkerchief, which he used to mop his brow. "Terrible business. We are all shocked, Curran."

"He was, I believe, president of this club?"

"Indeed. Had been for this last year."

"And what was his claim to membership?"

"There is a Mt. Newbold in northern Burma. Named for him during his explorations in the '70s."

Remembering the map of the Mogok valley in Newbold's study, Curran maintained a bland expression.

"What was the nature of his explorations in that area?" he inquired in a neutral tone.

Carruthers ran a finger around the stiff high collar of his shirt and cleared his throat. His obvious discomfort intrigued Curran.

"Northern Burma was still an independent state but a dashedly wealthy one, based on rubies and sapphires, mostly. The British were keen to exploit that wealth."

Curran sat forward. "Go on."

"A syndicate was formed in London—the Burmese Ruby Syndicate. It commissioned a small expeditionary force in Rangoon to infiltrate the northern Burmese territory in secret and report back on the location of the mines. Of course, it all had to be very hush-hush. The Burmese would not have been pleased."

Possibly not, Curran thought. "And was it successful?"

"Depends how you measure success," Carruthers remarked with a twitch of his lips. "The expedition consisted of Newbold, an army officer, a clerk and three servants. Only two returned . . . Newbold and the army officer."

"What happened?"

Carruthers shrugged. "It's bloody thick jungle up in those parts, Inspector. Accidents, disease, run-ins with the locals . . . Newbold had a story to account for all of them."

The man could not disguise the bitterness in his tone and Curran felt the instinctive prickle of a story withheld.

"Is there something you're not telling me, Carruthers?"

Carruthers stood up and walked over to the window. He stood for a long moment with his back to Curran.

Curran had found through long experience that silences had to be filled and said nothing.

Eventually Carruthers turned back to face him. "You'll find out anyway. The clerk who went out with them was George Carruthers, my father. According to Newbold, Father contracted some sort of hemorrhagic fever and died in days."

"How old were you?"

"Eleven. My mother and I were living in Rangoon at the time."

"Who was the army officer?"

"A man called Kent. Don't know what became of him."

"What about the reports Newbold brought back?"

"He didn't just bring back reports. He brought back proof. A huge ruby. I saw it once it had been cut and polished. I think the syndicate sold it to a German royal family. Newbold had discovered extensive mines in the area just north of Mogok. That was all the British government needed. They annexed northern Burma and brought it under the administrative control of British India. Once the area was secure, the Burmese Ruby Syndicate went in with Newbold as the principal. A lot of people made a lot of money. Newbold was quite the hero. Got his knighthood for it."

Curran's nerves tingled at the undisguised hatred on Carruthers's face.

"And your father was forgotten?"

As if realizing he had given too much away, Carruthers straightened and held up a hand. "Please don't mistake me, Inspector. I bore Newbold no ill will. Father made his choice to go, knowing it was a dangerous mission. My mother and I were looked after by the syndicate. We went back to England and my mother settled in Bournemouth, where she ran a lodging house. I sat for my Indian Civil Service exams and came back out East about fifteen years ago, just after she died." He smiled. "Have to admit, I never got used to the weather in England."

Curran agreed with that sentiment.

"How long have you been secretary here?"

"Not quite a year."

"And how did you get on with Newbold?"

"Well, it came as something of a shock when I found out he was a member. Not just a member, the president. Of course, he knew who I was. Spoke very highly of my father and to be honest I probably have to thank him for the post."

"You didn't answer the question," Curran prodded.

"He could be very demanding. A man used to getting his own way." Carruthers's neat moustache twitched. "Mind you, that probably describes most of the membership."

Enough chat. Time for the business at hand.

"When did you last see Sir Oswald?"

"Saturday night. We have a monthly members' dinner."

"What time did Sir Oswald leave?"

Carruthers shook his head. "It would have been well after midnight. He takes a room at the Van Wijk on the nights we have these dinners."

"Walking distance?"

"Precisely."

"You didn't see him on Sunday?"

"No. It is my day off, Inspector."

"What were you doing on Sunday night?"

The man started, half rising from his chair. "You don't think I . . . ? That is quite impossible . . . Actually, I was here until midnight."

Curran held up his hand. "It is just a routine question, Carruthers. If it was your day off, why did you come in to the club?"

"I had paperwork I wanted to get out of the way by Monday. Since you'll find out from the other committee members, Newbold had raised a concern over the accounts and I wanted to ensure I had all the figures correct before the committee were due to meet on Monday."

"Anyone who can confirm your presence?"

"At least half a dozen members. The club doesn't close, Inspector, and life in Singapore can be . . . lonely."

"I would be grateful if you can give me their names and I will send someone to take statements and to take your fingerprints."

Carruthers's eyes widened. "Fingerprints?"

"Yes, it is a new technique we have introduced." Curran looked at his hand. "Every person in the world has different fingerprints, did you know that, Carruthers? And whenever you touch something." He picked up the cup. "You leave traces of those fingerprints that can be seen with the right techniques."

"Really?" Carruthers said without enthusiasm. He glanced at the fingers of his right hand. "How interesting."

"It is," Curran said with a reassuring smile. "Back to Newbold. Did he have any enemies in the club?"

Carruthers shook his head but there was the faintest hesitation before he said, "Not at all. He was respected by everybody."

Respected but not liked?

"Could you supply me with a membership list and indicate on it those who were particular friends of Sir Oswald?"

"Friends?" The concept seemed strange to Carruthers.

"Members he spent more time with than others," Curran clarified.

Carruthers shifted in his seat. "We are very exclusive. I'll have to ask the committee. The members won't be happy."

"One of your members died violently, Carruthers."

"Of course, but I will have to clear it with the committee and the incoming president."

"Who is?"

"Colonel Augustus Foster'

Curran brightened. He knew Foster from the cricket club. The colonel never missed a game and he had enjoyed some good chats with the man on one of his own favorite subjects—cricket.

Carruthers pushed his chair back from the desk, signaling that in his opinion the interview was over. "Is there anything else I can help you with, Inspector?"

"One last thing." Curran patted his pocket, remembering the bag with the knife he had retrieved from Mackenzie that morning. He pulled it out, holding the knife carefully with his handkerchief. "Have you seen this before?"

Carruthers recoiled, his lips drawn back against his teeth. "Is that the . . . the . . ."

Curran ignored the question. "Can you tell me what sort of knife it is?"

"It's a *dha*," Carruthers answered without hesitation. "A Burmese weapon." He squinted and peered closely at the knife. "Of some antiquity," he added.

"Have you seen it before?"

Carruthers straightened. "Yes. Sir Oswald kept it in his study in his home. He used it as a sort of paperweight."

"You've visited Newbold's house?"

"Yes, several times, on club business, you understand."

"When were you last there?"

Carruthers shrugged. "Two, three weeks ago?"

"Were you aware Newbold had written his memoirs?"

Carruthers's moustache twitched and he nodded. "Everyone knew. In fact, I was rather looking forward to them. Sort of hoped he showed my father in a good light. I suppose they will be published posthumously now?"

Curran crossed his arms and after a pause, he said, "If we can find the manuscript."

Carruthers's graying eyebrows shot up. "It's missing?"

"Would there be anything in that manuscript that would be worth killing for?" Curran asked, fixing the man with an unblinking gaze.

Carruthers frowned. "Inspector, I'll be honest with you. I knew Newbold well and I doubt that the memoirs are anything more than the boastful ramblings of an old man. He was given to exaggeration. I didn't have any great hopes of it."

Curran kept his gaze on Carruthers. The bitterness in the man's voice had not escaped him. Carruthers's father had died on Newbold's expedition to northern Burma in 1876 while Newbold had returned a hero and a wealthy man. He could understand the man's curiosity in the portrayal of his father.

Carruthers stood up and faced Curran. "Is that all, Inspector?" Curran shook the man's hand. "For now, Carruthers."

"Let me see you out."

As Carruthers shepherded his unwanted visitor out of the front door, they encountered Colonel Augustus Foster coming up the front steps.

"Curran!" Foster exclaimed. "Good to see you, man. What brings you here?"

"The inspector was just leaving, Colonel," Carruthers said.

"Leaving? Nonsense. It's nearly lunchtime and the man must be starving. We do one of the best curry tiffins in Singapore, Curran. Come and join me. My guest."

Curran, conscious that Carruthers was all but hopping from one foot to the other in his anxiety to be rid of his unwelcome visitor, extended his hand to the colonel and said, "I'd be delighted."

Foster guided Curran into the dining room, a timber-paneled room lined with framed maps, each one surmounted with an embossed brass plate.

Curran wandered over to one wall and inspected the maps closely. Each brass plate bore a name and a date.

The colonel laughed. "Every new member has to present the club with an official map proving their eligibility for membership." He pointed to one particular map that, on closer inspection, appeared to be a part of British East Africa. "River Foster. That's mine. Now, do take a seat, dear boy."

As Curran settled himself the colonel returned to his favorite subject. "Big game this weekend, old chap. Johor Cricket Club. You'll be opening for the SCC?"

The annual Johor cricket match. He'd forgotten all about it. Curran cursed to himself. "I doubt it, Colonel. I have Sir Oswald's murder investigation . . ."

"Oh yes, rum business," the colonel said. "But before we start

on that, as I'm sure you have questions for me, let's order. Abdul"—
he summoned one of the white-clad club servants—"two chicken
curries and beers."

With an afternoon of interviews stretching ahead of him,
Curran wasn't sure a heavy curry meal and a beer . . . or two . . .
would help much, but while he had the colonel's ear, he might as
well take advantage of it.

"How well did you know Sir Oswald?" he asked, after the
servant set down the huge platters of meat and rice.

"Well enough. Met him a few times when I was posted to
Rangoon, but only really got to know him through the club."
Foster tore a piece of naan bread and dipped it into the fragrant
sauce.

"When were you in Rangoon, Colonel?"

Foster chewed on his naan. "Moved around a bit between
Burma and India. Never in one place for very long. Decided to
retire to Singapore about three years ago. Had enough of the
wandering life."

"Were you there around the time of Newbold's exploration of
northern Burma?"

Foster finished chewing his mouthful. "No. I was posted in a
bit later. You can imagine the natives weren't too pleased about
the annexation. Had to spend a few months up there myself dealing with a bit of insurrection. Did Carruthers tell you his father
was one of the party that went with Newbold?"

"He did."

Foster frowned. "Good chap, Carruthers. Newbold did pretty
damn well out of the ruby syndicate. Between us, from what I
gather nothing much flowed the way of Carruthers's widow and
child."

That seemed to contradict what Carruthers had told him.

"Why didn't Newbold retire back to England?" Curran changed
the subject.

"Good God, man. You of all people to ask that question. Nothing in England except miserable weather and miserable people. Told me he decided to retire to Singapore and write his memoirs. Now, they'd make interesting reading."

They would if we could find them, Curran thought.

"Have you read any of his writing?" Curran ventured.

Foster shook his head. "He was being very close with it."

"Did the memoirs contain anything that would cause concern?"

Foster's sharp eyes fixed Curran in a hard glare. "Do you mean was there anything in his memoirs that may have led to his death?"

Curran left it to Foster to answer his own question.

"Look, between us, the man was a crashing bore and prone to exaggerating his own importance, but would anyone kill him for it? You've got the manuscript, you can read it and tell me."

"We don't have the manuscript. It was the only thing taken from the bungalow."

Foster's fork fell back onto his plate, causing drops of yellow sauce to splatter on his pristine linen suit. "The manuscript? Who would take that?"

"That's what I would like to know," Curran replied, sopping up the last of his curry with a piece of bread. "Was he greatly liked by the club membership?" Curran lowered his tone as a group of men entered the dining room.

"Not that sort of place, Curran." Foster also lowered his voice. "You don't have to be loved to be president of the Explorers." Foster leaned forward. "Frankly, all he had to show for his record was that one expedition in Burma and any expedition where good men are lost is not successful, whatever riches you may find."

"You were in the army. What became of the other man . . . Kent?"

Foster shrugged. "Died of fever a few years later, I believe. Didn't know him myself. Another beer?"

Curran shook his head and thanked the colonel for the meal. He had left his chestnut gelding, Leopold, tethered at the front gate and the horse gave Curran a reproachful glance as Curran swung himself into the saddle.

"Sorry, old chap, didn't mean to be so long," he said to the horse as he turned back toward South Bridge Road to write up his notes and check on the progress of the rest of the investigation.

Harriet had been unable to settle into any serious work and she stood in the shelter of the porte cochere of the school building, her arms folded, watching a group of sweat-soaked boys playing rugby on the playing fields. A curiously inappropriate game for the climate, she thought.

As she turned to return to the office, a *ricksha* trundled through the gates and she heard her name called.

An Englishman in neat flannels and a white shirt waved at her and jumped down from the *ricksha*. He paused to give the *ricksha wallah* orders to wait and the man set down the conveyance and squatted in the shade of the porte cochere, his jaw moving rhythmically as he chewed on his betel nut. The Englishman turned to Harriet, whipping the hat from his head.

"Mrs. Gordon, how are you this afternoon?"

It took a moment for Harriet to recognize John Lawson, the parent of one of their boarders. They had only met once, briefly, at the end of the previous term but she knew the name well enough. It headed the list of tardy fee payers.

"Mr. Lawson. Have you come to see Will?"

"Yes, but first I need to settle some outstanding school fees with you."

She smiled at the man and gestured at the rugby players. "Will's out there getting hot and muddy. Do come in. You've saved me the trouble of writing you a letter."

She opened the door to the study to admit him into the relative cool of the room, seated herself behind her desk and opened the ledger. "You are now two terms in arrears and the board of governors are not"—she paused, searching for the right word—"always inclined to be charitable." She looked up, seeing the frown creasing his brow. "We would hate to lose Will. My brother tells me that he is one of our brightest students."

Lawson beamed with paternal pride. "He is a smart little chap. I wanted to send him to England to school but Annie, my wife, wouldn't hear of it and after she died, well, I couldn't bear to be parted from him." Beneath his straggly moustache, the corners of his mouth turned down and the lines of his face lapsed into heavy folds that belied his age. Even accounting for the heat, he had a high color and the whites of his eyes were shot with an unhealthy red. "Sorry for the delay. The price of rubber, y'know . . . To be honest, it's a struggle sending him down here to school."

She recalled that Lawson managed a rubber plantation in the north of the island not far from Kranji. As the price of rubber seemed to be a main preoccupation of the *Straits Times*, even she had not failed to notice the dire prognostications for the price of the commodity.

"Unfortunately schooling for English boys beyond the age of eleven is very limited in Singapore, Mr. Lawson. You may have to consider some options in England."

"I know, but I've two years to think about that . . . and save the money," he said with a sigh.

"There should be every chance he could win a scholarship if money were short, Mr. Lawson," Harriet said. "You should talk to my brother."

He looked at her and grinned again, his lugubrious features brightening. "He's that smart?"

Harriet nodded. "I'm not a teacher, of course, but I hear them talking about him and I see the school reports."

He nodded. "Annie would be proud."

From what Harriet knew of the family, Lawson's wife had died about twelve months ago. Grief still leached from him and in the confines of the room a fug of alcohol hung over him, which might have accounted for his high color and bloodshot eyes.

She named the outstanding amount and Lawson reached into the jacket of his crumpled linen suit and produced a bulging leather wallet. He counted out the notes, adding in the fees for the following term, and as Harriet wrote a receipt she asked what had brought him into town.

"I brought a load of rubber down on Sunday and then I had a meeting with the board on Monday morning," he replied without enthusiasm. "At least I was paid for the shipment."

Harriet handed him the receipt, which he tucked into his now much depleted wallet.

He rose to his feet. "Can I see Will?"

"Of course. They must have just about finished their game. Let me see you out."

She walked with Lawson to the door. The *ricksha wallah* had dozed off, leaning against the wheel of his conveyance. Harriet crossed her arms and watched as Lawson strode across the field to where the boys were coming off the playing field.

Will broke away from his fellows and came running across to meet his father, who swung him into his arms, even though the boy looked like he had been in a mud bath. Harriet looked away, tears starting in her eyes. Sometimes the most inconsequential action reminded her of what could have been.

She returned to the study and began typing up the letters to fill in the time until the bell rang at four to mark the end of lessons for the day.

The boys at St. Tom's numbered fifty youngsters aged between five and eleven. Twenty of the boys were boarders, the rest arrived daily, generally collected in the afternoons by their *amahs*,

Chinese women in the ubiquitous uniform of black trousers and white tunics, who waited deferentially with their master's carriages while their young charges ran out to meet them.

Harriet hurried outside to supervise the collection process to find that instead of the *amahs*, several mamas had arrived in person to collect their darlings. A gaggle of the good ladies hurried across to her before she could make good her escape back into the house.

"My dear, it's all over Singapore. Is it true you found . . . the body?" Mrs. Bryce began the cross-examination.

"How did you know?"

Mrs. Wilson laughed. "No secrets in Singapore, Mrs. Gordon. But how simply dreadful for you!" The woman's eyes were bright with feigned concern.

"Did you see the body?" Mrs. Chatham asked, her gaze sliding around the other women.

"Well . . ." Harriet considered lying but ultimately prevarication would look worse than the truth.

"I heard the body had been mutilated, is that true?" Mrs. Wilson interrupted.

"They said his head had been completely severed," Mrs. Bryce took up before Harriet could answer.

Harriet stared at her.

"Mercy! We could all be murdered in our beds if this villain is not found." The excitable Mrs. Chatham declared, her hand flying to her throat.

"I heard that Robert Curran is in charge of the investigation," Mrs. Bryce said with the faintest note of disapproval in her tone.

"Is he not a good policeman?" Harriet inquired.

"Oh, very good, from what I hear," Mrs. Wilson said. She leaned in closer. "But, my dear, he's a little odd. Gone native, if you know what I mean."

"No, I don't," Harriet lied. She had lived in India for nearly ten years and knew very well what *going native* meant but the good ladies of Singapore assumed her to be a newcomer so she might as well play on it.

"Lives by himself with only a . . . female servant," Mrs. Bryce said with pursed lips and a raised eyebrow that put the words *female servant* in quotation marks.

"I heard," Mrs. Chatham put in, "that he's a grandson of Lord Alcester. Terrible scandal. His daughter married"—she paused for dramatic effect—"the son of the groom. A stable boy, my dears! Eloped, they say."

"No!" the Mrs. Wilson and Bryce chorused. "Do tell more."

Primping herself with the importance of having such juicy gossip to impart, Mrs. Chatham took a breath. "Well, according to Chatham, she died in childbirth and Curran's grandfather took him in and brought him up with his cousins. He got sent down from Cambridge after a scandal of some sort and joined the army, the Military Mounted Police." Mrs. Chatham, the wife of an army major, sniffed.

"But how does he come to be in Singapore?" Harriet asked.

"Cuscaden recruited him from the London constabulary a couple of years ago," Mrs. Chatham continued, her tone even more disapproving.

Harriet considered this piece of information. She had met men of Curran's type during her time in India. Independent loners with little or no time for the niceties of society. He certainly carried himself as a gentleman, not like the rough bobbies it had been her misfortune to encounter in London.

It was at this point that Louisa Mackenzie sailed into the conversation.

"My poor Harriet," Louisa declared. "There you are. You promised to lend me that new book by Baroness Orczy." Louisa smiled sweetly at the other mamas. "I did like her *Scarlet Pimpernel* but her later works are not so engaging."

"What about Rodney?" Harriet protested, referring to Louisa's eight-year-old son.

"I've sent Roddy home with Ashok and told Ashok to come back and fetch me in an hour. You need tea, my dear."

Linking her arm with Harriet's she steered her across the playing fields to the little gate in a wild hedge that stood between the school and St. Tom's House.

"Thank you for saving me." Harriet sank into the cushions of her favorite rattan chair on the wide verandah while Louisa dispensed orders to Huo Jin to fetch tea.

Harriet had few friends in Singapore, but Louisa Mackenzie, the wife of Dr. Euan Mackenzie, had proved her worth as a trusted confidante. She had first met Louisa in India when Euan Mackenzie had brought her to stay with Harriet and her husband, James. The two women were much of an age and the four had got on famously. The Mackenzies' presence in Singapore had been one of the lures that had drawn Harriet back to the East.

Louisa was, of course, equally agog to hear all the gruesome details.

"My dear, how perfectly frightful for you," she said after Harriet had finished recounting the events of the previous day. She leaned forward and, lowering her voice, said, "Confidentially, and Euan will be terribly cross if he thinks I've told anyone, but you're not just anyone. Euan told me at lunch that Sir Oswald had over a dozen stab wounds on his body and one of his fingers had been almost completely severed."

Harriet looked at her friend with wide, horrified eyes. "Louisa, what on earth do you and Euan talk about?"

Louisa sat back and shrugged. "Don't tell me your James didn't share the details of his occupation with you?"

"Well, yes, of course he did but he wasn't the police surgeon and didn't deal with mutilated corpses on a regular basis."

Louisa took a decorous sip of her tea. "Neither does Euan. That's what makes it so interesting when he does." She set her cup down and the two women turned their conversation to more innocuous topics.

"You have a visitor," Louisa remarked as a *ricksha* turned into the drive, carrying a solitary male passenger. The man jumped down and told the *ricksha wallah* to wait. He bounded up the stairs, pulling an incongruous bowler hat from his head.

With mixed feelings Harriet rose to her feet to greet the journalist Griff Maddocks.

"Mr. Maddocks, what brings you here again?"

Her cool greeting did not deter the journalist who smiled. "I came to tell you that Sir Oswald's funeral is set for Thursday. St. Andrew's at eleven."

"Thank you. Do you know if the boy has turned up yet?"

Maddocks shook his head.

"What boy?" Louisa inquired.

Maddocks turned to Louisa. "Mrs. Mackenzie, how lovely to see you."

"Mr. Maddocks, you can take your charm and your *ricksha* and leave us in peace. I have never met a journalist without an ulterior motive for everything they did," Louisa scoffed. "News about the funeral, indeed. Now, what boy are you talking about?"

"I thought I heard voices." Julian came around the side of the house and joined the party on the verandah. "I'm gasping for a cup of tea. Maddocks, will you join us?"

"Mr. Maddocks was just leaving . . ." Harriet began, but Maddocks had already joined them, sitting down unbidden in one of the rattan chairs and crossing his legs.

"Griff, you are incorrigible," Harriet said. Giving in, she sent Huo Jin for fresh tea.

"What's the news on the Newbold case?" Julian asked.

Griff shook his head. "None. Funeral's Thursday at St. Andrew's. It will probably be the social event of the month."

"Surpassing the opening of the Anderson Bridge?" Louisa inquired, a mischievous twinkle in her eye.

Griff pulled a face. "The editor has put me on reporting on the frills and furbelows of that little event, Mrs. Mackenzie. Me! An investigative reporter who would rather have his nose in Sir Oswald's murder."

"Give me frills and furbelows!" Louisa declared, with a quick conspiratorial glance at Harriet. "What about you, Harriet?"

Harriet shook her head. "I'm afraid as the daughter of a crown prosecutor, I would much rather spend my evenings discussing father's cases than my sister's wardrobe."

"Hopeless!" Louisa said. "I think after this week we all need a little fun. How about we make up a party for the musical evening at the Van Wijk this Saturday night? The Austrian Ladies' Orchestra will be playing."

Julian pulled a face. "Not that dreadful oompah band."

Louisa tapped his arm. "It's not an oompah band." She paused. "Well, it is, but I assure you it's great fun. The food is good and there will be dancing."

Harriet did not miss the quick glance Maddocks cast in her direction. An unfamiliar thrill of excitement ran down her spine at the thought of getting dressed up in the maligned frills and furbelows and being in the company of well-dressed and charming men, like Griff Maddocks.

"I think that sounds like an entertainment not to be missed, particularly after the unalloyed excitement of the bridge opening," Griff said.

"Excellent. I shall book some tickets. Julian, Harriet?"

"You know how I love that band," Julian groaned. He looked at his sister and smiled. "But you're right, Louisa. We need some fun. Of course we'll come."

The Mackenzies' carriage turned into the driveway and Louisa rose to her feet, securing her hat with a long pin. "We shall see you on Saturday night and just to make quite sure you don't miss a minute of the Austrian Ladies' Orchestra, I will send the carriage to collect you. Do walk me out, Harriet," she commanded, and took her friend's arm, bending her head close to Harriet's so they would not be heard by the men on the verandah.

"So, Mr. Maddocks is paying you court?"

"He is not!" Harriet declared, feeling the heat rushing to her cheeks. "I'm a story, that is all. He wants information on Sir Oswald's death."

Louisa gave her a knowing glance. "Oh, Harriet. Why not? You're still young and he is fun and charming and quite good-looking."

Harriet's eyes widened. "Louisa Mackenzie. I will not be match-made, not by my mother or my sister and certainly not by you."

But as she waved her friend off, she admitted to herself that Louisa was right, there were times she had to remind herself that she was still a comparatively young woman and she had every right to have fun and enjoy being treated as a lady, rather than as an unpaid skivvy.

She turned back to rejoin her brother on the verandah. That last thought had been unworthy. She had chosen to come to Singapore and it was not Julian's fault that the board of governors did not think her deserving of being paid. That was what she had been fighting for when she had joined the WSPU back in London and, God willing, one day it would come but for now, she had to be content with her choices in life and what little she could make from her private clients, not that she had any that were not recently deceased.

Griff jumped to his feet, his hat in his hand, as a growl of thunder shook the house. "It looks like we're in for a storm. I'll bid you farewell too," he said. "Shall I see you at the funeral?"

Harriet glanced at Julian and nodded. "I think it would be right to pay my last respects," she said, and held out her hand. "Good-bye, Mr. Maddocks."

He shook her hand and clapped his hat onto his head. "Good evening, Harriet, Reverend."

Harriet stood watching him until he had turned out of the drive and onto St. Thomas Walk. The dark, lowering clouds of the evening thunderstorm closed in overhead with a sharp crack of lightning, followed closely by a rumble of thunder.

❧ NINE

Wednesday, 9 March 1910

Death, exacerbated by a tropical climate, had its own sickly pungency, and the stench hit Curran even as he pushed his way through the crowd that had gathered in the still, pale early-morning light on the banks of the Stamford Canal. Owing to the early hour, the crowd comprised mostly *dhobi wallahs*.

This stretch of the canal was one of the *dhobis'* favorite spots. They had easy access to the water and could set their washing to dry on the open land that ran up from the bank of the river toward the Indian community, clustered around Serangoon Road and Bencoolen Street. Now they jostled against the restraining arms of a small cohort of police for a better view of what looked like a pile of wet, stinking rags that had been pulled from the canal and lay amidst the bundles of laundry.

Curran had been woken at first light by a depressingly bright and eager Constable Tan. He had time to shave and dress but had to eschew breakfast, a fact of which he was glad as he crouched down and turned the corpse over. He composed his own expression to one of professional neutrality as he considered the bloated, mottled face, the hair darkened to anonymity by the water. Male, European and fully dressed in the clerical uniform of once-white linen jacket and trousers. One shoe was missing, the stockinged foot looking strangely pitiful as it lolled to one side.

Fighting back his natural aversion that even after all his years in the military and policing he could not quite overcome, he probed the trouser pockets, producing a soggy notebook and a wallet. He would have to wait until the objects dried before they would be of any use, but he suspected the immersion in the water would have destroyed anything of evidentiary value. Nothing about either object confirmed the identity of the corpse but he knew he was looking into the ravaged face of Hans Visscher.

He handed the notebook and wallet to Singh and indicated to Greaves that he should take his photographs. The young man busied himself with his tripod and plates.

"Is it the missing boy?" the sergeant asked.

"I fear so." Curran rose to his feet with a sigh.

In a rare show of emotion, Singh tutted and shook his head. "So very young," he said.

With his hands on his hips Curran surveyed the scene. The rain of the previous night had caused the river to rise and it had brought with it the usual rubbish and detritus from farther upstream. Singapore conspired against good policing on every level.

"Who found him?" Curran inquired of the crowd.

The *dhobis* clamored for attention, pointing fingers at one another. The discovery of a body was not all that unusual and it probably provided them with the most excitement they would see in weeks.

Singh indicated a *dhobi wallah* of indeterminate age, clad in a short sarong and so thin Curran could count his ribs beneath his threadbare tunic. Singh nodded and one of the constables pushed the man forward. He dropped at Curran's feet.

"I have done nothing wrong, sahib," he wailed in Tamil.

"No one is accusing you of anything," Singh responded in the same language.

"How did you find the body?" Curran asked. His own Tamil was basic but sufficient for the purpose.

The mention of "body" set the *dhobi* howling and wringing his hands to emphasize his horror, and he began, "Oh, sahib, I will never forget this terrible thing. Not to my dying day."

"Just tell us what happened," Singh said.

"I came early to get the best spot." The *dhobi* cast a baleful eye at his fellows. "And I saw what I thought was a pile of washing caught on that log." He indicated a half-submerged tree that had become snagged across the canal as the water level had fallen. "I used my hook." He pointed at a long stick with an evil-looking hook on the end that lay on the ground beside the body. "And as it came closer I realized it was, it was . . ." Here he burst into rapid speech, accompanied by eloquent gestures that left Curran in no doubt about his reaction to coming face-to-face with a rotting corpse. The *dhobi* sank to his haunches, his arms over his head, rocking as he wailed, "I swear to you, sahib, it gave me such a fright, I nearly let it go."

"Was the body floating faceup or facedown?" Curran indicated with the palm of his hand.

"Facedown as you found it, sahib."

Curran looked around at the other *dhobis*, about two dozen of them, listening in on the testimony with ghoulish grins on their faces.

"Ah, sahib"—one of them swept the length of the canal with a dramatic gesture—"if it had not been for that log, the poor man would have been swept out to sea."

Curran thanked the man for the observation and gestured at the corpse. "Have any of you seen this man before?" he inquired without much expectation of an answer.

Glancing from one to the other, they shook their heads. Further questioning of the *dhobis* led to the inescapable conclusion the body had not been in the water the night before. Someone had dumped Visscher like a piece of refuse into the Stamford Canal at some time during the night, probably in the expectation that the flow of water and tide would carry the body out to sea.

He forced himself to look down at the corpse again. Decomposition had already begun to set in, indicating Visscher had been dead at least twenty-four hours, if not longer. His eyes were wide open and already turning opaque like a fish too long out of water, the mouth wide in the rictus of death.

Curran did not need Mac to tell him how the boy had died. A gash across the young man's throat, washed clean of blood by the water, revealed a severed windpipe. The wound gaped like a second mouth. Curran shuddered and turned away.

"Finished, Greaves?" he inquired.

The young constable nodded, already folding the legs of his tripod.

Curran indicated for the canvas sheet to be put over the body, reducing the hideous sight to an anonymous lump.

"Get him straight back to the morgue. Leaving him here won't give us any more information and we don't need any more sightseers," Curran said to Singh, glancing at the crowd, which had swelled considerably since his arrival.

Singh signaled for the men with the handcart to come forward. Three of the regular constabulary had the unpleasant task of manhandling the flaccid corpse onto the back of the cart, pulling up a greasy, stained tarpaulin.

One of the younger regular constables turned away, his face green. He hurried behind a bush, from where the sound of vomiting could be heard. Curran cast a sympathetic glance at the man's pasty face when he reemerged, wiping his mouth with the back of his hand.

After the cart had trundled off, bearing its grim occupant, Curran and Singh remained at the scene, wandering up the canal to see if any obvious signs of a struggle or blood or Visscher's missing shoe could be located but they found nothing. Curran had not expected they would. It seemed far more likely that the boy had died somewhere else and been dumped.

Several bridges crossed the canal. The body could have been dumped off any one of them. Curran stood on the Bencoolen Street bridge and looked around at the now-peaceful sight. To his right was the grand, new museum and behind it the Explorers and Geographers Club. Downstream, just visible behind the vegetation, the Van Wijk Hotel.

"It would have taken only a moment to stop whatever vehicle he had been conveyed in and slip the body into the water, but why here?" he said aloud. "Why in the boy's own neighborhood?"

Singh stroked his moustache. "Coincidence? The water flow in the canal here is stronger than other rivers in Singapore."

"Do you think it reasonable to conclude that the perpetrators intended for the body to be carried out to sea or found?"

Singh shrugged. "Often the simple solution is the correct one."

Curran huffed out a breath. "The question is how this death is tied to Sir Oswald's. If at all."

Singh's moustache twitched. "That is indeed the question, sir."

Curran paused at one of the street stalls in Chinatown and bought a simple breakfast of rice and vegetables, washed down with tea, before entering the impressive portals of the Police Headquarters. As he walked into the office, Ajiad, the Malay administrative clerk assigned to the division, looked up.

"Inspector, General Cuscaden wants to see you, *tuan*," he said.

"He can wait," Curran said, flinging his hat onto his desk. "I have work to do."

The clerk stood up, his eyes widening. "Now, *tuan*. He was most insistent. As soon as Inspector Curran arrives."

Curran took a moment to brush the dust off his boots, collected his hat and made his way to the inspector general's grandiose office at the front of the building. Cuscaden had recruited him from the London Metropolitan Police and he had the greatest respect for Tim Cuscaden, as he was known to his friends. Curran only ever called him *sir*.

Cuscaden had introduced a number of excellent reforms to policing in the Straits Settlement but he had a weakness for minutiae and Curran knew what the peremptory summons concerned and he suspected he would not like it.

The inspector general looked up from behind his enormous teak desk that occupied an equally impressive office overlooking South Bridge Road and scowled as Curran entered the room. Curran saluted and stood rigidly to attention, his hat under his arm.

"Where have you been?" Cuscaden snapped. From the man's florid, sweating face and knitted eyebrows Curran's guess had been right. The inspector general of police in the Straits Settlements was in a vile temper.

"Investigating a murder, sir," Curran responded in a sharp military tone. "Another murder. A body was found this morning."

Cuscaden snorted. "You missed the meeting about the Anderson Bridge yesterday afternoon."

"Sir, with respect, I had been interviewing witnesses all day," Curran protested. "An autopsy—"

But Cuscaden was clearly in no mood to listen. "This bloody bridge opening will be the death of me. I need everyone on board for it, Curran, and that includes you and your men."

"Sir, we are the Detective Branch not the Traffic Branch," Curran ventured, and instantly regretted his words.

Cuscaden's luxurious moustache bristled. "You are policemen, every single one of you and if I say you will be at a meeting or your men will be on duty on Saturday then they damn well will be. Understood, Curran?"

Curran opened his mouth to argue but seeing Cuscaden's thunderous expression, thought better of it.

"And while you're here"—Cuscaden waved a sheaf of papers—"the paperwork coming from your department is not up to standard. Damn it, man, I can't even read this report." He peered at a single page. "Looks like the scratchings of a drunken spider. Didn't you go to a decent school, Curran?"

Curran recognized the handwriting as his and felt the heat rising to his face.

"Sir, we need more administrative—"

Cuscaden cut him off by slamming the papers back on the desk. "Dismissed, Inspector."

Curran snapped a sharp salute with an acknowledging "Sir!" and turned gratefully for the door.

As his hand touched the doorknob, Cuscaden said, "Did you say 'another body'?"

Curran turned back to face his superior. "Yes, sir. Dragged from the Stamford Canal this morning."

"European or native?"

"European. I think it is the missing hotel clerk, Hans Visscher."

Cuscaden sat back in his chair, steepling his fingers together. "Brief me."

When Curran had finished his report, Cuscaden huffed out a breath and leaned back, smoothing his thinning hair with his hand.

"Is this boy's death related to Sir Oswald Newbold's murder?"

"Early days, sir, but I think so, yes."

"Damn it, we can't just have respectable English gentlemen being stabbed to death in their own homes. People will get worried." Cuscaden's eyebrows furrowed. "Find who did it and find them fast and, Curran, I want the report on Chin Lee's stolen vases on my desk by five this evening. If he rings me one more time . . . Oh, and make sure I can bloody well read it this time."

"Sir." Curran turned again for the door, this time making it out into the corridor without further delay. He took a deep breath and composed himself before making his way through the rabbit warrens of corridors back to the office of the Detective Branch.

He strode across the wooden floorboards, his boot heels sending an echo around the cavernous room. The clerk appeared to be catching up with his filing, while Tan must have been out following up on this morning's discovery. Sergeant Singh stood in front of the Newbold murder case board, lost in rapt consideration of the growing information that had been added to it since the previous morning.

He looked around as Curran joined him. "Did you see the IG?"

Curran pulled a face. "Every member of the Detective Branch is to report for duty on Saturday in ceremonial dress. See to it, Sergeant."

It is good to know we have our priorities, he thought as he stomped into his office and closed the door.

✇ TEN

Julian had woken with one of his migraines and long experience told Harriet that nothing would relieve it except complete immobility in a darkened room for the day. She brought
him a wet compress and laid it across his brow.

"Tell Pearson to hold the fort today," he murmured.

She assured her brother that George Pearson was more than
capable of holding the fort, and stopping only long enough to
give the cook Lokman orders to prepare a light soup for Julian,
if he felt up to eating, Harriet strode through the garden and the
small gate that led into the school grounds.

The boys were in class and she could hear the tedious repeti-
tion of Latin conjugations issuing from one of the four class-
rooms. "O, as, at, amus, atis, ant . . ."

In the headmaster's study she found Ethel, the wife of the
senior master, George Pearson, seated in one of the chairs, her
foot tapping impatiently on the rug. The Pearsons occupied a
suite of two rooms upstairs and Ethel, a large, motherly woman,
fulfilled the role of surrogate mother and matron to the boarders. Before her marriage, Ethel had been a nurse and despite a
predilection for reading them religious tracts before bed, the
boys adored her.

The older woman stood up, peering around Harriet. "Headmaster not with you?" she said, her accent betraying her North Country origins.

"No, I'm afraid he's down with a migraine today."

Ethel shook her head sympathetically. "Poor man. I'll pop in later and check on him for you if you like?"

"Thank you, but I think he will be fine. Is there anything I can help you with?"

Ethel heaved a sigh, her massive bosom constrained even in the heat by formidable stays, rising and falling. "I am afraid we have a case of thieving, Mrs. Gordon."

"Oh dear, what has been taken?"

"Someone has been pilfering food from the kitchen. Nasim saw a boy running from the kitchen this morning."

"One of our boys?"

Ethel's lips pursed. "I'm afraid so, Mrs. Gordon. Growing boys—they're like bottomless pits, but still, you wouldn't think they'd take to thieving."

"Did Nasim see who it was?"

Ethel shook her head. "No, it was dark. He just saw fair hair."

"I suppose that narrows the suspects a little. What was taken?"

"A cup of milk and some of last night's leftover shepherd's pie."

Harriet considered for a moment. "You're right, Mrs. Pearson. He was probably hungry."

Ethel pursed her lips. "Stealing is still stealing, Mrs. Gordon."

Before the godly Ethel could remind her of the eighth commandment, Harriet said, "Leave it with me, Mrs. Pearson. I'll try and flush out the culprit."

Ethel sniffed. "And when you do be sure to tell Mr. Pearson and ensure the proper punishment is administered."

The "proper punishment" being a few righteous strokes of the cane, something Julian loathed inflicting and generally delegated to his senior master.

Harriet waited until the bell rang for lunch and the boys were seated at the long tables in the large room at the back of the old house that served as assembly hall, gymnasium, dining hall and wet weather play area. They recited the grace but before Mr. Pearson gave them permission to eat, Harriet stepped forward.

"May I have a word with the boys?"

Pearson deferred to her and she looked around at the young faces, eager for their lunch.

"Boys," she said, "it has come to my attention that someone is sneaking into the kitchen and taking food. Now, we all know that is wrong. It is stealing. If there is a good reason for this pilfering, the boy concerned can come and speak to me in absolute confidence. He won't get into trouble." She paused, looking down the tables, searching out the guilty face.

She spotted it immediately.

Ignoring the quiet rumble of disapproval from George Pearson, she continued. "But if the boy doesn't come forward by tomorrow morning, you will all be kept in for double prep on Monday."

Pearson cleared his throat. She had no authority to issue such dictates and supervising double prep would probably be as much a punishment for one of the masters as the boys.

With a beatific smile at Mr. Pearson, Harriet swept from the room. As the boys were released into the grounds to play, she lingered in the garden at the front of the school, with a pair of pruning shears, tending to the orchids lovingly cultivated by the last headmaster's wife. Harriet had no talent for gardening and if the orchids survived it was despite her care, rather than because of it.

"Miss?"

Without looking up she said. "Yes, Lawson. Shall we take a little stroll?"

In the shelter of a bright-pink bougainvillea, Will Lawson looked down at his scuffed shoes. "How did you know it was me?"

She smiled down at the bowed fair head. "Because, Will, you

have a face like a book. Now, are you going to tell me why you've been stealing food?"

Will stuck his hands in the pockets of his shorts, still not meeting her eyes. "I didn't think anyone would notice. It was just a little, tiny bit and it wasn't for me."

Now he looked up at her, his blue-gray eyes brimming with unshed tears.

"Then, who was it for?"

He hesitated.

"Will, you can trust me. I promised you wouldn't get into trouble."

He nodded. "If you come with me, Mrs. Gordon."

Skirting around the side of the schoolhouse so his fellow students would not see them, Will led her to the shed at the back of the oval where the cricket pitch roller and sports equipment was kept. The shed itself was locked but Will went behind it to a pile of old boxes, overgrown with creeper.

"Careful of snakes," Harriet warned.

Will nodded, apparently unconcerned. "There's a big old python around here. I think it ate the mother and the other babies."

He reached into a box and pulled out a kitten, of indeterminate color, probably five or six weeks old. It mewed, its little paws paddling at the air. Harriet's heart melted as she took the tiny creature from him.

"Oh, Will, is this why you were taking the food?"

Tears started in the boy's eyes. "It drank a bit of the milk but I couldn't get it to eat anything. I'm afraid it's going to die, miss."

"Not if I can help it," Harriet said. "I'll take it back with me and see if it can be saved." They both started at the clanging of the bell, signaling the end of the lunch break. "You get back to the boardinghouse and I will tell Mr. Pearson you're not in trouble."

"Thanks, miss. Can I come and visit and see how it's going? I know the house is out of bounds, but I miss my animals . . ." A shaming tear spilled down the boy's cheek and he manfully sniffed it away. It was all Harriet could do not to fold the child in her arms but she didn't think he would thank her for acknowledging his weakness.

"Of course, you may visit but I warn you this poor little thing is very dehydrated and weak. It will be lucky to survive."

Back at the house, Harriet made up a bed for the kitten in a cardboard box and with difficulty persuaded Lokman to part with some of the precious milk. This she fed to the tiny animal from the smallest teaspoon she could find. Gratifyingly the kitten took in everything that was given to her.

"Filthy thing," Huo Jin pronounced from the doorway, a look of utter disgust on her face.

"He is a bit dirty," Harriet conceded.

Huo Jin clucked her tongue and huffed off back to the kitchen.

Wetting a facecloth Harriet cleaned the kitten with small strokes like a mother cat would, revealing a patchwork pattern of brindled fur.

"I think I shall call you Shashti," she said.

Like many of the local cats, Shashti's tail was no more than a little stub that wiggled in appreciation as the tiny creature began to purr, her little paws working against the wool of the cloth.

Holding Shashti close to her chest, she pushed open Julian's door and found him awake.

"Meet our newest resident," she said, placing the kitten on the bed beside him. His hand moved, the fingers seeking out the kitten's soft fur, stroking Shashti's tiny head with his forefinger and provoking purrs completely out of proportion for the size of her small body.

"And where did this little chap come from?"

Harriet smiled. "I think this little chap is a girl. I have called her Shashti."

Julian frowned. "Shashti?"

"Shashti is the Hindu goddess of children," Harriet replied. "There was a temple in her honor very close to where we lived in

Bombay with a marvelous statue of her carrying a child in her arms and riding a cat."

She didn't add that all the offerings to Shashti laid at her feet during the typhus epidemic had not saved her own son, Thomas, or the hundreds of other children, rich and poor.

Julian said nothing for a long moment, his gaze fixed on her face. He had an uncanny knack of knowing exactly what she was thinking.

"And how has Shashti come to live with us?" Julian returned his attention to the kitten.

"She is the reason behind some pilfering in the kitchen," Harriet said. "All resolved now. I hope you don't mind."

Julian looked up. "And the culprit?"

"I did tell the culprit he wouldn't get into trouble."

"Harriet . . . you have no authority . . ."

"It was Will Lawson. He rescued the kitten from a python."

"Ah, Will," Julian said. "Just this once, Harriet, I will turn a blind eye . . ."

Harriet smiled. "Will has my permission to come and visit Shashti. We'll be sort of co-owners."

Julian smiled and closed his eyes. "Small children and animals will always be your downfall. Do you remember that hedgehog you rescued off the gardener?"

Harriet sat down in a chair beside her brother's bed and they engaged in an exchange of happy memories of their childhood, a diversion from the nagging concern about young Visscher and the brutal murder of Newbold and his servant.

✦ ELEVEN

"I tell you, there are some jobs that even turn my stomach." Euan Mackenzie's professional mask slipped as the first slice of his scalpel expelled a cloud of noxious gas from the stomach cavity.

Curran fought down an acrid wave of nausea and steeled himself. The normally phlegmatic Greaves rushed out of the morgue, abandoning his photographic equipment.

Mac looked up as the door slammed shut behind the constable and shook his head.

"I don't know, Curran. The lad needs to toughen up."

Resisting the urge to press his own handkerchief to his face, Curran replied with a noncommittal grunt and stood back to let Mac work. He thought longingly of a strong whisky which, even at this hour of the morning, would go down very well.

"Do you know who this boy is?" Mac asked without looking back.

Curran coughed. "I'm reasonably certain it's Hans Visscher, the missing clerk from the Van Wijk Hotel."

Mac straightened and he frowned as he looked down at the bloated face.

"Hmm. European, right age. Pity. If it's the lad I'm thinking of, he was always polite and eager to help. A nice lad. He shouldn't have had to die like this," Mac said, probing the wound in the neck in a way that made Curran grimace.

"Any similarity with Newbold?" he asked.

Mac shook his head. "The attack on Newbold was frenzied. This is calculated and efficient. One quick slash left to right with a very sharp knife." Mac demonstrated on his own throat. "Nasty, Curran, very nasty."

Curran jotted this unpleasant piece of information in his notebook.

"There would have been a lot of blood," Curran said.

Mac nodded. "A right royal mess." He lifted one of the boy's hands and indicated dark mottled bruising circling Visscher's wrist. "Same on the ankles and there is bruising around the chest. If you are asking me," Mac continued, without waiting for Curran to voice the question, "he was tied to a chair or something similar for a considerable period of time."

"Time of death?" Curran inquired.

Mac shrugged. "When was he last seen?"

"Monday evening."

"I'd say he's been dead twenty-four hours. No longer."

Curran did a quick mental calculation. Twenty-four hours meant he had probably been killed sometime on Tuesday and the body dumped into the canal under cover of darkness. It raised the unpleasant question of where he been held between Monday night and his death.

Mac, engaged in tidying his work, looked up. "Do you think there's a connection with the other murder?"

"I'm certain there's a connection with Newbold but I've no idea what it is." Curran closed his notebook with a snap.

Mac nodded to his assistant and walked outside with Curran.

Both men lit cigarettes, letting the smoke overcome the stench of death.

"Days like today, I regret taking on the role of police surgeon,"

Mac said. "A young man with his whole life ahead of him, dead in the worst way possible."

Curran shot him a sympathetic glance. He knew from his time in South Africa there were worse ways for men to die. At least Visscher's death had been quick.

"Why did you become a policeman, Curran?" Mac asked.

Curran shrugged. "I needed a job," he said.

Mac cast him a skeptical glance. "If you needed a job, there were plenty of others. Bank clerk, for example."

Curran laughed. "Can you see me as a bank clerk?" He stubbed out his cigarette and sighed. "In South Africa, I saw a great deal of injustice meted out by our side as well as the Boer. I decided there had to be ways of seeing justice done properly."

"You could have become a lawyer."

Curran curled his lip in distaste. "I'd rather be a bank clerk. In my opinion lawyers are responsible for some of the gravest injustices I've seen."

Mac flicked his cigarette stub into the nearest bougainvillea. "It's been a bad week for both of us, Curran. I tell you what, Louisa is putting together a party for the Van Wijk musical evening on Saturday. Care to join us?"

It was on the tip of Curran's tongue to decline. He had seen enough of the Van Wijk and the week wasn't over yet. Then again, a social evening could serve the purpose of allowing him to observe the workings of the Van Wijk while he was out of uniform.

"Thank you for the invitation. I'd be delighted. Who else is going?" he inquired casually.

"I think she's invited Maddocks, you know—the journalist fellow—and Harriet Gordon and her brother."

No invitation would be extended to Li An, although Mac, more than anyone on the island, knew about the nature of their relationship. However, it was easier to ignore any social improprieties if they weren't being forced into the public eye.

As if reading Curran's thoughts, Mac asked after Li An, his faded-blue eyes creasing at the corners.

"She's well, thank you," Curran said, oddly grateful to Mac for being the one person who at least acknowledged Li An's existence.

Mac straightened and huffed out a breath, the stiff, formal police surgeon once more.

"We will need the body formally identified. Is there someone at the Van Wijk? Someone with a strong stomach, preferably." As he spoke his gaze traveled to a woebegone Earnest Greaves, who crouched in the shade of a tree, his head in his hands.

Curran's lips tightened in a grim smile. He knew just the person.

Curran found Van Gelder in the kitchens, supervising the lunch menu. Despite his lack of breakfast, the unpleasant morning had taken the edge off Curran's appetite and the smell of rich curry for once did not provoke a visceral response. A kitchen skivvy working near to where he stood, glanced at him with an inquiring look in his eye. Curran indicated the harassed hotel manager.

"This is not a good time, Inspector," Van Gelder, red-faced and sweating in the heat of the kitchen, steered him out into a hallway. "My best chef is late." He mopped his streaming face. "Have you found Visscher?"

"Yes," Curran replied.

"You can tell him from me he is out! He will be on the next boat back to Rotterdam without a reference." Van Gelder punctuated his words with a dramatic flourish. "He cannot leave me in the lurch like this—"

"He's dead, Van Gelder." Curran cut across the manager's outrage.

Van Gelder stared at him, all his pomposity and arrogance leaching from him. He took a step back, leaning against the wall, and despite the heat, his face appeared to drain of color.

"Dead? An accident? Please tell me it was an accident."

"I need someone to identify the body."

"Of course, I . . ." Van Gelder glanced back at the kitchen.

"Mr. Paar will do."

Van Gelder looked relieved. "He will? Then, you will find him at the house, taking an early lunch."

Perfect, thought Curran as he crossed the gardens.

The door was answered by the little Chinese maid, who glanced at him fearfully.

"Who is it?" Mrs. Van Gelder's voice came from inside.

"The policeman, *mevrouw*," the girl said.

The lady appeared behind her maid, her plump cheeks pink with the midday heat. "Inspector. How can I help you?"

"Is Mr. Paar within?"

"He is having his lunch."

"Then, I am afraid I must interrupt. May I come in?"

"Of course." Mrs. Van Gelder stood aside, admitting Curran into the living room. She led him to a room at the rear of the house, where Paar sat by himself at a table, using a piece of bread to mop his plate. He rose to his feet, the chair scraping on the boards.

"Inspector?"

"I apologize for interrupting your lunch, Mr. Paar, but I was hoping you would be so good as to accompany me."

"Accompany you where?" Paar's eyes widened. "I've done nothing wrong."

Curran held up a placating hand. "We've found a body and I was hoping you might help with the identification."

Mrs. Van Gelder gave a sharp cry, her hand going to her mouth. "I heard stories this morning of a body being found in the Stamford Canal. Is it . . . could it be . . . Visscher?"

"We believe it is."

She lowered herself onto the nearest chair, fishing in the sleeve of her blouse for a lace-edged handkerchief, which she employed in dabbing at the corners of her mouth and eyes.

"How . . . ?" she began. "An accident? Did he take his own life?"

Startled by her response, Curran asked, "Why do you think he would take his own life?"

Her lips quivered. "Homesickness? Zis infernal heat? Maybe his girl has found another?"

"He was murdered," Curran said bluntly, and Mrs. Van Gelder closed her eyes, crossing herself, her lips moving as if in prayer.

"Why do you need me to identify him?" Paar glared at Curran from under his thick, dark brows. "Surely Mr. Van Gelder . . ."

"Mr. Van Gelder is unable to get away from the hotel and I can hardly ask Mrs. Van Gelder." Curran shot the woman a sympathetic glance, although he would bet a pound that Mrs. Van Gelder would be more than up to the task.

"We go now?" Paar looked less than enthusiastic.

"First, I would like to look at Visscher's bedroom," Curran said.

Paar glanced at his landlady and Curran added, "In the presence of both of you."

Mrs. Van Gelder rose to her feet, nodding.

"Poor boy, poor boy," she muttered as she led them through a door at the far end of the living room and up a set of narrow stairs. She threw open another door at the top of the stairs and stood back.

"We have beds for four clerks but at present we have only Mr. Visscher and Mr. Paar."

Curran stood at the door and surveyed the gloomy, hot, airless attic room. Four small, mean windows shut tight with wooden shutters appeared to be the only means of ventilation. Mrs. Van Gelder hurried into the room, throwing open the shutters to allow the light in.

The room reminded Curran of his boarding school. It was sparsely furnished with four iron cots, surmounted by mosquito nets, wrapped out of the way and tied into a knot. Two washstands, four bedside tables and four small wardrobes completed the furnishings. The mattresses on two of the beds were rolled up and unoccupied. Two traveling trunks stood at the foot of the other two beds, which were neatly made up with sheets and a light cover of a cheap, colorful, cotton material of the sort sold in Little India.

Mrs. Van Gelder indicated the bed on the left side of the room. "That is where Mr. Visscher sleeps." Mrs. Van Gelder ran a hand over the bed, smoothing an imaginary crinkle from its impeccable cover. "Slept." Her voice cracked.

Curran directed both Paar and Mrs. Van Gelder out of the room and they watched from the doorway as he went through Visscher's meager possessions. The wardrobe contained a number of sets of white ducks, the universal uniform of the clerical class in Singapore, but there were gaps in the wardrobe and shelves and no sign of a razor or other personal paraphernalia.

Curran gestured for Mrs. Van Gelder to join him. "What is missing?"

She frowned. "He had a linen suit and collars and his nightshirts. They are gone."

Paar glanced up at the top of the wardrobe. "His suitcase is missing."

Curran followed his gaze. "Suitcase? Describe it."

Paar shrugged. "Leather, so big . . ." He indicated a small rectangle with his hands.

Curran looked at the young man and his landlady. He could conclude only that Visscher must have returned at some time on Monday night and packed a bag. Someone was lying.

He questioned Mrs. Van Gelder and Paar again but they were both insistent that they had not seen or heard from Visscher all evening. Curran did not press them further and turned back to his rudimentary search.

The drawers in the bedside table were empty. No photographs or letters or personal items of any description confirmed that

Visscher had packed to leave permanently. He glanced around the room. He would need to return and do a proper search, but for the moment he had other matters to attend to.

"Mr. Paar, if you are ready we will go."

Paar looked like a man being led to the gallows as he climbed into the motor vehicle.

Stefan Paar vomited in the sink of the hospital morgue while Mac and Curran watched without sympathy.

"Get him outside. Fresh air will work wonders," Mac said.

Curran put his hand on the young man's shoulder and marched him out onto the broad, relatively cool verandah. The stench of the mortuary still lingered in the air and Paar produced a crumpled and none-too-clean handkerchief, wiping his sweaty, pasty face.

He fixed Curran with a malignant glare. "Dear God, why did you make me do that?"

Curran regarded him without sympathy. "Someone had to identify him and you knew him as well as anyone."

With a shaking hand, Paar restored his handkerchief to his pocket.

"I have something to tell you," he said.

Curran regarded the man's ashen face. "Sit down before you fall down."

Paar complied, collapsing onto a wooden bench and burying his head in his hands.

Curran stood over him. "What do you have to tell me?"

"I might have forgotten to mention that I did see Visscher on Monday night."

Curran fought down the rising anger. "Forgot?"

Paar did not meet his gaze. "I did not want to get into trouble with Mrs. Van Gelder. She can be . . . difficult."

Curran had some sympathy with that sentiment.

"And?"

"Do you have a cigarette?"

Curran obliged, holding a match for the young man, whose hand shook so badly he had trouble holding the cigarette. When it was lit, Paar sat back, taking several draws and blowing out the smoke as Curran waited patiently for him to compose himself.

"What happened?" Curran inquired.

Paar's lips curled in a humorless smile. "When I came home, he was hiding outside the house. He begged me to let him in after the Van Gelders had gone to bed."

"And you did?"

"*Ja*. He asked me to keep watch downstairs while he went upstairs and packed." Paar's gaze dropped to his shiny shoes. "We argued."

"About what?"

"He was scared." All Paar's bravado had gone and the hand holding the cigarette shook. "But he wouldn't tell me what was scaring him. He just said it was out of his control and he wanted to get back to Holland. I pointed out that there were no ships due to sail for three days and told him to wait and sleep on his problem. It would not seem so bad in the morning but he wouldn't wait. He said he was catching the next boat to Batavia and he would go on from there. He had to get out of Singapore. He took his suitcase and that's the last time I saw him." He lowered his head, his hands hanging limply by his side.

Curran regarded Paar's bent head. The suspicion that Paar had been holding something back had now been confirmed.

"What time was this?"

Paar took another drag on his cigarette, and the ash fell onto the flagstones. "Well after midnight. One o'clock, I think. Yes. I heard the town hall clock strike the hour."

"Had you noticed anything unusual in his behavior over the last few weeks?"

Paar looked up, his eyes wet with tears. "He was ordinary,

Inspector. He wrote every week to his mother and went to church on Sundays. He talked about marrying Lissa. Everything he did was for that purpose."

"Are you aware of any dealings he had with Sir Oswald Newbold?"

Paar shook his head. "You have asked me that before. Newbold was a frequent guest at the hotel. That is all. Now can I go home?"

"Thank you, Mr. Paar. If you're feeling better, I will take you back to the hotel and break the news formally to your employer."

Paar nodded and remained silent, huddled miserably in the backseat of the motor vehicle for the trip back to the Van Wijk.

Van Gelder bustled out of his office as Curran walked into the hotel with Paar in tow.

"Really, Inspector," he protested. "I am trying to be as cooperative as I can but you have kept Mr. Paar away for too long. I simply cannot allow this on such a busy day, when I am already short staffed." He glanced at Paar's pale and miserable face. "Go and tidy yourself up. You look a mess. I want you back on the desk in half an hour."

"Yes, Mr. Van Gelder," Paar responded without enthusiasm, and turned to leave, his footsteps dragging.

"Don't be too hard on the lad," Curran said. "It was not a pleasant experience."

Van Gelder looked up, as if remembering the reason for Paar's excursion. "Was it . . . ?

"Shall we talk in your office?" Curran suggested.

"Yes, yes . . . of course."

Behind the closed door, Curran confirmed Paar's identification of Visscher.

Van Gelder shook his head. "How did he die?"

Curran judged it best to leave the details vague. "He was murdered."

Van Gelder blinked. "No. Not Visscher. Surely there is some mistake."

"Trust me, there is no mistake."

The hotel manager groped for the edge of his desk and leaned against it, pulling out the large, spotted handkerchief with which he mopped his face and blew his nose loudly. His distress seemed genuine and if anything, out of proportion for a young man who had been nothing more than an employee.

Van Gelder took a deep breath and pressed his handkerchief to his lips. "He was a good boy. Who would want to kill him?"

Curran said nothing and Van Gelder continued.

"No, indeed, Inspector Curran, a good boy who loved his mother . . . oh, his mother! I must write to her."

"I am just on my way to the Dutch consul to arrange for her to be advised."

Van Gelder shook his head. "She relied on him for her support. I must see that she does not suffer . . . oh . . . and I will see to the funeral too. Who do I need to contact?"

Curran left him with the details and, with a cursory nod at Stefan Paar, who had returned to his post on the reception desk, headed back to South Bridge Road.

❧ Twelve

Huo Jin didn't so much set the bowls down, as slam them down on the table. Julian raised his eyebrows and shot Harriet an enquiring glance as their *amah* stomped back to the kitchen, muttering under her breath.

Harriet sighed. "I think there is trouble in paradise. Huo Jin and Lokman were having a shouting match in the kitchen when I got home this evening. I found Aziz hiding in the stables."

"Ah." Julian poked at his bowl of rice accompanied by a stir-fry of vegetables and meat.

They had discovered early in their tenancy of St. Thomas House that the temperamental cook, Lokman, was quite capable of cooking excellent English meals but he chose to do so badly. Harriet had persuaded her brother that a local diet was far healthier and preferable to stodgy English fare and in the end Julian had capitulated.

Lokman had unbent enough to allow Harriet to accompany him to the local fresh food markets and in his uncertain English had taught her about the local produce. She still drew a line at pig entrails and tortoises but fish and chicken were fresh and plentiful.

"I do so long for a good old roast beef and Yorkshire pudding," Julian said.

"If you want English food, then eat in the boardinghouse," his sister chided.

He pushed the empty bowl away and ran a hand over his eyes, which seemed lost in the dark shadows left by the migraine. "Sorry, Harri. Are you all right, old thing?"

She smiled. "Just a little tired."

"I wouldn't be surprised if you weren't suffering delayed shock. Do you want to see Mac?"

Harriet shook her head. "I'm not sick. Just not sleeping well. Funny how the heat gets to you when you are feeling under the weather." And every creak and groan the house made sent shivers of fear down her as she imagined Sir Oswald's murderer stalking her in the dark.

"Well, if you don't feel up to it, just take it quietly at home tomorrow, old girl."

"I'm fine, Julian."

Her brother fixed her with a gimlet eye and Harriet found herself unable to hold his gaze. Julian knew her too well. She often wondered if taking holy orders gave a person instant insight into the darkest thoughts of his fellow man.

"I really am better if I'm busy," she said with what she hoped was a reassuring smile.

The sound of tires crunching on gravel made a liar of her as she dropped her fork onto the plate with a clatter. She was definitely jumpy. Julian waved her back in her seat.

"I'll go." He glanced at the clock. "Late for a caller."

He returned with a damp Inspector Curran in tow. Curran dripped water onto the polished floorboards as he removed his hat, shaking his wet hair like a dog.

"Hell of a night," he said. "I apologize for my appearance."

Harriet stood up to greet him. "Can I get you a towel?"

"I'm not staying. I must get the motor vehicle back to South Bridge Road. I'm afraid I've got some bad news. You asked me to tell you when we found—"

"Visscher?"

Harriet sank back on her chair as the policeman nodded. "He was found this morning. Dead, I'm afraid." Something in his hard, flat tone left Harriet with no doubt that Hans Visscher had met a violent end.

Harriet looked down at the half-eaten meal, remembering the distressed young man from Monday night. "He was so frightened... was it"—she looked up into the policeman's grim face, already knowing the answer—"foul play?"

Curran nodded. "Yes."

She stopped herself from asking how Visscher had died. She didn't want to know.

Julian waved at the table. "Have you eaten, Inspector? I'm sure the cook can rustle up a meal for you."

"Thank you, but no. I've my own meal waiting for me at home." He ran a hand over his chin, rasping the bristles that spoke of a long day.

After her conversation with the gossiping wives of Singapore, Harriet found her curiosity about him had been piqued and she took a moment to study him. She supposed he would be in his midthirties, touching six feet, with a lean, athletic build and neatly cut brown hair that now hung in damp strands around a clean-shaven face, gray with exhaustion.

His deeply tanned, rather aesthetic face spoke of a life largely lived outdoors and she wondered if he really was the grandson of an earl and how he had come to be in the Straits Settlements Police Force. Questions for another day and another time. In the meantime, his impeccable courtesy to her had forced her to reevaluate her opinion of the police. He did not resemble the narrow-minded, rough men she had encountered during the protests in London and she wondered how differently she may have been treated had it been an Inspector Curran who had dealt with her rather than the weasel-faced Sergeant Hodge.

"Is there anything we can help you with?" Julian inquired.

Curran screwed up his eyes as if trying to remember something. "Yes. Can you confirm what time Visscher was here and what he was wearing?"

Julian glanced at Harriet and answered for her. "The clock had just struck eight and he was wearing ducks, very wet ducks. No hat."

Curran nodded. "Thank you. That's helpful." He glanced at his watch. "I must be going." He glanced at Harriet. "Mrs. Gordon, are you all right?"

Harriet shook her head. "No. I just wish we had been able to persuade him to stay. He would have been safe with us. He wouldn't be . . ." She broke off, conscious of the crack in her voice.

Curran sighed. "There is nothing you could have said or done that would have changed what happened. None of us know our ultimate fate, Mrs. Gordon."

"Very philosophical but it doesn't make me feel any better," Harriet replied.

Julian and Harriet stood on the verandah, watching as Curran drove away, his constable huddled over the wheel of the vehicle as the rain slewed down on the inadequate canvas hood they had pulled up. Harriet slipped her arm into her brother's and leaned her head on his shoulder and they stood for a long time just watching the rain as it hurled itself relentlessly, as only tropical rain could, against the unresisting earth.

Long after Julian had retired for the night, Harriet sat at her dressing table, brushing out her hair. Even at this late hour, her nose shone with the sheen of perspiration that she had come to accept as part of life in the tropics. The rain had stopped and the open window let in a soft night breeze that stirred the mosquito net above her bed.

She set her hairbrush down and opened the top drawer of her dressing table. From it she pulled a slender box that had been used to pack gloves in another lifetime. She took the lid off and folded back the tissue paper to look at the objects packed away within it. At the base of the box the purple, green and white stripes of a sash, and resting on it the rosette proclaiming VOTES FOR WOMEN but it was not either of these objects that she sought.

She picked up a flat black box and opened it to reveal a medal, the sort awarded to soldiers, with a grosgrain ribbon of purple, green and white. It proudly proclaimed FOR VALOUR, a date 29 June 1909 and from it hung a simple circular disk that read HUNGER STRIKE. She snapped the lid shut and replaced it in the cardboard box, stowing it back in the drawer.

For a long, long time she sat quite still looking at her reflection in the mirror, brooding on her recent conversation with Griff and remembering those three awful months in Holloway when she had been strapped down and a tube forced down her throat. The experience had not strengthened her resolve. It had, as it was intended, broken her.

She had been returned to her parents' home in Wimbledon, close to death. As she lay in her childhood bed recovering from her ordeal, listening to the sounds of middle-class life in the house around her, she had made a decision. The fight would go on without her. Somewhere between James's death and that grim cell in Holloway she had lost her way.

She had to find it again.

She climbed under the mosquito net and curled up, lost in the vastness of her empty bed.

"James," she whispered into the dark. "Where will this end?"

But her husband gave her no reply and beyond the window the crackle of insects and chatter of monkeys reminded her she was indeed a long, long way from Wimbledon. She curled up around one of the pillows, burying her face in the cool linen so her brother would not hear her tears.

🎜 THIRTEEN

Thursday, 10 March 1940

Thursday morning began with a sound and light display from Mother Nature of such intensity that Li An squealed and hid her head under the sheet. Curran laughed and drew her into his embrace. She snuggled against him, her body soft and compliant within the circle of his arms.

"I like this," she murmured. "Must you get up?"

Curran disengaged her slender arms and swung his legs around to sit on the side of the bed as another low rumble of thunder rolled over the house.

He ran his hand through his hair and sighed. "Duty calls. I have a funeral to attend this morning."

Li An knelt up behind him and entwined her arms around his neck, kissing his hair and nibbling the tops of his ears. For a long moment, Curran almost succumbed to her wiles, but the clock in the living room struck seven and he knew he had to get moving.

Unlike England, it never just drizzled in Singapore. Outside the cathedral of St. Andrew's the rain came in torrents, as if God and all his angels sat above the hapless mortals and tipped buckets of water from the clouds, accompanied to a rhythm of thunder and lightning that drowned out the even the cathedral's organ.

Perspiration dripped from the end of Curran's nose onto the hymn book he held and he pulled out a handkerchief to mop his face.

Quite a crowd crammed into the pews in St. Andrew's Cathedral to honor the president of the Explorers and Geographers Club or, more likely, Curran thought, out of ghoulish interest in Newbold's violent end. Colonel Augustus Foster gave the eulogy, expounding on Newbold's courage and foresight in opening up the jungles of Burma for the advancement of the British Empire, a thought that made Curran's blood run cold. He doubted the people of Burma viewed the advancement of the British Empire with quite such equanimity.

As far as he was concerned the main interest in the man lay in what was not said about him. As Foster waffled on, from his position to the side of the church Curran scanned the faces of the mourners, looking for signs of guilt or remorse. All he saw were perspiring, beetroot-red faces set in expressions of deep gravitas, befitting the occasion. He glimpsed Harriet and Julian squeezed into a pew beside several gentlemen he recognized from the cricket club. Harriet fanned herself with the order of service and, catching his eye, smiled.

As the service concluded, he caught up with her. Despite the black, high-necked dress she wore, she appeared calm and unruffled by the heat. Her brother wore a clerical collar and in contrast to his sister, looked flushed and wilted after the oppressive humidity inside the church.

Harriet glanced around the departing congregation, "Inspector Curran, are you hoping to find the murderer among the mourners?"

Curran refrained from expressing his opinion that there was always a high probability the murderer was among the crowd. Instead he said, "You never know, Mrs. Gordon."

He walked with them out into the spacious grounds of the cathedral. At least the rain had stopped but the trees dripped moisture onto the departing congregation.

"I saw Visscher's death reported in the *Straits Times* this morning but it didn't say how he died. Was he drowned?" Julian inquired.

Curran shook his head. "No, he was dead before he was dumped in the canal."

Harriet's brow puckered but she was doing her best to contain her curiosity about the manner of Visscher's death.

"His throat had been cut," Curran said in answer to her unspoken question. "It would have been very quick."

"Oh, poor boy." Harriet's hand went to the high collar of her dress, closing over a small cameo pinned in the hollow of her throat.

Curran looked around the crowd. "Mrs. Gordon, unfortunately I must attend the internment. Good day to you."

"Inspector Curran." Harriet's hand on his arm detained him. "Hans Visscher. What are his funeral arrangements?"

Curran shook his head. "I haven't heard. Tomorrow, I believe, but I will send you word of the details."

"Thank you." Harriet removed her hand, tucking it into the crook of her brother's arm. She inclined her head to him as Julian led her away to the waiting pony trap being held by the boy Aziz.

Curran turned back to watch the crowd still gathering at the door around Colonel Augustus Foster, the man's bulk unmistakable among the dark-clad figures. Curran pushed his way through the crowd and found the colonel in conversation with the tall, fair-haired Dutchman from the Van Wijk Hotel, the Amsterdam antiquities dealer, Cornilissen. He allowed Foster to make the introductions.

"What brings you to Singapore, Mr. Cornilissen?" Curran inquired.

"Every year I visit," Cornilissen replied. "Cape Town, Rangoon, Singapore, Hong Kong and Canton."

"Do you not have agents to do your buying for you?"

Cornilissen's pale-blue eyes rested on Curran. "Of course, but I prefer the opportunity to view the best goods for myself."

Curran glanced at the hearse, drawn by two heavyset horses, decorated with black plumes, which had begun to move away from the church.

"Were you acquainted with Sir Oswald Newbold?"

Cornilissen's face assumed a suitable gravitas. "Of course. I knew him from his time in Rangoon. He was a good source of antiquities and in turn bought some good pieces from me. His death greatly saddens me." Cornilissen placed the neat bowler hat he carried on his head. "Now, if you will excuse me, Inspector—Foster, I have business to attend to. Good day."

Curran waited until Cornilissen had departed before turning to Foster. "How do you know Cornilissen?"

Foster's moustache twitched. "Newbold introduced us at one time. Cold fish but he does have an eye for the antiques. I've made a few purchases through him. I presume you are coming out to the cemetery?" Foster indicated a bright-red motor vehicle attended by a stony-faced man of unfamiliar ethnicity, incongruously dressed in an ill-fitting English driver's uniform. "This is my man, Zaw," Foster said as the motor vehicle started with a jolt. "Been with me since Rangoon. Can I offer you a ride to the cemetery?"

Curran declined.

Curran returned to South Bridge Road, damp and irritable. He hadn't expected any dramatic revelations at Newbold's graveside but formalities had to be observed. Only the hardiest had maintained a vigil by the graveside, soaked to the skin while an equally sodden priest committed the last earthly remains of Sir Oswald Newbold and his servant, Nyan, who shared his grave, to the heavy clay of the Singapore earth.

With every available man on his force engaged in trying to trace Visscher's last movements and the whereabouts of the suitcase he had taken with him, Curran found himself alone in the office. He flicked through the notes on his desk to find a message from the Dutch consul advising that Visscher's funeral would be at ten the following morning. A short service at the Catholic cathedral followed by internment in the Catholic section of the same cemetery that now held Sir Oswald Newbold. Curran's already gloomy mood sank farther as he thought of Visscher's mother and fiancée, so very far away.

He poured himself a finger of whisky from the hidden bottle in his bottom drawer, just as the clerk knocked on the window of the partition and entered, waving a telegram.

"For you, *tuan*. From Scotland Yard," the young man intoned, reverently setting the envelope on the desk.

Curran dismissed the clerk and scanned the telegram. He had sent a general enquiry to an old colleague and the reply came with some interesting information about his principal witness, a certain Mrs. Gordon. Nursing his whisky, he set the brief epistle down on the desk and sat back, considering the contents.

"My dear Mrs. Gordon," he said aloud. "No wonder you dislike the police."

He would have to confront her with what he knew, if only to assure her that it made no difference to her veracity as a witness in this case and to reassure her that he could be trusted with her secret. Not that it was much of a secret. No doubt anyone could find contemporary reports in the London newspapers if they cared to go looking.

He drained his glass and glanced at his watch. The clerk knocked on the window of his office again. "Sir, you're late for the meeting."

Curran frowned. "What meeting?"

"The arrangements for the bridge opening."

Curran swore, snatched up his hat and stomped off to the meeting room, where he knew he would be roundly chastised by

Cuscaden. Damn it, he had three murders on his hands—surely they took precedence over crowd control?

Apparently not.

He chafed through the endless discussion before excusing himself and returning to his own office, where Sergeant Singh greeted him with the news that they had been unable to trace Visscher's movements from leaving St. Tom's House at about eight on Monday night to his body being found on Wednesday morning.

Curran was not given to swearing. Instead he paced the length of the outer office several times before snatching up his hat and ordering Singh and Greaves to accompany him, announcing they were going to search Visscher's rooms more thoroughly.

Mrs. Van Gelder was not welcoming but between much sighing and wringing of her hands she agreed to allow the search of the attic room provided she was present.

The room seemed much as it had when Curran had visited on the previous day. Curran watched as Singh and Greaves worked their way systematically through what was left of Visscher's belongings. Drawers were pulled out and the cavities searched for hidden documents. The pockets of his abandoned clerical ducks were turned. They pulled the mattress from the bed, searching the bed frame.

They found nothing.

Curran ordered everything to be restored and as Greaves and Singh heaved the mattress back onto the bed, something caught Curran's eye. The walls were lined with timber, contributing to the dark oppressive atmosphere in the room.

Curran glanced at Paar's bed. If a young man had private correspondence he wanted to keep away from the prying eyes of his roommate, where would he hide it? He knelt on the bed and ran his hands along the boards beside the bed. His questing fingers found what he was seeking, a hole. He inserted a forefinger and pulled. The board came away, revealing a cavity beyond.

Behind him, Mrs. Van Gelder let out a gasp and he glanced in her direction. She stood in the doorway with one hand raised to her mouth, staring at the hole. She caught his eye and looked down at the floor.

"Anything in there, sir?" Greaves's voice broke the silence.

Curran slid his hand inside the cavity, his fingers closing on leather. He pulled the object out, a small soft leather satchel. He unbuckled it, emptying the contents onto the bed. A black leather book and two packets of letters fell onto the cover. He picked up the book first: a well-thumbed Dutch translation of the Bible. The name in the front was recognizably HANS VISSCHER. He picked up the first bundle of letters tied up with a blue ribbon and extricated the top missive. It was written in Dutch in a neat, educated hand. Curran had picked up enough Dutch during his time in South Africa to recognize the signature.

"*Uw liefhebbende moeder,*" he read. "'Your loving mother.' Am I right, Mrs. Van Gelder?"

She nodded. "She wrote to him every week and he to her," she said.

The second packet was thicker than the first. Curran unfolded the top sheet, *Mijn lieveling Hans* . . . it began. "My darling, Hans . . ."

He had found the letters written to Visscher by his now-grieving fiancée. The girl signed her name . . . "Your beloved, Liselotte" . . . *Uw geliefde, Liselotte.*

He replaced the items in the satchel and handed it to Greaves. "Take this back to Headquarters."

His gaze raked Paar's corner of the room. He would have loved to have searched that particular young man's belongings but he had no cause to do so . . . yet. Even as that thought crossed his mind, he felt the prickle of uncertainty. What had Paar said?

"He asked me to keep watch downstairs while he went upstairs and packed."

Surely the first thing the frightened young man would have packed would have been his most precious possessions, his letters and Bible?

"Have you finished?" Mrs. Van Gelder broke the silence.

"Yes. Thank you for your patience, Mrs. Van Gelder." Curran gave the woman what he hoped was an assuring smile.

"I will be in attendance at Visscher's funeral tomorrow," he said.

"*Ja.* We will both attend. He was a sweet boy." She lowered her gaze with a shake of her head. "The poor boy . . . his poor mother. I must write to her."

Back in his office, Curran opened the satchel containing Hans Visscher's few possessions and spread them out on the table. He began with the letters but his Dutch wasn't good enough for anything approaching a translation and no words like *Newbold* jumped out at him. He turned to the Bible, the gift of the boy's grandmother, he guessed from the superscription in the front: *Hans van zijn liefhebbende grootmoeder.*

The pages were well thumbed and some passages underlined and annotated in a boyish handwriting. Curran turned the book upside down and shook it. Scraps of paper, religious tracts and page markers fell to his blotter. He set the book down and sorted through the papers. They were mostly fragments used as bookmarks, probably torn from scrap paper the boy had to hand. One or two were inscribed with the letterhead of the Van Wijk Hotel, others looked older, the paper yellowed.

One caught Curran's attention. Again, it had been torn from the corner of another sheet of paper but clearly visible was a diagonal line superimposed with the letter O written in a bright-blue ink. The symbol looked familiar but he couldn't think where he had seen it.

He carefully stored the other fragments in an envelope and replaced them in the box along with the letters and Bible but kept out the paper with the strange symbol on it, staring at it and turning it in different directions. He had no reason to think it was any more significant than any of the other page markers but it didn't fit.

Opening his notebook, he copied the symbol and filed the original in a separate envelope.

❧ FOURTEEN

Friday, 11 March 1910

Harriet settled onto the hard pew, her gaze drawn to the image of a tortured Christ hanging from his cross above the altar. Beside her Julian knelt to pray while she scanned the small gathering scattered through the pews of the Catholic cathedral. Unlike yesterday's service for Sir Oswald, a humble clerk from the Van Wijk barely warranted the attention of a dozen people.

Mr. and Mrs. Van Gelder occupied the front pew. The Dutch consul sat beside Mr. Van Gelder and a pretty, blond woman in a wide, fashionable hat trimmed with a black ostrich feather sat beside Mrs. Van Gelder. She recognized the other clerk, Paar, looking hot and uncomfortable in a stiff collar and black suit. Others present looked to be staff from the Van Wijk, including, a small, sweet-faced Chinese girl who cried uncontrollably into the shoulder of an older woman.

Harriet nodded at Maddocks, who sat across the aisle from them and knew if she glanced behind her she would see Inspector Curran, watching them all.

The service concluded and the small congregation filed out of the church after the casket. Hans Visscher would begin his last, lonely journey on the earth to the cemetery on Bukit Timah Road, accompanied only by the Dutch consul, Mr. Van Gelder and Curran. Harriet wondered if his mother would pay for a headstone for her lost son or if he would lie unmarked and forgotten. Surely, he deserved more than that?

"Mrs. Gordon?" She turned at the sound of her name to see she was being addressed by Mrs. Van Gelder.

"I'm sorry we should meet again in these circumstances, Mrs. Van Gelder," Harriet said, pausing to introduce her brother.

"*Ja*. It is very sad. Poor boy," the woman replied, and raised a lace-edged handkerchief to her eye after the introductions were complete. "He had such plans. He was to be married, you know?"

"No, I really knew very little about him."

Mrs. Van Gelder heaved a heavy sigh, her not-insubstantial bosom rising and falling beneath a lace jabot. "God's will," she intoned.

"I am not sure God had much to do with it," Julian said. "The boy was foully murdered."

Mrs. Van Gelder nodded. "Of course, you are right, Reverend Edwards. Perhaps, Mrs. Gordon, you could come back with me now and I shall return the book you left with me?"

"Book?" Julian quirked an eyebrow at his sister.

Harriet glanced at Julian. "That book I promised to lend Hans, remember?" Julian, knowing his sister well, held his peace and she turned back to Mrs. Van Gelder. "Of course I will retrieve the book and I will see you back at the school, Julian."

She walked with Mrs. Van Gelder over to a *gharry*, an open carriage used as a cab, where the young, blond-haired woman already waited. She was introduced by Mrs. Van Gelder as Gertrude Cornilissen.

"Mrs. Cornilissen is a regular visitor to the Van Wijk," Mrs. Van Gelder said as she seated herself next to the young woman, leaving Harriet to sit across from them.

"Is this your first visit to Singapore?" Harriet inquired of Mrs. Cornilissen.

"Oh no." Mrs. Cornilissen's gaze drifted to the tall man talking to Mr. Van Gelder. "I come every year. My husband has business here."

"And what is his business?" Harriet inquired.

"My dear Nils deals in antiquities."

"What a wonderful opportunity to see something of the world," Harriet said.

The woman's lips tightened and she fanned herself with a lace-gloved hand. "I do not like this heat, the food or the smells or the people."

"I am sorry to hear that. One does become accustomed to it," Harriet said. "And have you have known Mrs. Van Gelder long?"

Gertrude Cornilissen cast the older woman a quick glance, a smile lifting the corners of her mouth. "*Ja.* I knew Mrs. Van Gelder in Rangoon."

"It is a lonely life, as you may have cause to know, Mrs. Gordon. I look forward to dear Gertrude's visits." Mrs. Van Gelder patted the younger woman's hand.

The distance from the Catholic cathedral to the Van Wijk hardly justified a carriage and they reached the manager's house in a couple of minutes.

The Chinese maid opened the door, her eyes widening at the sight of the visitors. At the clipped command from her employer, the girl scuttled away as Mrs. Van Gelder indicated that the visitors take a seat. Conscious that she could quite easily claim her book and leave, Harriet sat down as the girl returned, balancing a tea tray with three cups.

Mrs. Van Gelder pointedly set Harriet's book down on the table next to her and handed her a cup.

"You have some wonderful antiques," Harriet remarked, casting her gaze around the parlor. It reminded her of Sir Oswald Newbold's collection of statues and carvings.

"My husband has a good eye for value," Mrs. Cornilissen said. "Mrs. Van Gelder has been quick to take his advice."

"Have you been out east long, Mrs. Van Gelder?" Harriet took a sip of tea.

"Some years," Mrs. Van Gelder replied. "I lived for a short time in Batavia and then in Rangoon. My first husband, Klop, managed a tea plantation, but he died in Burma. Cholera."

"I'm sorry. I lost my husband in India," Harriet said. "Typhus." Both women nodded in sympathy.

Harriet set the cup down. "Did you know Sir Oswald Newbold in Burma?"

"A little." The two women exchanged glances. "The European community is small. It was Sir Oswald who introduced me to Van Gelder."

"You have no wish to return to Holland?" Harriet inquired.

Mrs. Van Gelder shook her head. "There is nothing for me in Holland."

"No children?"

The woman set her empty teacup down and fixed Harriet with a hard stare. "No. What of you, Mrs. Gordon?"

"My son died with my husband," she replied.

Just for a fleeting moment Mrs. Van Gelder's mask slipped and something like genuine compassion softened the prim, little mouth. "I am sorry," she said. "I lost a son in Batavia."

Gertrude Cornilissen set her cup down, the delicate china clattering in the saucer, breaking the mood. "I hope I never have a child," she declared.

The two older women looked at her. "Why?" Harriet asked.

"They just break your heart," Gertrude said. "Is that not so, Viktoria? I think of that poor woman in Rotterdam mourning her boy who will never come home to her."

Harriet made a show of glancing at her watch. "I must get back to the school." She rose to her feet. "Thank you for the tea. It was most welcome after such a sad morning."

Mrs. Van Gelder saw her to the door with an almost indecent haste, pressing the book into her hand with a reminder that she had almost forgotten it.

As the dark descended on a soft, clear Friday evening, Harriet and Julian sat with the junior master, Michael Derby, on their verandah enjoying a predinner drink. Shashti lay curled up on Harriet's lap and she let her finger trail across her soft fur. Just a couple of days of proper nutrition and love and the kitten had already gained weight and condition.

Julian and Michael were discussing school matters and Harriet only listened with half an ear.

Julian's chair groaned as he rose to his feet. "I think we've time for another drink. Harri?"

"Mm," she concurred, "and I think it might be prudent to find an extra glass. Unless I am greatly mistaken we have a visitor."

A horse and rider had turned into the driveway. Aziz ran around from the back of the house to take the reins of the horse, as Inspector Curran swung easily to the ground.

Holding the kitten pressed against her chest with one hand, Harriet rose to greet him. Curran took the steps up to the verandah two at a time, whipping off his pith helmet, which he tucked under his arm.

"It's a lovely evening for once," he said.

"You look tired, Inspector," she remarked.

"It's been a difficult day—a difficult week." Curran ran a hand across his brow, pushing back the dark lick of hair that fell across his forehead.

Julian handed him a glass. "You look like a man who could do with a whisky. Take a seat, Curran. Have you met Michael Derby? He's the junior master at the school."

Michael half rose to his feet. "I should go . . ." he began but Curran waved him back.

"Don't leave on my account." The policeman sank into the spare chair with a sigh, clutching the glass Julian had handed him as if it were a life preserver.

Harriet resumed her seat, resettling Shashti on her lap.

"You've acquired a new resident?" Curran observed, indicating the kitten.

"One of the boys from the school found her abandoned and we've taken her in. We think the mother and other kittens were eaten by a python."

To her surprise, Robert Curran's lips curled in a smile and he reached out a finger, gently stroking the kitten's head. He had long, elegant fingers, better suited to the drawing room than the rough work of policing, Harriet thought, taken by the expression on the man's face as he took the little animal from her.

"He has a name?" he asked.

"She . . . Shashti. I would have thought you a dog man, Inspector?"

To her surprise the policeman laughed. "I like dogs but I prefer cats," he said, scratching Shashti behind the ears. "They're independent animals."

In their short and dramatic acquaintance, she'd never seen him remotely relaxed but the little cat seemed to have broken down Curran's professional reserve and she liked the way he smiled as he stroked the small animal.

"No motor vehicle tonight, Inspector Curran?" Harriet said.

"No, I prefer my horse on short errands such as this. I like horses too," he added. "In fact, there are days I think the company of animals is infinitely to be preferred to that of humans."

He took a sip of the whisky, his eyes widening with pleasure. "Good stuff, this."

"The advantages of a Scottish husband," Harriet said. "He taught me to appreciate good Scottish whisky drunk with just a dash of water. Of course finding pure Scottish peat water in Singapore is a challenge but we make do."

"It is most welcome," Curran said. "Visscher's internment was a sad affair. Just myself, Van Gelder and the Dutch consul at the grave."

Shashti abandoned Curran and climbed back up Harriet's skirt. She turned her attention to the kitten, gently stroking its tiny head, feeling the rumbly purrs. This little animal was real and alive. Hans Visscher was dead and buried thousands of miles from the people who loved him.

"All that time you were looking for him, was he dead in a canal?" she asked.

Curran shook his head. "Not in the canal. We think his body was put there sometime on Tuesday night or early Wednesday morning."

A cold shiver ran down Harriet's spine. "Poor boy. Dumped like refuse," she said.

"Do you mind if I ask you something?" Curran reached into his jacket pocket and unwrapped a notebook from an oilcloth. He flicked through the pages and, glancing up at Harriet, he said, "I think I should get you to teach me shorthand, Mrs. Gordon. Now, what exactly did Visscher say about his visit to Newbold the previous night?"

Harriet frowned. "Something like 'I tried to warn him but he said I was a fool.'"

"And that nonsense about the VOC," Julian added.

"The VOC?" Derby put in. "You mean the Dutch East India Company?"

Curran turned to the young man. "That's right. What do you know about it?"

Derby shrugged. "Only what I read in the history books. It was a powerful consortium of merchant venturers in the seventeenth century. The VOC pretty much controlled most of the East Indies."

Curran turned to a page in his notebook on which was drawn

a diagonal line superimposed with an O. "I don't suppose any of you recognize this symbol?"

The three craned forward.

"Of course," Derby said. "It's part of the insignia of the VOC. The letter V for 'Vereenigde—United,' the straight lines of the V superimposed with an O for 'Oost-Indische—East Indies,' just like this, and a C for 'Compagnie.' United East India Company."

Curran turned the book back and added the second diagonal line forming the V and superimposed a C. "Like this?"

Derby nodded. "Just like that, Inspector." He laughed. "But it's a nonsense, of course. The VOC has been nonexistent for one hundred and fifty years."

"So everyone says," Curran said. "Oh, hello, little one."

Shashti had given up on Harriet and returned, mewing, to Curran. The policeman scooped up the kitten and turned it on its back, scratching the kitten's little round belly while Shashti tried to catch his fingers with her tiny paws.

"I think you need to get a cat," Harriet said.

"Li An is not very fond of them," he said, and as if he realized he had spoken out of turn, he set the kitten down and rose to his feet, once more the policeman. "Actually, Mrs. Gordon, there is another matter I need to speak to you about alone, if that's all right?"

Harriet shot Julian a glance. Indecision flashed across her brother's face.

"Of course," she said. "Julian, perhaps you and Michael could adjourn to the study for a few minutes."

Michael Derby had one of those open friendly faces that concealed no guile. He looked from Harriet to the policeman and back again, curiosity burning in his eyes.

"Derby." Julian stood up and indicated the front door. "We do need to discuss the upper thirds' Latin results."

Harriet retrieved Shashti from her endeavors in trying to stalk a lizard on the wall and rose to face the policeman, her arms crossed. "What do you wish to talk to me about that requires such privacy?"

"I'm sorry, I had hoped to catch you alone . . . at least I presume your brother knows . . ."

She'd never seen him discomfited before. "Knows what? What are you talking about?"

"Mrs. Gordon, I know what happened in London last year."

He may as well have hit her in the stomach. The breath left her body and she sank back onto her chair. "Oh . . . how . . . ?" was all she could say.

"I telegrammed London for information on all the parties involved in the Newbold affair—not just you."

Harriet glared at him, furious that he did not trust her and had gone in search of her past, but then he was a policeman, what could she expect? She, in turn, should have known better than to trust him.

Her mind raced with the implications of his knowledge. Disgrace, dismissal, the end of Julian's career.

She straightened and took a deep steadying breath. "Inspector Curran, please understand . . ."

He held up a hand. "Please trust me, Mrs. Gordon. What occurred in London is of no relevance to my investigation. I just wanted you to know that I am quite in sympathy with the suffrage movement." He paused. "Can you tell me what happened? I am curious about the assault charge that was dropped."

She hesitated, her heart racing as the memories flooded back. "It was supposed to be a peaceful rally but the police charged us. A policeman was hit over the head with an umbrella. The police were . . ." She gave a shuddering sigh. "You see, it was my umbrella but I swear to you that it was not wielded by me. I had brought it home from India and it had a distinctive elephant handle. I dropped it in the chaos and someone else must have used it as a weapon. Mercifully the man was not badly hurt and my father—"

"The crown prosecutor?"

She nodded. "He was able to persuade the authorities of the truth of my story. Unfortunately he could not get me off the other charge of affray so I went with my sisters in the movement to Holloway."

Curran considered her for a long moment before he cleared his throat and said, "Do you know my cousin? Lady Eloise Warby. Apparently she chained herself to the railings of Westminster a few months ago."

Harriet stared at him. "Lady Warby is your cousin? I heard her speak at the first gathering I attended in Hyde Park. I liked her enormously."

She could still see Eloise, hatless, her hair coming down from its pins, screaming the WSPU slogans as the bobbies dragged her away.

Curran smiled. "The family does not take well to rebels in their midst so Ellie and I have always been close." He paused, his lips tightening "When I last heard, she was still in Holloway. Is it true? The stories about how they are dealing with the hunger strikers?"

Harriet's hand went to her throat, as if she could still feel the feeding tube being forced down. "Yes. They're force-feeding the women. Please don't tell me she is on a hunger strike?"

Curran glanced at her, a flicker of understanding and deep concern in his eyes. "I don't know. It's hard being so far away. If I was still in London I could probably do something . . ."

Harriet swallowed back the bile induced by the memory of that rubber tube. "Inspector Curran, not all the governors of the school know about my past. The bishop knows but he's the only one and it would be a disaster if they were to find out."

"What would they do?"

"Probably fire Julian."

He shook his head. "That seems a bit drastic. Does anyone else in Singapore know?"

Harriet shrugged. "My brother, of course, and Griff Maddocks. He's a journalist. He recognized my name from the papers."

Curran nodded. "Is there a reason you have not been entirely forthcoming with the school governors?"

Harriet bit her lip. "I wanted to put it all behind me. Start afresh."

Curran regarded her, his expression unreadable. "That is a risk you're taking, Mrs. Gordon."

"We know, but Julian is a good man. A really good man."

Curran grunted. "They'll hear nothing from me. I just wanted to clear the air between us. Now, I've taken up enough of your time. I should be getting home."

"Mrs. Curran will be wondering where you are," Harriet said, fishing.

He glanced at her and she thought she saw the faint glimmer of a smile. "There is no Mrs. Curran, something I am sure you already know from the local gossips."

Harriet smiled. "I try not to listen to gossip."

"Please thank your brother for the whisky and give him my regards," he said, clapping his hat on his head.

"Will you be at the bridge opening tomorrow?" Harriet asked.

Curran pulled a face. "On duty but I believe we will meet in more congenial circumstances tomorrow evening at the Van Wijk. The Mackenzies have added me to the invite list."

"I look forward to it," Harriet said, and meant it. "Good night, Inspector," she added as he took the steps down to the driveway two at a time.

He swung effortlessly into the saddle of his horse, raised his hand and turned the magnificent animal's head toward the road.

Harriet stood on the verandah for a little while trying to reconcile the gentle handling of a small, vulnerable kitten with the hardened policeman.

"I wonder," Harriet said to Shashti as she clambered back up her skirt, "who is Lee-Anne? Or is it Lee An?" Remembering the whispered gossip of the school mothers, she decided the latter was far more likely. The mysterious Chinese housekeeper, perhaps?

Was it possible that she had been wrong about Curran? Was he a policeman she could trust? Certainly no policeman she had met in London would have sympathized with the cause of the suffragettes, but then no policeman in London could claim Lady Eloise Warby as a cousin.

Even as she thought of Lady Warby, she felt a stirring in her blood. She may have been driven into the arms of the suffragettes by her own loneliness but she had come to embrace their beliefs and they had come to represent everything in her life that had frustrated her. Why couldn't she have become a lawyer like her father? Why did she, as an independent-thinking woman, not have the right to vote on matters that affected her and the thousands of other women?

She may have left London but it seemed the cause had not left her.

✧ FIFTEEN

Saturday, 12 March 1910

"**M**y goodness, what a crowd."

Louisa Mackenzie skillfully elbowed her way through the well-dressed men and women to join Harriet on the temporary tiered platforms that had been erected on the north bank of the Singapore River. From here they had a fine view of the new bridge.

Louisa let out a breath as she surveyed the elegant truss arches and fine fluted piers. "So glad it is finally opening. I must say it is rather splendid."

"Worthy of the Thames perhaps, rather than this unassuming stream?"

As one Louisa and Harriet turned their heads. Robert Curran, resplendent in his white ceremonial uniform with gleaming, freshly polished brass buttons and epaulettes, stood behind them. He tipped his fingers to the brim of the slightly preposterous white sola topee.

"My dear Curran, shouldn't you be off investigating murders?" Louisa inquired.

Curran's mouth tightened and he cast a baleful glance at the official dais, where a similarly resplendent inspector general of the Straits Settlements Police sat just behind the governor, Sir John Anderson. Cuscaden appeared to be deeply engaged in the prattle of an overdressed matron in a large hat surmounted with peacock feathers that kept hitting the IG's nose every time she bobbed her head.

Harriet raised a gloved hand to her mouth to stifle the giggle.

"I wonder," Curran murmured, "if having a bridge named after you would make Sir John eligible for membership of the Explorers and Geographers Club."

"I'll tell him you suggested that." The soft lilt of a Welsh accent alerted them to the presence of Griff Maddocks, who scrambled up beside the ladies.

"Maddocks, you should not sneak up on people unannounced," Louisa chided, hitting the journalist playfully on the arm with her furled parasol.

Maddocks grinned. "But that's how I hear the best gossip, Mrs. Mackenzie. Mrs. Gordon, you look lovely today."

Compared to Louisa in her soft cream muslin tea gown, Harriet felt like a frump in a plain navy drill skirt, starched white blouse and a utilitarian straw hat trimmed with a navy ribbon.

Griff smiled at her. "What brings you to the social event of the year?" he asked.

"The unbridled excitement of watching our governor cutting a ribbon," she replied. "And the school choir is singing the national anthem in the Memorial Hall. I came along to keep them all in line but found I was not needed."

"I gather things got a little rowdy last night. Some idiot decided to go across it riding on the bonnet of a motor vehicle. Now, that would have been a story, not this . . ." Maddocks' lip curled as he gazed around at the stiff, formal pageantry. "Anyway, why are you here, Curran? Don't you have a couple of murderers to catch?"

"I do," Curran said, "but Cuscaden was concerned there would be trouble today."

Maddocks gave the policeman a sharp, journalistic glance. "Is the case of the boy fished out of Stamford Canal connected to Newbold?"

"Couldn't possibly say." All humor had gone from the policeman's face and he stared ahead with a stony countenance, once again the professional dealing with an irritating member of the press.

Maddocks smiled. "Oh, come on, Curran, give me something to write about other than this damned bridge."

Curran brought his attention back to Maddocks and his lips twitched. "Oh, I'm sure by the time you've reported on the jollities in Memorial Hall and who said what about whom, you should have several good inches of column space."

Maddocks rolled his eyes. "Spare me! One gets bloody weary of reporting about rubber prices and who is staying at what hotel."

"Now, now, Maddocks watch your language, there are ladies present."

Maddocks mumbled his apologies to Harriet and Louisa.

"What would you say to a trade of information?" Maddocks addressed Curran.

Curran stiffened. "What do you mean?"

"I've been doing a little research into Sir Oswald Newbold. If I let you have what I've got, you give me the exclusive to report on the progress of the case."

"Oh, how thrilling," Louisa interposed. "What have you found out, Maddocks?"

Harriet elbowed her friend in the ribs. "None of your business, Louisa," she said in a low voice, not wishing to interrupt the interesting exchange between the men.

Curran regarded the Welshman, his eyes narrowed. "How good is your information?"

"It'll save you months of research."

Louisa smiled coquettishly at the reporter. "Do tell!"

Maddocks inclined his head. "Another time, Mrs. Mackenzie.

Curran, meet me in the Long Bar at Raffles for a beer this afternoon about three. Right now, I have a story to write. I see His Excellency is armed with a vicious pair of golden scissors. Ladies."

Maddocks tipped his hat and pushed his way through the crowd to get a closer view. Harriet stood on her tiptoes in time to see His Excellency, Sir John Anderson, the feathers on his hat blowing in the wind, step forward with the scissors poised, ready to cut the ribbon across the new bridge, the *jambatan bahru*.

"I'm pleased you will be joining us this evening, Robert," Louisa said.

An unfamiliar prickle ran down Harriet's spine as Louisa used the policeman's first name.

"I have heard that the Austrian Ladies' Orchestra is not to be missed," Curran replied with a straight face.

Louisa flicked his sleeve. "I think a good oompah or two would do you good. The entertainment begins at seven. Bollinger champagne is promised. Don't be late, Curran."

Scattered applause and a halfhearted cheer roused the crowd as the ribbon fell away from under the governor's gold scissors. One of the brightly decorated new trams waiting on the south bank and driven by a stony-faced European driver, rang its bell and began to rattle slowly across the bridge, followed by the still oddly respectful crowd.

"It looks like the fun is over. Come, Harriet, I'm sure you wish to hear the boys' rendition of 'God Save the King.' Until tonight, Curran." With a twirl of the lace parasol she carried, Louisa slipped her hand into the crook of Harriet's arm and they pushed through the crowd toward the Memorial Hall.

"You're wrong to tease him, Louisa," Harriet said.

"Nonsense. I've known Curran since he arrived in Singapore. I know exactly how far I can push him but he does need to learn to relax more. It will be good for him to have a night out."

"Will his . . . umm . . ." Harriet stumbled on the right word.

"His paramour? His native woman?" Louisa suggested. "No,

she won't accompany him and not because she would not be welcome. She lives her own life quite away from Curran's. You will know why when you meet her."

"If I meet her. If I am unlikely to encounter her in social settings, I don't see when our paths will cross."

"True," Louisa said. "And perhaps that is for the best. Oh dear, I can hear the band striking up. We'll miss them."

The two women had to push their way into the crowded, stuffy hall, just in time to hear the cherubic voices of the boys of St. Tom's beginning "God save our gracious king. Long live our noble king . . ."

✸ SIXTEEN

At three in the afternoon Curran found Maddocks in the Long Bar at Raffles. The journalist had arrived before him and was already on his second beer. Curran set his hat down on the table and gave his order to the waiter.

"How were the speeches?" he asked.

Maddocks pulled a face. "Obsequious. His Excellency won a rather large, ugly silver platter for his skill at wielding the scissors. Important matters first, are you playing cricket tomorrow?"

Curran nodded. "That is my intention. I'm waiting on information from Rangoon on Newbold. Other than that, I have no clear leads."

The Johor Cricket Club had sent across its best team to match up against the Singapore Cricket Club in the annual "grudge" match. Murder or not, he didn't intend to miss the game. If he did he would probably have to add his death to the mounting list.

The captain of the Singapore Cricket Club team would kill him.

"And the Dutch boy, Visscher? Cause of death?" Maddocks continued.

"Suspicious."

Maddocks set his beer down and rolled his eyes. "Suspicious? From what I could gather his head had been almost severed."

"Who have you been talking to?"

"The *dhobis*."

Curran rolled his eyes.

"Officially all I can tell you is that his death is suspicious."

Maddocks grunted and took a swill of beer. "Tell me honestly, do you believe the two deaths are connected?"

Curran swirled the amber fluid in his glass. "You're not to write this down—of course they are, but at this stage I have nothing to link them."

Maddocks straightened in his chair. "Maybe I can help."

Curran shot him a glance. "What do you know?"

Maddocks produced a notebook and flicked through several pages until he came to the part he was looking for.

"I have a colleague on the *Times* in London. He's been working on a story coming out of Amsterdam concerning illicit Burmese rubies."

"Rubies?" Curran's hand jerked, slopping beer onto the table.

Maddocks grinned. "That got your attention, didn't it?"

"Yes, but Amsterdam is noted for diamonds, not rubies."

Maddocks shrugged. "Primarily diamonds, but the cutters also deal with high-quality gems of other types, particularly Burmese rubies and sapphires."

"Go on."

"Rubies of a particularly high quality have been coming into Holland through the black market for the last two years. There's no official records and corresponding tax paid on them. The authorities believe they are coming out of the mines in northern Burma and being smuggled through Singapore. Now, tell me how long Oswald Newbold has been living in Singapore?"

"About three years."

"Correct. He arrived three years ago, after a life spent in

Burma. Did you know it was Newbold who led an expedition into northern Burma in the 1870s to discover the extent of the ruby mines?"

"Yes, and I also know he and one other were the only ones to come back alive."

"One of the expedition was a George Carruthers. According to the official report, he died of fever. Newbold's only surviving witness was a military man by the name of Kent."

"I know all this. Carruthers's son is the secretary of the Explorers Club."

Maddocks's eyebrows shot up. "Is he indeed? That I didn't know."

"And he told me Kent died a few years later."

Maddocks shrugged. "Kent went off on another exploration to northern Burma and didn't return. It was widely assumed he was dead."

Curran shot the journalist an appraising glance. "He's not?"

"No reason to assume otherwise. Kent's loss meant that Newbold had no witnesses to his discoveries and no one to share the glory. As a direct result of his expedition, Britain annexes northern Burma and the Burmese Ruby Syndicate sets up a mine in the Mogok region. Newbold was the Burmese Ruby Syndicate's man on the spot. He commissions the mines, gets a knighthood and amasses a fortune."

Curran frowned. "A fortune? I'd have said he was comfortably well off but from what I've seen he didn't have a fortune."

Maddocks's eyes gleamed. "This is where it gets interesting. It's not common knowledge but he lost a large part of it in a speculation on ruby mines in Indochina. My source in London tells me his management of the mines came under suspicion in the early part of this century. Ill treatment of workers and the like and he was quietly persuaded to retire. From what I can find he arrived in Singapore, if not quite destitute then pretty badly off but in three years he's gone from a room in the Hotel Van Wijk to a bungalow on Bukit Timah Road."

Curran held up his hand. "Did you say the Van Wijk?"

Maddocks consulted his notes. "He lived there for just over a year before he bought the place up on Bukit Timah. You know, for a policeman you have a face like a book, Curran. What's the connection?"

Curran schooled his face to behave and shook his head. The Van Wijk again. All paths seemed to lead back to that respectable establishment.

"It seems more than a little coincidental that his arrival in Singapore overlaps with the illegal rubies arriving on the Amsterdam gem market. Wouldn't you agree?" Maddocks continued.

Curran considered the information. "He has precious few personal records of any kind, for a man writing his memoirs. Some story about a fire in Rangoon?"

"That may be true," Maddocks said. "His bungalow burned to the ground, the same month he was to leave for Singapore."

"An accident?"

"Spilled oil lamp, so the story goes."

Curran shook his head. "I would appreciate it, Maddocks, if you kept this information out of your paper for the time being."

Maddocks shrugged. "It's just supposition, Curran. Until I can back it up with some decent facts, it won't be going to print." He returned his notebook to his pocket and picked up his empty glass. *"Satu empat jalan?"*

Curran smiled. "For a man who has only been in Singapore a few short months, Maddocks, you've a pretty good grasp of the lingo."

Maddocks's neat dark eyebrows rose in mock surprise. "And for a policeman, you've obviously neglected to investigate my past. I was born here, Curran. Went back to dismal Wales with my family when I was twelve. I'm afraid it's in my blood."

"Satu empat jalan." Curran raised his glass and repeated the

anglicization of the Malay. A not-so-subtle play on words. *Satu* meaning "one" and *jalan* meaning "road." The Anglo community used *empat*, the number four, instead of "for." *One for the road.*

Curran waved a waiter over and ordered another round of beers . . . for the road.

Maddocks pulled out a pipe and began to pack it with tobacco from a leather pouch as he said, "Back to my original question. What's your feeling about the match tomorrow?"

Curran's mood lifted. Cricket had been the one part of his life he had clung to wherever he had been and whatever the circumstances.

Li An tied Curran's bow tie and smiled as she ran a finger down his freshly shaven cheek.

"You look fine, Curran," she said.

He caught her face in his hand and gazed at her, the old anger rising to the surface. "Li An, you understand . . . tonight is business."

"And this Gordon mem, is she business?" Li An asked, her wide eyes belying the knife edge to her tone.

"Purely business," he assured her.

Mac had sent a message earlier in the evening. He was delayed at the hospital and had promised to collect Mrs. Gordon. Would Curran oblige, as her brother was indisposed and she could hardly arrive alone. Curran wondered about the propriety of openly socializing with a key witness to his current investigations and decided he didn't really care. He liked Mrs. Gordon and she intrigued him. The policeman in him yearned to know more about her past and what had occurred in London twelve months previously. The man in him responded to her keen intelligence and her independent spirit.

He could hardly arrive in a *ricksha* or a *gharry* so he had sent for the departmental vehicle, knowing Tan relished any opportunity to drive the damn thing. Even as Li An brushed an imaginary piece of lint from the sleeve of his evening jacket, he could hear the hideous rumble of the machine coming up the hill.

He bent his head and kissed her. "Good night. Don't wait up for me."

Although he knew she would—she always did.

❧ SEVENTEEN

Julian managed a low, unclerical whistle as Harriet swept into the living room.

"You look smashing," he said.

Harriet twirled to show off the à la mode dress of black satin and lace, chosen for her by her sister, Mary, before leaving London. Ever bossy, Mary had insisted on taking her younger sister on a shopping expedition to ensure, if nothing else, Harriet did not disgrace the family even further with her choice of drab clothes.

Even the phlegmatic Huo Jin had stood back, nodding as she considered her mistress.

"Very pretty" was her conclusion.

Harriet patted her hair, swept up into an elegant chignon and held in place with a tortoiseshell comb. Huo Jin had shown a hitherto undemonstrated talent with hair.

Harriet glanced at the front door as the grumble of an engine announced the arrival of a motor vehicle.

"That must be the Mackenzies. They must have borrowed a motor vehicle," she said. "Are you sure you don't mind me going by myself?"

"Quite sure. An afternoon in the hot sun at the bridge opening was a bit much and I can feel the start of a headache, Harri.

I really can't face the Austrian Ladies' Orchestra." Julian smiled. "I trust Mac and Louisa to keep you out of trouble."

Firm footsteps crossed the verandah, followed by a sharp rap on the door. Huo Jin answered it, standing back to admit not Euan Mackenzie but an almost unrecognizable Robert Curran. The man standing on the doorstep, in full, starched white tropical evening dress, bore more resemblance to his purported aristocratic roots than to the policeman Harriet had come to know over the last few days.

A small "Oh" escaped Harriet before she had a chance to restrain it.

Curran must have misinterpreted her exclamation. "Sorry to disappoint you. Dr. Mackenzie is detained and has sent me in his stead. I have the motor vehicle outside."

"I am not disappointed. Just surprised," Harriet said. "I hardly recognized you out of your uniform, Inspector." She glanced at Julian. Her brother raised a questioning eyebrow.

"You're not joining us, Reverend?" Curran inquired.

Julian patted the book by his chair. "No, it will just be me and Virgil tonight."

"Each to their own," Curran responded. "Will you be coming to the match tomorrow?"

"Wouldn't miss it!" Julian declared. "Bringing some of the boarders with me, so you better put on a good show, Curran."

"Mrs. Gordon . . . ?" Curran turned to Harriet.

"Not me, Inspector. As my brother will tell you, cricket is not my game and I refuse to be one of those women in the stands who turn up to look decorative and sip tea."

Curran's eyes rested on her face for a moment, the corners creased in amusement. "I imagine you're not," he agreed. "Far better at making the tea . . ."

"Inspector Curran, if I had a cushion handy I would throw it at you."

"Fortunately for me you haven't."

It had been a long time since a man had presumed to tease her and she rather liked it.

Julian laughed. "Challenge Harriet to a tennis match one day, Curran, and you'll soon discover where her talents lie."

Curran raised an enquiring eyebrow at Harriet. "Tennis?"

Harriet glared at her brother. "I do enjoy a game of tennis," she mumbled. "Shouldn't we be going?"

"Have a wonderful evening," Julian said. "I'm certain I can trust you, Inspector Curran, to see to my sister's safety?"

Curran smiled. "She has the full protection of the Straits Settlements Police, I assure you, Reverend."

"Oh dear, that makes it sound like I'm under arrest," Harriet said.

Robert Curran smiled and crooked his elbow. "Mrs. Gordon, I am off duty tonight and I assure you it is my absolute pleasure to have your company for the evening."

She allowed herself to smile in response and took his arm in her gloved hand. Even in the tropics, correct dress had to be observed.

As they walked down the front steps toward the car, Curran said, "I have ordered the car for eleven. If that is too early for you, I am sure Mac . . ."

"No, eleven is fine. I have the unenviable job of organizing the boarders for church in the morning and I will need all my wits about me. They're already overexcited after singing today and the cricket match tomorrow."

Curran handed her into the car. "What is your aversion to cricket, Mrs. Gordon?"

She settled herself on the hard leather seat. "Years of being forced to watch my father and brother playing the game. I am sure that is why I married a Scot. James professed to loathe cricket." She laughed. "But too late I discovered he adored rugby, which has the benefit of being considerably shorter in duration and therefore almost bearable." She paused. "Julian says you are very good."

"At policing?"

"At cricket."

"In my younger days," Curran said, settling himself next to her. "I'm afraid old age is creeping up on me. I still enjoy a hit but the fire has burned down."

"Where to, sir?" the young constable at the wheel asked without turning his head.

"Hotel Van Wijk, Tan."

The weather being fine, the canopy had been lowered and the warm evening enveloped them as the motor vehicle purred along Orchard Road and into Stamford Road. Harriet glanced at the dark snaking line of the Sungei Stamford.

"Is that where Visscher was found?" she asked.

Curran nodded. "He was found just beyond the Serangoon Road bridge by one of the *dhobi wallahs.*"

"What did he do to deserve such a death?"

"He was a threat to somebody, Mrs. Gordon."

"But what sort of threat? He was only a boy."

"Mrs. Gordon. I am off duty tonight. Can we talk about something else?"

She glanced at his profile. "I don't believe you are ever really off duty, Inspector Curran. By the way, I did a little research on the VOC."

"And?"

"They were powerful, Curran. The most powerful single company in the world, particularly this part of the world. Whole populations of islands were simply wiped out in the East India Company's quest to secure the spice trade."

"Someone told me they swapped Manhattan for one of the Spice Islands." Curran tilted his head and looked at her. "I wonder if they would make the same decision today?"

"Probably, if it meant world domination," Harriet said. "Do you think it is possible that the VOC has been reconstituted in some way?"

Curran shook his head. "No. I suspect the name has been appropriated for some reason best known to whoever is responsible for these crimes."

"But, Curran, if they have, what is their connection with Newbold? He wasn't Dutch."

"I don't know," he said.

Something in his tone made her pause. She glanced at him.

"You're lying to me, Inspector."

"Lying?"

"I was right. You're never off duty."

"I am when I'm playing cricket."

"Then, perhaps I should come and watch you play. It could be interesting. Assuming you will be working in whatever capacity tonight, is there anything I can do to assist you?"

"Good Lord, Mrs. Gordon. You are a guest at a party. The last thing I want to do is ruin your evening. You enjoy yourself."

Harriet stiffened. "Don't patronize me, Curran."

"I wasn't."

"I'm not just a simpering female."

"Oh, I know that," he replied with a smile. "But to answer your question, I intend only to observe the interactions of several people."

"Suspects? Am I a suspect?"

He shook his head. "No, but you're a witness and it would be improper of me to jeopardize your evidence." He paused. "However, if I were to need your assistance . . ."

"I want to help. I would like to find the person responsible, if not for Newbold's death but certainly for the cold-blooded murder of that poor old man, Nyan, and young Visscher. Neither of them deserved to die."

Curran didn't respond immediately. Propping his arm on the door of the car, he looked out into the night.

"Yes, we owe them justice, don't we, Mrs. Gordon?"

* * *

The exterior of the Hotel Van Wijk had been hung with bright Chinese lanterns and from beyond the open windows of the ball-room, the music of a fox-trot drifted out onto Stamford Road as Robert Curran helped Harriet out of the motor vehicle.

She hesitated before taking his proffered arm. It would be easy to forget that this handsome man, cool and elegant in his tropical evening kit, was a policeman and worse, a policeman who knew her history.

Too many people already shared the knowledge. Louisa and Euan Mackenzie, of course, the journalist Maddocks and now Curran. She wondered how long it would be before it spread through the close Anglo community. Nothing the "mamas" would like better than a scandal of such magnitude involving someone they knew. She had visions of outraged mothers removing their darlings from the school in protest at having a convicted criminal in the employ of St. Tom's. The board would surely sack Julian.

As if he could read her thoughts, Curran's hand closed over hers. "It's a lovely evening, Mrs. Gordon. There is a band playing so let us put the cares of the world behind us and enjoy the night."

These monthly soirees at the Van Wijk were popular and quite a crowd pressed into the ballroom and spilled out onto the terrace and gardens. A placard at the entrance proudly declared that the AUSTRIAN LADIES' ORCHESTRA OF THE GRAND CONTINENTAL HO-TEL UNDER THE BATON OF BANDMASTER L. HOCKMEYER would be the entertainment for the evening and indeed, the band comprising ladies in Austrian national dress were already hard at work.

Mr. Van Gelder met them at the door, his eyes widening as he recognized Harriet's companion.

"Inspector, I hope you are here for pleasure, not business?" Van Gelder asked with a forced laugh.

Curran inclined his head. "Even policemen are entitled to a few hours off."

He introduced Harriet and Van Gelder clicked his heels together as he bowed over her hand, affording her a view of well-oiled hair that had been combed across a nascent bald patch.

As he straightened, he said, "Did I not see you yesterday at the funeral of poor Visscher?"

"Yes. My brother and I both attended," Harriet replied.

"*Liefste . . .*"

Harriet and Curran turned as Mrs. Van Gelder joined them. Her hair had been styled in a fashionable coiffure and she wore a low-necked, royal blue satin evening gown. It set off her eyes and, Harriet considered, in her youth Viktoria Van Gelder must have been quite a beauty.

"The kitchen," Mrs. Van Gelder said, and her husband excused himself, hurrying away in the direction of the hotel kitchen.

Mrs. Van Gelder acknowledged Harriet with a polite smile and turned to Curran, tilting her head to look up at the tall policeman. "Inspector. Do you have any news about our poor Hans?"

Curran shook his head.

The woman fumbled in her beaded reticule for a handkerchief with which she dabbed decorously at her eyes.

She sighed, restoring the handkerchief and forcing a smile. "My apologies, tonight is not the night for such gloomy thoughts." She gestured at the ballroom. "Please enjoy yourselves."

As they entered the ballroom, Curran left Harriet to go in pursuit of a waiter with a tray of champagne glasses, allowing her an opportunity to peruse the room. The band were now playing a cheerful polka and she caught sight of Louisa talking to a group of women on the far side of the room.

"Good evening, Mrs. Gordon."

Harriet turned to smile at Griff Maddocks, who had slipped into place beside her.

"Good evening, Mr. Maddocks. Did you finish your story on the bridge opening?"

Maddocks pulled a face. "The story is filed and my evening is my own. Can I prevail on you for the next dance?"

Harriet looked around but couldn't see Curran. She allowed Maddocks to lead her out onto the floor as the band struck up a waltz. They had partnered each other at several dances on board the ship from England and Maddocks had a deft touch and light feet. They chattered about the bridge opening.

When the dance ended Harriet looked around for Curran once more. He stood in the doorway to the terrace, clutching two glasses of champagne, talking to the Mackenzies. To judge from his perspiring face and crooked tie, Euan had only just joined the party.

Maddocks had seen them too. He took her arm and they strolled over to join their party.

"There you are," Louisa said. "Poor Curran has been holding this glass for so long, it is probably quite warm."

"Your champagne, Mrs. Gordon." Curran handed her the dripping glass and she took a sip, expecting the tingle of bubbles but the humidity sapped even the fizz from champagne.

"Glad Curran managed to deputize for me," Mac said, taking a glass from the tray of a passing waiter. He downed it in one gulp to a disapproving glare from his wife.

"What detained you?" Harriet inquired.

"Babies. They come when it suits them, not when it suits everyone else."

"All well?" Harriet inquired.

"Yes, mother and baby both fine. Good to share a happy occasion after the week we've had." He glanced at Curran and sighed. "I'm here now and let me just say, my dear Harriet, you look bonny tonight. No Julian?"

"No. It's been a hard week and he was all done in tonight."

"That brother of yours needs to watch his health." Euan waylaid a second waiter and scooped up a glass of champagne which again he downed in one quaff. He waved his empty glass in the direction of the door. "Haven't seen them before."

All heads turned to look at the elegant couple who had entered the ballroom. Gertrude Cornilissen wore a filmy gown of pale-blue silk and languidly waved a matching fan. Her lip curled in disdain as she surveyed the gathering, much as Harriet imagined Mr. Darcy's had on encountering the Bennet family in one of her favorite novels. Like his wife, Cornilissen was tall and blond haired, but some years older, the blond hair fading to silver.

"That's Nils Cornilissen and his wife. They arrived on Monday on the *Europa*," Maddocks put in. "I had to do the write-up for the *Times* on arrivals. He's some kind of antiques dealer. Dutch."

"I met his wife, Gertrude, at Visscher's funeral yesterday," Harriet said.

Harriet caught a quick glance that passed between Curran and Maddocks and Curran set his now-empty glass down on the nearest table. "May I prevail on your company for a moment, Mrs. Gordon?"

They excused themselves and Harriet took Curran's arm. They circled the dance floor, just like two casual attendees, looking for friends and familiar faces.

"What would you like me to do?" Harriet asked in a low voice, guessing that Curran was not interested in pure social engagement.

"I wish to pass some time with the Cornilissens," he said.

"Why? Do you think they are connected in some way to Sir Oswald? Oh . . . They are or at least they were in Rangoon at the same time as Mrs. Van Gelder."

He glanced at her. "How do you know that?"

"I took tea with both ladies yesterday."

"Ah, that confirms what Cornilissen told me."

They had reached the Dutch couple, who had moved to one side of the room, watching another vigorous polka. The Austrian Ladies seemed very partial to their polkas.

Curran feigned surprise and recognition. "Cornilissen, isn't it?" he said.

168 ◆ A. M. Stuart

The man straightened and frowned.

"Curran." Curran held out his hand. "We spoke at Newbold's funeral on Thursday."

Cornilissen smiled. "Ah *ja*, Inspector Curran. Are you here in an official capacity?"

Curran smiled and shook his head. "I'm here only to forget my concerns for a couple of hours. It's a popular event."

"There are a lot of people," Mrs. Cornilissen agreed, her gaze scanning the room.

"Allow me to introduce Mrs. Gordon." Curran presented Harriet.

"We've met," Harriet said, smiling as she took Gertrude's hand.

Courtesies were exchanged and fresh glasses of champagne procured.

Harriet gave the young woman an appraising look. Several years younger than her husband, tall and almost impossibly slender, her blue silk dress perfectly matched the blue of her eyes and set off the heavy sapphire earrings and necklace he wore. A jaunty blue feather headdress adorned her thick, fair hair.

"Having much luck?" Curran inquired.

Cornilissen smiled and shrugged. "Some interesting pieces from Indochina that will sell well. I did better in Batavia this trip."

"Ah yes, that little bit of old Holland still in the East," Curran said. "The old Dutch East India Company pretty much owned this part of the world for a while there. What was it called . . . the VOC? Now, they were a ruthless bunch. Stopped at nothing to secure the spice trade."

"And it made them the most successful enterprise of the time, if not all time," Cornilissen said with a smile. "Those days are gone."

"Do you wonder what it would have been like to live at that time?" Harriet asked.

Cornilissen smiled. "I think I would miss the modern conveniences of life, Mrs. Gordon."

"Indeed," Curran agreed.

"Why your interest in the VOC?" Cornilissen asked, draining his champagne glass.

Curran smiled. "No particular interest. I am a student of history and I like to understand the places that I live. Here in Singapore we are at the crossroads of so very many cultures—the Chinese, the Indians, Indochina—all different, all having their own histories. Throw in the Dutch, the Spanish, the French, the English and even the Arabs and it is a fascinating place to live."

"The VOC marked the heyday for the Dutch," Cornilissen said, with a soft reminiscent look in his eye. "The East Indies and South Africa. Even here in Malaya. The Dutch ruled the world, Mr. Curran, but that was a long time ago and as you intimate, sometimes it is best to leave the past where it belongs . . . in the past."

"I think you might be right," Curran said.

"That is the most exquisite necklace," Harriet addressed Gertrude.

Gertrude's long fingers played with the jewels at her neck. "My dear Nils deals in antiquities, but his brother, Anders's interest is in precious stones."

Her gaze dropped to Harriet's pearl strand, the gift of her late mother-in-law on her marriage to James, and one of her few good pieces of jewelry.

"Lovely sapphires," Harriet remarked. "Are they Burmese?"

The woman smiled. "They are. There is such depth to the Burmese stones. Have you ever seen a Burmese ruby, Mrs. Gordon? The color of blood."

"My dear, you are boring these good people," Cornilissen cut in, his tone clipped. "If you will excuse us, Inspector, Mrs. Gordon, I think I would like to dance. My dear . . . ?" He held out his hand and led his wife onto the floor.

"She's not a very happy woman," Harriet remarked.

"I agree," Curran said.

"And not all the beautiful jewelry or fine silk gowns will buy happiness."

Harriet turned her attention back to the dance floor, her fingers tapping the rhythm of the waltz beat on the stem of her glass.

Curran coughed. "Would you . . . umm . . . care to dance?"

She looked up at him and smiled. "I would, Inspector Curran. That would be most pleasant."

He offered her his arm and they joined the couples on the dance floor.

She had expected him to be a stiff, awkward dancer but he had been taught well and his timing was impeccable. Harriet let herself relax under the guiding pressure of his sure hand.

"You dance well," she remarked, conscious that the eyes of the nondancers were following them around the floor.

"I'm sure my grandfather would be pleased to hear you say that. Heaven knows, he expended enough money on trying to turn me into a gentleman."

"On which point he largely failed?" Harriet suggested.

"Indeed. As my aunt is at pains to point out, there was little point making silk purses out of a stable hand's son."

"Oh. I'm sorry, I didn't mean . . ."

He smiled down at her. "It's fine, Mrs. Gordon. I am sure the local gossips have acquainted you with my family history. It's quite true. My mother was the daughter of Lord Alcester and my father the son of the head groom. Lord Alcester, my grandfather, God rest him, was good to me and took me in but I was always the cuckoo in the family nest and since his death, I have been well and truly expelled. What else do the gossips say?"

"That you have a local woman as your mistress."

Curran missed a step and trod on her foot.

"You are nothing if not forthright, Mrs. Gordon," he said as he picked up the rhythm again.

"I apologize. That last piece of gossip is nothing short of scurrilous and I should not have repeated it," Harriet said.

"Her name is Khoo Li An."

"Li An who doesn't like cats?"

He smiled. "She considers them bad luck. Are you shocked, Mrs. Gordon?"

She pondered this question. "A hundred years ago in India, it was almost to be expected that the young men would take a local woman as their wife or mistress but the denizens of the Raj today are far less forgiving." She looked up at him. "I am not like them, Curran. As far as I am concerned this is the Far East, not Wimbledon and I have no right to judge anyone."

"Thank you," he said. "It is only my small talent at cricket that saves me from total social ostracism but Li An is more important to me than social acceptance."

He trailed off and she saw something in his face that surprised her. A fierce light in his eye and a grim set to his mouth. Whoever Li An was, this man loved her with a fierce protective love.

"Where did you meet her?" Harriet asked.

"Penang."

The abruptness of his response indicated he had no further wish to discuss Li An so Harriet changed the subject, asking him about the hope for success against the Johor Cricket Club. He humored her and as they danced for a little longer in silence, Harriet noticed Curran's gaze kept drifting to the Cornilissens, who stood together in a corner, apparently deep in conversation.

"You keep looking at the Cornilissen woman," Harriet said. "What are you thinking?"

Curran frowned. "Very little," he said. "The trouble is, Mrs. Gordon, I need firm evidence, not just my gut instinct."

"And what is your gut instinct telling you?"

"The murders of Newbold and Visscher are connected to this hotel in some way." He smiled ruefully. "You didn't hear me say that, Mrs. Gordon. I tend to talk too much in your presence."

"I heard nothing," she agreed.

The music ended and they drew apart, politely applauding the band.

"I think this may be my dance." Griff Maddocks's voice came from behind them.

Harriet turned and looked up at the tall policeman, who inclined his head. "I cede my place, Maddocks."

"An interesting chap, Curran," Maddocks remarked as they watched Curran push his way through the crowd, out onto the terrace, to be swallowed up by the night.

"As I am coming to discover," Harriet said.

They chatted about inconsequential matters and when the music ended, Euan Mackenzie claimed her for the next dance. As he whisked her out onto the floor in an enthusiastic polka, Harriet abandoned herself to the enjoyment of the evening.

❧ EIGHTEEN

Sunday, 13 March 1910

The sun beat down remorselessly on the heads of the "flannelled fools" who graced the Padang, the large field that served as both playing field and military parade ground for the annual match against the Johor Cricket Club. A large crowd had turned out to watch from the grandstand or from beneath umbrellas or in open carriages, in the shade of the young rain trees that had been planted along Connaught Drive.

The Singapore Cricket Club had the home ground advantage but the Johor side were putting up a sterling attack. A big brute of a man with a large moustache clean bowled Curran for thirty-four runs. He retired to a smattering of polite applause and resounding cheers from the little group of St. Tom's boys who sat with their headmaster and young Michael Derby. Curran smiled and lifted his bat to acknowledge the boys.

On his return to the pavilion, he removed his pads and sat down in the players' ranks to watch the game. He always found the gentle click of willow and leather soothing and it afforded him the opportunity to ponder on the confused events of the week.

"Deep in thought, Curran." A large shadow loomed over him.

Curran squinted upward and smiled at Colonel Foster. "Rather a lot on my mind, Colonel."

"Yes, of course. Mind if I join you, old chap?"

Without waiting for a response, Colonel Foster squeezed onto the bench beside Curran, juggling a cup of tea and a biscuit, which he dunked in the tea and munched thoughtfully as he watched the match.

"Tricky bowler, that one. Caught you with a clever inswinger," he said at last as the Johor player thundered in on his run-up. The batsman at the crease swayed away just in time to avoid being hit on the body. The crowd oohed its collective disapproval as the bowler trudged back to his mark before turning to run in again.

Curran shrugged. "He's fast and I just didn't see it."

"Oh, well played, sir!" Foster spat biscuit crumbs as the batsman sent a ball from Curran's nemesis to the boundary for four runs.

Foster drained his teacup and brushed the biscuit crumbs from his moustache. "I've been thinking about our conversation of the other day, Curran. And I've remembered something."

Curran shot his companion a quick glance. "Yes?"

"Carruthers."

"What about him?"

"He was absent sometime during the evening the night Newbold died."

Curran's instinct prickled and he gave Foster his full attention. "Absent? How do you know? He tells me he had a club full of members all attesting to his presence."

"Not all. It was sometime after dinner. Carruthers said he had some work to catch up on in the office and would prefer not to be disturbed, but Ginger Smitherton, you know old Ginge? Discovered some ruins in Thailand or something."

"Err . . . no."

"Anyway, Ginge remembered he had to pay his dues so he went to Carruthers's office. Door was locked so he knocked. No reply.

One of the servants said he thought Carruthers had gone 'out the back,' you know, to visit the conveniences, so Ginge gave up."

"If Smitherton didn't pursue Carruthers to the conveniences, what makes you think he would be anywhere else?"

"About an hour later, Carruthers comes back into the parlor with wet hair. Didn't think anything of it at the time but now I think it's a rum thing. If he'd just been out the back, there's no reason for his hair to be wet. Covered walkways and all that."

Curran's fingers clenched on the handle of his bat.

"Does Carruthers have any transport?"

"He does. Rather a nice little motor vehicle. He brought it in from America a couple of months ago. Had the whole club agog. Must have cost him a year's wages."

"Where did he get the money from?"

"An inheritance from an uncle, he said."

Curran's pulse quickened. Carruthers was a paid employee of the Explorers and, according to his own story, his father's untimely death in Burma had left him and his mother destitute, dependent on the charity of the BRS. How had he come into money? This was a kernel of real evidence and Curran had to speak to Carruthers without delay.

"Thank you, Foster. That's most helpful. Any idea where Carruthers will be today?"

Curran stood up. The batsman at the crease had just gone out to a rising ball. The innings would be over shortly. The cricket match would have to continue without him.

Foster looked bemused. "At the club, of course. Hates cricket. I say, you're not leaving, are you?"

"I've done my bit and they can manage without me for the next innings. Twelfth man can field."

"But, damn it, you're the best slip fielder . . ." Foster's words were lost in the applause of the crowd for the change of batsman. Curran pushed his way through the crowd to find his captain and excuse himself from the rest of the game.

* * *

Still wearing his cricket flannels, Curran turned up at the door of the Explorers and Geographers Club. The *jagar* eyed him askance.

"Cannot let you in. Not properly attired."

"I'm not going to argue with you. Fetch Mr. Carruthers."

As he had on Curran's previous visit, the *jagar* moved into the doorway and stood there solid, silent and implacable, with his arms crossed. As he topped Curran by at least a head, any chance of taking him on physically did not seem like a good idea. Instead Curran shouted.

"Carruthers? Anyone? Please tell this oaf to let me in!"

He heard hurried footsteps on the passage and Carruthers's pink face peered around his doorman. "Inspector Curran, I do apologize. Let him through."

Curran passed into the hallowed halls of the Explorers and Geographers Club without further hindrance.

"What can I do for you?" Carruthers asked. Sweat sheened his forehead and he produced one of his endless supply of handkerchiefs to mop his face.

"I need to speak to you urgently. In your office."

Carruthers led the way and Curran shut the door behind him as Carruthers settled himself into his chair behind the vast expanse of desk.

"Please take a seat, Inspector, and tell me how I can be of help."

Curran remained standing.

"Where did you go on the night Newbold was murdered?"

Carruthers visibly flattened in his chair. "What do you mean? I was here all night. Didn't leave until after midnight. People will vouch for me . . ."

Curran put his hands on the desk and leaned forward so his face was within inches of Carruthers's.

"No, you weren't, Carruthers. You disappeared in your motor vehicle for at least an hour. Where did you go?"

"Nonsense! Who says, I . . ." Carruthers looked up into the policeman's unsympathetic face and crumpled. "I . . . I . . ." Sweat ran in runnels down the man's jowly face. He swallowed. "I went to see Newbold."

Curran had what he came for. He straightened and sat down in a chair across the desk from Carruthers, schooling his face to impassivity.

"But . . . but . . . I didn't kill him. He was already dead."

"Why did you go to see him?"

Carruthers licked his lips. "I could lie and tell you it was club business but I've already been a little economical with the truth." He hefted a deep breath. "I told you that my father was part of the expedition that went out with Newbold and that he never came back. Newbold was going on and on about his memoirs and I wanted to confront him about my father. You see, I always believed there was something odd about the whole affair."

"In what way?"

"Newbold got all the accolades and made a fortune from those bloody ruby mines whereas Ma and I got nothing." An old bitterness cramped the man's face. "I intended to ask Newbold for money to help us out. We only have what I earn from here and Ma is living in penury in Torquay. He owed us something."

Anger now suffused Carruthers's face so Curran moved the subject along, leaving the question of the money to buy the motor for the moment. His own pulse raced and had to be careful not to push too hard, just hard enough to get a confession.

"I know you own a motor vehicle so I assume you drove up to Bukit Timah Road. Where did you park the vehicle?"

"Halfway up the drive," Carruthers said.

That accounted for the vehicle tracks Curran's men had found.

"What time did you get there?"

"About nine thirty. I saw a light in Newbold's study and found the front door open. I knocked but no one came so I walked in. He was . . ." Carruthers mopped his brow again, pressing the linen to his mouth. ". . . lying on the carpet with that, that thing in his throat."

"Why didn't you summon the police?"

Carruthers's inadequate moustache quivered. "I know I should have done and I thought about it but then I realized that you might think it was me."

Curran could not prevent one of his eyebrows lifting in sarcastic surprise.

Carruthers noticed the gesture and turned a deeper shade of crimson. "I saw the safe behind the desk. It was unlocked so I took a look. Couldn't believe my luck when I found the manuscript. I thought maybe if I took it, the answer would be in there."

"And?"

"I left, Inspector. It was raining when I got outside and I got wet trying to raise the canopy on the motor vehicle. I left the vehicle a little way from the club and entered through the back. No one saw me. Not even the servants. I tried to dry myself as best I could but I feared my hair might still be damp." His mouth drooped. "I just hoped no one would notice."

"That was naive in the extreme," Curran observed. "Do you still have the manuscript?"

Carruthers bent down and a key clicked in a lock. The rasp of wood indicated a desk drawer being opened and Carruthers lifted out a large packet of papers, bound together with string, and set it down on the table in front of him.

He laid a hand on the packet and sighed. "This is it. I swear it's all I took."

"Did you find what you were looking for?" Curran inquired.

Carruthers shook his head. "No. The whole damned thing is written in shorthand. May as well be written in Sanskrit." He pushed it across to Curran. "Take it."

"I intend to."

"Are you going to charge me?"

Carruthers looked so miserable that Curran felt inclined to believe his story.

"Not right now. I'll continue to make inquiries, Mr. Carruthers. In the meantime, please attend at Central Police Station tomorrow and give a written statement to Sergeant Singh. We will consider any criminal culpability for theft, if for nothing else."

Carruthers looked up at him with watery eyes. "I'll never forget seeing him there, Inspector. It was horrible . . . horrible . . ."

As he stood up, Curran said, "One last thing, Carruthers. Where did you get the money to purchase your motor vehicle?"

Carruthers's eyes widened. "My uncle Cyril died and left me something in his will," he said.

So much for the mother living in penury in Bournemouth, Curran thought. That was a question that could wait for another day. Carruthers was still lying about something, either where he got the money or his penniless, widowed mother.

"Please give all the details of Uncle Cyril's will to Sergeant Singh tomorrow," he said.

He tucked the parcel under his arm and left the man blowing his nose on his handkerchief.

❦ NINETEEN

Sunday was the servants' day off and Harriet was on kitchen duty, making scones to go with the chicken soup Lokman had left for their supper. In a corner of the kitchen, a small domestic altar had been sent up by Huo Jin, presided over by the faded photographs of an elderly Chinese couple in stiff robes and an even stiffer pose. The burnt-down stubs of the incense sticks placed on the altar before the ancestors left a lingering sweetness that mingled with the kitchen smells. The honored ancestors scowled at Harriet, while at her feet, Shashti chased a scrap of paper around the tiles. Aziz sat in a corner, polishing boots and humming to himself, even though he too should have been enjoying some free time.

"Have you no family to visit?" Harriet inquired.

Aziz looked up, his eyes wide with surprise. "No, mem. No family. You give me time to go to the mosque on Friday. That is all I need."

Beyond the kitchen door, the heavy leaves of the tropical foliage that fringed the school dripped with moisture from an evening rainstorm and hidden in the canopy the *ulu* resonated with the shrill cries of the macaque monkeys, birds and the chirrup of myriad insects. When she had first gone to India it had surprised her to find that the jungle was such a noisy place.

"Mrs. Gordon?"

At the sound of a boy's voice, she poked her head out of the kitchen. "In here, Will."

Will Lawson hesitated, looking around the unfamiliar room. "Can I come in?"

"Of course. It's only a kitchen."

The boy entered the room, his nose twitching at the pleasant baking smells. Aziz looked up from his task and, seeing Will, grinned broadly.

Will raised a hand to acknowledge the other boy. "Hello, Aziz."

Aziz ducked his head and returned to his task.

"Good evening, Mrs. Gordon." Will stood very straight, his hands behind his back. He seemed a very well-brought-up young man. Annie Lawson had done a good job.

"Good evening, Will. Did you come to visit Shashti?"

Harriet placed a second batch of scones on a tray and thrust it into the oven.

Shashti appeared from under a kitchen cabinet and Will's face lit up. He picked up the kitten and sat down on a kitchen stool.

"She's getting fat, Mrs. Gordon."

Harriet looked at the little round kitten tummy and smiled. "She's doing just fine, Will. How's school?"

"It's all right," the boy said but his shoulders slumped and he turned all his concentration to the cat in his lap.

"Something wrong?"

"Daddy says I have to go to school in England."

Many of the children of planters and officials got sent to school in England from the age of eight so Will had been fortunate he had been spared for at least a couple of years. She wondered how John Lawson could afford the school fees for a school in England when he struggled to pay St. Thomas.

"I don't want to go to England. Papa says it means I will have to stay there and live with my aunt and uncle during school holidays."

Although she couldn't see his face the quaver in his voice told her he was crying and a large tear plumped onto Shashti's soft fur.

She squatted down in front of him and lifted his face with her floury finger.

"You will still have next term here, Will. Plenty of time to get used to the idea."

His face crumpled. "You don't understand. He's sending me away this week."

"This week?"

Harriet sat down on the nearest stool. This seemed completely at odds with her conversation with John Lawson. He had paid until the end of the school year. They had talked about scholarships.

"He wrote me a letter."

"Do you have it?"

Will stood up and, still clutching a compliant Shashti, dug in the pocket of his shorts with his spare hand, producing a crumpled and stained envelope. Harriet wiped her hands on her apron before pulling out the equally crumpled and stained letter.

"Dear boy," she read. *"Sorry to break this news to you by letter but I may not get a chance to get down to town to tell you myself. I have decided the best place for you is in England with your mother's family and I have booked a passage for you on the* Europa, *which sails on Thursday. Mr. And Mrs. Banks will be looking after you on the voyage and I have telegraphed your aunt and uncle to expect you. They will be at Portsmouth to meet the boat. You will live with them while I sort out the school for you. I have written to my old school, Winchester, and I know you will like it there and make lots of good chums. I will ring the school and try to speak with you before you leave. Be a good, brave little chap. This is for the best and it won't be long before I will be in England to visit you and we will make a new home together. Much love, Papa."*

Another large tear dripped down Will's face. "I don't want to go."

Harriet stared in disbelief at the letter. "Oh, Will, I don't know what to say. He hasn't said anything to the school about this."

Will wiped his nose with the back of his hand. Harriet rose to her feet and handed him her clean handkerchief. He looked so woebegone she just wanted to take him in her arms and tell him it would be all right.

"Let's go and speak to Reverend Edwards," she said, laying a hand across his shoulder and propelling him out of the kitchen. She paused to look back and issue Aziz with strict instructions about the scones.

They found Julian on the front verandah, reading Virgil.

"Hello, Will." Julian's smile died at the sight of the boy's bereft face. "I say, what's the problem?"

Harriet handed her brother John Lawson's letter. Julian read it in silence and handed it back to her.

"First I've heard of this," he said. "What say if your father's too busy to come down to town then I go up and see him tomorrow and see what this is all about?"

Will's lip trembled but hope gleamed in his eye. "Will you?"

Julian smiled. "Of course I will. Doesn't seem any point sending you away with only one term left of this year. I'll see if he can't be persuaded. I say, we've got another visitor, Harri. Inspector Curran is becoming an evening institution."

Robert Curran drew his chestnut horse to a stop and dismounted, looping the reins over a carved Chinese lion at the foot of the steps. He was not in uniform, favoring an open-neck shirt, riding breeches and highly polished boots.

"Good evening, Reverend Edwards, Mrs. Gordon and who do we have here?"

Will shrank back, clutching Shashti tightly to his chest.

Julian gently but firmly pulled him forward. "One of my boarders, William Lawson. His father manages a rubber plantation up near Kranji. Lawson, this is Inspector Curran of the police. Lawson is a rescuer of small animals, Curran."

"Pleased to make your acquaintance." Curran smiled and stooped to scratch the kitten's head. "And how is Shashti tonight?"

The boy grinned. "You know her name?"

"I do indeed."

"It was Will who saved the kitten from the python," Harriet said. "I consider him a part owner."

"I saw you bat today," Will said, undisguised admiration in his eyes.

Curran's face softened. "Not one of my better innings. Do you like cricket?"

"I do." The boy's face brightened. "I'm opening bat for St. Tom's against the Raffles Institution next week . . ." He trailed off, his face falling with the realization he would not be in Singapore to play the rival school.

"Perhaps when he is a little less busy, we could prevail on the inspector to come and do some coaching," Julian said.

A distant bell clanged, announcing the boarders' supper.

"Give me Shashti." Harriet held out her hands to take back the kitten. "Off you go and don't worry about the other matter. We will speak to your father."

"Thank you, Mrs. Gordon." The boy handed the kitten back to Harriet and scampered down the stairs and around the corner of the house, back to the school.

"Will you join us for a preprandial drink, Inspector?" Julian asked.

"That would not be unwelcome," Curran replied.

"Take a seat and I shall see what I can organize. Being Sunday, we've been left to our own devices."

Curran sat down on the top step, resting his forearms on his knees.

"Pretty part of Singapore, this," he said, looking out over the still-unspoiled jungle that fringed the house.

"Where do you live, Inspector?" Harriet asked.

He took off his hat and ran a hand through his hair, making

it stick up on end. "I've a small bungalow at the back of Chinatown, off Cantonment Road. I prefer to leave my work behind
me at the end of the day."

"Good match today." Julian returned with a tray with glasses,
whisky and a soda siphon.

Curran took the proffered glass Julian held out to him. "How
did it end? I played dismally and then I got called away."

"Johor took the honors, Curran. You won't be popular with
your teammates."

Curran shrugged. "They've learned to take me as they find me."

"And what brings you out to River Valley Road tonight?"
Harriet asked.

"I've a commission for you, Mrs. Gordon." He rose and returned to his horse, producing a parcel from the saddlebag.

He handed her a heavy package bound with string, which,
from its weight and shape, she guessed contained papers. She
looked up into Curran's gray eyes.

"Is this . . . ?"

He nodded. "The missing manuscript."

"Where did you find it?"

"It was given to me."

Harriet smiled. "By the murderer?"

A corresponding smile twitched the corner of his mouth.
"No . . . or at least I don't think so. I would like to commission
you to continue the task you started. I will pay whatever you
would have charged Newbold."

"Oh, but . . ."

Curran held up his hand. "This is a business proposition,
Mrs. Gordon. You don't have to do the lot. However, it's evidence in the case and I'm particularly interested in everything
involving the 1872 expedition and the establishment of the Burmese Ruby Syndicate."

"Newbold's dead. Why do you want it translated?" Julian
asked.

Curran shrugged. "There is probably nothing in it, beyond the grandiose imaginings of a self-important man, but there are others who are looking for peace of mind and there may be something in it of interest to them."

Julian sat back in his chair and crossed one leg over the other. He nursed his whisky and studied the policeman. "So, Curran. You have Sir Oswald Newbold and his servant murdered sometime on Monday evening by someone Newbold knew. The Visscher boy is seen at the house and then later here, babbling nonsense about a defunct trading company and he turns up dead two days later. What do these crimes have in common?"

"Are you turning detective, Reverend?" Curran inquired.

"I must confess I'm very partial to the writings of Conan Doyle," Julian replied.

"Unfortunately, I'm not Sherlock Holmes," Curran replied. "I'm just a common policeman."

Harriet considered the man and decided there was nothing common about Robert Curran.

"It's Burma, isn't it?" she ventured. "Burma and the ruby mines."

"Possibly, but I've nothing to link Visscher to either," Curran said.

"Except the Van Wijk Hotel, where a Dutch antiquities dealer with an interest in gems just happens to be staying," Harriet said.

Curran turned his gaze back on the garden. "I've probably said enough." He rose to his feet, setting his empty glass down on the table. "Thank you for the drink. Good evening to you both."

Harriet and Julian sat in silence for a long time after Curran had left. Harriet told Julian about Mrs. Cornilissen and her expensive jewelry.

"Sapphires, Harri, not rubies," Julian pointed out.

"They all come from the same place. Burmese sapphires are as sought after as rubies and surely it's no coincidence that this man Cornilissen is in Singapore."

"But he wasn't here when the murder occurred," Julian pointed out.

"I wonder—" Harriet began but Julian raised his hand.

"Don't speculate, Harri, and as interesting as it is, solving murders is Inspector Curran's job, not ours. I am far more concerned about Will Lawson. Why on earth is his father pulling him out of school and packing him off to England in such a hurry? Particularly when the school fees have all been paid up? I will go out to Kranji tomorrow."

"Would you like me to accompany you?"

Julian considered for a long moment. "I think that's an excellent idea. You may have more success with the man than me. Now, tell me more about last night. Did you have fun?"

Harriet smiled. It had been a long time since she had enjoyed an evening more. The attentions of two attractive men, both of whom seemed to seek out her company, gave her an unexpected thrill, reminiscent of her first season.

But she wasn't seventeen any longer and she had learned to appreciate such moments as they presented. She knew that happiness was only an illusion and it could never last.

❦ TWENTY

Monday, 14 March 1940

The train pulled away from the station at Tank Road at nine forty-five sharp and commenced its fifty-minute journey, winding up through the island past *kampongs*, gambier and rubber plantations and thick jungle. The train line terminated at Woodlands on the north coast, the jumping-off stop for the ferries, imaginatively named *Singapore* and *Johor*, which plied the short distance to Johor Bahru on the tip of the Malay Peninsula.

As they disembarked, Julian pointed out the *Johor*, bobbing peacefully at its mooring on the far side of the railway station, ready to take its passengers onward to Johor Bahru and the train to Kuala Lumpur and Penang. Much as Harriet would have loved to have spent the morning sightseeing, particularly with the Malay Peninsula so tantalizingly close, they were here on business.

Julian had telegrammed ahead and an ancient *gharry* driven by a local Malay awaited them.

"Very far away," the driver complained as the old horse plodded along at a snail's pace down narrow country lanes shaded by jungle and rubber plantations.

And indeed, the Lawson plantation took them well over three quarters of an hour to reach, culminating in a long driveway that wound up through rubber trees, skirting a river edged with mangroves.

"Sungei Kranji," the driver rasped in answer to Julian's enquiry about the name of the river.

"I don't know much about rubber plantations, but there seems to be an air of neglect over this one," Harriet remarked, indicating the weeds and creepers that had claimed the orderly rows of straggly rubber trees incised with the V-shaped cuts that allowed the sap to run into the collection cups.

Julian agreed, his lips tightening as they passed a *kampong* of derelict huts where once the workers may have lived.

The familiar shape of a long, low plantation house came into view as they rounded a bend. In an earlier time, it would have been a pleasant house with its outlook over the river. Now the paint on the wooden boards cracked and peeled and the neglected *atap* roof probably leaked and housed who knew what vermin. Untamed purple bougainvillea circled the verandah posts, casting it into a deep shadow. Like the garden that surrounded it, the house looked lonely and uncared-for.

John Lawson waited for them on the steps to the bungalow, his hands on his hips. Julian ordered the driver to wait for them and helped Harriet dismount from the buggy. They stood on the overgrown driveway and looked up at Lawson. Harriet raised her hand to shield her eyes but Lawson did not move or stand aside to offer them hospitality out of the bright midday sun.

"Headmaster. What are you doing here? Is everything all right with Will?" Lawson's tone held no welcome.

Julian mopped his forehead. "Will's fine. Do you mind if we come in, Mr. Lawson? It is a trifle warm out here."

Lawson twitched and, as if recalling his manners, stood aside and spoke to a white-robed house servant who appeared at the door.

"Of course, come in."

Rather than show them into the house, he gestured to the odd assortment of chairs on the verandah. Julian glanced at Harriet. She quirked an eyebrow but kept her face impassive as she sat down in one of the heavy planters' chairs. These reclining wooden chairs were meant for taking one's ease in and, trying to keep an upright posture, she perched awkwardly on the seat.

"I'll come straight to the point," Julian said. "Why did I have to hear it from your son that you intend to withdraw him from the school this week and send him back to England?"

Lawson ran a hand through his hair. Harriet tilted her head and considered him. The change in him in just over a week was dramatic. His bloodshot eyes were lost in dark smudges and heavy bags, and the very muscles of his face had sunk into bristly jowls. His clothes were crumpled and stained and up close he had the stale odor of a man who had not washed for several days.

"I was going to telegram the school today," he mumbled, and gestured at the house. "No telephone."

"Is there a problem with the school, Mr. Lawson?" Julian pushed.

Lawson shook his head. "No, no. I just . . . it's something I have to do. He'll be safer in England."

Harriet frowned. "Safer? Are you concerned about the security at the school?"

"No. It's not that." Lawson rose to his feet and paced the length of the verandah. "Things have been getting on top of me. I've already lost a wife and three children to this damned climate. I cannot . . . I dare not risk the life of my only remaining child."

"I understand," Julian said, "but stop and consider how disruptive it will be for the boy to arrive at a new school in England in the middle of the last term. At least let him finish his school year here."

Lawson shook his head, fumbling in his trouser pockets for a tortoiseshell cigarette case. His hand shook as he took several attempts to light a cigarette. He leaned on the verandah, his right foot tapping impatiently as he took a deep draught, watching the smoke dissipate.

He glanced back at Julian. "If it's the fees you're worried about, Headmaster, then don't. I don't give a toss for them and I don't expect them to be refunded. Will is going to England this week, and that's the end of it."

A desperate need to defend the rights of a small boy who had no say in the matter overcame Harriet's good manners. She rose to her feet to face the man.

"Mr. Lawson. Please spare a thought for Will. He has taken his mother's death hard and now he feels like you're sending him away as some sort of punishment."

Lawson threw the half-smoked cigarette into the tangle of bougainvillea and turned his red-rimmed eyes on her, his mouth working as if he struggled to control his own emotions.

"With respect, Mrs. Gordon, what decisions I make about my son are none of your business." He waved a hand at the world beyond the verandah. "He's a damn sight better off in England than he is in this godforsaken hole. If I'd stayed in England, Annie would still be alive and so would the children who are buried with her. I want Will somewhere safe. Every minute he stays on this island, I am in fear for his life." His lip curled in a sneer. "And who are you to lecture me on how I should bring up my son? You have no children."

A hurt and furious response formulated in Harriet's heart but before she could say a word, Julian laid his hand on her arm and shook his head. Little would be gained by retaliation. This had to be about Will, not Harriet and not Thomas Gordon.

"I assure you, Mr. Lawson, we take very good care of Will," she said.

Lawson turned his head so he wasn't looking at them as he said, "I'm not questioning the care he is getting at St. Thomas, Mrs. Gordon. Believe me, he will be safer and happier in England."

Harriet tried one last time. "Mr. Lawson, I will be frank. Will thinks he has done something to make you angry. Won't you at least come back with us and take the time to explain it to him?"

This time the anguish on Lawson's face as he turned to look at her was raw. "I can't . . . I can't go into Singapore." He broke eye contact and looked away.

Julian glanced at the *gharry* driver squatting in the shade of a rain tree. "Nothing more to be done here, Harriet. We better get moving if we want to make the one thirty train."

Lawson leaned both hands on the rail of the verandah, his shoulders sagging. "There is something you can do for me," he said. "I've packed a trunk for Will to take on the boat. Can you take it with you?"

"Of course," Julian said.

Lawson seemed to brighten and summoned the servant. Like his master's clothes, the servant's once-white robe looked stained and crumpled.

Harriet glanced at the front door, which the servant had left open as he went to fetch the trunk. "If you don't mind, Mr. Lawson. I wish to avail myself of . . ."

Lawson reddened. "Of course, Mrs. Gordon. At the back of the house. You can go around the verandah."

But Harriet had no intention of going around the verandah. Before he could stop her, she had marched through the front door, stopping at the sight that met her. Books and papers littered every surface along with empty whisky bottles and ashtrays filled to overflowing. The room smelled of stale cigarettes, alcohol, damp, dust and decay. Despite the cloying heat, she shivered. Little wonder he wanted to be rid of the boy. This was not a suitable home for a child.

As she passed a side table, a small pile of papers balanced precariously fluttered to the ground in her wake. Automatically she stooped to pick them up, intending to restore them to their place. Glancing down at the topmost paper, she took a breath. The paper had had only four words, written in a bright-blue ink and a firm hand. Unless she was very much mistaken, Sir Oswald Newbold had written, *Consignment 6: 5 March.*

"I apologize for the mess." Lawson stood in the doorway behind her. "I wasn't expecting company."

Harriet turned to face him, setting the papers down without glancing at them again. She brushed her hands and looked around her with what she hoped seemed like disapproval.

"Clearly," she said in an icy tone.

Drawn by several photographs in tarnished silver frames, she crossed to a pine dresser that stood against the wall, its homey Englishness so out of place in this setting. All the photographs were heavily mildewed but she could make out a family picture of a man, a woman and four small children with a female servant standing to one side. She picked the frame up, peering closely at the faces. She recognized a younger and happier John Lawson and assumed the woman to be his wife, Annie.

"When was this taken?" she asked.

Lawson swallowed. "Four years ago, in Mogok."

Harriet looked up. "Mogok?"

"You've heard of it?"

"Yes. Burma, isn't it? Your family . . ."

Lawson took the photograph from her. "The baby . . ." His voice cracked. "The baby Annie is holding died a few weeks after that photograph was taken. Annie was distraught. She wanted to go back to England then and there but I persuaded her to stay. I'd been offered this job in Singapore. It was a compromise but it killed Annie and the other two children as surely as if I had stayed in Burma."

"Did you know Sir Oswald Newbold?"

"I worked for him." Lawson glanced at his watch and said, "You better hurry if you're going to make the train."

Harriet availed herself of the bathroom, an experience she did not wish to repeat. In a generally disorganized and uncared-for home, the bathroom facilities were always the first to suffer.

The driver had brought the *gharry* around to the front door and a medium-size metal-bound trunk had been placed in the footwell.

Julian clapped his hat on his head and held out his hand. "Thank you for your time, Mr. Lawson. I shall inform the board of governors of your decision but I would appreciate confirmation in writing."

"Will is booked on the *Europa* on Thursday. I've arranged for him to be properly escorted and he will be met by Annie's sister in Portsmouth." Lawson's lips tightened. "I have every intention of getting down to see the little chap off myself, but if I don't . . ."

Julian frowned. "Please make that effort, Lawson, but you have my assurance that everyone at St. Thomas will try to make it as easy as possible for Will."

Lawson clasped Julian's hand. "Thank you for giving up your valuable time to come all this way. The boy will be right as rain as soon as he gets to England and I will sleep sounder for knowing he's there."

Lawson helped Harriet into the carriage. She maneuvered herself around the trunk and unfurled her parasol. "Mr. Lawson, I want to assure you that my brother and myself are very fond of Will and there is nothing we wouldn't do for his happiness."

The man nodded. "Thank you. A letter of recommendation to the school in England is all I need from you but . . ." He paused, the muscles in his throat working. ". . . tell the little chap that I miss him and I'll join him in England as soon as I can. I just need a bit of time to wind up things here. Oh, here's the key for the trunk, Mrs. Gordon. Might be better if you keep it at your house until it comes time to leave and then it can go straight into the hold. There's nothing in there he'll need."

Harriet took the small, flat key and secured it in her reticule as Julian climbed into the carriage beside her.

"Wait!" Lawson turned and ran back into the house, returning out of breath. He held up a small leather-bound, traveling photo frame. "Can you give this to Will? It's his mother. He might like to have it with him."

"Of course," Harriet said. "Good-bye, Mr. Lawson."

As the *gharry* turned away, Harriet glanced back. Lawson stood in the driveway, his hands thrust into his pocket, his shoulders sagging, a picture of abject misery.

They made the train in good time and on the trip back to Tank Road, Harriet sat with her chin propped on her hand, staring out with unseeing eyes at the passing countryside.

"Harri, he's right, you know, it is none of our business," Julian said at last.

She turned to face her brother. "I know that. I just need to be sure that the decision has been made for the right reasons. Didn't you think there was something odd about Lawson?"

"Clearly he's been drinking," Julian replied, with a faint sniff of disapproval.

"He seemed to be afraid of something."

Julian scoffed. "He's been through hell. To lose three children and his wife? Snakes, tropical diseases . . . of course England looks like a safe alternative for his son. I must agree with him, it is his son's best interests he has at heart. Plenty of other boys of Will's age, and younger, get sent home. It's a sensible thing to do." He paused. "Particularly the state he's in."

"That all sounds perfectly acceptable, Ju, but why pay up two terms of school fees only last week, if he was intending on sending the boy away? The decision has been made in haste."

Julian leaned forward and laid a hand over hers. "Harriet, don't get emotionally involved."

"Easy for you to say," Harriet said, and sniffed, fighting back a sudden urge to cry.

Her brother squeezed her fingers. "I understand. Will reminds you of Thomas and God knows, you have better cause than I to know how quickly this climate can kill."

The sob that had been scratching at the back of Harriet's

throat escaped. She shook off Julian's sympathy and scrabbled in her reticule for a handkerchief. "Tom would be the same age as Will now."

"I know."

She blew her nose and wiped her eyes, stowing the handkerchief in her sleeve. "You're right, Ju, I'm letting my emotions cloud my judgment. If John Lawson thinks the best thing for Will is to go back to England, then that is his decision and all we can do is make the transition as painless as possible."

Back in Singapore, they hailed a *gharry* at the station, which, like its dilapidated counterpart in Woodlands, barely fit the two of them and the trunk. Lokman and Aziz were summoned to carry the trunk into the house and over their complaining, Harriet ordered it to be taken to her bedchamber and stowed under the bed.

Alone in her room she removed the hatpins and tossed her hat onto the bed. Sitting down at her dressing table she stared at her reflection in the mirror and wondered what, if anything, she could do to prevent what seemed to her an inescapable descent into tragedy. The state of the plantation house and John Lawson's obvious distress concerned her, and why send his child away?

The heat did that, it got inside people's minds like an insidious worm, twisting and turning until there was no escape but oblivion. She had seen it in Bombay often enough among the expatriate community. The misery ended with a revolver to the temple or a rope over a beam.

She placed the photograph Lawson had given her on her dressing table and unhooked the frame, opening it to reveal a daguerreotype of a young woman still in the flush of her youth, her unbound hair proclaiming her single status. Annie Lawson had probably never been a beauty but she had a bright, lively face and a wide smile. Harriet touched the glass with her finger.

"Oh, Annie," she said. "We have more in common than you will ever know."

She closed the photo frame and decided it should be put away safely with the rest of Will's things. She took out the trunk's key, weighing it in her hand as she wondered about whether she was breaching a confidence. Then again, it would be the responsible thing to look through the contents of the trunk and ensure that Lawson's packing was appropriate for a child heading back to England.

Kneeling on the floor, she pulled the box out from under the bed. The key turned stiffly in the lock but that was no surprise. Everything rusted so quickly in the humidity. She tutted with disapproval at the state of the interior. The contents of the box appeared to have been flung in with no particular order or symmetry. A man's idea of packing or a man in a hurry? she wondered.

Her opinion of Lawson worsened as she shook out each article of clothing. Most would have been far too small for Will and few were appropriate for a new life in the colder English climate. She decided she would take the boy shopping on Wednesday to ensure he had at least a few decent clothes for his arrival in England. April could still be cold and nothing in the trunk would provide the boy with any warmth for the hideous voyage around the Bay of Biscay.

Among the clothes were a box of tin soldiers and a selection of children's books—E. Nesbit and a well-read copy of Shakespeare inscribed with Annie's name—and, poignantly, a disreputable cloth rabbit. It looked homemade and had been much patched and was missing an eye. She wondered if this beloved object had been made by Annie Lawson for her son.

At the bottom of the trunk she found a wooden box about eighteen inches square. Harriet grunted as she lifted it out of the trunk and onto her bed. Whatever it contained was heavy and accounted for the weight of the trunk. She shook it but nothing rattled.

Curiosity overcame her. The lid had been nailed shut and she went in search of Julian's toolbox. Julian liked to tinker with woodwork in his spare time and had set up a workshop in one of the outside sheds.

Using a screwdriver, she carefully pried the lid off without damaging the nails and stood back, puzzled by the contents. Nestled in the sawdust shavings the benign face of Buddha smiled serenely at her. She brushed the dust from his face.

"I know you," she said aloud.

Without pulling the statue from its resting place she recognized the same long earlobes and tightly curled hair as the Buddha Sir Oswald had kept in pride of place on his desk. Only this one was on a smaller scale.

She shouldn't be surprised. The Lawsons had lived in Burma and from what she could see of the house, under the dirt and detritus, they had accumulated one or two nice pieces. It was probably an antique purchased by Will's mother.

Guiltily Harriet nailed the lid back on and replaced the box in the chest, followed by the rabbit, the toys and the books and added the photograph Lawson had given her to the top of the pile. She locked it returned it to its place under the bed.

She carried the pile of discarded clothing out into the parlor for discussion with Will tomorrow. Needing a distraction, she dispatched Aziz to the school to fetch her typewriter while she began sorting through Newbold's papers, trying to distinguish a starting point for the task Curran had set her. The sight of the firm penciled strokes of Newbold's shorthand, interspersed with notes written in a now-familiar blue ink, gave her pause.

Consignment 6: 5 March.

5 March had been the day before Newbold had died. Lawson had worked for Newbold in Burma but there was nothing to link the two now . . . except that note.

Aziz, carrying the folding typewriter, her father's parting gift to her, returned from the school. She set the typewriter down on the table and went to work, plunging herself into Newbold's dreary recitation of life in Rangoon.

Harriet pushed the overcooked vegetables around her plate with her fork. Lokman had excelled himself with the awfulness of his cooking that night and all because Julian had expressed a desire for roast chicken.

"Harriet, you can't change the world," Julian said at last.

She looked up. "I'm not trying to. I just don't think it's fair that Will has to be punished for his father's inadequacies."

"It's John Lawson's decision and he honestly believes he is doing the right thing by the boy. Plenty of English lads are sent back to England at a younger age than Will and they survive."

"Survive!" Harriet said. "Julian, you remember how you hated school . . . the bullying, the cold baths, the awful food . . . at least you could come home for the holidays. Will won't even have that. He will be bundled off to an aunt and uncle he doesn't even know."

"Harriet, it's none of your business . . . Damn it . . . Who is that at the door?"

Julian stood up, flinging his napkin onto the table. "Huo Jin, whoever that is . . ."

"I'm sorry, Headmaster." Pearson stood in the doorway, flushed and panting as if he had run from the school. Pearson, being of a corpulent build, never ran anywhere.

Harriet rose to her feet and went to her brother's side.

"What is it, Pearson?" Julian's clipped tone reflected the obvious urgency in Pearson's demeanor.

"One of the boys is missing."

"Who?" Julian and Harriet chorused.

"Lawson. He didn't come for dinner and at first I thought he may be sulking somewhere. He's very upset by the news that he is being sent to England, but I didn't think for a minute that he'd run away."

Harriet let out an involuntary cry. "Have you searched?" she demanded.

Pearson turned a baleful gaze on her. "We've turned the school and the outbuildings inside out, Mrs. Gordon."

Julian glanced at his watch. "It's eight thirty. When was he last seen?"

"Prep."

"So, he's been missing for three hours and nobody thought to tell me?" Julian's normally imperturbable countenance flushed dark with anger.

"I'm s-s-sorry, Headmaster," Pearson stammered. "I honestly expected him to return."

"Harriet, ring the police," Julian ordered. "I'm going back to the school."

Harriet telephoned the Central Police Station and asked to speak with Inspector Curran. To her immense relief she was connected to him.

"You just caught me," he said. "I was catching up on paperwork."

Harriet explained what had happened and Curran assured her he would come at once. She set the telephone down and a wave of unjustified relief washed through her. Curran was on his way. Surely now all would be well.

On the chance that Will might be hiding somewhere around the house, she lit a lantern and with Aziz for company searched St. Tom's House and the outbuildings but they found no sign of the boy.

There being nothing more she could do at the house, she hurried up to the school. Lights blazed from every window and lanterns bobbed in the jungle behind the school.

She found Julian in the office, talking with the two junior masters.

"Is there anything I can do?" she asked.

Her brother glanced at her, the lines of his face tight with concern.

"Can you help Mrs. Pearson and see if you can settle the boys down? They're in a terrible state."

Harriet found the boarders gathered in the dining room with Mrs. Pearson. They all wore pajamas and several were crying. Mrs. Pearson had two of the younger boys on her knees, comforting their obvious distress.

"Now, then, what's this?" Harriet said. "It's past bedtime and tomorrow is a school day. Mrs. Pearson, do you think you could rustle us up some cocoa and then we'll get everyone into bed."

Mrs. Pearson set the two little boys down. One of them immediately ran to Harriet, wrapping his arms around her legs.

"The bogeyman will come and get us," he sobbed.

Harriet disengaged the child and crouched down to his level. "Don't be silly. There are no bogeymen. Go and sit next to Pritchard. Pritchard, make room."

"Have they found Lawson yet?" Simpson, one of the older boys, asked. He sat a little apart from the others, his hands moving restlessly along the well-worn tabletop.

"Not yet, but he won't have gone far," Harriet said. "Here comes Mrs. Pearson with cocoa. Everyone, sit down at the table."

The boys brightened. Despite a climate that did not lend itself to the consumption of hot beverages, cocoa remained a perennial favorite and was allowed only as a very occasional treat at the school.

"Can I speak with the boys?"

At the sound of a now-familiar voice, with its cadences of a well-bred upbringing, Harriet turned to see Curran standing in the doorway. Relief washed through her. Curran was here and all would be right.

"Boys, this is Inspector. Curran. He's a policeman." She paused and added, conscious of a new realization, "And a friend."

"I'd like to ask you boys a couple of questions," Curran said.

"How about we put the chairs in a circle. It makes it easier for me to talk to you all."

As the boys obediently pulled up their chairs around him, Curran perched himself on the edge of the table.

He leaned forward, his hands clasped. "Which one of you is Will Lawson's best friend?"

All eyes turned to Simpson.

"I am, sir," Simpson confirmed.

Curran smiled. He had a good way with the children, Harriet thought. The boys had instantly relaxed with his air of calm authority.

"Good lad, Simpson. Tell me, when did you last see Lawson?"

"After prep, sir," Simpson said. "We went outside to practice hitting a cricket ball around. Lawson was in a very bad mood."

"Why?"

"He didn't want to go to school in England," Simpson replied.

Curran shot a quick glance at Harriet.

"His father has him booked to sail on the *Europa* on Thursday," she said.

Curran's face betrayed nothing but she saw the flicker of interest in his eyes.

He turned his attention back to Simpson. "So, the two of you were outside hitting a ball . . . What happened next?"

"The man came . . ." Simpson began.

Curran straightened.

"The bogeyman," one of the other boys said, and the littlest boy began to cry again.

"Don't be ridiculous," Harriet said. "There is no such thing as a bogeyman."

"Well, there is," David Allen, one of the older boys, always ready with a quick answer, interposed. "They are the Bugis pirates who roam these seas and steal small children and grind their bones for flour."

"That is enough, Allen!" Harriet said as a boy screamed and

flung himself at Mrs. Pearson. "Boys, he is just trying to frighten you. The Bugis pirates are long gone. Inspector Curran?"

He stared at her for a moment before guessing what she required of him. "Indeed, the Bugis are peaceful fishermen who cause me no trouble whatsoever." He rose to his feet. "Mrs. Gordon, I think you and I should talk to Simpson in private."

Harriet nodded and turned to Mrs. Pearson.

"Mrs. Pearson, can you see the boys go back to bed?" Harriet said. She put her hand on Simpson's shoulder. "I think we'll be more comfortable in the headmaster's office."

"Am I in trouble?" Simpson looked up at her with wide, worried eyes.

Harriet shook her head. "Not at all."

They found Julian pacing his office, his hair sticking up on end as if he had been running his fingers through it. He whirled on his heel, his gaze traveling from Harriet to Curran and down to the boy between them.

"Come in and sit down in that chair, Simpson," Harriet said, pointing to the large overstuffed leather chair. "It's Reverend Edwards's favorite chair."

Simpson complied, even though the chair seemed to swallow him up and his feet didn't touch the floor.

Curran leaned his hip against Julian's desk.

"Now, Simpson, you were telling us that you were playing outside and a man approached Lawson."

Simpson nodded. "He had a note for Lawson."

"What did this man look like?"

Simpson looked blank. "Just a native, sir."

"English, Chinese, Malay, Indian?"

Simpson narrowed his eyes. "Not one of us and not a Malay or an Indian," he concluded.

"Chinese?"

Simpson shrugged. "Anyway, he handed Lawson the note and went away."

"Did you see the note?"

Simpson shook his head. "Lawson said it was from his father and his father was waiting for him and he had to go and see him now but he wasn't to tell anyone."

The three adults in the room stiffened.

"And?" Curran prompted.

"The bell rang for washup. I said he should tell Mr. Pearson but Lawson told me to go inside and not tell anyone. He would see me later."

"And is that the last time you saw him?"

Simpson nodded. "When I looked back he was walking across the cricket pitch to the jungle behind the school." Simpson pointed in the general direction. "When I got upstairs I looked out of the window to see if I could see him but he'd gone."

Curran glanced at Julian. "What time would this be?"

"Supper is at six. The bell for washup is rung at ten to six," Julian said.

Curran glanced at the clock on the table behind the headmaster's desk. "So, he's been gone over three hours?"

"Did I do wrong, sir?" Simpson asked.

Curran shook his head. "You did what your friend asked you. Now, go to bed and maybe we'll have another chat in the morning. You might have remembered something else about the man who gave Lawson the note."

Simpson struggled out of the chair. At the door he turned around and looked back at the grown-ups. "I'm scared, sir."

Curran's lips compressed. "There'll be policemen here to keep guard, Simpson. You will be quite safe."

Simpson's shoulders visibly relaxed. "Will he have a revolver, sir?"

Curran nodded. "Yes."

Simpson slipped out of the room and Curran sat down in the nearest chair with his hands behind his head.

"I'm missing something here. Who is this John Lawson?"

"John Lawson manages a rubber plantation on the north of the island, near Kranji." Julian said. "In fact Harriet and I went out to see him today. This decision to send his son away is very sudden and quite frankly, Curran, he struck us both as a man under a great deal of pressure."

"Is it possible that Lawson could have taken his son?" Curran asked.

Julian and Harriet exchanged glances. "No," they chorused.

Julian continued, "Why would he do that, when he was quite clear today that he had no intention of coming into town and he wanted the boy on the next ship to England?"

Harriet sank back against her own desk. "I thought Lawson was frightened of something and we were left with the impression that he felt his son wasn't safe at the school. He wanted the boy off the island. We promised . . ."

Curran straightened, every inch the policeman. "Does this Lawson have a telephone?"

Harriet shook her head. "No. That was why we went to see him in person."

Curran glanced at his watch. "I'm going to telephone the Kranji police post and send them out to the plantation. Meanwhile I've mobilized a search party for the boy and they'll do what they can tonight, but other than that I don't think there's much else we can do before daylight."

Harriet ran her hand across her eyes, hoping the men could not see the tears that had gathered and threatened to betray her. She took a deep breath and looked from Julian to Curran. "I have a terrible feeling, Curran."

Curran met her gaze, his expression revealing nothing. "Mrs. Gordon, Reverend Edwards, I suggest you go home and get some sleep. I'll return first thing in the morning."

Harriet glanced at her brother. "He's right, Julian. Let's go home."

Julian shook his head and indicated the sofa. "I'll sleep here,

Harriet. You go home. No point in both of us staying here. Curran, do you mind walking Harriet back to the house?"

Harriet opened her mouth to protest but common sense prevailed. Even though it was just a few hundred yards, with a possible kidnapper lurking in the shadows, she really did not want to walk by herself or, if she was honest, be at home alone.

"I'll put a police guard on the house tonight," Curran said, as if he had read her thoughts.

Julian nodded. "Much appreciated, Curran. Try and sleep, Harri. I am sure it will all look less bleak in the daylight."

Curran replaced his hat and held the door open for them.

As they crossed the sports field, lights bobbed in the jungle behind the school and voices called the child's name. Harriet wrapped her arms around herself, as if a chill breeze blew across the field.

"My brother is an eternal optimist. It won't be better in the morning. He's gone, isn't he?"

Curran drew in a deep, audible breath. "I fear so."

Those maddening, betraying tears threatened again as she thought of Will alone and terrified. If he was still alive . . .

"Poor boy. He must be so scared. Why would anyone take him?"

Curran cleared his throat. "Tell me more about John Lawson."

"I don't really know him as anything more than a parent I've met on a couple of occasions. In fact, I only saw him last Tuesday— he came to pay the outstanding school fees." She paused. "That's an odd thing. He not only paid the outstanding fees but also the fees for next term. That's why I don't understand this sudden haste to remove William."

"Interesting," Curran said. "Had he come to town on that errand?"

"No. He said there had been a meeting of the board that own the rubber plantation he manages. I wouldn't be surprised if the board were less than happy. Even I could see that his plantation is in an appalling state but then I don't suppose he knew much about rubber planting. He was a mine engineer."

Curran stopped. "A mine engineer? Where?"

Harriet turned to face him. Although his features were shadowed in the dark, the fingers of his right hand tensed around the strap of his Sam Browne.

Her own voice sounded small and tight in the echoing cavern of the night. "He worked for Newbold on the Mogok mine."

Curran huffed out a breath as if he had been holding it in anticipation.

"He worked for Newbold," he echoed. "What brought him to Singapore?"

"They lost a child and his wife insisted they move so they compromised and came to Singapore a few years ago. Is this significant?"

Curran started walking again, his pace lengthening so that Harriet had to scurry to catch up with him.

"Two, possibly three, people with a connection to the Burmese Ruby Syndicate are dead and the child of another has been kidnapped. I think that is significant, don't you, Mrs. Gordon?"

"As soon as he told me he had worked for Newbold I had a feeling there had to be a connection."

Curran turned to her and in the dark she sensed, rather than saw, the quirk of his eyebrow. "Do you get these feelings often?"

She allowed herself a smile. "Call it woman's intuition, Inspector. Now everything else makes sense. Lawson told us that he was frightened of something happening to Will. He covered it with his own tragic history—losing three children and his wife to disease—but do you think someone may have threatened the child directly? Do you think Lawson had something that Newbold's murderer wants?" She stopped, her hand seeking out the comfort of the brooch at her throat. "Do you think they will harm Will?"

Curran opened the gate in the hedge, which squeaked on its

protesting hinges, and let Harriet pass through. "Unlike you I do not have the luxury of jumping to conclusions," he said. "But what is clear is that we are looking at something far deeper and more complex than we first thought."

He walked her up to the house, where Huo Jin waited.

"I'll send a constable around to watch the house tonight," he said.

"Thank you. I'll sleep better for knowing we have a guard." Harriet managed a humorless laugh. "At least I have no connection with the Burmese Ruby Syndicate."

Curran cast her a glance, unreadable in the dark, tipped his fingers to his hat and turned back toward the school.

Harriet stood on the verandah and watched him until the black, unforgiving night swallowed him and she heard the squeak of the gate. Cold fingers of fear ran down her spine. Only ten days ago she had no connection with Burma or rubies, but it seemed like a vortex had sprung up that threatened to drag her down into its depths. The deaths and the disappearance of Will had shaken her. Particularly the latter. That touched her heart.

"You are being ridiculous," she said out loud.

"Is everything all right, mem?" Huo Jin asked.

"No, it's not," Harriet replied. "Tea . . . no . . . make it a whisky, please, Huo Jin."

✸ TWENTY-ONE

Tuesday, 15 March 1910

O n Curran's return to St. Thomas's in the morning, accompanied by Tan and Greaves, he found an air of unnatural calm hung over the school. Harriet Gordon met him at the door. Her hair had been coiled into an uneven bun on top of her head and the dark circles that ringed her eyes spoke of a restless night. All her confidence seemed to have been drained from her.

She ushered him into the headmaster's study. Constable Greaves followed.

A neatly folded blanket and pillow on the sofa indicated that Julian had followed through with his promise and spent the night at the school.

"Where is the headmaster?" Curran asked.

"Teaching," Harriet replied. "He said it was important to appear normal."

"Can you fetch him?"

Harriet nodded and slipped out of the room. The brisk tapping of her heels on the floorboards was followed by a rapping on a distant door and then silence. She returned with her brother. If Harriet looked haggard, Julian Edwards looked like a man twice his age.

"Any news?" Edwards asked.

"My search party confirmed that they found fresh wheel tracks and evidence of a horse on a track a hundred yards from the school. A closed carriage was sighted on River Valley Road about the time Will went missing." He took a breath. "We can assume that whoever took the boy had him well away from here before the alarm was raised."

Julian sunk into the chair behind his desk, his mouth set in a grim line. He leaned his elbow on the arm of the chair and ran a hand across his chin as he looked up at Curran. "There's more, isn't there? I haven't heard from Lawson. I would have thought he would have been here as soon as your chaps passed on the news."

Curran steeled himself. "It would appear Lawson is missing as well." Julian shook his head and Curran continued, "The local constables went out to the plantation the moment they heard from me. They would have got there close to midnight and reported to Headquarters the moment they returned to the post. The plantation was deserted. I have men at the docks and the station all on the lookout for the child. What I need is a description of his father."

Julian tugged at his moustache. "Not quite six feet, sandy thinning hair, blue eyes. When we saw him yesterday it didn't look like he'd shaved for a few days."

Greaves jotted down the description in his notebook.

"Thank you, I will add that to the bulletin about the boy," Curran said.

Julian's lips twitched. "You don't suppose that the boy could be with his father, after all?"

"I don't suppose anything, Headmaster. I am going out to Kranji now. If anything should happen here, please advise one of the constables on duty. He will know how to get in touch with me."

"Thank you, Curran." Julian's face relaxed into a wry smile. "In my profession, all I can do is pray that the boy is with his father and all is well."

"Amen to that," Curran said.

He clapped his hat on his head and turned for the door. As he opened it, he glanced back. Harriet stood with her back to the window, her arms wrapped around her body.

"Mrs. Gordon, can you be spared?"

Harriet glanced at her brother. "Julian?"

"Of course, but what on earth for?" The headmaster frowned.

"It might be useful if Mrs. Gordon comes out to Kranji with me."

"Why?" Harriet asked.

"Because you are an observant woman and you can tell me what, if anything, has changed since your visit yesterday."

Harriet nodded. "Meet me at the house. I must fetch my hat."

Curran paused to give instructions to the two constables he was leaving on duty at the school and by the time the motor vehicle turned into the driveway of St. Thomas House, Harriet waited by the front steps, a practical pith helmet secured to her head with a scarf and an umbrella clutched in her hand. Tan opened the door and she slid into the backseat next to Curran.

The morning rain had turned Bukit Timah Road and the country tracks into a muddy trap for motor vehicles and Tan and Greaves had to stop and dig the motor vehicle out of the mud on two occasions. Neither of Curran's constables were in a good mood when they arrived at the Lawson plantation.

A local police constable waited for them on the verandah. He came down the steps to meet them, sparing Harriet no more than a cursory glance as Tan held the door of the motor vehicle open for her.

"The place is deserted, sir," the local man said in Malay.

"What about the house servant?" Harriet asked.

Curran repeated the question in Malay and the constable shook his head.

Curran turned to Harriet. "Shall we look inside?"

As they stepped through the front door into the gloom of the living room, she recoiled, turning to look at him, the color draining from her face. "It was a shambles but it was nothing like this."

Curran surveyed the room. Furniture had been overturned, lamps and ornaments lay smashed on the floor and papers had been pulled from the desk. Every drawer and cupboard had been opened and rifled. His nose twitched at the dusty smell of mold, neglect and unwashed human.

"Sir." Tan crouched by the doorway to the main bedroom. "I think we have blood."

Curran crouched down and looked at the dark stains and spatter. He nodded. "Definitely blood."

Harriet leaned over him. She carried with her a soft scent of sandalwood. He hadn't noticed it before.

"Is he . . . dead?" He detected a tremble in her voice.

Curran straightened. "No, I don't think there's enough blood. Greaves, get your photographic equipment out and photograph the bloodstains. Tan, take the local boys, and I want you to search every outbuilding."

"And you?" Harriet asked.

"I'm going to see what I can find among Lawson's papers."

"Can I help?" she asked. "I saw a note yesterday that I would swear was Oswald Newbold's handwriting."

Curran frowned. "What did it say?"

"Consignment 6: 5 March."

He nodded and the two of them gathered the scattered papers up from around the living room, setting them out on the dusty dining table. It was all that he would have expected: personal letters from family in England, letters of condolence on the death of Lawson's wife and business correspondence relating to the plantation. The latter confirmed Harriet's earlier observation. The letters from the managing company expressed great dissatisfaction with the returns and the running of the plantation.

"Nothing," Curran said aloud. "Not a damned thing. No sign

of that note you saw. He must have destroyed anything incriminating."

"Or taken it with him," Harriet responded.

"Sir. I think you should come." Constable Tan appeared in the doorway, puffing and sheened with sweat as if he had run some distance.

"Lawson?"

Tan shook his head. "No. Something odd."

Curran turned to Harriet. "Wait here."

She glared back at him and he knew his directive would be disregarded. Ignoring her, he followed the young constable down to the water. This was not the Sungei Kranji itself but a narrower creek. A path led through the undergrowth along the bank, culminating in a small wooden hut, half-hidden by creepers. Here the foliage had been cleared from the bank of the river and a rope tied around the bow of a nearby tree to provide mooring for a boat, no doubt.

Harriet crashed through the undergrowth behind them, swatting at the mosquitoes that rose in her path.

Tan pushed open the door to the hut and the men stepped inside, taking a moment to allow their eyes to adjust to the gloom.

At first the hut appeared to be empty except for a rickety table against one wall. Several paint pots and brushes lay on the table along with an almost-empty paper sack of grayish powder and a metal container in which something had been mixed. Curran touched the dried scum around the edge.

"Plaster of paris, I think," he observed, crumbling it in his fingers.

"What's this, sir?"

Tan crouched down and from a pile beneath the table retrieved a lump of what looked to be stone.

"It appears to be a piece of a statue," Tan said.

He handed it to Curran, who carried it over to the doorway. His breath caught as he recognized the long, elegant carved fingers.

"Any more?" Curran asked.

"Quite a few pieces, sir." Tan carried out more bits of broken statue, laying them on the ground in front of the hut.

"It looks like a Buddha statue." Curran turned a piece over in his hand, the tight curls of Buddha unmistakable. "But this isn't stone. It's some sort of concrete. See, the interior is a different color to the exterior. It's been deliberately aged."

"A forgery?" Harriet came to stand beside him.

"A very good one."

"I've seen it before." Harriet crouched down beside him and turned over a shard. A fragment of a benign face smiled up at them.

"Where?" Curran asked.

"Two places. Sir Oswald Newbold's study and in a trunk belonging to Will Lawson. His father sent it back to Singapore with us yesterday. We were to ensure it went on the boat with Will."

Curran could have kicked himself. The very same statue, only twice the size, currently occupied shelf space in his own office.

"Well spotted," he said. "But may I ask how you know what was in the trunk?"

Harriet had the grace to look a little shamefaced as she said, "I had to open it to put something in and when I saw what his father had packed, I thought I should sort it out and repack it properly. I found the statue in a wooden box at the bottom of the trunk."

"You didn't think to mention this before?" Curran inquired.

"I didn't think it was important. Not until I saw this." Harriet had begun methodically piecing the shattered statue into a cohesive whole. "There is something strange about this, Curran. Look. The center appears to be hollow."

Curran joined her, running his finger around the hollowed space in the pedestal of the statue. "It wouldn't hold much," he observed. "The statue in the trunk, was it the same?"

Harriet shook her head. "It was well packed in sawdust so I

didn't take it out of the box, but I would say yes, from what I could see, it was identical."

Curran stood up. "You . . ." He indicated the local constable, and addressing him in Malay, said, "I want every piece collected and packed back in boxes and sent down to Singapore, along with the other contents of that hut."

The man saluted and nodded. "Yes, *tuan*. When . . . ?"

"As soon as possible."

Curran turned to Tan. "I want you to stay here and make inquiries of the neighbors and locals."

"Any particular line of inquiry?"

Curran surveyed the river that snaked through mangroves. As he watched, a sleek furry head broke the water, looked around and disappeared again. An otter. Despite the circumstances, a surge of wonder flashed through him. Seeing one in the wild like this was a privilege.

"Inspector?" Greaves's voice shook him out of his reverie.

"This creek runs into the Kranji River and out into the Straits of Johor. With the mangroves and mudflats, a boat can enter easily without being seen," Curran said.

"Are you thinking that this is some sort of smuggling operation, sir?" Greaves asked.

Curran drew in a deep breath. The heavy air smelled of decay. He gave an involuntary shiver. "There is something very wrong here, Greaves, and to answer your question, yes."

"What would they be bringing in?" Harriet asked.

That, Curran couldn't answer. The police had been working hard to cut out the opium importation into Singapore but it didn't feel like an opium operation. Was it something to do with the rubies Maddocks had talked about? If illegal goods came in here, it would be easy for Lawson to carry them down to Singapore in rubber consignments. No one would check until the shipment reached the dock and by then the boxes of statues, if that's what they were, would be gone. Like the shattered statue itself, the pieces of the picture were spread out before him. He just had to put them back together in the correct order.

He glanced at Greaves and Harriet Gordon, who stood back from the group, her eyes heavy with fatigue. "I've detained you here long enough. We'll get going, Mrs. Gordon. Greaves, get us back to town in one piece."

As they settled back into the car, Curran glanced at Harriet. "I think the first thing we need to do is have a look at that statue you found in Lawson's trunk."

She nodded and after a little while he noticed that despite the jolting car she had fallen asleep, her hat slipping awry. He moved closer to her, allowing her head to rest against his shoulder. She wouldn't thank him for the unwanted physical contact but he wasn't going to wake her.

Harriet sat up with a start as the motor vehicle jerked to a halt in the driveway of St. Thomas House. Greaves lacked Tan's touch with the vehicle.

Julian was already hurrying down the stairs to greet them, his face pale and drawn.

"Any news?" he asked, holding the door open for Harriet.

Harriet shook her head. "Not really. I'm desperate for something to eat and drink. Inspector?"

Curran nodded, conscious that they had not stopped for anything to eat and it was long past lunchtime.

As Harriet went in search of her *amah*, Curran filled Julian in with their discoveries at Kranji.

"That's extraordinary," Julian said, sinking into one of the verandah chairs. "Are you looking at a smuggling operation?"

"I'm not making any assumptions yet, but I would like to see the trunk John Lawson sent down with you."

Carrying a tray with a large teapot and a plate of sandwiches and cake, Harriet came out through the house.

"It's in my bedroom, but please, let's eat first before I start gnawing my arm off."

Chafing with impatience, Curran swallowed some sandwiches and a cup of tea and rose to his feet. "The trunk?"

Stepping into Harriet's bedroom, Curran genuinely felt like an intruder. Like its occupant, the room was decorated with practical purpose. No unnecessary frills or lace but plenty of books and solid, comfortable furniture decorated with colorful throws and cushions, probably reflecting her years spent in India.

Harriet indicated the trunk and Curran dragged it out from under the bed, grunting at its weight as he carried it into the small room that appeared to be used as Julian's study. Julian joined them and Harriet closed the door behind them and handed Curran the key to the trunk.

It contained books, a set of soldiers and a wooden box about eighteen inches square. Curran extracted this and set it on the table. It had been roughly made and nailed shut.

"No clothing?" He looked at Harriet, who must have done a little more than just glance at the contents. A fetching shade of pink tinged her cheeks.

"None of it was suitable for the child. I was going to take him shopping . . ." Her mouth twisted in sudden distress. "We have to find him, Curran."

Will Lawson had been missing nearly twenty-four hours and Curran didn't seem any closer to restoring the boy to safety. He tried not to think about it as he levered the lid off the wooden box with his penknife. He drew a sharp breath as he recognized the smiling face of the now-familiar Buddha nestled in its bed of sawdust and shavings.

Curran lifted it out and set it on the desk. Through a patina of age Buddha smiled beneficently at the paltry humans.

Julian let out a low whistle. "That looks old."

"It's a forgery," Curran said. "A very good forgery."

"We found bits of a broken statue on Lawson's property at Kranji. It's made of some sort of concrete," Harriet said. "I would swear it was identical to the one in Newbold's study, only half-size.

Do you think Newbold's statue might have been used as the pattern?"

"It seems likely," Curran agreed. "The Kranji statue was hollow. Let's see."

He picked the statue up and shook it. Nothing rattled. He turned it over. Nothing distinguished the base from the rest of the statue and it was only when he tapped it with the hilt of the knife that he detected a difference in the resonance between the base and the side.

Harriet let out a breath. He glanced up at her, catching her bright, rapt gaze.

With the point of his knife he dug into the "stone" of the base. It gave easily, a grayish powder spilling out as he scratched it away. Damping his finger, Curran dabbed it in the dust and held it up to his nose.

"Plaster of paris, painted to match the rest of the statue. Very well done."

Gently he pried the plaster out and all three craned over to see what lay tucked into the Buddha's pedestal. It appeared to be kapok, the seedpod fluff from the silk cotton tree, commonly used for filling or packing. Curran pulled this out, sneezing as some of the down went up his nose. With it came a small velvet bag.

Curran weighed it in his hand, feeling something hard and solid, about the size of a quail's egg. He undid the drawstring and laid a large uncut stone on Julian's blotter. Julian picked up the stone and held it up to the light, catching the deep-blue heart of the stone in a shaft of sunlight. He let out a whistle worthy of one of his pupils.

"It's a sapphire."

"A sapphire?" Curran frowned. "I thought I was looking for rubies."

Harriet took the stone from her brother and cradled it in the palm of her hand. "It's huge. Do you know anything about precious gems, Curran?"

Curran shook his head. "No, but I do know enough to say that one must be worth a fortune."

Julian sat down and ran a hand over his forehead. "What does it all mean, Curran?"

Harriet shot her brother a look of sharp reproach. "Really, Julian, it's obvious. Our Mr. Lawson is involved in some sort of gem thieving. Am I right, Inspector Curran?"

Curran took the stone from her, turning it over in his hand. "You could be right, Mrs. Gordon."

"Of course I'm right." Harriet glanced from her brother to Curran. "But he's not working alone, is he? He worked for Newbold in the ruby mines of Mogok. They have to be connected."

Julian's eyes widened. "I fear Mr. Lawson has failed in an attempt to outwit his partners in this venture. Whoever killed Newbold wants this stone and they now know Lawson had it."

Privately Curran agreed with them, but he was a policeman first. "That's a good theory, Reverend."

He dropped the stone back into its pouch, repositioned the bag back inside the Buddha and replaced the statue in its box.

"What are we going to do now?" Harriet inquired.

Curran's eyebrow quirked. "We?"

"Julian and I are involved, Curran," Harriet said.

Curran caught the defiance in her gray eyes. They *were* involved and the thought troubled him. He had allowed them both to be dragged further into the investigation then he should have done. A fledgling friendship had crossed the lines of professionalism and he needed to step back.

He shook his head. "I'll take the statue and stone away with me and request you both carry on with your normal routines."

"What about Will?" Julian challenged.

"There's nothing more you can do, Edwards, except trust me and my men . . . and pray."

Julian Edwards's lips twitched into a smile. "That goes without saying, Curran."

Curran tucked the box under his arm, adding with more confidence than he felt, "I am returning to South Bridge Road. Thank you for your help today, Mrs. Gordon."

"You will tell us if you hear anything about Will?"

He gave a curt nod and bid them a brusque farewell.

As the motor vehicle pulled out of the driveway of St. Tom's House, Curran glanced back. Harriet and Julian stood on the top step of the verandah. Just ordinary people caught up in an extraordinary problem. Three people were dead and two were now missing, including an innocent child. He needed to bring this to a conclusion fast, before anybody else got hurt.

🦋 TWENTY-TWO

A fter Curran departed, taking the statue with its hidden sapphire, Julian returned to the school to check that the boys were settled and the place secured for the night. Harriet, her mind racing from the day's revelations, sank into one of the wicker chairs on the verandah. She sat bathed in the soft light of the kerosene lantern, listening to the now-familiar sounds of the fine, warm night.

From the back of the house she could hear a low murmur of voices drifting through the open doors from the kitchen where the constable Curran had left to stand guard, shared food with the staff in the breezeway outside the kitchens.

Shashti dozed on her lap as she mechanically stroked her little head. The presence of the kitten reminded her of Will, who was . . . where? The thought of the boy tore at her heart and she choked back the prickle of tears.

She couldn't think of him as dead. Surely, whoever they were had taken the boy to use as bait for his father, not to do the child harm.

Whoever had taken Will, and possibly his father, wanted the sapphire. That had to be it. Lawson had tried to cheat them and had been discovered and the price was the life of his child. And if the sapphire was now safely in police hands, what would become of father and son? By handing the stone over to Curran, had she signed the Lawsons' death warrants?

She thought of Visscher, his throat slashed for what little knowledge he must have had. No, there was no guarantee they, whoever they were, would not hurt Will Lawson.

She closed her eyes. After a largely sleepless night and a long day, weariness washed over her.

"Shashti," she said aloud, because talking to a cat was better than talking to herself. "Just a few more minutes, then bath and bed. Hopefully there will be better news in the morning."

Another sound broke the rhythmic peace of the night—horses' hooves and the rattle of carriage wheels turning into St. Thomas Walk from River Valley Road. She straightened in her chair, peering out into the darkness as a closed carriage drawn by two matching chestnut horses turned in through the gates and came to a stop at the foot of the verandah stairs.

A closed carriage? Her blood ran cold and she rose to her feet, ready to call out for the constable as the carriage door swung open and a man stumbled out onto the driveway, almost falling. He caught himself in time and straightened, swaying on his feet, looking up at the house.

The cry for help stuck in her throat as John Lawson raised a heavy revolver in his left hand.

"Not a word, Mrs. Gordon," Lawson said as he advanced up the stairs toward her, a humorless smile fixed to his bloody, bruised and unshaven face. His shirt was crumpled and stained and he held his right arm pressed to his chest, a crude bandage, stained dark, tied around the upper arm. As he approached, she caught the odor of stale sweat and something else that she could not readily identify. Fear?

The driver, a short, stocky man, jumped down from the box and remained in the shadows out of the light thrown by the kerosene lamp on the verandah but not before she caught the glint of a second revolver the driver held in his hand.

"Mr. Lawson." Harriet tried to sound untroubled by the hideous weapon now pointed in her direction. "You look like you need help. Do you want me to send for a doctor?"

In the dull light of the kerosene lamp, his eyes were sunk into dark pools, giving him the look of something unreal, a corpse come back to life.

He shook his head. "I've only come for the box."

Harriet's heart skipped a beat. "The box?"

"The boy's trunk. You have it?"

"Yes, but . . ."

"Where is it?"

"In my bedroom."

She took a step back but was stopped by the chair. Lawson loomed over her and pressed the muzzle of the revolver against her throat. She swallowed, feeling the heavy metal cold against her skin.

"Trust me, I'm desperate, and I will kill you if I have to. Not a sound," he said. "Bring the lamp."

She picked up the kerosene lamp in her right hand. Lawson gripped her left forearm, pushing her ahead of him into the house. Their feet echoed hollowly on the floorboards and the door to her bedroom opened with a creak. Every noise seemed to be amplified tenfold.

The second man followed, heading for the back door and the kitchen.

Huo Jin's cry of alarm was cut short and Harriet heard the sound of scuffling and slamming doors coming from the servants' quarters.

Harriet pointed at the trunk Curran had restored to its place underneath her bed. Lawson let out his breath in a long sigh and the hand holding the weapon to her throat dropped away.

He waved the revolver at the box. "Open it."

When Harriet hesitated, he brought the weapon up again. "Open it!"

She set the lamp down on the chest of drawers and with shaking fingers located the key in the top drawer of her dressing table. The back door slammed and the driver stood in the bedroom door. He addressed a few curt words to Lawson in a language Harriet did not recognize.

Lawson replied in the same language without looking at the man.

"What did he say? Are my servants all right?" Harriet demanded.

"They're fine. My friend has locked them up with that useless police constable. They won't be bothering us."

Lawson's breath came in audible gasps as she dragged the box out, fumbling with the key in the lock. She threw the lid open and stood back, her heart thudding in her chest. Lawson laid the weapon on the bed and knelt, rifling through the contents with his left hand. Harriet glanced at the discarded revolver but the coach driver now stood in the doorway watching, the muzzle of his own weapon pointed at Harriet. Now that she could see him, he frightened her all the more. His dark face betrayed no emotion and his eyes were fixed on her without blinking.

Lawson looked up at Harriet, his face glistening with perspiration and his eyes wide with horror. "Where . . . is . . . it?"

Harriet swallowed, her mouth dry. "Do you mean the box with the statue? The police have it."

A roar, like that of a wounded animal, issued from Lawson and he seized up his revolver, lunging at her and forcing her back against the wall.

"What have you done?" he screamed as he pressed the muzzle of the revolver to her throat.

"Harriet?" Julian's voice came from the hall. He must have returned home and entered by the front door.

The driver in the doorway swung around, raising his weapon in Julian's direction.

"Harriet, are you all right!" Julian sounded desperate.

"Julian. It's Lawson. He wants the statue," Harriet gasped.

"Where's the police constable?" Julian demanded.

"Locked up with the servants," Lawson replied. "Stand aside, Edwards. I don't want to hurt your sister."

"Please do as he says, Julian." Harriet's voice sounded high and tight, even to her own ears.

Lawson wrenched Harriet forward by the arm, forcing her in front of him, the revolver pressed into her skin, just behind her left ear. He pushed her toward the bedroom door and out into the hall.

The driver jerked his revolver, indicating for Julian to move. Faced with the weapon, Julian had no choice and backed into the unlit living room. Lawson followed, shoving Harriet ahead of him. As he reached the living room, he turned to face Julian, pushing the revolver harder into Harriet's neck. She yelped as the metal bit into her flesh. She had no doubt that in his present state of mind, Lawson was quite capable of killing her.

"Take me instead," Julian said.

Lawson shook his head. "No. Mrs. Gordon makes a much better hostage and she's my guarantee they don't hurt my son. I want the sapphire, Edwards. Tell Curran, I want the stone."

"How do we get it to you?"

"You'll get a message. Now, get down on your knees, Reverend, and don't move."

Harriet screamed as the shadowy figure of the driver moved behind the kneeling man, bringing the butt of his weapon down on the back of Julian's head with a sickening crack and Julian fell forward, hitting the floor with a dull thump.

Tears of panic and fear pricked the back of Harriet's eyes as Lawson dragged her down the front steps toward the waiting carriage. He pushed her into the darkened box and up against a corner, pulling the door shut behind him.

The carriage jerked as the second man swung into the driver's seat above them. He cracked the reins and the carriage jolted forward, carrying them out into the dark night.

✖ TWENTY-THREE

Harriet shrank back against the dry and cracked leather of the seat. The shutters on the English-style carriage had been closed, making the interior of the carriage dark and unbearably hot and stuffy. Perspiration had already begun to sting her eyes and she fumbled in the pocket of her skirt for her handkerchief.

"Don't do anything stupid," Lawson said from the gloom.

"Do you really think I have a weapon concealed in my skirt?" Harriet demanded as she dabbed her face. "What do you mean by . . ." She struggled for the word. There seemed no polite way to put it. ". . . kidnapping me? I've never done you any harm."

"Mrs. Gordon." Lawson's voice cracked. "This is a damnable mess. If you only had the sapphire none of this would have happened."

"The sapphire I presume you stole!" Harriet said.

"I only took what I considered was owed to me." Lawson sounded petulant.

"And now your thieving friends are holding Will as a surety for the sapphire?"

In the gloom, she heard him swallow hard. "Yes."

"So, who are these friends of yours?"

"They're not friends," Lawson said, his tone bitter. "Once

they have their cursed sapphire and I have Will back, I'll be on the next boat to England."

Harriet wondered if people with the ruthlessness to murder Visscher and Newbold would let him go so easily . . . or her. The sour tang of nausea rose in her throat and her fingers tightened on the handkerchief she held, twisting it hard.

She straightened in the seat and took a deep breath of the cloying air. "Mr. Lawson, where am I being taken?"

"I don't know," Lawson mumbled. "I'm as much a dupe in this as you. They sent me to get the statue back. That's all I know."

In the suffocating dark, she could make out no more than his shape on the seat across from her and now that his fear and anger had passed, he slumped back in the corner. The light from a streetlamp briefly illuminated his face, contorted in pain as he clutched his right arm and groaned.

"How badly are you hurt?" she asked.

"When they came for me I stupidly put up a fight and he . . . the man out there . . . he stuck me in the arm with his knife," he said. "They only let me live on condition I retrieved the sapphire and now . . ." His voice cracked. "They will kill William." He straightened, the anger back in his voice as he said, "What right did you have to open that trunk?"

"I . . . I just wanted to check that Will had suitable clothes for the journey. I was going to take him shopping . . ." Betraying tears pricked at her eyes and she looked away, swiping at them with the sodden handkerchief.

"Mrs. Gordon . . . I . . . please don't cry . . . I'm sorry to drag you into this mess. You and your brother are good people. I should never have involved you."

"No," Harriet agreed. "And you should never have got yourself embroiled in the first place. It is too late to consider the might-have-beens."

"I just wanted enough to set William and myself up in comfort back in England. That's all," he said.

"Was the sapphire Newbold's?"

"Yes. He told me he found it on that first expedition to northern Burma and he'd kept it safe and hidden all these years."

"Why?"

Lawson sighed. "It's difficult to sell a stone of that quality and he couldn't bring himself to break it up. Over the years I think it had become his talisman. I didn't think the others even knew about the sapphire."

Lawson slumped lower on the seat, stretching his legs out and forcing Harriet to move her feet. "My life has been a failure, or should I say a long succession of failures. I . . . I got into trouble in England over gambling debts so I took Annie out to Burma for a fresh start but it didn't take long before the old habits took hold. Newbold was good to me, settled the creditors and gave me a good talking-to. Little did I know there would be a price to pay for his kindness. I can't say I was even a very good mine engineer and certainly I'm a worse rubber planter."

"What is the VOC?" Harriet cut across him, weary of his maundering self-pity.

The man gave a visible start. "What do you know about the VOC?"

She shook her head. "Nothing, except it is the acronym for an old company of Dutch merchants. What was your role?"

The silence that followed her question prompted her to kick his leg. "Lawson?"

"Your brother is a clergyman. They say confession is good for the soul?"

"Julian would say God forgives even if you can't forgive yourself."

Lawson gave a snort of laughter. "That is an easy platitude." He sighed. "The price Newbold demanded of me? I stole the rubies, Mrs. Gordon. All I had to do was select the best stones, falsify the entries in the ledger and hand them over to Newbold."

"How many stones?"

Lawson shrugged. "Sixty, at least. It was done slowly over the five years I was tied to Newbold."

"And what did Newbold do with them?"

"I don't know. He couldn't sell them. It would have attracted attention so he bided his time. After the baby died, I got into an awful funk. Started going down to town, drinking and gambling again. Annie persuaded me it was time to move. She wanted to go back to England, but I couldn't. The creditors would have pounced the moment the ship docked, so I accepted the rubber plantation contract here in Singapore."

"Newbold let you go?"

"Yes, or so I thought, but then he turned up in Singapore. He said I still owed him for the debts he'd paid in Burma." He laughed bitterly. "Oh, I repaid that debt with interest. Newbold had found a way to get his rubies onto the market and needed someone like me to do the hard work."

"How was he going to sell them?"

"A little partnership with a couple of others of a similar disposition. That's your VOC, a little play on their names. They thought themselves so clever." Lawson gave a hollow laugh and Harriet caught her breath.

"O stood for Oswald Newbold?"

Lawson grunted assent.

Her heart hammering, Harriet said. "Who are V and C?"

Lawson shook his head. "I can't tell you that."

"Do you know?"

"No."

Harriet wondered if he was lying but judged it best to hold her peace.

There had been no more streetlights for a little while and the road beneath the wheels had become rougher, forcing Harriet to reach for the strap as the carriage jerked through a pothole.

"Where did the rubies come from?"

"Newbold brought them into Singapore."

"And your part in the plan? The statues you were forging on your property?"

He didn't answer for a long moment and then sighed deeply. "You know about those?"

"Yes, and so do the police."

"They're good, aren't they?" She detected a note of pride in his voice. "Whatever my other failings I always had an aptitude for art. Maybe I should have stuck to the forgery business. Newbold had them cast in Rangoon and shipped to me—only enough for every consignment. I did the work of making them look authentic."

"If there were only enough for each shipment, how did you end up with a spare one?"

"I just told him I needed a few spares. There were some breakages."

"So Newbold had the rubies and you put them in the statues?"

Lawson seemed quite happy to talk. "The VOC couldn't flood the market with rubies or suspicions would be raised so they have been filtering them out over the last two years. Newbold would give me rubies and I would hide them in the statues and then bring them into town with the rubber shipments. Newbold had a *godown* on Clarke Quay which he used for different business interests and the box with the statues would be stored there as just another shipment of antiquities."

Harriet tried to rally her tired mind to recall a recent conversation about antiquities. "Cornilissen?" she ventured.

Lawson shifted in his seat and his silence gave her the answer. C *for Cornilissen?*

If O was Newbold and C possibly Cornilissen, then who was V?

Visscher was dead, probably killed by this gang. Van Gelder? He had connections to both Cornilissen and Newbold. Had Newbold been killed by the members of his own syndicate? She screwed her eyes shut. The key to this was *V*. Like the insignia of the VOC, *V* controlled everything.

She turned to the window, trying to make out something . . . anything in the glimpses between the shutters. They were in the country and through the darkness she had a sense of palm trees rustling and the tang of sea. She had not been in Singapore long enough to be familiar with the geography outside of the township and she wondered if they were traveling east or west.

The pace of the carriage had slowed over the rougher road and her gaze fell on the handle of the coach door but even as she had the thought, she heard a click and glancing around she had the sense that Lawson had raised his revolver.

The coach lurched to the right onto an even rougher track.

Out of the dark, the stark horrifying image of Sir Oswald's bloodied corpse came into her mind and she stifled a gasp.

"Surely they won't kill your son?"

"Yes, they will." Lawson's voice twisted in pain. "They're ruthless. They've killed before. After the Visscher boy's death I realized I had to send Will away but I was too late. They came last night. They told me they had Will and that they would hold him until I agreed to give them the sapphire. I'm so sorry, Mrs. Gordon. Oh God, my life is a mess."

Harriet regarded the man. She found herself unable to muster any sympathy for John Lawson. She had her own worries.

The carriage came to a jerking halt and the door swung open. Harriet peered out into the dark, seeing the looming outline of a bungalow against the night sky. No lights burned in the windows.

The driver let down the steps and stood holding his weapon, the sleek modernity of the revolver at odds with his native dress and the knife tucked into his waistband.

He didn't speak, just jerked the revolver, indicating they were to alight from the carriage. Lawson climbed out first, holding out his hand to assist Harriet but she ignored it, jumping lightly to the ground. She looked around her, trying to take in as much detail as she could. They had stopped in the compound of a modern house. Probably one of the many seaside villas being built by the wealthy of Singapore, be they Chinese, English or Armenian, along the east and west coasts.

"What now?" Lawson asked the driver.

For reply, the man swung his revolver to aim at Lawson and snapped out a command in the same language he had used before.

When Lawson protested in the same language, the man drew the hammer back with a click. No more words were needed. Lawson handed over his revolver. The man tucked the second weapon into his waistband and Harriet knew that the VOC now had a third hostage. Despite the warmth of the night, she shivered.

At an abrupt gesture by their captor, she and Lawson walked up to the front door. It stood slightly ajar and Harriet pushed it open.

The man barked out what sounded like a command.

"Inside, Mrs. Gordon," Lawson said.

"What language is he speaking?"

"Burmese."

In the dark passageway, they stumbled past shut doors, coming to a halt against a firmly closed door of some solidity. The Burmese man pushed past her and opened the door, ushering the two captives into a large room.

He pushed Lawson down onto a dining chair, indicating with a grunt and wave of his revolver for Harriet to do likewise. She complied while he lit a kerosene lamp, its soft light spilling out across a pleasant room furnished with well-padded sofas and chairs and elegant Chinese furniture. The long front windows stood open, letting in a soft sea-tinged breeze. In normal circumstances it would have been a lovely room, one in which Harriet could happily have passed the time with a good book.

Lawson gave a sharp cry as his wounded right arm was wrenched behind the back of the chair. The Burmese ignored

Lawson's cries as he used a curtain cord to fasten the man's wrists to the chair back. Lawson looked up at her, his face gray and drawn even in the warm light thrown by the lamp.

"This man is hurt. Let me see to his arm," she said, attempting to rise only to be pushed back into her chair.

The chair chosen for her was a Carver, and unlike Lawson, her captor contented himself with tying her wrists to the arms of the chair. Harriet flexed her hands but the knots did not give.

An elegant French clock on a side table chimed midnight as their captor, grunting with exertion, turned the chairs with his captives so they stood side by side facing the door. He sat down cross-legged on the floor facing his captives, his weapon across his knee.

"We wait," he said in English.

Lawson raised his head and glanced at Harriet, despair written in the line of his shoulders but Harriet had little pity for him. He had drawn this trouble down on himself and ensnared the boy and her in a web of his own device.

She swallowed, desperate for a drink of any description.

"Excuse me, my good man," she addressed their captor. "Could we have something to drink?"

The man didn't move. She tried the question in Malay but he didn't even glance at her. Lawson addressed him in Burmese but the man remained implacable.

"It's no good, Mrs. Gordon," Lawson said. "We just have to wait."

"Wait for what?"

"The VOC," he mumbled, and his head fell forward.

❧ TWENTY-FOUR

St. Tom's House was in uproar. In the kitchen, Tan was interviewing the hysterical servants who had been found locked in the pantry and outside, Sergeant Singh was dressing down an embarrassed and contrite police constable. In the living room Dr. Mackenzie tended to the bump on Julian Edwards's head.

Curran stood in Harriet's bedroom looking down at her dressing table. The jumble of hair- and hatpins in the china bowl made him smile. He liked the disorder; it lent a humanity to the private Harriet Gordon that she hid so very well in public.

Three photographs in well-polished silver frames had been pushed to the back of the table. The first was of a broad-faced, ruggedly handsome man with sandy hair and wearing a kilt, taken in a setting that had to be the Scottish Highlands. Her husband, he supposed. The second was a family group, a middle-aged couple and their three grown children wearing tennis clothes and posed around a tea table in a well-ordered garden, a respectable Victorian home visible in the background. He recognized a much younger Harriet and Julian, who wore a university striped blazer, with a heavy lock of fair hair falling across his eyes. The third, older girl must be a sister, he thought. He picked up the last photograph. A chubby, smiling child on the lap of a thin-faced Indian woman wearing a sari.

"They called him Thomas," Julian said from the doorway. "Her son."

"She lost a child?" Curran stared at the photo of the happy child. He knew she had been widowed but not about the child. How did she live with that grief?

Julian nodded. "Thomas and her husband, James died of typhus in India about two years ago. Harriet couldn't stay in India and went back to England." He straightened. "Curran, I fail to see what an examination of Harri's personal effects has to do with finding her?"

Curran set the photograph back amidst the clutter.

"You're right, it has nothing to do with it," Curran admitted. He glanced down at the open trunk on the floor. "It was definitely Lawson?"

Julian removed his glasses and ran a hand across his eyes. "Yes. He was in a bad way. Looked like he'd been in a fight and his right arm had a rough bandage tied around it, over his shirtsleeve. The other man, a native. Not Chinese but not Malay. He's the one who clocked me." He rubbed the back of his head and flinched.

"We found blood at the house in Kranji. Looks like his friends paid him a visit out there," Curran said. He didn't add that since he had left Kranji, Lawson's house servant had been found hiding in the *ulu*. He had been outside in the kitchen when Lawson's visitors had arrived and when he had heard the sound of fighting, had fled.

"Shouldn't you be doing something other than standing in my sister's bedroom?"

If Julian sounded terse, no one could blame him, Curran thought.

"Edwards, I have every able-bodied constable on the lookout for a dark carriage. There is nothing I can do until I start to get the reports in from the outlying police posts."

"I'm sorry." Julian slumped against the door frame. "I just feel so . . . useless."

Curran walked over to him and put a hand on his shoulder.

It was pointless telling the man to go to bed, despite the fact he looked dead on his feet. He left him in the care of Mac and left St. Thomas House with a promise to send word as soon as he heard anything.

He returned to South Bridge Road but no reports of any substance had come in. Tempted as he was to sit and wait, he would be no good to anyone in the morning if he didn't try and get some rest, so he left Singh in charge and returned to his bungalow, so exhausted he could barely put one foot in front of the other.

Li An met him, as she always did, at the front door. He dropped his hat on a table and folded her in his arms, burying his face in her hair. She wrapped her arms tight around him as if she would shield him from the outside world.

"Are you hungry?" she asked at last.

He shook his head, but she led him into the living room, sitting him in his favorite chair while she busied herself in the kitchen. The simple *mee goreng* she produced revived him and while he ate she poured water into a tin bathtub in the bedroom. He let himself be led into the haven of their bedchamber and Li An undid the silver buttons of his uniform, slowly divesting him of his clothes until he stepped naked into the tub, shivering slightly at the tepid water.

She knelt beside him and plied a loofah, sloughing away the dirt and care of the day. Her slender fingers slid down his torso, lingering on the scar just above his right hip, a parting gift from her murderous brother. He erupted from the bath, seizing her in his arms. She responded, soft and compliant beneath his questing hands and seemingly oblivious to the water that streamed from his body and hair. He needed her. In her arms he could forget, even for a little while. And he needed to forget.

But he lay awake long into the night, in the stuffy darkness of the mosquito net, thinking about Harriet, Lawson and the boy, lost somewhere out there in the dark on this benighted island.

He thought of Newbold and Visscher, dead in their graves. If only he could make the pieces fit. Rubies . . . it was the rubies. Ruby mines . . . Burma . . . The connection between Lawson and Newbold loomed clear in the darkness. An illicit ruby trade . . . the same one Maddocks had mentioned. But where did the sapphire fit into the puzzle?

Holding that thought, Curran drifted into a fitful sleep.

❧ TWENTY-FIVE

The tick of the little clock marked every second, every minute and every hour of the interminable wait, driving Harriet to distraction as she tried to counteract the pins and needles in her fingers. As the clock chimed the second hour, Harriet glanced at her captor, who had not changed position once in the long wait. She had thought him in some sort of trance or asleep but he returned her gaze with unblinking eyes and a countenance that told her nothing.

Across the sigh of the wind, the rustle of dry palm fronds and the gentle swoosh of waves breaking on the shoreline that seemed to echo around the silent room, Harriet heard distantly at first, but growing stronger, the whine of a motor vehicle's engine, followed by the hiss of the gravel as it drew to a halt.

The Burmese man heard it too. He rose from the floor and opened the door, revealing the dark corridor beyond. With a quick backward glance at his prisoners, he slipped into the darkness, leaving the door slightly ajar.

Across from Harriet, Lawson seemed to have fallen asleep, or more worryingly, to have lapsed into unconsciousness. Harriet straightened in her chair and, stretching out a foot, she found she could just reach him. She nudged Lawson and he stirred, opening bleary eyes.

"Lawson," she whispered. "A motor vehicle has just arrived."

Voices, too distant to make out the words, drifted in on the night air.

Lawson, wide awake now, flexed his shoulders and winced.

"Your arm?"

He nodded with tight lips. She didn't like the look of his face, pasty beneath the grime and bruises.

There were footsteps in the corridor, floorboards creaking as they passed. One of the doors along the corridor opened on protesting hinges and Harriet squeezed her eyes tight shut, trying to make out the voices from the room next door. A man . . . no, two men, but no recognizable words drifted out.

"Can you understand what they're saying?"

Lawson shook his head. "My Burmese is not that good."

"They are all talking in Burmese?"

"I think so."

Then a voice, higher than the other two. "The fool!"

Harriet's breath caught in her throat. "A woman." She glanced at Lawson. "Who is she?"

Lawson shook his head. "I don't know, believe me, I don't."

In the list of possible suspects she had been compiling in the time Harriet had been tied to a chair, not one woman had made an appearance. Her world shifted slightly on its axis as she reeled through the women she had encountered since Newbold's death. Surely not that vapid Cornilissen woman?

The door opened and Harriet held her breath.

She didn't know who she had been expecting but the young man, dressed in a sweat-stained, open-necked shirt had not appeared on her list of suspects either.

The clerk from the Van Wijk, Paar, held a struggling Will Lawson firmly by the collar. Will's face, streaked with the track marks of tears through dust, lit up when he saw his father.

"Papa!" Will's tremulous voice broke the silence of the room.

"Let the boy go." The words came from Lawson, forced out

between tight lips. He strained against his bonds with a renewed vigor. "Have they hurt you, Will?"

Will glanced up at Stefan Paar and shook his head.

Harriet strained to see past Paar but the woman, if it had been a woman, did not appear. Instead she heard the front door slam shut and the distant sound of a motor vehicle starting up.

Paar looked at Harriet and frowned.

"You were sent to get the stone and you bring the woman. Why?"

Lawson glanced at Harriet. "She makes a better hostage than Will. You can let the boy go now."

Paar glared at Harriet. "Is it true, the police have the stone?"

"Yes," she replied.

Paar looked up at the ceiling and his Adam's apple moved as he swallowed. "They're not pleased."

Lawson glanced at Harriet. "For God's sake, man, she only did what was right. What I should have done in the first place. You've got the rubies, surely that's enough?"

Paar flung Will away from him into the arms of the Burmese man, who had followed him into the room, and advanced on Lawson, leaning over him, so close that Lawson had to lean his head back.

"It's a little late to develop a conscience, Lawson."

Lawson snorted. "No honor among thieves, Paar. You should know that."

Paar responded by spitting in Lawson's face. Restrained as he was, Lawson could do nothing to wipe the spittle away from his eyes.

Paar turned to Harriet. She shrank back against the chair, her stomach churning.

"What are we supposed to do with you?"

"I told you, she's a better bargaining tool, Paar."

"I agree. Let the child go," Harriet said.

Paar glanced across at Will, who hung limply in the Burmese man's grasp, and shook his head. "I have no authority."

"From whom?" Harriet demanded. "Who is behind this mess?"

Paar snorted. "You will find out soon enough," he said. "They had to return to Singapore to finish off some business but they'll be back in the morning."

Harriet strained against her own bonds, trying to ignore her spinning head. "At least give us something to drink," she murmured. "We've been here hours."

"Are you going to faint?" Paar inquired.

Harriet raised her head to look at him, hoping her face gave him the answer.

Paar gestured at the other man and their guard released the boy.

"Fetch something to drink," he said, and the man moved silently out of the room.

Paar looked from Harriet to Lawson and then to Will and gestured at the floor at his feet. "Sit down, boy."

Will complied, his anxious gaze fixed on his father.

"So, we have two hostages and no sapphire. How exactly are you proposing we retrieve the missing property, Lawson?"

Lawson replied. "I've said they are to expect a message. The boy for the sapphire."

Paar shrugged. "We will see what they say in the morning."

Paar stood aside as the Burmese man returned, carrying a tray on which balanced a pot of tea and teacups. It made such an absurd sight that if the circumstances had been different, Harriet would have laughed.

He set the tray down on the table and with a gesture from Paar, untied Harriet's restraints. Harriet let out a sigh of relief, moving her fingers to try and restore the circulation. Paar poured the tea and handed her the cup. She drank thankfully and greedily, holding out the cup for more.

When Paar had poured it, she stood up and leaned over Lawson, holding the cup to his lips.

"Drink," she said. "You're badly dehydrated."

As her hand brushed the man's unshaven cheek, heat radiated from him.

"Are you feverish?" she asked.

He closed his eyes. "Could be," he said. "Head aches like the devil."

Harriet straightened and looked at Paar. "Untie this man. He's hurt and ill."

Paar ran a hand through his dark hair. "My orders are to keep you restrained. You will have to wait until they return."

"Who are 'they'?" Harriet demanded. "Who are the VOC?"

Paar's eyes widened. "What do you know about the VOC?"

Harriet shook her head. "Only what Visscher told me."

Paar threw his head back. "Visscher! Visscher poked his nose in where it was none of his business. He should have just turned away."

"Is that why he had to die?" Harriet asked.

Paar's silence gave her the answer.

She sank back on the chair. "What now?"

Paar glanced at his companion. "Take the woman and the boy and lock them up." He addressed Harriet. "They won't be here until the morning so I suggest you get some rest."

The Burmese man hauled Will up by his arm and, pulling one of the revolvers from his waistband, he gestured at Harriet. She rose to her feet and with a quick backward glance at John Lawson, preceded her captor out into the darkened corridor.

The door slammed shut behind them.

The only relief from the darkness seemed to be a small square high up in the wall, through which she could glimpse a few twinkling stars. These rooms were not designed for comfort, they were merely shelters for the servants. At best they might contain a bed or a sleeping mat but not much else.

Beside her, Will gulped and she drew the boy into her, allowing them both to sink down to the floor.

She sat with her back against the wall, holding Will as the child finally gave in to the stress and misery of the last twenty-four hours. He had been so brave but he was still only a nine-year-old child, lost in a confusing world where the adults in his life had only ever let him down. His mother had died and now his father, wounded and beaten, had been the cause of the most terrifying time of his life. He needed to cry, he needed to be held, comforted and told it would be all right.

Exhausted and emotionally battered, Harriet thought of happier times when she had been part of a family. James Gordon, laughing as he lifted his baby son up. She could not have imagined that it would ever be any different.

James had left her and Thomas, that happy child who would throw his arms around her and tell her how much he loved her, taken from her too. She, more than anyone, understood the desolation of desertion.

Now she held another woman's child in her arms and she knew she owed it to that dead mother to do everything in her power to shield this child from fear and danger.

She bent and kissed Will's hair. "It's all right," she whispered. "It will be all right."

🍀 TWENTY-SIX 🍀

Wednesday, 16 March 1910

As day broke over South Bridge Road, Curran paced his office. All the available information indicated that the carriage had taken the Beach Road heading east. East to where? He surveyed the map on the wall in his office and shook his head. Jungle and fishing villages. They could be anywhere.

He slumped down on his chair and rested his elbows on the desk, running his fingers through his hair. He had rarely felt so useless in his life. Until he received a message from the kidnappers, all Curran could do was sit and wait.

To occupy his mind, he laid the physical evidence out on his desk and his focus moved to the two identical statues of the Buddha, one the genuine antique from Newbold's study, the other a smaller replica. He tapped his pen on the original, antique statue. It was undeniably beautiful, the long fingers of the Buddha curled in his lap, his closed eyes downcast.

He picked up the replica. It had been very neatly done and, viewed by an inexperienced eye, apart from size, the two were nearly identical. There would be several homes on the Continent now boasting a genuine forged antique Burmese statue.

Newbold—Newbold was the key to the whole conspiracy.

The man with the painted face, Li An had called him on the first day. She had been right.

Drawing a sheet of paper toward him, he wrote *NEWBOLD* and *LAWSON* and drew a line between them. He drew a circle around Lawson's name and added notes. *Motive: Connected to the ruby-smuggling operation? Stolen sapphire? Means: Dha already used to finish off Newbold but second knife used in initial attack on Newbold and to kill servant? Opportunity . . .*

Lawson's movements on the weekend Newbold died had not been hard to track. He had arrived in town with the rubber shipment on Saturday morning. It had been delivered to a *godown* on Boat Quay and Lawson had taken a room at a nearby hotel. In the afternoon he had met with the owners of the plantation. According to the chairman, the board was not pleased with Lawson and were considering sacking him. He had persuaded them to keep him on for a little longer.

Lawson had retired to a bar to drown his sorrows, not returning to the hotel until the early hours of Sunday morning. He had not reappeared until the early afternoon when he had left his hotel and returned to the same bar, where he spent the afternoon drinking alone, and heavily, until around five, returning once more to the hotel around eleven. The hours between six in the evening and eleven on that Sunday night, the hours when Newbold had died, were unaccounted for.

Curran wrote, *Opportunity: No alibi for night of murder.*

He sat back and considered the paper and underlined the word *Motive*.

Lawson was cheating the thieves. He had stolen the stolen sapphire. At least, Curran assumed, it was a stolen sapphire.

He picked up the scrap of paper he had found in Visscher's Bible with the remains of the initials VOC and studied it thoughtfully. Lawson had been back in Kranji on Monday so even if he had something to do with Newbold's death, he was innocent of Visscher's.

He dipped his pen in the ink and down the side of his paper he wrote the initials *VOC*.

Against *O* he wrote *OSWALD NEWBOLD?* And against *C* he wrote *CARRUTHERS?* Carruthers. Yes, there was a strong connection to Newbold and the man may have had a motive to kill him, based on his father's participation and death on Newbold's expedition.

That left *V* . . . the dominant letter. Who was this *V* that held them all together?

Leaving that for a moment he went back to his conversation with Maddocks and wrote *AMSTERDAM* in capital letters and circled it. Gem dealers or . . . ? He straightened in his chair. Cornilissen, the dealer in Asian antiquities and gems. Was it coincidental that Cornilissen was in Singapore?

Another C. He wrote the name beside Carruthers's.

Newbold, Cornilissen, Visscher all had one thing in common. A connection with the Van Wijk Hotel. The proprietor of the Van Wijk Hotel was . . . *VAN GELDER*.

He let out a deep breath and wrote the name next to the initial *V*.

Jumping up from his desk, he threw open the door to his office and yelled for Singh and his constable.

❦ TWENTY-SEVEN

Harriet sat up, stiff and sore from sleeping on the unyielding wooden floor. She swallowed, trying to restore some moisture to her parched mouth, and pushed her disordered hair out of her eyes as she surveyed her prison. A fitful daylight struggled in through the only window set high up in the wall of the tiny and airless room. As she had surmised in the dark, it contained no furniture except the one thin sleeping mat which she had given to Will.

Exhausted from the ordeal Will slept, curled up like a little dog on the mat. Harriet smiled and pushed a lock of matted hair away from the boy's pale, tearstained face. Let him sleep. She just hoped his dreams were pleasant.

The atmosphere in the room was close and stuffy and smelled of bad drains. A jug of water and a tin cup had been placed by the door and a covered bucket stood in one corner. She realized with mingled horror and relief that it was there for her convenience.

Her watch showed the time as seven thirty. By the time Will had settled, Harriet had been so weary that she had no problem falling asleep. Lying awake and worrying did not help the situation and she would need all her wits about her to get through the day ahead.

She stood up and stretched her cramped limbs. Stepping over the still-slumbering child, Harriet poured a cup of water. She forced herself to drink it slowly, savoring each mouthful before swallowing. Who knew how long she needed to make it last?

The sound of the water hitting the tin cup woke the boy and he sat up, looking around him with red-rimmed, bleary eyes.

"Where's Papa?" he asked.

"I'm sure he's not far away," she said, hoping that John Lawson had been similarly incarcerated and was no longer tied to a chair in the living room. She didn't like to think about the alternative, but she was under no illusions. They had fallen into the hands of ruthless individuals who would not quibble at the life of a man who had tried to cheat them at their own game.

"Papa's in trouble, isn't he?" Will said.

Harriet nodded. No point in making light of the situation. They were all in trouble.

Will's mouth tightened and Harriet, familiar with the bashfulness of small boys, understood his dilemma. She explained the delicacies of the bucket and the boy flushed beetroot red. Harriet promised not to look and busied herself pouring him a cup of the tepid, brackish water.

Lacking a comb or a washcloth, she did the best she could to tidy her hair and her clothes and their ablutions complete, there seemed nothing for it but to sit and wait . . . and wait.

TWENTY-EIGHT

B reakfast was still being served in the dining room of the Van Wijk as Curran marched into the reception area, followed by Sergeant Singh and Constable Greaves. An unfamiliar Chinese clerk on the desk scuttled into the back room in response to Curran's demand to see Van Gelder. Curran didn't wait. He followed on the boy's heels and arrived at the door of Van Gelder's office just as the hotel manager rose to his feet.

"Inspector Curran, it's very early . . ." Van Gelder began, a whine of annoyance in his voice.

"Sit down," Curran ordered. "Singh, stay with me. Greaves, clear the office and make sure no one comes in."

Van Gelder subsided into his chair and mopped his forehead with a spotted handkerchief as with a curt nod Curran turned to his sergeant. Singh set the large parcel he carried down on the desk and pulled off the wrapping to reveal Lawson's forged statue.

"Have you seen this before?" Curran inquired.

Van Gelder stared at the object for a long moment and shook his head. "No, should I have?"

Curran had hardly expected a full admission but the bewilderment in the man's eyes seemed genuine and a nagging doubt tugged at the back of his mind where previously he had been so certain.

He changed the subject, hoping to catch Van Gelder off guard.

"Where's Cornilissen?"

Van Gelder, his gaze still riveted to the statue, mopped his face once more and stuffed the handkerchief in his pocket. He straightened his shoulders and looked up, on surer ground now.

"He will be at the *godown* on Clarke Quay. He has a shipment of antiquities being loaded this morning."

Curran's mind raced. He wanted to question Van Gelder but if the rest of the rubies were in Cornilissen's shipment, it had to be stopped.

"Which ship?" Curran demanded.

"The *Tasman*. It sails tonight."

Curran turned on his heel. "Singh . . . take Mr. Van Gelder straight to South Bridge Road. No phone calls, no contact with anyone."

Van Gelder rose to his feet. "Inspector, I must protest . . . I have done nothing!"

"Protest all you wish, Mr. Van Gelder. I will speak with you later." He threw the office door open. "Greaves, with me." Halfway across the office he turned and looked back at Van Gelder. "Do you know which *godown*?"

Van Gelder's neat moustache twitched. "It is a private *godown*. Toward Ord Road with a green door."

As Singh took the man by the elbow, preparatory to leading him out, Van Gelder pulled back. "Please, not through the hotel. It will upset the guests." He gestured at a side door. "We can go out that way."

Singh glanced at Curran, who nodded, and as Singh and Van Gelder crossed to the door, it opened and Mrs. Van Gelder stood framed in the doorway. She looked from her husband to the policemen and back to her husband.

"Henrik? What is happening?"

Van Gelder held up a hand. "Nothing to concern you, my dear. These gentlemen have some questions for me and I am going with them to the Central Police Station."

Mrs. Van Gelder turned her blue eyes on Curran. "Are you arresting my husband?"

Curran shook his head. "No. He is merely helping us with our enquiries."

Van Gelder attempted to wrest his arm from Singh's grip. Singh glanced at Curran, who nodded. The large policeman released his hold. Van Gelder straightened his collar and drew himself up, his head barely reaching Singh's shoulder.

"Please, just one thing before we go. My dear, have you seen Paar this morning?" Van Gelder sounded querulous. "I need him to cover for me, while I am away."

Mrs. Van Gelder shook her head. "It is his day off. I have no idea where he is. He did not come down for breakfast this morning. I will return to the house and see if he is there." She turned and looked back at her husband. "And if he isn't? You know what he is like on his days off."

"Then, you will have to cover for me, my dear."

Mrs. Van Gelder stiffened. "But I am going out. I am meeting friends at John Little's tearoom."

"Then, you will have to send word that you are detained. Nothing is more important than our guests."

Mrs. Van Gelder's rosebud mouth turned down at the corners. A morning rendezvous with friends spoiled, Curran thought.

Singh bustled Van Gelder away, leaving Curran alone with Mrs. Van Gelder. He was not greatly versed in the ways of women but she didn't seem dressed for an excursion to Raffles Place. Apart from the practical but inelegant sola topee and the large, leather handbag she clutched, she wore a plain dark-blue skirt and a light-blue shirt, more like the sort of working dress that Harriet Gordon would wear.

"You surely don't suspect my husband of involvement in anything illegal, do you?"

"I am investigating serious crimes, Mrs. Van Gelder, and your husband can probably help me."

She shrugged. "That is doubtful. He notices nothing. Now, if you will excuse me, Inspector, I should see if I can find that lazy boy."

Catching her skirt in her hand, she turned to head back toward the manager's bungalow.

"Let me escort you," Curran said.

She paused and looked back at him. "There is no need. I am sure the idle lad is still in bed."

"I have one or two questions for him," Curran lied. He didn't know himself quite why he needed to see Stefan Paar but his policeman's instincts prickled, his sense of unease growing as he mounted the steps and Mrs. Van Gelder ushered him into the parlor.

"You wait here. I will fetch him," she said, turning for the stairs, but Curran moved ahead of her, taking the stairs two at a time.

He flung open the door without knocking. In one sweep of the room he saw Paar's bed had not been slept in. Clothing lay scattered around the room and the door to Paar's wardrobe and the drawers of his chest stood open, clothing spilling from them, as if the occupant had rushed into the room and changed hurriedly. On the other side of the room, Visscher's bed had been stripped of all bedding, the mattress rolled up.

"See." Viktoria Van Gelder shrugged. "He probably spent the night with a girl in Serangoon Road. He is a godless heathen."

Curran walked over to Paar's bed and stooped to pick up the crumpled, sweat-stained white jacket of his uniform.

"Was there anything else, Inspector?" Her foot tapped. Clearly she was in a hurry to be somewhere.

Curran hesitated. "With your permission, Mrs. Van Gelder, I would like to search this room again."

Mrs. Van Gelder scowled. It was not an attractive look on her round face. "Why?"

"I am still investigating the death of Visscher and I want to be sure my men didn't miss anything."

He thought he detected the faintest flicker of hesitation in her eyes. "Of course, but I will stay."

"It would be quite proper for you to do so," Curran gave her the benefit of his most charming smile.

Paar's wardrobe, like Visscher's, contained the usual clerks' white ducks. He searched pockets and shoes and, finding nothing, turned to the chest of drawers. Paar's sparse possessions were jumbled into the drawers without any order or concern. Curran searched each drawer from corner to corner, turned over the mattress, went through the nightstand and learned nothing about Paar. There were no personal letters, no photographs, nothing. Like Visscher, any item of personal use, such as a razor, was also missing. Paar had gone.

Curran stood in the middle of the room, looking at the young man's world.

Where would I hide something I didn't want anyone to find?

He turned back to the chest of drawers, removing all the drawers and checking the undersides. With the drawers out, he ran a hand across the internal spaces of the chest and gave a grunt of satisfaction as his questing fingers touched leather. Peering up, he could see that a space had been made between the two top drawers, allowing a leather folio to be secreted securely, invisible to the curious eye.

He pulled it out and smiled as he scanned the documents it contained. Trust a clerk to keep an accurate record of the illegal transactions. Here he had it all right there in neat columns: the date the "goods" (which lacked any further description) arrived, the quantity, the amount paid to *JL*—John Lawson, he assumed—and the outgoing manifest right down to what ship it had been transported on.

On a separate sheet of paper, folded and tucked into the back of the book, he found the details of the payments made to Paar for his role. What the records didn't tell him was who was paying the young man. The only indication were three letters: *VOC*.

Everything came back to VOC.

The last piece fell into place as he withdrew a sheet of paper, the corner of which had been torn away, leaving only the diagonal line of the V and its superimposed letter C. Without doubt it matched the torn scrap Visscher had secreted in his Bible. Had Visscher found the ledger and made the connections?

He turned to Mrs. Van Gelder, who stared at the folio in his hand, her expression unreadable.

"What is that?" she asked.

"Have you ever seen it before?"

She raised two wide blue eyes to meet his. "Never."

"It is evidence that your Mr. Paar and possibly Visscher were involved in something illegal, Mrs. Van Gelder. Tell me, have you ever heard either of them mention the word VOC?"

She laughed. "The VOC is the old Dutch East India Company, Inspector. It has been defunct for years. Now, if you have what you want, I must return to the hotel."

Curran replaced the drawers and turned to the woman. "If Mr. Paar returns here or to the hotel, you are to say nothing to him. Telephone the Detective Branch at the Central Police Station and leave a message for me that he has returned."

She nodded but said without enthusiasm, "This is all terribly inconvenient, Inspector."

Curran raised his eyebrows. "Murder is," he said, and bade her good morning.

Singh had taken Van Gelder away in the motor vehicle but there were plenty of *rickshas* waiting at the stand outside the hotel. Before he followed after Van Gelder, he took Greaves aside, silently cursing not bringing one of the local constables with him. A European policeman loitering outside the hotel was more likely to attract attention.

"Stay here and watch the hotel," Curran ordered. "Keep yourself out of sight. I'll send one of the undercover constables to relieve you shortly."

"What am I watching for?"

"I want to know if Stefan Paar returns and, if he does, bring him into custody. And"—he lowered his voice—"if Mrs. Van Gelder leaves the hotel, I want her followed."

"But I can't follow Mrs. Van Gelder and watch out for Paar," Greaves pointed out. Curran frowned and said without conscious thought, "Follow her."

As Curran strode across to the *ricksha* stand, a familiar red motor vehicle, driven by Colonel Foster, pulled up beside him. Foster pushed up his driving goggles and hailed Curran.

"I say, Curran, what brings you here at this hour of the morning?"

"Colonel, good morning," Curran said.

Foster glanced in the direction taken by the police motor vehicle. "What's going on here? Was that Van Gelder in your motor vehicle that I just passed?"

Curran had no interest in indulging the idle curiosity of passersby, however well acquainted he was with them.

"If you'll excuse me, Colonel, I don't have the time to stop and chat."

"Of course." Foster glanced up at the hotel. "Can I give you a lift somewhere?"

Curran hesitated. "If you can drop me back at South Bridge Road?"

"Of course, hop in, my boy."

As Foster turned back into Stamford Road, Curran came to regret his decision as the colonel wove in and out of the traffic, scattering pedestrians and scaring *ricksha wallahs*.

"Where's your driver?" Curran gasped.

"On other duties. Anyway, I like to drive this beauty. One of the first motor vehicles on the island." He patted the steering wheel affectionately.

With white knuckles Curran gripped the side of the vehicle and could not restrain a yelp as a hapless *ricksha* was sent skittering to the side of the road, almost tipping its passenger into the drain.

With a squeal of brakes Foster drew up in front of the Central Police Station and Curran dismounted to solid ground and with some relief thanked the colonel. Foster fired the vehicle back up and with a cheery wave and a cry of "My breakfast calls," executed a turn across the traffic and disappeared back in the direction of the Van Wijk.

Curran hefted a thankful sigh for his safe delivery and turned to enter the building and organize his forces.

❧ TWENTY-NINE

Normally Curran enjoyed the shifting tide of humanity to be found crowding the quayside down on the Singapore River. Chinese, Malay, Indian, Arab and African cultures met on the slimy steps leading down to the river, where the little bumboats crowded the water, waiting for the consignments of goods to be loaded so they could take them out to the cargo ships waiting in Keppel Harbour. The goods themselves, everything from rubber and gambier and spices through to fine china and antiques were housed in *godowns*—warehouses fronting the quay—owned by shipping companies or private individuals.

But today the stench from the river and the crowds caused even Curran's nose to twitch. He made his way to the customs office to wait for his men.

Singh, Tan and two other uniformed constables arrived within the half hour.

"Expecting trouble, sir?" Singh inquired after Curran had ordered his men to unbuckle the holsters of their Webleys and have the weapons ready.

"Yes. We are looking for a *godown* with a green door near the Ord Road bridge," Curran replied.

"And what will we find there?"

"We are looking for the forged statues Lawson brought to town on Saturday," Curran said.

The men glanced at one another and Singh nodded. Accompanied by a sweating customs officer clutching bills of lading, Curran and his men plunged into the crowd.

The authority of uniform caused the crowd to part like the Red Sea. Many of the men of all races who inhabited the port area preferred not to be seen, let alone spoken to, by the police and slunk away into the shadows and alleyways as the officials passed.

Nothing distinguished the *godown* they were seeking from its neighbors, except the faded and chipped paint on the door. It had long since ceased to have any natural affinity to the color green. Indeed, the color of the mold and damp that stained its walls was brighter.

Curran did not knock. With his hand on the butt of the Webley, he opened the door and stepped into the gloomy interior.

It took a moment or two for his eyes to adjust but the unmistakable tall, angular figure of Cornilissen standing in the middle of the floor immediately caught his attention. Cornilissen was neatly dressed in a frock coat and he held a leather folder. Around him were tea chests and other wooden boxes of varying sizes, some with their lids still ajar, fresh straw spilling out onto the floor.

As the door swung open, Cornilissen removed his glasses and set the folder down on the nearest box.

His eyes flicked to the party of officials now blocking the doorway. "Inspector Curran, is there a problem?"

"Your bill of lading?" Curran held out his hand.

"I must protest!" Cornilissen exclaimed. "This cargo must be loaded this morning. My ship sails this evening."

When Curran did not reply, Cornilissen glared at him and handed over the leather folder. Curran flicked through the papers. They contained an impressive list of objects d'art that would, no doubt, fetch a pretty penny on the European market.

He handed the papers to the customs official to compare against his list.

"Search," he said to his men, adding, "gently," as one of the larger constables bumped against a chest, causing Cornilissen to gasp and reach out a hand as if to steady the box.

The men began cracking open boxes to reveal elegant rosewood furniture, no doubt pilfered from China, as well as fine china and statuary that had probably been looted from temples in Indochina.

The customs man handed back the bill of lading, indicating a line that read: *Statues, stone, Shan period Burmese. Quantity four.*

Curran gave a grunt of satisfaction and pointed the item out to the agitated Dutchman.

"It would save us time and you further expense and the risk of damage if you were to indicate which box these statues are in."

Cornilissen glanced at the policemen with their crowbars surrounded by splintered wood and sawdust. He heaved a sigh and indicated two wooden chests.

Curran nodded and one of the men stepped forward, levering open the lid of the first chest. He stood back to allow Curran to search the box.

Curran pulled out the packing straw, revealing two wooden boxes, identical to the one he had found in Will Lawson's trunk. The lid had been secured with screws. A screwdriver lay on the table and he undid the screws and lifted off the lid. With the sense of anticipation he had as a child for a long-awaited Christmas present, he slowly unwrapped the well-shrouded figure, setting the smaller copy of Newbold's statue on its waisted podium on the table. Buddha's closed eyes inclined downward as if looking at the long-fingered hand that lay in his lap. The elongated lobes of his ears rested on his shoulders.

"That's what you were after?" The customs officer leafed through his own file. "Receipts look to be in order."

"I think you'll find they're forged," Curran said. He turned the statue upside down and, using the screwdriver, began to scrape at the plaster of paris that concealed the hidden cavity. Cornilissen let out a squawk and lurched forward but Singh's heavy hand on his shoulder prevented him from reaching Curran.

As the powdery flakes drifted to the table, every head in the room strained forward for a better look. Curran eased the well-wrapped package from its hiding place. He undid the string securing the package and let the stones fall to the table. The gentle thunk of the uncut rubies hitting wood echoed around the silent room. Someone gasped and every face turned from the stones to Cornilissen.

Cornilissen's face shone with perspiration in the close gloom of the *godown*.

"I must speak with my wife," Cornilissen demanded. "She knows nothing, Inspector. I need to reassure her . . ."

"About what precisely, Mr. Cornilissen? You've been caught in the act of smuggling stolen goods out of Singapore. You will certainly be going to prison. I'm not sure how she would find that reassuring."

A muscle in Cornilissen's cheek twitched.

"Tan, secure this man and take him to South Bridge. You men, I want those two boxes resealed and brought with him."

"Sir . . ." Singh had pulled back the lid from another wooden box and he gestured for Curran to inspect the contents.

Curran let out a snort of laughter. Two large Chinese vases of some antiquity nestled in the straw and sawdust. Another mystery solved. Cuscaden would be pleased.

"Chin Lee's stolen vases, unless I am gravely mistaken." Curran turned back to face Cornilissen. "My dear Mr. Cornilissen, you will not be leaving Singapore for quite some time."

Cornilissen sank down onto a stool and covered his face in his hands.

Curran waited patiently as the formalities were concluded and

Cornilissen and the men with him had left. Alone with Sergeant Singh and two remaining constables, Curran surveyed the gloomy, dank interior of the *godown*. As the heat of the day intensified, the atmosphere inside the building grew more unpleasant.

Curran looked up at the heavy beams of the old building. There would be another floor above this one and he had a feeling that this *godown* had more secrets to reveal.

"I want every inch of this building searched from top to bottom," he ordered.

"What are we looking for?" Singh inquired.

"The boy," Curran replied grimly.

He remained downstairs, intending to go through boxes while Singh led the search on the upper floor.

After only a few minutes, Singh summoned Curran to a small room on the top floor at the back of the building. Singh had lit a lantern and held it up. Curran recoiled, holding his sleeve to his nose at the rotting stench of the slaughterhouse.

The dark, oppressive, windowless space contained nothing except a table and a chair. Ropes had been piled on the table and around the chair. A dark, noisome substance stained the floor around the innocuous piece of furniture. A man's shoe had been kicked under the table.

Curran stooped and picked it up, knowing that he had seen its pair. It had been Visscher who had been tied to that chair and had bled to death, his throat cut to the bone.

He skirted the chair with its grisly patina of dried blood. As if he needed confirmation that it had been Visscher who had been held and died in this room he found a small leather suitcase, thrown into a corner of the room, its contents strewn around it as if it had been hastily searched. He turned to Singh, who stood in the doorway, his face, as usual, implacable.

"Pack this up and bring it to South Bridge and when Greaves gets back to Headquarters, send him down here. We need photographs and fingerprints."

At the door, he took one last look around the miserable room, raising the lantern high above his head. The swinging light illuminated something he had not noticed before. It had been kicked against the far wall and lay half-hidden among a pile of leaves and other debris, a flash of red among the dust and detritus. Curran stooped and picked up the St. Thomas school tie. His lip curled in anger.

The bastards had kept William Lawson in this ghastly room.

❦ Thirty

A lthough Harriet schooled herself not to look at her watch, the minutes and the hours dragged with leaden feet and by midmorning her patience with inaction had worn thin.

If they're going to kill us, why not do it now? she thought as she looked up at the window.

It was too small and too high off the ground for a grown woman but a small boy could, with a bit of help, probably squeeze through it. She glanced down at Will.

"If I lift you up, can you tell me what you see out of that window?"

The boy nodded and Harriet hoisted him up on her shoulders as she used to do with Thomas. Will was older and a little heavier than Thomas. The badly healed wound in her heart gaped open and she had to swallow back the old grief that sometimes threatened to engulf her as it had done in the long days and weeks after her stay in Holloway. She could not succumb to it now. It was a self-indulgence that, under the circumstances, she did not need.

"What do you see?" she asked.

The boy craned his head. "We're at the back of a big house. The kitchen is on our left."

"Are there any other houses nearby?"

"Can't see any. Just palm trees and jungle at the back."

"How far to the ground?"

The boy craned forward. "There's a big bush underneath."

"Does the window open?"

Will jiggled the latch.

"It's stuck," he said.

"Damn," Harriet swore. "It's probably rusted shut. I'm going to let you down and see if I can find a tool we can use to loosen the catch."

After casting around the cell and finding nothing useful, she pulled out a long, glass-headed hairpin and inspected it. While it might not be of much use as a tool for moving rusty windows, it could make quite a useful weapon. She tucked it into the top of her boot and pulled out one of her ordinary pins, causing her hair to tumble down her back.

"You have long hair," the boy observed. "So did Mama. I used to watch her brushing it. Papa said it looked like spun gold."

No one had ever described Harriet's ordinary brown hair as "spun gold." She pulled the boy in toward her and kissed the top of his head.

"Are you feeling brave?" she whispered.

He looked up at her, his eyes huge in his dirty face. "What do you want me to do?"

"If we can get that window open, I want you to squeeze through it and then run as hard as you can, as far away from this place as you can get."

A grave little face seemed to consider her for a long moment before he said, "What about you and Papa?"

"We're adults; we can take care of ourselves."

And we will both be much better off knowing that we are not worrying about you, she thought.

She hoisted Will back up onto her shoulders. Weakened by lack of sleep and food, Harriet had to keep letting the boy down to allow herself to gather her strength. He scraped and scratched but the window remained obstinately rusted shut.

"It's no good," Will admitted, sinking to the ground with his back to the wall. "It's stuck."

Harriet swore volubly and slammed her hand impotently against the door.

"I didn't think ladies knew words like that," Will said with a look of mingled shock and admiration.

She allowed herself to smile. "I know worse," she replied.

Sinking down beside him, she pushed the damp strands of hair away from her face. She made an attempt to coil her heavy locks into a knot at the base of her neck but her hands shook with the effort she had expended in hoisting Will up to the window and the resultant mess did little to alleviate her discomfort.

Lacking any thoughts about what to do next, she clasped her hands together and, closing her eyes for a moment, she prayed. *Dear Lord, please keep us safe.*

As she opened her eyes, the world tilted and spun. It had been hours since she had last eaten and Harriet never did anything without a decent breakfast. She tried not to think about fresh coffee and toast with marmalade.

"I'm awfully hungry," Will said, echoing her own thoughts.

"So am I," she admitted, and poured another cup of water to share with the boy.

He took a sip and looked up at her. "What do we do now?"

"Do you know any good games?"

"You could test me on my French vocab," Will said.

"Your French vocab?" Harriet asked in astonishment. She would have thought French vocab would be the last thing on the boy's mind.

"Please. If I am going to go to Papa's big school in England I don't want to be behind in anything."

Harriet laughed.

"Very well, Master Lawson. French it is. Let's begin with *aller*—'to go.'"

🈺 THIRTY-ONE

Curran sat down at his desk to drink the lukewarm cup of tea the elderly servant, allocated to the detectives, had brought him. Van Gelder and Cornilissen were in custody—in cells as far apart as they could be to discourage any collusion. As he contemplated his next move, he pulled his pipe from his desk drawer and carefully filled it with tobacco from the leather pouch Li An had given him.

He rarely smoked a pipe and only on occasions when he needed to think. He sat back in his chair, watching the puffs of smoke floating up toward the ceiling, his feet on his desk.

"You look bloody relaxed for a man with three missing people and three murders on your hands."

Curran brought his booted feet back to the floor with a thump and jumped to his feet, expecting Cuscaden but it was James Carruthers who stood at the door, his pith helmet in his hand, his face flushed with heat and anger.

"Mr. Carruthers, who let you in? This is none of your business—"

"Yes, it bloody well is," Carruthers responded in a tone that oozed with an authority he had not shown before.

Unbidden, he stepped into the office and shut the door with a thump that rattled the partition. "Sit down, Curran, and hear me out."

Curran remained standing while Carruthers fumbled in his pocket and produced a letter, which he handed across the desk. Curran unfolded the letter, noting the embossed letterhead bearing the imprimatur of the Home Office. He read the contents and, with mounting anger, carefully refolded the letter granting the bearer immunity from prosecution and free carriage in any investigations he wished to carry out.

He handed it back to Carruthers and, keeping his annoyance in check, said in a low, controlled voice, "If I had known this when I first came to see you, Carruthers, we could have worked together and three people would not now be hostages."

Carruthers restored the letter to his pocket with a casual shrug that had the effect of making Curran want to launch himself across the desk and shake the man. "I couldn't give my cover away," he said. "I've been working too long and hard on this case to risk involving a clod-footed policeman."

Curran's jaw clenched hard and he said between gritted teeth, "So, if you are not James Carruthers, who is Archibald Symes?"

"As the letter says, I'm an agent of the Burmese Ruby Syndicate, employed to investigate the appearance on the Dutch gem market of rubies of the same geological composition as those found in the Mogok mines owned by the syndicate."

"And the real James Carruthers?"

The man shrugged. "Died in Bognor in 1895, five years after his mother."

Curran took a steadying breath and controlled his anger by casually tapping the contents of his pipe into the ashtray. "And I take it your prime suspect was Oswald Newbold?"

"After Newbold moved to Singapore, the new chap at the mines picked up on stories going around the mine workers of the best stones mysteriously not making it into the inventories. Thousands of pounds' worth of rubies had disappeared over a number of years preceding Newbold's departure. Problem was, Newbold's reputation was unimpeachable and the BRS wanted to be sure that this wasn't just a fabrication. After all, there was no real evidence. Two years ago, rubies of the quality of the Mogok stones began appearing on the Amsterdam market. Rubies with no known provenance. I was sent to keep an eye on Newbold."

"And what did you discover in your time in Singapore?" Curran could barely keep the ice out of his voice.

Carruthers's mouth tightened. "To be honest with you, Inspector, very little. The operation was a tight one. I have been unable to discover how Newbold smuggled the stones into the country. I do know a man called Cornilissen seems to have been involved in the Amsterdam end of the operations but again I don't know how he got the rubies out." He paused. "I'm also fairly certain that Newbold's former mine engineer, John Lawson, was also involved, a fact that seems to now be confirmed by the disappearance of Lawson and his son."

Curran stood up and set the forged Buddha statue on the desk. "This is Lawson's involvement or part of it—there may be a longer, more heinous involvement but until I can find Lawson I can't confirm it. What I know is Lawson packed these forgeries on his property and brought them into Singapore with the rubber shipments. Cornilissen then exports the statues to Amsterdam. I believe he has a brother in the gem industry. There you have it, Carruthers."

Carruthers let out a low whistle. "We knew Lawson was in Newbold's pocket over some indiscretion Newbold had covered up for him. Lawson was a gambler and a drinker. Easy prey."

Curran's eye drifted to the larger, original, antique statue that had stood on Newbold's desk. He carried it over to his own desk and set it down on its back. At first glance the underside seemed to be solid, natural stone. Curran scratched the bottom with his penknife but, unlike the forgeries which betrayed themselves immediately, his knife encountered only solid stone. He ran his fingers across the base, with its pits and imperfections, his nail catching in what looked to be a natural indentation.

He grunted and inserted the blade of the penknife in the indentation and, with a grating of stone, a circular piece of the base worked free, revealing a large cavity in the pedestal of the statue. The breath stopped in his throat as he thought of the other statues still at the Bukit Timah house. How many of them had been similarly doctored?

He swung it around to face Carruthers.

"That is how Newbold brought the rubies into Singapore," Curran said.

The rubies and the sapphire. His mind flashed back to the scene of the crime. Newbold's bloodied fingerprints on the statue. Had he died trying to save his precious sapphire?

Carruthers shook his head. "Ingenious."

Curran sat down and surveyed Carruthers from over his steepled fingers. "The question I want answered is why you went to Newbold's home the night he was murdered?"

"I genuinely went on club business." Carruthers spread his hands. "I often went out on a Sunday night with invoices to sign off. I used it as an excuse to look over his place, if I got the opportunity. But this time I found him dead, exactly as I said."

"It was you who ransacked the room?"

The man shook his head. "Someone had already done that. I had some notion that if I took the manuscript it would look like a burglary gone wrong and it was consistent with my cover story." Carruthers spread his hands in an unconvincing apology.

Curran regarded him without humor. "All you did was muddy the waters, Carruthers . . . Symes . . . or whatever your name is . . ."

He drew the VOC symbol on a piece of paper and turned it to face the man.

Carruthers picked it up, frowning. "Isn't this the old Dutch East India Company?"

"A little joke by our conspirators. Assuming O stands for Oswald, the provider of the rubies, and C for Cornilissen, the contact in Amsterdam. V is the contact here in Singapore. Do you have any idea who V is?"

Carruthers shook his head. "Van Gelder?"

Curran took the paper back and squinted at the V. It dominated the insignia. V was the key who held the whole plot together. Instinctively he felt Van Gelder did not have the intelligence—no, the rat cunning—to coordinate the plan.

He pushed back his chair, the legs scraping on the polished floorboards. "I have Van Gelder in custody. Shall we go and ask him?"

"We?" Carruthers rose to his feet.

Curran shrugged. "Why not?"

✿ THIRTY-TWO

A s the heat in their prison rose with the sun, it sapped Harriet of energy and hope. Will curled up with his head on her lap and slept. Absently she stroked the boy's soft fair hair and closed her own eyes, allowing herself to doze, conscious that she needed to rest in order to have the strength to face what lay ahead.

The sound of a motor vehicle cut through her torpor and she sat bolt upright, her heart thudding. Every nerve in her body strained but she could hear nothing useful, beyond the rattle of insects, through the thick walls of her prison. Her watch told her it was now midday.

Will sat up, rubbing his eyes.

"What's the matter?"

"I thought I heard a motor vehicle." Harriet rose to her feet and banged on the door. "Is anyone out there?"

But no one came and she leaned her head against the door, fighting a sudden terrible fear that she and the child may have been abandoned and that their decomposing bodies would be discovered in months to come. Dead from starvation and thirst.

She considered the contents of the jug. Even if she eked out the water, it would be gone within twenty-four hours. Stupid, weak tears sprang into her eyes. She wanted to go home. She wanted to be safe in St. Thomas House with Julian and Shashti and Huo Jin, Lokman and Aziz.

She sank down against the wall and put her head in her hands as the tears began to flow. Pointless to try and be brave. She would need whatever courage she had for later. A small hand touched her shoulder.

"It will be all right, Mrs. Gordon. They won't kill us. They want the sapphire."

She sniffed and looked up at the boy. "What do you know about the sapphire?"

He shrugged. "I heard them talking."

Adults forget children have ears, Harriet thought. She patted Will's hand. "You're right, Will. They do want the sapphire. Did you see them at all?"

Will shook his head. "I was blindfolded until I got here and then that man took the blindfold off just before he opened the door and I saw you and Papa. I heard them talking. There was a man and a woman."

Harriet's heart jumped. A woman? The woman she had heard last night?

"What did they say?"

Will frowned and shook his head. "I don't know. They were not talking in English. Sorry, Mrs. Gordon."

The man would have been Paar but the woman . . . ?

Harriet summoned a smile and patted the boy's hand. "It doesn't matter, Will."

Whoever they were, if they were here now she would find out soon enough.

❧ THIRTY-THREE

C urran let his fingers play over the stones he had set out on the
table of the room they used for interviews with the better
class of villain. Even uncut and unpolished, the quality shone
through, casting a red glow on the blotter. The man sitting across
from him followed his movements with curious eyes.

"What are those?" Van Gelder asked.

Curran regarded Van Gelder. Something in the man's demeanor made him pause. If he was acting, he was very, very good.

"Uncut rubies of the highest caliber. Have you ever seen them
before?"

Van Gelder looked up at him. "No. Where did they come from?"

"A shipment of forged antique Burmese statues."

"Really?"

Van Gelder looked more interested than guilty.

"Your guest Cornilissen, had them in his possession."

The man's eyes widened and his mouth fell open. "No!"

Curran glanced at Carruthers, who shrugged.

"How many times has Cornilissen stayed with you?"

Van Gelder considered the question.

"Since I took over as manager, three years ago, he has come at
least once a year. On buying expeditions, you understand. He

was a generous guest." The man's eyes slid sideways and the sweat shone on his forehead. He was a terrible liar.

"How do you know Cornilissen?"

Van Gelder said nothing and Curran let the silence stretch between them. Behind him, Carruthers fidgeted, his chair squeaking as he shifted his weight.

Van Gelder wiped his forehead with a crumpled handkerchief and a shaking hand. "His wife is the daughter of my wife," he blurted out at last.

"Mrs. Cornilissen is your stepdaughter?" Curran struggled to keep the incredulity from his voice. Now he thought about it, he should have spotted a likeness at the Van Wijk on the night of the musical diversion, the two fair-haired women in blue gowns.

Van Gelder shrugged. "She was a grown woman, already married when I met her mother. I do not think of her as my daughter but, yes, she is family."

Curran's instincts prickled. At last—a connection. Keeping his face and tone neutral, he asked, "And how did you meet your wife?"

A deep flush colored Van Gelder's already scarlet cheeks. "It was Sir Oswald Newbold who introduced us, Inspector. I was managing a hotel in Rangoon. He would always stay with us when he came to town and he brought her to dinner one night. Viktoria Klop, she was then."

Viktoria?

The breath stopped in Curran's chest and he cursed himself for not making the connection earlier.

He thought of the ordinary little woman he had met during his enquiries, so easily overlooked. Viktoria Van Gelder. Viktoria Klop. *V* for Viktoria.

"And how did Sir Oswald know your wife?"

Van Gelder frowned. "He told me her husband managed a tea plantation in Burma but he had died a few months previously."

"And the widow Klop did not wish to return to Holland?"

"That is right. She said she had fallen in love with the Far East. I told her I had accepted a post in Singapore and she . . . we . . . decided it would suit us both to marry. It was a marriage of convenience, you understand."

Very convenient, Curran thought.

"One last thing." Curran reached in his pocket and set the uncut sapphire down among the pile of rubies.

Van Gelder's eyes widened. "*Mein Gott*, is that . . . ? Is that a sapphire?"

"Do you know anything about it?"

The man shook his head, his eyes riveted by the stone. "It must be a hundred carats, at least. A fortune."

Curran abruptly terminated the interview and packed away the stones. He wanted to reinterview Cornilissen but there was a greater urgency in detaining the Van Gelder woman.

Accompanied by Singh and Tan they took the motor vehicle to the Van Wijk.

Greaves had been replaced by a local constable dressed in plain clothes who lingered in the shade of one of the rain trees that lined Stamford Road. The man confirmed that he had not seen any European women leaving the hotel.

Curran gave orders to Tan to take Gertrude Cornilissen to South Bridge Road and he and Singh headed for the manager's residence. The door was answered by the Chinese maid.

"Mem is not here. She is gone."

Curran drew himself up to his full height and glared down at the girl.

"What do you mean 'She is gone'?"

The girl began to tremble. "She packed a suitcase, changed her clothes and she is gone."

She began to weep but Curran did not have time for tears. He pushed past her, into the house, throwing open doors until he came to a bedroom. At first glance it looked like it had been ransacked. Wardrobes stood open and drawers had been pulled out.

Mrs. Van Gelder's packing had been rapid. Toilette items were gone and, according to the maid, enough clothes to indicate a journey. A little writing desk contained nothing of interest. No doubt any evidence of her involvement with the VOC had also gone in the suitcase.

"What was she wearing?" Curran rounded on the maid.

The girl licked her lips and she looked at the floor. "She was dressed as a *tuan*," she said.

Curran stared at her. "A man?"

The girl nodded. "Often she dresses as a *tuan*. She tells me it is funny to fool people. She has the . . ." The girl tugged at her chin.

"Beard?" Curran asked between clenched teeth.

The girl nodded and Curran swore under his breath.

Outside he accosted the plainclothes constable he had left on watch.

"Did a short man with a beard and carrying a suitcase leave the hotel?"

The constable thought for a moment and nodded. He glanced up at the sky. "An hour or more ago. He got into a motor vehicle."

"A motor vehicle."

"*Ya, tuan.* A red motor vehicle."

Curran's blood ran cold. There were not many motor vehicles in Singapore and only one person he knew drove a red vehicle.

"Did you see the driver?"

"A big *Inggeris*." The young man put his hand to his face, mimicking driving goggles, and made a gesture in imitation of a large moustache.

A red motor vehicle? A large Englishman with a moustache?

Curran's mouth went dry. Foster? Surely not. If someone had punched him in the stomach, he could not have felt more winded.

"Are you all right, sir?" Singh asked.

"Augustus Foster," Curran said aloud, and turned back to the constable. "Did you see which direction the motor vehicle went?"

The constable waved in the direction of Beach Road. "That way." He frowned. "Have I done wrong, *tuan*?"

Curran shook his head and clapped the boy on the shoulder. "No. You did nothing wrong. You didn't know. None of us did."

✲ THIRTY-FOUR

Harriet wiped the perspiration that dripped off her nose, rolled her sleeves up over her elbows and undid another button on her blouse. Nothing made a difference. The heat in the little room had risen to a suffocating level, draining her of what little energy she had. Will slumped against the wall, his arms around his knees. All pretense at practicing French grammar long since abandoned.

It took an effort to rise to her feet and Harriet paced the little room several times, pausing only to pour a ration of the precious water. She gave some to Will before swallowing the remaining mouthful herself. Hot and stagnant, it still had the power to refresh.

Will stiffened. "I can hear someone," he said.

Harriet held her breath. The boy had heard right. Heavy determined footsteps approached on the flagstones of the covered breezeway that led to the house.

She pushed Will behind her and stood with her back to the farthest wall as the key rattled in the lock. Her head spun and for a dizzying moment she thought she might be sick or faint . . . or both. She swallowed back the bitter bile and struggled to control her breathing as the door flung open, letting in some fresh air.

For some absurd reason, she was almost pleased to see the young Dutchman Paar rather than the grim Burmese man.

But Paar's brashness of the previous night seemed to have deserted him and the hand holding the revolver shook. He jerked the weapon, signaling for them to leave the room.

When Harriet didn't move quickly enough, he leveled the revolver at her. "Out, now."

"I do not respond to being spoken to in that tone, young man," Harriet said.

Paar's mouth dropped open. "Please . . . Mrs. Gordon."

"Much better. Come, William."

With her head held high, she swept past Paar out onto the covered walkway that separated kitchen and servants' quarters from the main house. In daylight she could see the house was one of the fine holiday villas that lined the east coast of the island. In other circumstances it would be considered idyllic, set in an isolated grove of palm trees that fringed the white sands of the beach. A pleasant place for rest and recreation, with no nearby neighbors.

Now it might be the last place on earth she would ever see.

They entered the house and she found herself back in the elegantly furnished living room. It didn't look as if John Lawson had been moved. He remained tied to the same dining chair, with his arms fastened behind him, his feet tied to the legs of the chair and a gag wound tightly around his face. His chin rested on his chest and only the very slightest rise and fall of breath indicated he still lived. In a corner the Burmese man crouched on his haunches, running his thumb along the edge of his knife. He looked up at Harriet and his cold, dead eyes knocked the confidence from her.

"Papa!"

At the sound of Will's voice, Lawson raised his head. Harriet put a restraining hand on the boy's shoulder to prevent him running forward. Above the gag, Lawson's red-rimmed eyes filled with tears. Harriet drew the boy in to her, and Will buried his face in her skirts, his shoulders heaving with dry sobs.

A movement by the wide-flung French windows diverted her attention. A short, rather dumpy man wearing a floppy double felt hat that shadowed his face, entered the room from the terrace. He stood, feet apart, the fingers of one hand playing with the short goatee beard on his chin as he surveyed the prisoners.

"*De gevangenen,*" Paar said.

The man gave a curt acknowledgment and swept the hat from "his" head, allowing a long, fair plait to fall across "his" shoulder.

"Good morning, Mrs. Gordon."

Harriet gasped, taking an involuntary step backward, only to be brought up short by Paar's hand in her back, propelling her forward into the middle of the room. She stumbled, straightened and raised her chin to face the woman she knew as Mrs. Van Gelder.

THIRTY-FIVE

Curran returned to South Bridge Road and left Singh to see to
Mrs. Cornilissen's incarceration in a different part of the
building from her husband's.

He found Carruthers sitting on the bench outside his glass-
partitioned office. The man jumped to his feet at the sight of Curran.

"I thought you'd gone back to the Explorers?" Curran said.

Carruthers ignored the question. "Do you have the women?"

"Mrs. Cornilissen is enjoying our hospitality but the Van
Gelder woman got away"—he paused—"and it looks like Augustus Foster is involved."

Carruthers sat down with an audible thump. "Foster? Good
God," he said.

Curran ushered him into the office and related the morning's
doings at the Van Wijk Hotel, glad that Carruthers's reaction had
been the same as his. Utter incredulity.

"But if Foster is involved, why would he risk being seen col-
lecting the woman in such a distinctive vehicle?"

Curran had the answer. The conspirators knew that the need
to maintain the deception had passed. If he did not move fast,
they would be off the island and lost in the souks and alleys of
some other colony or backwater and Harriet, Lawson and the
boy could be . . . He didn't want to dwell on their fate.

He found his voice and said bitterly, "I think I will find when I get to Foster's house, that he is gone too."

"But I don't understand. What's Foster got to do with it?"

Curran shook his head. "Damned if I know. I am going up to his house now."

Curran ignored the man's request to accompany him. He knew where Foster lived, had attended a Singapore Cricket Club function at the comfortable bungalow on Mt. Elizabeth.

As his men conducted a cursory search of the deserted house, Curran stood in the bedroom and swore. Like Viktoria Van Gelder's bedchamber, there was evidence of a hurried departure but little else.

A shelf of books caught his attention and he walked over to it, running his eyes over the titles. One stood out. *Explorations of Burma* by C. Kent. Kent—the name sounded familiar. It had come up at some point in his investigations. The name of the army officer who had accompanied Newbold on his Burmese exploration. It couldn't be coincidence that two men named Kent had been involved in such an exploration.

On a whim, he pulled the slender volume from the shelves and flicked it open to a fuzzy image of the author and for a heartbeat his breath stopped. A younger, slimmer version of the man he knew as Augustus Foster, wearing a military uniform with the rank of major, stared back at him. He would need to telegram Rangoon as soon as he got back to the office.

In the meantime, a full search would have to wait. He was rapidly running out of time. Foster and Viktoria Van Gelder had shown their hands and were now on the run. Their fugitive status meant only that Harriet, Lawson and his son were now in very real danger. The conspirators had nothing to lose and everything to gain from hanging on to their hostages.

Would they be prepared to leave the island without the sapphire?

Thirty-six

The Van Gelder woman stood with her hands on her hips, her gaze raking Harriet from the top of her head to her toes. Any resemblance between the soft fluffy woman Harriet had first met at the Van Wijk and this hard-eyed female was purely coincidental. Harriet felt any hope begin to fade in the shadow of that cold gaze.

"Good afternoon, Mrs. Gordon. I trust you have enjoyed your stay at our humble establishment?"

Harriet straightened. "I must say, Mrs. Van Gelder, I found the bed somewhat hard, the food lacking and the staff extremely rude."

Something that might have been a smile twitched the woman's false beard and moustache. She fingered the facial hair and jerked her head at Paar. "Fetch me a bowl of water and a cloth."

As the door closed behind Paar, the woman inclined her head to Harriet, her hands rubbing together in an obsequious parody of her husband. "On behalf of the manager, please accept our apologies," Mrs. Van Gelder said, "but I am afraid you may find the discomfort of which you complain will seem like a pleasant dream." Her eyes narrowed. "You are a meddling fool, Mrs. Gordon. You and that idiot." She jerked her head at Lawson. "If you had not interfered, you would even now, be safe at home with your loved ones."

Paar returned carrying the requested bowl of water, which he set on the table, and Mrs. Van Gelder crossed to it. With a grimace, she pulled the beard from her chin and moustache from her upper lip, dabbing with the dampened cloth at the glue that had held the facial hair in place.

"That's better." She stood, drying her hands on the cloth. "It never ceases to amaze me that people see only what they want to see. I walked straight past that foolish police constable but he had been told to look for a woman, not a man. By the time they realize I am gone, it will be too late. Your friend the handsome police inspector will be less than pleased."

"Mrs. Van Gelder—" Harriet began, but the woman held up her hand.

"Viktoria," she said. "Thank the Lord I no longer need to pretend an affection to that foolish man, Van Gelder. My name is Viktoria Klop."

Viktoria's gaze moved to Lawson. "What a mess you have made of things," she said, addressing Lawson, her tone chiding rather than angry. "He is very angry and you know what he is capable of doing when aroused."

Harriet pulled Will in tighter as Viktoria glanced at the door into the hallway and raised her voice. "*Mijn geliefde*, the woman and boy are here."

The door opened and a large man with a military bearing entered. Harriet recognized him from the church congregation and the cricket club and felt her knees go weak, tears of relief welling up behind her eyelids.

"Colonel Foster! Thank heavens you're here. Are the police with you? These people . . ."

She trailed off as Foster walked over to Viktoria Van Gelder, putting an arm around her shoulder.

"Ah, sadly, I fear you may be mistaken, Mrs. Gordon," he said. "I am, alas, not your rescue party, but your host."

🕱 THIRTY-SEVEN

It had long gone past midday and the hubbub of Clarke Quay had died down in the hottest part of the day. Even so, there were plenty of interested eyes peering around doors or through shuttered windows as Curran and a handcuffed Nils Cornilissen alighted from the motor vehicle.

"Why are we back here?" Cornilissen demanded.

The short sojourn in the cell had given Cornilissen time to compose himself and he emerged from the vehicle with the serenity of a man who had just walked out of his hotel suite rather than a prison cell. He may have appeared calm but he did not look quite so dapper. He had abandoned his frock coat and his shirt and waistcoat were grimy and sweat soaked.

Curran did not reply.

With a curt nod, Curran led Cornilissen down the quay and past the police guard he had left on the door, into the dark interior of the nameless *godown*.

He indicated the rickety stairs leading up to the loft and the rooms above.

"Up there."

"Why . . . ?" Cornilissen began, only to be given a gentle shove in the back by Curran, causing him to stumble on a broken stair tread.

At the top of the stairs the men crossed the open loft to the door at the far end that stood open, revealing a sweating Constable Greaves working on fingerprinting the room. The constable looked up but did not stop his work.

Curran shoved Cornilissen inside. The man recoiled.

"What is that?" he demanded, holding a manacled arm against his face.

"That is the smell of blood . . . a lot of blood. Hans Visscher's blood. His throat was cut from ear to ear. What do you know about his death?"

Cornilissen's face drained of color. "Nothing," he said between tight lips. "I had nothing to do with the boy. She told me he had left the country."

"She?"

"Viktoria. Viktoria Van Gelder."

V *for Viktoria*, Curran thought again.

"What is your relationship with Viktoria Van Gelder?" he demanded.

Cornilissen licked his lips. "I am married to her daughter."

That confirmed Van Gelder's story.

Curran just let the man talk.

"She is . . . was . . . I knew Viktoria back in Amsterdam when she ran a number of successful and exclusive establishments for gentlemen, you understand?"

"Brothels?" Curran knew he could not allow his surprise to show on his face. He tried to imagine the plump, fair-haired matron he had met as a brothel keeper. Of all scenarios, that had not been one he would have expected.

Cornilissen must have sensed Curran's shock and straightened his shoulders. "Oh yes, Inspector, Viktoria Klop was a well-known madam and as well as the brothels, she headed a very successful gang of housebreakers, but all good things come to an end and when she thought the authorities might catch up with her, she disappeared from Holland."

"And turned up in the Far East?"

Cornilissen nodded. "Batavia at first but she didn't stay there long. There was a fortune to be made in Burma as the British opened it up. She set up in Rangoon, where she met Oswald Newbold."

"And how did you get involved?"

Cornilissen glanced at the chair with its grisly reminders of how Visscher had died. He gave a bitter laugh. "Never fall in love with a beautiful woman, Inspector."

❧ THIRTY-EIGHT

Colonel Foster looked around the pleasant room and rubbed his hands together. "Do you like my little villa? I am very sad to be leaving it, but, as Viktoria has just pointed out, the unfortunate interference in our plans by you and Lawson"—he gestured at Lawson—"necessitate our hasty departure from this pleasant island."

Harriet glanced at Lawson. His eyes above the gag were wide, as if Foster's involvement also came as a surprise to him.

Viktoria Van Gelder glanced at the window. "Time to go, Charles. The boat is here."

He shook his head. "I told you, Vik. I'm not leaving without the last shipment of rubies and that sapphire."

"But the police will have them all by now," she protested. "We have enough and Curran is no fool. He'll have worked it out by now."

"Yes, but we still have them—" Foster gestured at Harriet and the child.

Viktoria Van Gelder tossed her head. "We could kill one and leave the body to be found by the police. That way they will know we are serious."

A muffled protest rose from John Lawson and he strained against his bonds.

Augustus Foster withdrew his arm from around the woman's shoulders. "I don't kill women or children," he said.

"You are too soft." Viktoria's lip curled in derision.

Harriet forced her tired mind to a solution that would save at least Will.

"If you want the stones, then you need to get a message to the police," she said. "They are expecting some sort of communication from you. Killing one of us serves no purpose and you won't have another murder to your name. Send the boy."

Viktoria glanced at Foster and shrugged. "The child is nothing but a nuisance. If we let him go, we still have the woman."

"And Lawson," Harriet pointed out.

Viktoria cast the bound man a look of pure indifference. "He's worthless. He is as guilty as the rest of us."

"What about me?" Paar's voice rose an octave. "You promised . . ."

"Of course you are coming with us, *mijn kleine* Stefan," Viktoria said. "You have been so very useful."

She approached the young man, laying her hand on his chest and looking up into his sweating, pimply face. Harriet shivered. The gesture left her in no doubt as to how Viktoria had coerced the young man into assisting the conspirators. Paar swallowed, his Adam's apple convulsing.

Without warning Viktoria struck him across the face, a stinging blow that knocked him back several steps and reverberated around the room.

"It is your foolishness that has brought us here, *mijn kleine* Stefan." This time the endearment was spat out. "Leaving the journal where any foolish policeman could find it."

Clutching his face, Paar whimpered an apology. Viktoria regarded him with a curl of her lip and turned back to Foster.

"What do you want to do, Kent?"

Kent? Harriet closed her eyes.

"Who are you?" she demanded of the man.

He swept her a bow. "Major Charles Kent, late of the South Sussex Infantry Regiment."

Before Harriet could ask any more, the man she now knew as Kent jerked his head at Will. "You, boy, come here."

Will glanced up at Harriet and, with great reluctance, she withdrew her arm from around his shoulders. Will straightened and obeyed the command, stopping an arm's length from Van Gelder and Kent, his feet apart and his hands behind his back. If the boy was afraid, he showed no sign of it. Viktoria Van Gelder put a finger under the boy's chin and tilted his face up. Harriet held her breath but Will did not flinch.

"Give me your word you won't hurt him," Harriet said.

Viktoria glanced across at Harriet. "Really, Mrs. Gordon, you are hardly in a position to bargain with me. If I want to hurt him there is nothing you can do to stop me." She turned her attention back to the boy. "I have a little task for you, young man. Come with me, I need to write a note, which you will deliver for me." She gestured at the Burmese man. "And you, Zaw."

Viktoria laid her hand on Will's shoulder and the boy grimaced as her fingers bit into his flesh. She steered him toward the door, followed by the stone-faced Zaw.

Kent sat down in a rattan armchair and crossed his legs. "You may as well sit down, Mrs. Gordon."

Harriet complied, sinking into a comfortable chair as if she were about to take tea with her genial host. After the hard floor of the servant's cell, the chair felt almost civilized. She took the opportunity to glance at the clock. It showed nearly one o'clock, earlier than she had thought.

"Paar, there is a hamper in the car. I am sure Mrs. Gordon must be famished." Kent gestured in the direction of the front door.

"I'm not a servant," Paar responded, his flushed face a darker red where Viktoria had struck him.

"Do as I say," Kent purred in a low voice that held more

menace than if the order had been shouted. Muttering under his breath, Paar left the room. Distantly, Harriet heard a door slam.

"What a pity things have come to such a pretty pass," Foster said. "We were doing so nicely."

Harriet glanced at Lawson. He was watching the door through which Viktoria had disappeared with his son.

"I would appreciate an explanation of your involvement, Colonel . . . or is it Major?" Harriet said.

"That is a very long story, Mrs. Gordon, and I'm not sure we have the time." He glanced across at the clock as it struck the hour.

"Did you kill Newbold?" Harriet demanded.

Kent's moustache twitched. "You are very direct, Mrs. Gordon. No, I didn't"—he paused—"although I might have done. He had served his purpose."

"And that was?"

Kent smiled. "Viki and I had decided it would be pleasant if the proceeds of our little enterprise were not shared three ways."

"What about Visscher?"

"That was unfortunate," Kent said. "The stupid boy overheard a conversation he shouldn't have and went running off to Newbold. He made the mistake of confiding in Paar and Paar delivered Visscher straight into our hands. We had no choice but to silence the boy. Pity. I deplore violence. The trouble with enterprises of our nature is that once too many people are involved there is always the risk of a weak link." He jerked his head at Lawson. "Like that fool."

Harriet glanced across at Lawson. His head had sunk onto his chest and at the mention of his name, he groaned.

"Please, release Mr. Lawson's bonds. I fear he is not well."

Kent rose to his feet and walked across to Lawson. Seizing a handful of hair, he raised his head. "I think you might be right, my dear." He shrugged and let the man's head fall again. "If he dies, no loss."

Harriet took a deep, shuddering breath, her gaze scanning the room, looking for an opportunity to make good her escape. The doors to the terrace stood open, beckoning her. She rose to her feet, stretching her stiff back. Kent moved with remarkable agility for a big man. He pushed her back in the chair and leaned in to her, his hands on the arms of the chair. She could smell garlic and onions on his breath.

"Don't even think about it, Mrs. Gordon. I told the truth when I said I don't like harming women or children but I will if I have to."

The unexpected domestic clink of china interrupted Kent and he straightened, looking over Harriet's head toward the door. "Ah, Paar. Thank you. Set the tray down on the table and undo Mr. Lawson's restraints. I don't think he will be giving us any trouble. I suggest you eat something, Mrs. Gordon. It could be a very long day for you."

Harriet glanced at the tray Paar carried. If she were to get through the next few hours she needed all her wits about her and that required food and drink. Without interference, she rose to her feet and crossed to the table where Paar had set down the tray on which were bottles of warm ginger beer and digestive biscuits. As she started to eat, Paar undid Lawson's restraints. His head fell back and he gasped as he took in deep breaths. Harriet filled a cup with the ginger beer and carried it over to him.

"Drink," she whispered. "You need your strength."

Lawson looked up at her. His hair clung damply to his forehead and the heat that radiated from him came not from the humid atmosphere but fever. He raised his left hand to take the cup but his hand shook too badly. Harriet held the cup to his lips and he drank greedily, forcing Harriet to pull back.

"Don't make yourself sick."

When she had got some food and drink into the man, she turned to Kent. "His wound needs dressing."

Kent stood up and walked across to the sick man. Without any emotion on his face he looked down at him.

"Very well. Paar, you will find some bandages in the bathroom. Bring those and some fresh water."

"Thank you," Harriet said, and began unwinding the fetid cloth that had been used to bind Lawson's arm. As it came away he cried out in pain and Harriet flinched in sympathy, her nose twitching at the familiar smell of a wound gone bad. She had seen enough untended injuries in her husband's little clinic in the slums of Bombay to recognize the symptoms. The long, nasty cut, no doubt inflicted by Zaw's knife, oozed pus, and the skin around it was inflamed.

She looked up at Kent. As a soldier, he must have known what he was looking at—a wound that was threatening to turn gangrenous.

"He needs a doctor," she said.

"He will have to make do with you, my dear. Here's Paar with the contents of my medicine cupboard. Do what you can."

Relieved to see carbolic among the items Paar dumped on the table, Harriet cleaned and dressed the wound properly. Lawson did not utter a sound until she had finished.

"It's bad, isn't it?" he whispered at last.

She nodded. "You've lived in the tropics long enough to know what happens to untreated wounds."

He looked away and Harriet straightened. She turned to face Kent.

"Let him go," she said. "He needs a doctor. You still have me."

"I don't think so, Mrs. Gordon." Viktoria cut in from the doorway. "Zaw has returned and we will be away."

Kent jerked his head at the French window. "Time to go."

Paar glanced out the window. "A boat, but we have the carriage and the motor vehicle—"

"You are a stupid boy." Viktoria's voice dripped with ice. "You don't think we could use the carriage again, let alone such a distinctive motor vehicle? Every police officer on the island will be looking for it. No one will suspect an innocent fishing boat."

"Where are we going?" Harriet found her voice.

"A quiet little place we know. However, it will take us some hours to reach our rendezvous."

Viktoria turned to look at Harriet, and Harriet returned her gaze without blinking, gratified to see Viktoria's eyes slide away.

"I gave the police until midnight to turn up with the stones, Charles."

Kent snorted. "*The Spartan* won't wait forever."

Harriet's mind churned. The police still had to find the boy before they could take action on the instructions Viktoria had sent with him.

"And if the police don't come?" Harriet asked through tight lips.

Kent shrugged. "Then, we will have to cut our losses, my dear." The smile he gave his mistress turned Harriet's blood to ice.

"You haven't hurt Will?" Lawson half rose from his chair.

Viktoria turned her gaze on Lawson. "No. Annoying brat, but no, he's still in one piece. We've left him where someone will find him soon enough. Enough talk. It's time to go. Zaw . . ."

Kent barked out an order in a language Harriet now assumed to be Burmese.

Zaw hauled Lawson to his feet and wrenched his arms back behind his back, tying his wrists, oblivious to Lawson's yelp of pain. Satisfied Lawson had been secured, he turned to Harriet, tying a dirty piece of rag around her mouth. She gagged at the sour taste of the cloth but he ignored her muffled protestations, securing her wrists behind her back with the cords that had bound her the previous night.

The fingers of his right hand closed around her forearm and he jerked her forward. As he pushed her toward the door onto the terrace, one of her last remaining hairpins tumbled to the floor with a gentle ping. She cast a quick glance around but nobody else seemed to have noticed it.

A humble native fishing boat had been pulled up onto the beach. Harriet cast frantic glances to her right and left but the beach was deserted. It appeared to be a small private beach framed by two rocky points with only Kent's villa fronting it. Even if she could scream she doubted anyone would hear her and even if they did she would be dead before anyone could come to her aid.

The prisoners stumbled forward onto the warm sand. Lawson staggered and would have fallen if Zaw hadn't caught his bad arm and hauled him upright. Lawson cried out in pain, audible despite the gag.

As they reached the shoreline, Zaw picked Harriet up bodily and threw her into the bottom of the boat, where she lay in a soup of tepid, stinking water. Lawson followed, forcing Harriet to wriggle over to make room for him.

Paar tossed two suitcases and a canvas bag into the boat, prompting a roar from Kent as the canvas bag landed in the bilge water that sloshed in the bottom of the simple craft. The luggage was rearranged and Paar clambered awkwardly into the boat, causing the small craft to rock. He settled himself in the stern, where he was joined by Viktoria, who pulled an *atap* screen partly over their heads to shield them from the sun and curious eyes.

Harriet could hear Kent arguing in Malay with the boatman but the words were indistinguishable.

The boat scraped along the sand and shuddered as Kent vaulted after them, landing with surprising agility beside Harriet's head. There could be no disguising the large *Inggeris* as a local fisherman and as there was no room for him beside Viktoria and Paar, he settled down beside Harriet, apparently impervious to the seeping water.

He bent down and solicitously lifted Harriet into a sitting position.

"More comfortable?" he inquired as he unrolled a second *atap* screen to pull over them.

If Harriet had been able to summon a sharp retort, the gag prevented her from doing anything more than glaring at him.

As the sail on the heavily laden vessel kicked out with a slap of canvas, she closed her eyes, tying to visualize a map of the island. Changi lay on the far northeastern end of the island. According to Julian it was nothing more than a fishing village as far away from the main settlement as it was possible to travel. The coastline was dotted with islands where a larger steamer or boat could hide. If *The Spartan* had been commissioned by Van Gelder and Kent to carry them away then it probably lay offshore. From there it could go anywhere.

As for Lawson and herself, if the police did not bring the stones in time, they would be disposed of and their bodies would never be found. Julian would blame himself. Her parents would be distraught.

Nothing, not even the blackest moments in Holloway, had provoked such a sense of despair as that which overwhelmed her at that moment. Harriet turned her face to the side of the boat, trying to focus on the sodden, stinking wooden boards but exhaustion had begun to catch up with her and the tears began to seep from beneath her tightly closed eyes, silent tears born of hopelessness.

&ۤ THIRTY-NINE

Hot, tired and frustrated by the lack of communication from the kidnappers, Curran returned to South Bridge Road to find he had visitors. The Reverend Edwards, Dr. and Mrs. Mackenzie and the journalist Maddocks were sitting in a row on a bench in the detective's outer office. They rose as one as he entered and began firing questions at him. Curran held up a hand and they fell silent as he gestured them into his office.

It was not a large room and with five people in it, it felt even smaller. Louisa took the only spare chair and the three men stood behind her, all of them fixing Curran with anxious and fearful gazes.

"You promised to give me news," Julian began, pushing his glasses back up the bridge of his nose.

"I know," Curran said. "Forgive me, but I haven't had a moment to myself. We've arrested Cornilissen and recovered the rest of the ruby shipment."

"Cornilissen?" Euan Mackenzie raised a shaggy eyebrow.

Before Curran could respond, Louisa chimed in, "And Harriet? Have you found her?"

Curran shook his head. "I know who has her."

"John Lawson." Julian ran a hand through his hair, making it stick up on end. "We know that, Curran."

"Yes and no. I have made some progress. Cornilissen, Viktoria Van Gelder and Augustus Foster are the chief perpetrators of the events of the last weeks. Newbold, to a certain extent, was their dupe And Lawson was just one of their underlings."

Four thunderstruck faces stared at him.

"Viktoria Van Gelder?" Louisa's mouth fell open in genuine surprise. "I know her from one of my charities. She always seemed nice enough but a little dim."

Curran gave a snort of laughter. "Far from it, Louisa. I'm only beginning to learn about Viktoria Van Gelder and one thing she isn't, is dim."

"What about Foster?" Maddocks put in. "He's a harmless old buffer."

Curran picked up a telegram from London that lay on his desk. "That harmless old buffer is a man by the name of Charles Kent. He was asked to leave the army after a particularly nasty incident involving the massacre of an entire village in northern Burma. Newbold may have been the instigator of the scheme but this man Kent and the Van Gelder woman had their own plans for the stones."

"So much for honor among thieves," Mackenzie remarked.

"Quite. I have the last ruby shipment and the sapphire and I've no doubt our friends would like them back. I anticipate they will offer Harriet and the boy in return for the stones but I'm yet to receive the ransom demand so that, if nothing else, is good news."

"It could mean they're already dead," Julian said, a sharp edge to his tone.

"I don't think so." Curran dismissed that suggestion with a shake of his head. "For the moment assume the best. Now, please, can I ask you all to return home? I have an interview I need to conduct and every moment is precious."

"Of course," Julian said. "If you want me, Curran, I will be with the Mackenzies."

At the door Curran put out a hand to detain Maddocks. "And

you, Maddocks, not a word . . ." he said in a low voice. Maddocks opened his mouth to protest but shut it again as Curran said, "Anything you write could potentially endanger Mrs. Gordon."

Maddocks shook his head. "I have the highest regard for Mrs. Gordon. I would never . . ."

"Good."

Curran began his interviews with Viktoria Van Gelder's daughter. Gone was the soft, frilly creature of silks and satins. The woman sat across the table from him, her arms folded and her mouth in a hard line. The cornflower blue eyes were as cold as a Scottish loch in the middle of winter. Curran greeted her with a smile.

"Your charm is wasted on me," Gertrude Cornilissen said.

"Where is your mother?"

"I don't know."

"Do you care?"

"Of course I care. I care because she has the money owed to Nils and me."

"I have your husband in custody, Mrs. Cornilissen. He will be charged with theft and being an accessory to murder . . ."

"Murder?" The blue eyes widened. "We were not even on the island when Newbold died."

"But you were when Visscher was killed . . . in the *godown* used by your husband. Where are your mother and Charles Kent?"

A muscle twitched in the woman's jaw at the mention of Foster's real name but she looked away. "I don't know."

Curran could not waste any more time on her. Clearly cut in her mother's image, Gertrude Cornilissen would not betray the other conspirators. He left her in the hot, airless room to consider her options and turned his attention back to Van Gelder.

The hotel manager sat on the edge of the hard platform that served as a bed in the cell. Sweat streamed from him and the room stank of fear and the contents of the bucket in the corner.

Van Gelder rose to his feet as Curran entered. "When will I be free to go, Inspector? My hotel . . . my guests . . . Viktoria hates being left in charge—" He began to whine but something in Curran's face stilled his tongue.

"Has something happened to my Viktoria?"

Curran resisted the urge to tell him exactly what he thought of *his* Viktoria.

"Nothing has happened to your wife, that I know of," Curran said, "but I would like to know a little bit more about her."

Van Gelder frowned. "Viktoria? She has nothing to do with this."

"Sit, Van Gelder." Curran waved the man down onto the bench again. "Your precious Viktoria has played you for a dupe."

"What do you mean?" The man frowned.

"Did you know that before her marriage to you she was mistress of brothels from Amsterdam to Rangoon?"

Van Gelder stared at him, his mouth falling open. He blinked rapidly.

"A brothel keeper?" he managed at last, and sat back, his arms folded. "No, that is not right. Newbold told me she was the wife . . ." He trailed off. "Newbold?"

"Your wife has, as far as I can ascertain, enjoyed close relations with Oswald Newbold and Augustus Foster. Oh, by the way, that's not his real name."

"Close relations?" Van Gelder inquired in a shaky voice.

"Certainly close business relations," Curran conceded.

Van Gelder ran a hand over his eyes. "What are you implying, Inspector? I cannot deny that Colonel Foster dines often at the Van Wijk and he and my wife are, what would you say, good nodding acquaintances. Nothing more. He invited us to parties at his beach villa on a couple of occasions . . ."

Curran almost jumped to his feet. With difficulty he controlled himself. "He has a beach villa? Where?"

Van Gelder scratched his chin. "It's about four miles from the city, near Tanjong Katong. Very pretty spot."

Curran stared at him. Tanjong Katong was a pleasant native village just off the Beach Road. Over the previous few years it had become a popular spot for beach villas and he himself had enjoyed some pleasant nights off at one of the newer hotels that had been built on the beach.

The carriage that had taken Harriet away from St. Tom's had last been seen heading for Beach Road. He had no reports of it having passed through the village or any of the other villages along the road to the east of the island. If it had turned into one of the beach villas, that seemed a probable destination.

After extracting details of Kent's villa, he left a protesting Van Gelder in his cell. On returning to the detectives' office he found the clerk waiting for him, a piece of paper clutched in his hand, his eyes bright with excitement.

"*Tuan*, I have received a telephone call." He gestured at the device on the wall in the main office. "It was the police post at Tanjong Katong. An English boy calling himself William Lawson has just been picked up in the village. They have him at the police post."

⎈ Forty

Curran didn't wait for the motor vehicle. He wanted to be on the move and on the move fast and for that Leopold was a far better choice. Leaving orders for the others to meet him, he reached the police post at Tanjong Katong in just under half an hour, riding at a hard canter most of the way.

The village of Tanjong Katong had grown from being just a simple *kampong*. A row of shop houses now graced its main street but stringy chickens and mangy dogs still wandered across the rutted, muddy road. The police post, a simple two-room building with a primitive moat around it to catch the monsoonal rains, stood at the far end of town.

Curran swung himself off his horse and tethered the reins to the nearby hitching post. He strode into the little police station and found William Lawson sitting on the end of a desk, swinging his legs and drinking from a bottle of pop. The child was filthy, his school uniform torn and stained and his stockings hung down around his scuffed boots.

The boy's eyes brightened when he saw Curran. He set the bottle down and slid off the table and ran toward him, stopping short of throwing his arms around the policeman, a situation that would have completely discomposed Curran. He had little experience of children.

Instead he gave the boy's damp and sweaty hand a hearty shake. "William, it's good to see you. You had us worried. Are you hurt?"

The boy shook his head, belying the cuts and scratches on his arms and legs.

Curran perched on the edge of the desk and addressed the sergeant in Malay.

"Where did you find him?"

"Wandering along the side of the road. A passing chicken seller found him and brought him here. I recognized him at once from the description."

"Good work," Curran said, and turned to the boy. "Do you know where your father and Mrs. Gordon are?"

The boy nodded. "They're in the big house down by the beach."

"Who else is there?"

Lawson considered for a moment. "The nasty lady, the man calls her Vik, and the big man with the moustache. Then there is the man with the funny accent and the scary man."

"Tell me about the man with the funny accent. What did he look like?"

"He has dark hair and spots on his face and he sweats a lot." Paar.

"And the scary man?"

Will shuddered. "He was the one who took me away. He never talks. They call him Zaw. He tied me up and put a blindfold on me so I couldn't see where they took me." He shivered. "I was very scared."

"Can you tell me about this place?"

"I think it was near one of the quays—I could hear people shouting and I smelled the river. They took me up some stairs and put me in a horrible room." The boy pulled a face. "It was dark and hot and it smelled funny . . ."

"Good boy. It was a *godown* on Clarke Quay and it was a bad place for you, Will." A good thing the boy had been blindfolded. "What happened then?"

"The man with the funny accent came and took me away in a motor vehicle and when I got to the big house, they took off the blindfold and Mrs. Gordon and Papa were there." His face screwed up. "They were being horrid to Papa. He's hurt. I think he's going to die." Will's composure began to crumple and a couple of large tears tracked their way through the dirt on his face, following the path of others before. Curran could only imagine what the child had been through in the last forty-eight hours.

Curran gave the boy a pat on the shoulder. "We'll get him back. Just tell me what happened next."

Will swallowed. "They locked me up with Mrs. Gordon. We tried to escape but the window wouldn't open and then they told me I had to give you a message."

Curran's heart skipped a beat. "Do you have it?"

Will fished inside his trouser pocket and produced a crumpled piece of paper. Curran took it and smoothed it out on the desk. To judge from the neat, rounded writing, the note had been written by a woman. Viktoria Van Gelder, he surmised.

It said simply, *Bring the stones to Changi Beach at midnight. ALL THE STONES.*

Changi Beach? The note was vague in the extreme. Changi Beach was over ten miles to the east. Why Changi?

"Mr. Curran?"

The boy's voice brought him back and he looked down at the woebegone face.

"You did well, Will."

"Did I?" The boy's lower lip began to tremble.

"One last question. What can you tell me about this house?"

"It had big gates with lions on the gate posts," Will said. "I think it belonged to the big man."

Curran smiled and thanked the boy. He turned to the local police constable. "Are you married?"

The man nodded and smiled. He looked prosperous and well

fed, the sort with a good wife to ensure he never went hungry. Mercifully, it wasn't Ramadan.

"Take the boy to your house and ask your wife to look after him until we come and collect him. He needs food and rest."

"Yes, *tuan*." The police sergeant beamed at Will and said in English, "My Humaira is the best cook in the village."

Curran pulled on his riding gloves. "Tell my men, when they arrive, that I have gone to the house of *tuan* Foster. They have the details."

The man nodded. "You want me or one of my men to come with you, *tuan?*"

Curran shook his head. "No, I will go alone."

Curran had no trouble locating the house. A pair of fine gateposts surmounted by rampant lions brazenly fronted onto a narrow side road that led off the main Katong Road just before the village. He had ridden straight past the turnoff.

He dismounted and led Leopold down a long driveway toward the beach and an elegant, isolated seaside villa, out of sight and sound of the main road. Stopping well short of the house, he tethered Leopold in a grove of palm trees and drew his service revolver.

He made his way around to the back of the house under the cover of the undergrowth and secreted himself behind a hedge. No smoke came from the kitchen chimney and he heard no servants. Tightening his grip on the revolver, he entered the servants' area. The kitchen showed signs of recent use—a picnic hamper and an open packet of digestive biscuits, already overrun with ants, provided an incongruous note to the seriousness of the situation.

He searched the kitchen and laundry and the little rooms that served as servants' quarters. In one room he found evidence of recent occupation, a sleeping mat and a nearly empty jug of water. Several bent and broken hairpins littered the floor beneath the high window, indicating that a woman, most likely Harriet, had been incarcerated here. He picked up one of the pins and looked up at the window, allowing himself a smile at the evident scratch marks around the catch. Harriet Gordon was not a woman to sit meekly by while her fate was decided.

The back door leading into the house was shut but unlocked. He opened it slowly, relieved that it moved easily on oiled hinges. With every nerve tensed, he stepped into the cool hallway. At each door he stopped and checked the rooms beyond before coming out into a spacious living room with long French windows opening onto a terrace overlooking the beach. A half-eaten platter of biscuits, the same as the ones he had found in the kitchen, had been placed in the middle of the table, along with five empty ginger ale bottles.

He swore aloud. He had missed them, but by how long?

A motor vehicle grated to a halt in the courtyard and Curran abandoned his reconnaissance. Moving silently to the front of the house, a quick glance through the glass-paneled door confirmed the arrival of the Detective Branch motor vehicle. He threw the front door open to admit Singh and Greaves. Greaves carried his black leather case with the fingerprinting powders. After the hours he had already spent in the *godown*, the young man looked drained.

"We're too late," Curran said. "We've missed them. Now we need to know how they are traveling. Search the house."

He led them into the main room and Greaves set to work.

"Someone was hurt," Singh said, indicating a bowl of bloodied water and soiled dressings on the table beside a dining chair. Severed cords lay on the floor around the chair.

Blood and ropes—someone had been tied up for a considerable time. Lawson?

Curran walked over to the doors leading out onto the terrace.

As he stepped forward into the doorway, something under his foot crunched. He stooped and picked up a long, decorative hairpin, its glass end now turned to dust under his boot. Had Harriet left him a clue?

As he stood contemplating the pin and its significance, Constable Tan confirmed he had found horses and a carriage in the stables, the carriage matching the description of the one that had taken Harriet away.

"What about a motor vehicle?"

The constable nodded. "A red motor vehicle is there too."

Curran inspected the stables and carriage house, ordered Greaves to dust the carriage and motor for fingerprints and gave orders for the horses to be taken back to the Tanjong Katong police post.

There was only one other way they could have left the building, and Harriet's discarded hairpin had pointed in that direction . . . the sea.

Back at the house he traced a path from the terrace to the beach. Scuffed footprints in the otherwise pristine sand indicated that a sizable party of people had passed that way only recently. The footprints ended at the water's edge and a long scrape showed a boat had been drawn up on the sand.

"They've gone by boat," he said to Singh and Tan as they joined him.

Singh looked up and down the beach. "Not a big boat. It would be riding low in the water. They cannot have gone far."

"Given their note, I can only presume somewhere near Changi," Curran said.

He walked down to the water's edge, letting the benign water lap at his boots as he twirled Harriet's hairpin in his fingers. The sun had already begun to dip and it would be dark within a couple of hours.

Why Changi? There were plenty of small islands off that part of the coast that could hide a small coastal trader and give easy access to the Straits of Johor and escape. Whatever their plans, he could be fairly certain they did not include Harriet or John Lawson.

"*Tuan?*" Tan's voice jerked him from his reverie.

"We are awaiting your orders."

"I want the three of you to return to South Bridge Road and bring the stones and reinforcements to Changi Village," Curran said. "All the police outposts along the east coast need to be notified to keep an eye out for a native fishing vessel behaving suspiciously. It's carrying at least five people as well as the fisherman so it will be low in the water. We will liaise at the Changi police post at 2200 hours."

"What are you doing, sir?" Singh inquired.

"I'll take my horse and go on to Changi."

Singh nodded. "You have a revolver and ammunition?"

Curran nodded and patted his holster.

Singh regarded him for a long moment. "You will be careful? It would be tiresome to have to deal with a new inspector."

Curran put a hand on Singh's shoulder. "If it were up to me, you would be the next inspector. Now, get going."

Turning on his heel Curran strode back through the house to retrieve Leopold.

FORTY-ONE

Harriet sat with her back to the *atap* wall of a rough fishing hut. It smelled of rotting vegetation and fish and she could feel insects running down her back, even if they didn't really exist. The dank, heavy smell of mangroves and the high humidity made her think they must be on a river, rather than on the beach. Any semblance of hope she may have been holding on to had vanished and she let her head hang in exhaustion and despair.

It had probably been late afternoon when they had arrived at this secluded spot but she had no way to check her watch. Paar had left her hands secured behind her back and her feet tied. Her clothes, soaked through with the refuse from the fishing boat still felt damp and stank. At least they had removed the noisome gag but she could still taste the revolting fabric and she was desperate for something to drink. Every muscle in her body hurt and she had a pounding headache.

Lawson, similarly bound and slumped against the wall across from her, was in a bad way. It didn't take wounds long to turn septic in this climate and the knife wound to his arm had been untreated, beyond Harriet's rudimentary attention, for forty-eight hours at least.

"I'm sorry," he mumbled, tossing his head and causing the *atap* walls to rustle. "So sorry."

Harriet didn't respond. He must have repeated the apology several times in the last hour. Forgiveness took energy and she had none left.

It had long gone dark and a lantern's glow permeated the gaps in the *atap* walls, casting a faint illumination on Lawson's sweating face. The thunk of a metal shovel in dirt sent a shiver up her spine and she squeezed her eyes tightly shut, trying to block the noise, which had cut through the buzz of the jungle for most of the previous hour.

They're digging our graves, she thought. *I'm going to die here. No one will ever find my body. My mother will say* I told you so . . .

At the thought of her mother, a sob rose in her throat.

Lawson spoke again, "Mrs. Gordon . . ."

She turned her head away and fought down the tears.

"Harriet?"

John Lawson's voice sounded husky and weak. She wanted to be angry with this man but could not find it in her heart. She could feel only pity.

"Yes, John."

"I keep thinking how angry Annie would be with me."

"Why?"

"I've broken all the promises I made to her."

"If you are looking for forgiveness, John, you need to ask my brother."

"I wanted to keep Will safe. Give him a future." He paused and drew a labored breath. "You're fortunate."

"In what way?"

"You have no children."

Harriet gave a choking sob. "There you're very wrong. We have more in common than you think, John. My son, if he had lived, would be nearly the same age as Will now and every time I see Will, I think of Thomas. Don't talk to me about the responsibility a parent owes a child. If you cared about Will, you never would have got yourself tied up in this business."

"I had no choice," he whimpered.

"Of course you did. We all have choices and now your son is suffering for your own poor judgment. I'm suffering for it."

"Oh, God. I'm sorry, Harriet."

"Stop apologizing!"

A long pause before he said in a quiet tone, "Can I ask how your son died?"

Harriet swallowed back the tears. If the circumstances had been anything other than what they were, she would never have said a word about her son but now, as these were possibly her last few hours on earth, she felt the need to talk.

"Typhus. It took my husband and my son within days of each other. I survived."

John Lawson sighed deeply. "Harriet—"

"If you apologize one more time, I will . . . I will . . ." Harriet drew her knees up and lowered her head, letting the tears fall onto her filthy skirt. She couldn't even wipe her nose.

"My, you two are surprisingly conversational." Viktoria Van Gelder pushed aside the ragged curtain that served as a door. She gave a harsh laugh. "If you believe in God, you best make peace with him now."

Harriet raised her head. "Are you going to kill us?"

Viktoria shrugged. "That depends on how cooperative your friends in the Straits Settlements Police are feeling." She pulled out a man's pocket watch and peered at it, squinting in the gloom. "Still some hours until midnight. We made good time to get here."

Harriet looked up at the woman. Despite everything she now knew about Viktoria Van Gelder, she still resembled a comfortable Dutch matron, albeit one in trousers and riding boots.

"Do take a seat, Mrs. Van Gelder," Harriet said, employing the tone her mother would use to invite an expected guest to take tea. "If I'm going to die, we may as well pass the time of day and I am curious to know a little more about you."

Viktoria let the curtain fall and in the dark, Harriet sensed the woman's gaze locked on her. "I have nothing better to do. As you are so curious, you may as well know I was born Viktoria Klop. My mother was a prostitute in Amsterdam and I grew up in brothels, scraping for every piece of food. Neither of you know what it is to have nothing," she said, the contempt spitting the words from her mouth. "My mother sold me to my first customer when I was eleven years old. I grew to hate men but I learned one thing. How to be a good businesswoman. By the time I was twenty-one I ran the best brothels in the Walletjes."

Harriet thought back to her earlier meetings with Viktoria Van Gelder. It was almost impossible to tell Viktoria's age. She may have still been in her thirties but early forties seemed more likely.

"What bought you to the Far East?" Harriet asked, in the hope that by keeping the woman talking, help might arrive in time to save her from the grave Zaw and Paar were digging.

"Opportunity, Mrs. Gordon. My clients in Holland had a taste for the exotic. I arranged for girls from Batavia to be shipped to my houses in Amsterdam and I also took the opportunity to open a few houses in Batavia itself. I was doing very well."

"What changed?"

Viktoria heaved a sigh. "I got bored and I saw an opportunity in Rangoon. There I did a foolish thing, Mrs. Gordon. I made the mistake of falling in love with a most unsuitable man."

"Van Gelder?" Harriet tried to picture what sort of man a brothel keeper would consider unsuitable.

Her suggestion was met with a peal of harsh laughter. "Van Gelder? No, Mrs. Gordon. Guess again."

"Newbold?"

Viktoria snorted. "Oswald Newbold was a means to an end but he wasn't very bright." She approached Harriet and bent down until she was on a level with her. In a lowered voice, she said, "Charles Kent."

"You do surprise me," Harriet responded in an icy tone.

"Never had I met a man so immoral and unprincipled as me. A match made in heaven."

"And what about Sir Oswald?"

"Kent told me of the expedition he had been on with Newbold. Of the stones they had found and the possibilities of playing on a man's greed. He introduced us and we saw at once that we could make a convenient business arrangement. I had the contact in Amsterdam—my son-in-law, Cornilissen. All we needed was a way to smuggle the rubies out of Burma and onto the gem market without suspicion. Newbold introduced me to Van Gelder as the respectable widow Klop, we married and moved to Singapore. The hotel was the perfect cover for the operation and I was the perfect hotelier's wife. The poor fool had no involvement in any of this."

Lawson groaned. "And I was the one who stole the bloody stones and this is how you reward me."

Viktoria laughed. She bent over him, lifting his chin so he looked her in the face. "You are a weak, greedy man, Lawson." She glanced at Harriet. "Has he been bleating to you about how much he loved his darling Annie? All the time I kept him supplied with pretty girls."

Harriet swallowed, trying to bring some moisture to her dry mouth. "And the sapphire?"

Viktoria released Lawson and his head fell back, causing the *atap* to rustle. "Newbold thought we did not know about the sapphire or where he hid it. The prize of the collection. It was the last stone we needed to seal our fortunes. That silly boy Visscher overheard a conversation between Kent and me. We were planning to snatch it from him that Sunday night but someone got there first. By the time Zaw reached the house, Newbold was dead and the stone had gone. Zaw covered up the location of the stone and left empty-handed."

"So, who killed Newbold?"

Viktoria straightened and took the few paces back toward the door. "I don't know but I can tell you it was not us."

"But you did kill Visscher?"

Viktoria's silence gave her the confirmation that she needed.

"Vik?" Kent called.

Viktoria pushed aside the curtain and paused in the doorway. "It has been pleasant passing time with you but we have preparations to make."

❧ FORTY-TWO

C urran reached the village of Changi just before nightfall. He found the constable in charge of the police post, a large man who clearly enjoyed his food, snoring peacefully on a bench outside the station. He rolled off the bench at the sound of Curran's voice.

"My apologies, *tuan*," he said, retrieving his hat from where it had fallen. "It has been a busy day."

"No doubt," Curran responded, his voice dripping ice. In this far-flung corner of the island the most exciting thing to happen would be a stolen chicken.

A second man, as thin as his colleague was fat, appeared at the door. He cast his colleague a sharp glance.

"You are Inspector Curran? I am Constable Musa bin Osman. This is Constable Najid bin Hasif."

The introductions made, Musa said, "I had word to look out for a suspicious boat in these waters and such a boat has been seen. We go now to talk to Aswad the fisherman."

They found Aswad the fisherman crouched beside his cooking fire, frying a fish.

He stood up, brushing his hands on his checkered sarong, as Curran and the constable approached.

"Aswad, you tell the *tuan* what you saw," Musa addressed the elderly man.

Aswad clearly enjoyed being the center of attention as he described in vivid detail, accompanied by extravagant hand gestures, how he had been out in his boat just past the point when an unfamiliar fishing boat had passed him. He had hailed the vessel, as was the custom, but the single man at the helm, whom he did not recognize, had not acknowledged him in any way. A second man, sitting in the prow of the boat, had turned to look at Aswad and Aswad had got a clear view of him. The description he gave could have matched that of Kent's man, Zaw.

"You saw no one else?"

Aswad shook his head. "He had *atap* screens over his catch and the boat was sitting very low in the water. A big catch," he added with admiration in his tone.

A very big catch, Curran considered. Five adults concealed in a small fishing boat. Here Aswad reached the climax of his story, his chest puffing out as he said, "I saw the second man had a gun, *tuan*. I saw the sun glint off it. A small gun . . . like yours . . ." He indicated Curran's service revolver in its holster.

Instinctively Curran's hand went to the butt of the Webley.

"Did you see where they went?"

"Ah yes, *tuan*. They sailed past the point and I believe the boat turned toward the Sungei Selarang."

Curran dispensed a few coins to the man. "You did well, Aswad."

Musa did a quick step beside him as Curran strode back to the police post. "What do we do now, *tuan*?"

"How well do you know the river?"

Musa laughed. "I have lived here all my life. I know the river as I know the lines of my hand. What are we looking for?"

"I believe there were five people hidden on that boat, the catch your friend Aswad spoke of. Three people who are wanted on suspicion of murder and two hostages."

Musa stopped in his tracks. "Murder? We have never had such a thing. What can Najid and I do to help?"

Privately Curran considered Najid to be more of a hindrance than a help but Musa seemed bright and keen. "My men will be here in a few hours," he said, glancing up at the sky. "Take me to the Sungei Selarang."

"There are fishermen's huts on the banks of the river. Would they be sheltering there?" Musa asked.

"Possibly. Draw a weapon, Musa."

The constable blinked. "A weapon? These men are dangerous?"

"Very."

Buckling the police-issue weapon onto his belt, Musa followed Curran out into the compound.

"We don't have time to walk. You can ride behind me," Curran said as he untethered Leopold's reins.

The constable drew back with a shake of his head. "I do not like horses, *tuan*. I have a bicycle."

Curran didn't argue but they must have made an odd sight, the tall European policeman in his khaki uniform on a chestnut horse led by a diminutive police constable on a bicycle that looked, and sounded, in sore need of mechanical attention. The uncertain light attached to the bicycle at least provided some illumination on the rutted tracks.

Curran glanced around as the jungle closed in around them, filled with the clatter and buzz of a myriad of insects and the calls of macaques and other wildlife. There were said to be no more tigers in Singapore but in this isolated corner of the island, who could say if that was true? He loosened the revolver in its holster.

The track ended in a clearing. Above them the sky arched clear and bright with stars and the waning moon rose slowly above the trees. In an hour or so it would provide good illumination.

Leaving the horse tethered to a tree, Musa led Curran on foot through the jungle that fringed the banks of the Selarang River. He could not see the water but the air became closer and he could smell the musky tang of mangroves and the drone of mosquitoes and knew they must be close.

Musa knew every hut along the high bank of the river. Most were unoccupied or the inhabitants quietly going about their evening routine. Careful questioning confirmed that an unfamiliar boat had been seen on the river that afternoon, heading upstream.

"I think I know where they will be," Musa said. "This way."

As they approached an isolated hut on the bend of the river, Musa signaled to Curran and both men went to ground. A casual observer would notice nothing amiss. A native fishing boat drawn up on the bank and two men crouched over a cooking fire in front of a derelict *atap* hut. Curran sniffed the air and smiled. Above the smell of the woodsmoke, the scent of English pipe tobacco drifted through the humid air. Foster/Kent's favorite twist. It reminded him, with a pang, of several pleasant afternoons in this man's company at cricket matches. He had few people he called friends, but he had always enjoyed the company of the man he had known as Colonel Foster.

Beside him Musa tensed. "*Hantu*," he murmured.

From the back of the hut a man appeared, shirtless and dirty, his thin torso so white, he could well have been mistaken for a ghost.

"Not *hantu*. His name is Paar," Curran muttered under his breath.

Stefan Paar crouched down next to the cooking fire and took a swig from a bottle.

Musa indicated that he was going to scout the direction from which Paar had come and Curran nodded. The minutes ticked past before Musa crawled in beside him.

"I do not wish to worry you, *tuan*," he whispered, "but at the back of the hut, they have dug a very large hole."

Curran's blood ran cold. There could be no other reason for a very large hole, other than the disposal of bodies. What was the plan? To kill Harriet and Lawson and turn up on the beach demanding the stones on the understanding that their hostages were safe and well? What sort of fools did they think the police were? Or maybe the stones were no longer the main game?

He tapped Musa's weapon and both men eased their revolvers from the holsters. Curran checked both his and Musa's Webleys to ensure they were fully loaded. Drawing a deep breath, Curran squashed a large mosquito on his bare arm and settled himself to watch and wait.

❊ FORTY-THREE

The sound of shoveling stopped and those outside must have moved the lantern. Except for the faint flickering from a fire, the dark inside the stuffy hut became absolute.

"Will the police come?" Lawson's voice cracked.

"Curran knows what's at stake. A few stones are not worth the sum of two people's lives," Harriet responded. "Yes, they'll come."

She hoped her newly kindled faith in the police in general and Curran in particular would not prove to be unfounded.

The flicker of the fire outside provided some illumination inside the hut and she could hear the murmur of voices but even straining her hearing she could not make any sense of the conversation. Across from her Lawson had fallen silent, either asleep or unconscious.

She shifted position and the wall behind her gave slightly under her weight. If her feet had not been tied, it would be a simple matter to push out one of the *atap* screens and make a run for it. She mused on this thought for a while and tried wriggling her hands to see if the knots would loosen but Zaw knew his business and the more she tried to loosen them, the tighter the knots became. She stopped struggling.

Despite the tantalizing smell of cooking fish drifting into the hut on the smoke from the fire, no one offered the captives food or drink. Harriet swallowed. She didn't believe it was possible to feel so desperately thirsty. She wondered if she should pray for rescue or if her prayers should be a plea to be admitted to heaven and that death, when it came, would be swift and painless. Her calm at this thought surprised her.

She closed her eyes and began to recite in her mind the Lord's Prayer, Psalm 23, and any other psalms she could remember. The patterns of the familiar words were oddly soothing.

She was not aware she had been voicing the words aloud until John Lawson joined in "Yea, though I walk through the valley of the shadow of death . . ." he murmured.

"Psalms?" The derisive snort came from the doorway. Viktoria again. "Spare me your religious ranting, Mrs. Gordon. There is no God."

She stood aside to admit Zaw.

Harriet caught the glint of the man's knife in a flicker of light from the fire and she cringed against the insubstantial wall, embarrassed by the sob of fear that escaped her as Zaw knelt and sliced through the ropes that bound her feet. As she stretched her cramped legs and feet, he turned to Lawson and repeated the action.

Zaw hauled Harriet up by her right arm. Her legs buckled underneath her but he dragged her upright and pushed her out of the door into the grip of Stefan Paar before going back for Lawson.

After the close, stinking hut, the breeze coming off the river lifted her hair and she took a deep, appreciative breath, praying that these would not be her last moments on earth.

Harriet glanced behind her. Zaw came out of the hut, half carrying John Lawson. They walked around the hut and Paar released her, pushing her to the ground. Lawson collapsed in a heap beside her. The smell of freshly turned dirt filled her nostrils and with difficulty she rose to her knees and found herself looking down into a gaping hole. Harriet recoiled, falling backward against Zaw, who stood behind her. For one of the few times in their acquaintance he uttered a sound. He laughed.

Now kneeling with her hands tied behind her, Harriet twisted slightly, her fingers closing on the glass head of the hairpin she had slipped into her boot. She withdrew it, clenching it tightly in her right hand.

Hard experience learned during her time as a suffragette came back to her and she flung her head back with all her force, feeling the satisfying thud of contact with a vulnerable part of the man's anatomy. Zaw gave a muffled cry and crumpled to the ground.

Harriet scrambled to her feet and took off into the dark while behind her she heard Viktoria screaming at Paar to follow her.

She knew she wouldn't get far . . . not in long skirts and with her hands tied behind her. Her foot caught a tree root that sent her sprawling, facedown, knocking the wind from her.

A man fell on top of her, a heavy hand pushing her face into the soft humus of the jungle floor. Her fingers tightening on the hairpin, Harriet jerked her bound hand with all the force she could muster. It may not have been as sharp as a hat pin but it had the desired affect. The man gave a howl of pain and his weight fell off her.

"You bitch!" Stefan Paar screamed, and grabbed her by the hair, hauling her to her feet. "I should kill you now!"

One look at his contorted face and Harriet believed him.

"Uh, uh . . . Paar, we need her alive." Kent's hard voice cut across the night.

"But she stabbed me in the leg . . ." Paar broke off into Dutch, an obvious collection of invective clearly aimed at Harriet.

"I have to admire a woman with spirit, Mrs. Gordon, but that little show of resistance is really no assistance to your cause. Come with me." Foster's hand closed on her arm and, without waiting for her to regain her feet, Kent dragged her, breathless and wheezing, back to the hut, with Paar limping and still cursing behind her.

Foster flung her back on the ground and Paar laced his fingers in her hair, jerking her head upward. Zaw had recovered his feet and his composure and addressed his master in hysterical tones, gesticulating and waving his knife in Harriet's direction.

Foster held up his hand and the man fell silent, his malevolent gaze fixed on Harriet.

"He would like to cut your throat, Mrs. Gordon, and my friend Paar here would happily hold you while he did it, but personally I prefer modern weaponry. So much quicker and effective and far less messy."

Foster drew the revolver from the holster he wore at his waist and lovingly stroked the barrel. Harriet whimpered as he brought it up, the muzzle pointed directly at her.

⸼ FORTY-FOUR

Musa's fingers tightened on Curran's arm and in the dark, the young constable's eyes gleamed. Curran nodded. He had been watching the scenario unfolding before them and knew that reinforcements would not arrive in time.

It had taken all his discipline not to go to Harriet Gordon's aid when she had made her bid for freedom but he relied on the knowledge her captors needed her alive and unhurt in order to retrieve the stones.

Now he was not so sure. They had to act and act fast.

The Webley was a good weapon but to be effective they had to be closer. He glanced at Musa and indicated they needed to move. Fortunately the *ulu* came right up to the campsite. They could be within ten yards and not be seen.

The noise and distraction from Paar and the Burmese man allowed Curran the opportunity for some whispered instructions to Musa, and on Curran's signal, they crept forward, taking up positions on opposite sides of the camp.

🎐 FORTY-FIVE

Harriet squeezed her eyes shut, certain now that she would die but the shot didn't come. Her breath coming in short, frantic gasps, she opened her eyes again. She blinked. The revolver was not aimed at her but at the man who stood behind her.

Paar had seen it too. "What are you doing?" His voice wavered with incredulity.

"Unfortunately, Mrs. Gordon needs to stay alive but you, alas, are an encumbrance."

"But . . . you can't kill me . . . I . . ."

"Zaw!" Foster barked the order and the man complied without hesitation. Paar struggled in the man's grip, protesting and whimpering as Zaw pushed him to his knees on the other side of Lawson. All his bravado gone, weeping and crying out in Dutch, Paar stared down into his grave, the grave he had dug.

John Lawson looked up. In the light of the fire, his face seemed calm and composed.

"Is this how it ends?" he inquired.

"You're no fool, Lawson. You knew this would be how it ended for you," Foster replied.

Foster turned to Harriet. "As for you, Mrs. Gordon. We need you alive to secure the return of the rubies. In a moment, we will be returning to that boat for a gentle moonlight sail around to

Changi Beach, where your policeman friend will be waiting. Rubies and a sapphire for you. Simple."

"And then?" Harriet ventured.

Foster glanced at Viktoria. "Viki and I have a boat waiting offshore to take us to pastures new." He swung his attention back to the two men. "Stop that pathetic gibbering, Paar, or I will let Zaw slit your—"

A single gunshot rang out into the night and Zaw gave a gurgle before toppling forward into the freshly dug grave. For a moment the reverberation of the shot hung on the air before the jungle came alive with the shrieks of monkeys and the crash of undergrowth as the animals charged through the trees above them.

A second shot rang out from a different direction. Foster began firing wildly into the dark. Paar screamed and went down, curling up in a fetal position, still screaming.

Harriet kicked herself backward until her back was against a tree as two men in blessed, familiar khaki, came into the circle of light. One tall, hatless Englishman and a slightly built Malay constable. Viktoria turned to run only to be brought up short by the constable. His size belied his strength and she struggled ineffectually in his arms as Kent turned and, moving with surprising speed for a large man, ran to the boat. The boat's owner had already begun to push the vessel out into the water. Whatever Foster had paid him, it did not include the possibility of death.

Curran reached Foster with the ease of a born athlete, bringing him down with what Julian would applaud as the perfect rugby tackle. They fell into the river, locked together as the boat drifted away into the center of the river, its owner already hard at work with a paddle to escape the scene.

Even with the waning moon now high, Harriet found it hard to make out the two figures thrashing in the shallows. Foster had size and weight but Curran was younger and fitter and it was Curran who rose from the river, like some sort of marine spirit, throwing back his head, sending sprays of water that sparkled in the moonlight as he hauled Kent to his feet, his arm twisted behind his back. Kent sagged at the knees, coughing and vomiting water.

Through all of this Paar lay curled up on the ground, his hands over his head, gibbering like a small, frightened child while Viktoria cursed and swore, kicking futilely at the constable who held her.

When Kent and Viktoria had been secured, Curran turned to look over the two wounded men, his service revolver still tightly clenched in his hand. For all his moans and cries, it looked like Paar had sustained only a flesh wound to the upper part of his right arm. Curran spared him little sympathy and trussed him up with the others. The three conspirators sat with their backs to the *atap* hut. Soaked and shivering, Kent glared at Curran, and Paar still sniveled. Only Viktoria Van Gelder held her chin high.

Lawson lay on the ground beside the grave, unmoving. Curran held up the lantern and crouched beside him. Lawson moved his head and groaned and Curran laid a hand on the man's shoulder. The grim look on Curran's face as he rose to his feet, confirmed Harriet's worst fears. Somewhere in the melee, John Lawson had sustained a bullet wound.

Leaving Lawson, Curran finally turned to Harriet, crouching down before her, flicking a lock of wet hair out of his eyes. A smile caught at the corners of his mouth.

"My dear Mrs. Gordon," he said. "That was a most unladylike act to perpetrate on a man. Remind me never to tangle with a suffragette." The smile faded and he reached out, lightly brushing her cheek with his forefinger. She leaned her head against his chest and his arms circled her. For a long moment, time stood still and she knew she was safe.

"You're wet," she murmured.

He chuckled. "And you don't smell very nice."

She sat up and directed her fist at his chest. "That is a rude thing to say, Inspector Curran."

His lips quirked. "Tact was never my strong point." He let her go and the policeman returned. "Turn around and let's see to those ropes."

She heard the click of a pocketknife and the blessed relief of freed hands. She shook her fingers and whimpered, as agonizing pins and needles marked the return of blood. Curran took her hands, chafing them in his own.

Lawson groaned and Curran released her hands, turning to look at the injured man.

"I know you've been through a lot but can you have a look at Lawson? I think he took one of the stray shots."

As pleasant as it was to be sitting with her back against a tree, having her hands held by a handsome man who had just saved her life, Harriet pulled away and scrambled to her feet.

She knelt beside John Lawson, and Curran held up the lantern. The growing stain across the front of John Lawson's shirt gleamed darkly wet in the light and told its own story. Curran was right, Lawson had been hit by one of the stray shots. However, he was conscious and raised his left hand, reaching out to Harriet. She took it, pressing it against her cheek.

"It's all over, John," she said. "We'll get you to a hospital."

"Will?" he gasped, his eyes seeking out Curran.

"He's safe," Curran said gruffly.

Lawson tried to speak again but Harriet put a finger to his lips. "Save your strength. Let me look at that wound."

Curran crouched down beside Harriet and peeled back Lawson's blood-soaked shirt, revealing a pistol wound to the abdomen. Harriet swallowed and her gaze met the policeman's. They both knew a wound like this would most likely be fatal.

"Is there something we can use as a dressing?" Harriet asked.

"Your petticoat?" Curran suggested with a cocked eyebrow.

Harriet indicated the lifeless body of Zaw. "His sarong will do."

She did what she could to stem the bleeding and make the dying man as comfortable as possible and when she was done she sat with his head in her lap.

She looked up at Curran. "What now?"

Curran straightened and looked around at the campsite, illuminated by the fire and the waning moon; at the three prisoners on the ground, bound hand and foot; the dead Burmese and the dying Lawson.

"I need the rest of my men," Curran said. He turned to the constable. "Musa, get back to the police post, bring my men and a stretcher for Mr. Lawson."

The Malay constable snapped smartly to attention and saluted.

Curran waved a hand. "Just go."

Harriet pushed her disordered hair back behind her ears and said with a heavy sigh, "I could really do with a decent cup of tea."

Curran fished in a pocket and held out a battered leather hip flask. He unscrewed the lid.

"Will brandy do?"

Harriet took the flask. "It will do nicely, thank you."

❧ FORTY-SIX

Thursday, 17 March 1910

Curran returned home for a few hours' rest, a bath, a shave and a change of clothing. Foster had managed to land some heavy blows to his ribs and now that the crisis had passed, he ached in every muscle. He found Li An asleep in her chair, curled up like a small, elegant cat, her beautiful hair falling across her face, hiding the terrible scar. With fingers that shook, Curran brushed the dark tresses away and bent and kissed her ravaged cheek.

She awoke with a start, her fingers tightening around the hilt of the knife she always carried.

"It's me," he whispered, taking a step back before she lashed out with the vicious blade.

"Curran! Don't do that," she chided, uncurling from the chair.

She rose to her feet and wound her arms around his neck. It still lacked a few hours to daylight and he could not see her face in the dark but she smelled of frangipani and all that was good. He buried his face in her hair.

"It's over," he mumbled.

"The man with the painted face . . . you have found his killer?"

"I think so, but it can wait till morning. He's not going any-where. I need some sleep now."

She slipped her hand into his and led him into the bedroom. He fell back on the bed and let her pull his boots off, her clever fingers working their magic on his tired, bruised body.

In the daylight, Li An lavished her attention on him, exclaim-ing over his injuries, however superficial, and refusing to let him out of the house without a decent meal. He arrived at South Bridge Road looking, even if he did not feel it, the cool, crisp, efficient police officer he needed to be.

He chose to interview Paar first. Fresh from the shock and horror of realizing that there really was no honor among thieves, the young man babbled out everything he knew, among tearful claims of being misled and expressions of remorse at his part in Visscher's death.

Paar admitted to being seduced by Viktoria Van Gelder and he blamed her for leading him into a life of vice. His role had been bookkeeper to the VOC. The kidnapping of Will and his father and Harriet Gordon had dropped him right into the con-spirators' dark well of deceit and he realized he had to play along or he too would be dead. He had packed his bag in haste, realiz-ing only after he got to the villa that he had forgotten the most important thing, the records of the transactions. He had sus-pected from that moment his life was forfeit.

Curran had little sympathy to spare for the boy's self-loathing and tears. He considered that luring Visscher to his death at the *godown* on Clarke Quay had been particularly reprehensible and despite Paar's protestations that he had no notion that the con-spirators would kill Visscher, it still made him an accessory to murder. He would hang if Curran had his way.

With the information from Paar, Curran turned his attention to Viktoria Van Gelder. Despite her unkempt appearance, she sat back in her chair, her arms crossed. Viktoria was no stranger to authority. She treated it with the contempt she felt it deserved and refused to answer his questions.

It didn't matter. He had enough to hang her or at least send her to prison for a very long time for the kidnappings and attempted murders of John Lawson and Stefan Paar and possibly being an accessory to the murder of Hans Visscher.

"Let's talk about the death of Oswald Newbold," he began, and, to his surprise, provoked a reaction from the woman.

She rose to her feet and slammed her hands down on the table. "I had nothing to do with his murder."

"Are you going to deny you intended to kill him?"

She shrugged. "It made little difference if he lived or died. We had the rubies and most of the profits from the sales of the other stones. We could have left Singapore and it would be too late for Newbold to do anything about it."

"But you didn't have the sapphire," Curran pointed out.

Viktoria turned to a corner of the room and stood facing the wall, her arms wrapped around herself.

"No," she admitted. "We didn't have the sapphire but we knew its hiding place."

She turned back to face him. Swinging her chair around she straddled it like a man, leaning her arms on the chair back. With a weary gesture, she brushed the thick matted hair from her eyes.

"We sent Zaw to retrieve the sapphire that night. That was the conversation Visscher overheard. It didn't matter, Newbold was dead when Zaw arrived and the sapphire was gone."

"But the base of the statue was intact when I found it."

"Zaw replaced it. He is . . . was very careful not to leave unnecessary evidence lying around. You may have discovered that little hiding place, Inspector, but I am guessing you did not check the other statues in Newbold's home. That is where he hid the stones and that is how he smuggled them into Singapore."

Curran nodded. He had already sent word to Clive Strong

that all the statues in the house were to be brought into South Bridge Road.

"So the VOC was composed of Oswald Newbold, you, Viktoria Van Gelder and Nils Cornilissen?"

"Nils? No. Guess again, Inspector."

In the clear light of day, it became clear. "Kent . . . Charles Kent. He was C. The VOC. Viktoria, Oswald and Charles."

"Newbold's little joke because of the Dutch connection." Viktoria's mouth curled in a humorless smile. "This is a plan long in the making, Inspector. Nils comes from a long line of thieves and swindlers. A perfect match for my daughter. I set him up with a reputable business as an antiquities dealer and he had a talent for it—looting the Orient of its treasures made a nice sideline for him. It also made him useful as a fence for certain objects that came into my possession. Newbold thought he was running the operation but the reality was we used him."

"And Cornilissen's brother, the gems dealer?"

"He really does have a brother in the gems industry." She smiled. "Another useful contact."

The reach of this woman stretched far and wide, Curran considered. He thought of the insignia of the VOC—the V really did control the operation with Oswald Newbold and Charles Kent as her creatures.

"And what did you plan to do once you had the last of the stones?"

"Kent and I planned to quietly slip away from Singapore. There are good opportunities in Argentina for enterprising people with our talents. Nils would gradually filter the rubies onto the market and we would get the money. A fine plan until some fool killed Newbold and you and that interfering woman started poking around in our business."

"Tell me about your relationship with Charles Kent."

"What do you think, Curran? If you have done your homework, you will know that Charles Kent is as venal as I."

So Curran had discovered from his contacts in Rangoon. The only other survivor of Newbold's expedition into northern Burma, Kent had been implicated in a massacre of villagers in the newly annexed northern provinces and left the army. He had stayed on in Burma, outwardly respectable but strongly suspected by the authorities of being behind several opium dens and gambling establishments in Rangoon and Mandalay.

Some three years ago he had vanished from Rangoon, only, it seemed, to reappear as Colonel Augustus Foster in Singapore. The real Colonel Foster, a perfectly respectable but little-known explorer, after whom a river had been named, had disappeared on an exploration in Africa some ten years earlier.

"Did Newbold know about your relationship with Kent?"

She shook her head. "As far as Newbold was concerned, Kent was just a friend, nothing more. The two of them were running illegal businesses in Rangoon. Newbold was a thief and a murderer too. The men who did not return from that initial exploration all died at his hand."

Curran pushed back his chair and rose to his feet. "We will talk again, Mrs. Van Gelder."

She looked up at him and for a fleeting moment her face softened. "My husband . . . Van Gelder . . . does he know?"

Curran nodded. "Yes, he knows."

He had released Van Gelder that morning, a sad, broken man. "Not my Viktoria," he had said repeatedly, as if trying to convince himself.

Curran strode out of the room, leaving Viktoria Van Gelder to consider the failure of her plans.

Foster/Kent was another matter. This was personal. He had considered Kent, or Foster as he had known him, a friend and felt the same sense of betrayal as any of Kent's Singapore friends would when the truth came out about his history.

He spent a long moment studying the man in front of him.

Kent bore little resemblance to the dapper member of the

Explorers Club and stalwart of the Singapore Cricket Club. His linen suit was crumpled and stained, his face blurred with graying bristle and he smelled rank. However, he still retained his upright bearing, and the gaze that met Curran's bore no trace of fear . . . or regret.

"VOC," Curran said, "spelled out the letters, Viktoria, Oswald and Charles. How did you know Oswald Newbold?"

"We were at Sandhurst together," Kent replied. "He was an odious little reptile then. What do they say, Curran? Birds of a feather?" He paused, a muscle twitching in his cheek. "Speaking of which, did I ever tell you I knew your father? He was an ensign in the South Sussex when I was with them on the northern frontiers."

Curran's blood ran cold. "My father has nothing to do with this affair," he said stiffly. "He's been dead nearly thirty years."

A humorless smile played around Kent's eyes. "Is he?"

Curran schooled his face to remain neutral, hoping Foster did not notice the betraying muscle in his jaw as he clenched his teeth. He knew the man was trying to disarm him, deflect him from the case in hand, but the calculated little barb had hit home.

Clearing his throat, Curran continued, "According to your military records you were in Rangoon at the time of Newbold's exploration of northern Burma."

A few beads of perspiration shone on Kent's forehead and he fumbled in his pocket, searching for but failing to find a handkerchief.

"Newbold recommended you join the expedition?"

"Yes."

"What happened to Carruthers and the other members of the expedition?"

Kent huffed out a breath. "Do you have a cigarette on you, Curran?"

Curran did not reply. He sat back with his arms folded, waiting for the response.

Kent shrugged. "We knew as soon as we saw the Mogok mines that there was an opportunity too good to miss. The others were an encumbrance we did not need and we ensured they did not return."

"You mean you murdered them?"

Foster shrugged. "Newbold thought he had paid me off in the rubies that we pocketed on that expedition but I the bastard had found that bloody sapphire and was hanging on to it. So, I bided my time. I knew once he had the mine operational, he could not resist pocketing the best stones but he lacked a means to do so. I introduced Viki to him and we came up with the plan to smuggle the rubies out of Burma using her contacts."

"What about his memoirs?"

"Of course I knew it would be a work of fiction, aimed at securing his place in history. It didn't bother me. Charles Kent was dead. When young Carruthers turned up at the club last year, I had a nasty moment. I remembered the lad in Rangoon. Fortunately he didn't recognize me."

Curran held his tongue. Foster didn't need to know that Carruthers had not recognized him because he was not Carruthers. So many lies and so much deceit had wrapped this case in a tangled web.

"You thought he may be interested that you murdered his father?"

Kent shrugged. "Don't think for a minute there are any confessions to be had in what Newbold was writing, Inspector. To all purposes Carruthers's father died of fever and that is what I will swear to. What Newbold's story may have been, we will never know."

"You were the one who told me Carruthers had gone out to Mandalay the night Newbold died."

"I mentioned Newbold's memoirs to Carruthers—thought he might be interested. Suggested he may like to talk to Newbold on Sunday night. It's always useful to have someone else to blame a dead body on. Although, let me get this clear, Curran. At the time I had no way of knowing Newbold was already dead. Zaw's instructions were . . ." He trailed off.

"Were?" Curran prompted.

Kent regarded him for a long moment. "We wanted the sapphire and Zaw can be very persuasive. However, if Newbold proved too hard, there is no doubt that Zaw would have persisted to the end. Believe me, Inspector, Newbold was dead when Zaw arrived. I honestly thought Carruthers had done him in for us."

"How many people have died for these rubies, Foster? I'm losing count. Carruthers's father, the other men on that expedition, Newbold . . ." Curran paused. "Why did the boy Visscher have to die?"

Kent crossed his arms and looked up at the ceiling. "Viki and I were a little indiscreet and it seems the boy overheard us discussing Newbold. Time was running out. The last of the rubies were already at the *godown* and we needed the sapphire. Visscher rightly assumed that Newbold was going to be cut out of the arrangement and went to warn him. I don't know what Newbold would have done with the information. He never got a chance to act on it. Someone else killed him that evening. As for Visscher, Paar had no trouble betraying the boy to us."

"So you deny killing Newbold?"

"I will say this again, Curran. It was not us. We would have been on our way to a comfortable life in Argentina within a few days—with the sapphire. I repeat, Newbold was dead when Zaw got there."

"So, who killed him?"

Kent shrugged. "No idea."

"Let's go back to Visscher. Who killed him?"

A muscle in Foster's cheek twitched and Curran answered for him.

"Zaw?"

With narrowed eyes Curran studied Foster. "Too grand to do your own killing?"

Foster shook his head. "Zaw has been my right-hand man for over twenty years, Curran. Why have a dog and bark yourself? It was quick. The boy didn't suffer. The body was supposed to be washed out to sea but . . ." He waved a dismissive hand and not a flicker of remorse crossed his eyes.

He was responsible for countless deaths in Burma, he had tried to frame the false Carruthers for a murder he didn't commit. He had ordered the murder of Hans Visscher and, like his lover, he was guilty of the attempted murders of John Lawson, Stefan Paar and Harriet Gordon. Charles Kent would hang.

Back in his office, Curran stood by the window. He looked out onto the courtyard below, without seeing the hustle and bustle of the busy police station, and for the first time in many, many years he thought about his father, dead on an obscure battlefield in the Afghan wars, or at least that was what he had been told. What had Kent meant by implying his father might still be alive? He lit a cigarette with hands that shook. It had been a diversion, nothing more. Edward Curran had been dead thirty years and no one, not even a venal murderer like Charles Kent, had the right to resurrect his memory. He owed his father nothing

He stubbed out the unsmoked cigarette and turned his thoughts back to the case. He had to concede that whatever else they may be guilty of, Viktoria Van Gelder, Kent and their accomplices did not seem to be responsible for the brutal attack on Oswald Newbold and his servant. They didn't need to kill Newbold and the way in which he had died suggested a frenzied, emotional attack, not the calm, ruthless efficiency of Zaw.

That left Carruthers/Symes?

He considered that possibility. If the man had really been James Carruthers then, yes, he had a motive—the death of his father, but Symes was merely an agent of the Burmese Ruby Syndicate. He had no reason to kill Newbold. In fact, he would have wanted him alive. If Carruthers was to be believed, Newbold was already dead when he got to the house that night. So somewhere between seven o'clock when Visscher had left and nine o'clock when Carruthers arrived, Newbold had entertained another visitor, one who had not given him time to act on the information Visscher had passed on.

Curran sat down and leaned back in his chair. Lacing his fingers behind his head, he ran through the list of suspects once more and sighed deeply and with genuine regret. He knew who had killed Newbold and possibly why and the knowledge brought him no satisfaction.

❦ FORTY-SEVEN

Harriet lay in her own bed, staring up at the mosquito net, while her fingers pleated the soft material of the clean, linen sheet that covered her. From the kitchens came the apparently tuneless twang of Huo Jin singing Chinese opera. At that moment Harriet considered the atonal screeching, as Julian rudely referred to it, could possibly be the loveliest thing she had ever heard.

She was in her own bed, in her own home. The nightmare that had begun when she accepted a commission to type Sir Oswald Newbold's memoirs, finally over.

After the terrifying end to her ordeal, she remembered very little. A tall figure brandishing a service revolver illuminated by the light of a fire, a horse and a strong arm to lift her down out of the saddle. She touched her cheek as if the memory of the damp khaki uniform and metal buttons pressed against her and the warmth of his body as he carried her into the police post, still lingered.

In the Changi police outpost, someone had brought her tea, Chinese tea, and she had drunk cup after cup. There had been voices, familiar, loving voices and Julian's arms around her. The sight of her brother's anxious face had been the last straw. She had broken down completely, sobbing into his shoulder until she had no more tears to shed.

Euan Mackenzie had given her a cursory inspection. He had been brisk and professional but he had not come for her sake. She saw him bent over the man who had been laid on the table in the center of the police station. John Lawson was still alive and Euan had come to take him to the hospital. She would have to wait.

In the end it had been the police vehicle that had carried her home. Despite the hour, Huo Jin had been waiting, her long graying hair tied loosely at the nape of her neck, and she was wearing a loose gown Harriet had never seen before. There had been more tea, fussing and warm, scented washcloths, a sleeping draught prescribed by Euan and then bed, blissful, lovely, wonderful bed.

She wondered what time it was. Well into the day, she thought, listening to the buzz of insects, the cries of the birds and the chatter of monkeys from the *ulu* behind the house. As if he had sensed her return to consciousness, the door squeaked open and Julian peered around.

"You're awake," he said, his face splitting into a grin. He turned back to address someone outside. She heard the words *tea* and *toast*.

Harriet pulled herself up on her pillows. Every muscle in her body ached. She rubbed her wrists where the bonds had left bruises and red raw marks. Julian crossed to the bed and lifted the mosquito netting away, tying it in a ball above her. He sat down on the edge of the bed and took her right hand in his.

Dark gray circles bagged under his eyes and the lines of strain pulled at his mouth.

"Harriet . . . I thought . . . I would never have forgiven myself . . ."

"I'm fine, Julian. A bit stiff and sore and I badly need a bath. How's Will?"

Julian smiled. "Louisa took him in. Like you, he needs a little rest and love and the distraction of being with other children but he's otherwise unharmed."

"What about Lawson?"

Julian shrugged. "Last I heard he was still holding his own. Euan got him to the hospital and operated straight away, but . . ." His lips tightened. "We don't hold out much hope. He was already in a bad way. Euan had to take his arm off."

Harriet looked away. "Poor man . . . poor Will." She turned back to look at her brother. "Julian, I want Will here. Can you ask Louisa to bring him?"

"But he's better off with Louisa."

She shook her head. "He needs me. That child and I have been through an ordeal and come out the other side. I owe it to him to have him beside me."

Julian considered his sister for a long moment.

"Are you up to it? You're not . . ."

He trailed off and Harriet knew he had been about to say, *You are not trying to bring Thomas back to life?*

He might be right. She squeezed her eyes tightly shut, remembering those long hours with Will and how she would have risked her own life to save him.

The door opened and Huo Jin, familiar again in her black *samfu*, her hair coiled in a neat bun, entered, carrying a tray. Harriet sniffed appreciatively as the scent of fresh toast drifted toward her. Huo Jin, grinning from ear to ear, set the tray down.

"You eat," she said. "I fix you bath. You smell." She clicked her tongue. "Now I have to wash sheets and nightdress. I am old woman. Too much work."

"Thank you," Harriet said. "I'm sorry to be such a nuisance."

With another click of her tongue, Huo Jin went into Harriet's bathroom. The bungalow had a rudimentary water system that allowed the luxury of lukewarm baths but as Harriet had quickly discovered, anything more than lukewarm was not really required.

Julian patted her hand again. "I'll leave you to it," he said. "I'll go and telephone Louisa."

Two hours later Louisa arrived, driving a pony trap with Will sitting beside her. Harriet waited for them on the verandah, sitting in her favorite rattan armchair in a loose peignoir, her still-damp hair unbound and Shashti in her lap. Will jumped down from the trap before Aziz had come out to take the pony from Louisa and help her out.

The boy bounded up the stairs and for a moment Harriet thought—hoped—the child would throw himself at her but long-ingrained English manners prevailed and he came to a halt a foot from her, his hands behind his back. He looked pale beneath his tan and there were dark-blue smudges under his eyes but apart from a few visible scratches and bruises, he appeared to have survived his ordeal quite well.

Harriet smiled and held out her hand to him. "There's room to sit down, Will," she said, squeezing herself along and patting the cushion beside her. To her surprise the boy complied and she handed Shashti to him.

"He's been asking after you," Louisa said as she joined them.

Will looked up from tickling Shashti behind the ears. "I want to go back to school, if that's all right?"

Harriet smiled. "Of course, Will. Your friends will be pleased to see you. I know everyone was very worried." She hailed Aziz and ordered him to escort Will up to Reverend Edwards at the schoolhouse.

She waited until she heard the gate squeak on its hinges. "He'll be better off in the company of his friends and normal routines," she said.

Louisa sighed and folded her hands in her lap. "I took him to see his father on the way here."

"And?"

"Lawson rallied for the boy, but from what Euan tells me it seems doubtful his father will see out the day. I think they both knew it was good-bye."

Harriet looked away, fighting back the tears, not for John
Lawson but for a child who had loved his father and would now
lose him.

Louisa reached over and took her friend's hand. "How are you?"

Harriet composed her features and managed a smile. "I'll be
just fine, Louisa. I'm just a little tired."

Louisa gave a dramatic shiver. "I think you're remarkably
composed."

Harriet glanced at her friend. In Louisa's comfortable middle-
class life, a tardy servant would probably be the worst thing she
would have to confront. Harriet had lost her world when James
and Thomas had died, and, tied up in a dark hut waiting for
death, she had realized that since those terrible days, she had
been merely going through the motions of life. She hadn't been
truly living. For the first time in years, she wanted to live, and in
Will Lawson she had something . . . someone . . . to live for.

Louisa took a genteel sip of her tea and Harriet decided
against trying to voice her thoughts. Louisa would never understand.

"I don't think there is much rest for the wicked, Harriet. Here
is your dashing Inspector Curran, the hero of the hour, by all
accounts."

Harriet glared at her friend as the familiar chestnut horse
came to a halt. "He's not *my* Inspector Curran, dashing or otherwise!" she said under her breath.

Louisa leaned forward. "Not what Euan told me . . ."

Harriet had no opportunity to ask what Euan had told his
wife as Curran, annoyingly crisp, clean and fresh for a man who
had probably not had any sleep in twenty-four hours, took the
steps up to the verandah two at a time and swept off his helmet,
running his hand through dark, damp hair. Harriet caught a
wince of pain but thought better of asking what injuries he had
sustained.

"I came to see how you are, Mrs. Gordon."

Harriet smiled at him. "I am as you find me, Curran. In one piece, on my own verandah, in the company of my friend, enjoying a spot of Darjeeling tea, sadly without the luxury of a lemon. Would you care to join us?"

Curran glanced down at the tea tray with its delicate porcelain and a smile tugged at the corners of his mouth.

"Thank you, but no. I don't have time to stop. I'll need a statement from you—"

"Of course." Harriet gestured at her shorthand notebook and pencil that rested on the arm of the chair. "I was just making notes."

"I won't bother you anymore today. Tomorrow will be fine. Can you come to South Bridge Road about ten in the morning?"

Harriet agreed and asked, "How are our friends faring this afternoon?"

Curran, catching her meaning, smiled. "Annoyed," he said. "No, I would go so far as to say they are livid."

"What will happen to them?"

Curran glanced upward as if the question required considerable thought. "I'm afraid there will be a trial which will involve you." He brought his gaze back to Harriet, a slight smile curving his lips. "But I think you are up to it. I saw what you did to that poor man last night."

Louisa raised her eyebrows and cast a curious glance at Harriet. Heat flooded Harriet's face and she glanced down at her hands, her fingers pleating the fine material of her peignoir.

"Inspector Curran, please . . ."

He smiled. "I'm teasing. Sorry I can't linger. Glad to find you in good spirits and"—he turned to Louisa—"good company."

"I've brought Will back to school," Louisa said. "He's said his farewells to his father—sadly."

All humor vanished from Curran's face and he nodded. "Yes. I think *tragic* is a better descriptor." He gathered himself together. "Good day to you, ladies."

Harriet watched him swing himself with ease into the saddle of the chestnut gelding and ride away.

Robert Curran. They were now bound together by the blood that had been spilled in the last few days and she owed him a debt she didn't think she could ever repay, except with her friendship, if he wanted it.

"So, is it true? Did he really carry you into the Changi police outpost in his arms?" Louisa inquired, fixing Harriet with wide, curious eyes.

Harriet felt another flush of embarrassment rise to her cheeks. "Someone did," she conceded. "It was probably that large constable he had with him."

Louisa's lips pursed in a moue of disappointment. "Oh, come on, Harriet, that's not what Euan said. Oh dear, another interruption."

The gravel on the drive crunched as a *ricksha* turned in. Griff Maddocks jumped down and strolled up the stairs.

"Mr. Maddocks," Harriet said. "What a surprise."

Maddocks bowed low and handed her a bouquet of orchids from behind his back. "Surely not, Mrs. Gordon. I'm a reporter. There must be only one reason why I would be here."

Louisa stood up, bristling like a mother cat. "If it's Harriet's story you want, Griff, you will have to wait. She is not up for visitors today."

Maddocks held up his hands. "I'm jesting, Mrs. Mackenzie. I have my story from Curran. I'm here merely to inquire after Mrs. Gordon's health, as a friend."

Harriet smiled at him. "Thank you, Griff. I'm quite well."

Maddocks tipped his hat. "I'm delighted to hear it." He hesitated as if expecting an invitation to sit down and join them for tea but one glance at Louisa's pursed lips dissuaded him of such a hope. "Now I'm satisfied that you have survived in one piece, I will take my leave and hope that next time I see you it will be in more pleasant circumstances. Perhaps another musical evening, Mrs. Mackenzie?"

"I rather think it will be a long time before I set foot in the Van Wijk again," Louisa said with a theatrical shudder. The two women watched him leave, with a backward wave to them, as the *ricksha* turned into St. Thomas Walk.

"Louisa, I could have invited him for a cup of tea," Harriet reproved.

Louisa turned to look at her. "It starts with a cup of tea . . . Are you blind, my dear? I think he is more than a little sweet on you."

Harriet fussed at the petals of the pretty purple orchid. "You're being ridiculous, Louisa," she said. "We're just friends. Sea journeys tend to do that. And, of course, I'm an interesting story."

Louisa huffed out a laugh. "Curran . . . Maddocks? You will have half the eligible men in Singapore beating a path to your door, Harriet."

Harriet made a pretense of rescuing Shashti from the lacy ruffles of her skirt but in her mind she saw Curran's smile in the firelight and remembered how he had taken her in his arms. She could not imagine the dapper Griff Maddocks, still damp from a fight to the death in the shallows of the river, carrying a half-conscious woman into a police station.

"I don't believe Inspector Curran falls into the category of 'eligible men,' Louisa," she chided, not without regret.

Curran belonged heart and soul to someone else, the mysterious Li An. She saw it in his eyes when he had spoken of her. She would like to meet Li An.

❧ FORTY-EIGHT

Long after Julian and Harriet had retired for the night, they were woken by the sound of furious knocking on the front door. Harriet's heart jumped to her throat as memories of John Lawson and Zaw's intrusion into her house, came flooding back. Julian, wearing his dressing gown, answered the door with a bravado Harriet certainly did not feel as she lingered at the door to her bedroom, ready to flee.

She could hear a hastily exchanged conversation and Julian came hurrying down the corridor.

"Get dressed, Harri. It's Euan's driver. Euan's sent a message to say Lawson won't make it through the night and he has asked to see us."

Harriet pulled on a simple cotton frock and tied her hair loosely at the nape of her neck. She had no time for anything else and was still lacing her boots in the motor vehicle as the driver took to the deserted roads at a breakneck pace.

In the quiet of the Singapore General Hospital, they were directed to a private room, easily found by the constable stationed outside in the corridor. Inside the small room, a single gas lamp cast a warm glow across the man's face but not even that forgiving light could hide imminent death. Harriet had seen it often enough to recognize it in John Lawson's sunken face. His eyes were closed.

The windows stood wide open and a gentle night breeze ruffled Euan Mackenzie's graying hair as he stood at the foot of the bed, contemplating his patient. Mackenzie's gaze was stern and professional. A nurse, crisp and cool in her uniform, waited with her hands folded, in a corner of the room.

"How long?" Harriet asked.

Mac shook his head. "A matter of hours, no more. He asked to see Curran too. I'll go and wait for him. Can I leave you with him?"

Harriet pulled up a chair and sat down, closing her fingers around the man's left hand, which lay outside the coverlet. Where his right arm should be the bedclothes lay flat and undisturbed.

Julian opened the small case he had brought with him in which he carried the sacrament for the visitation of the sick and for last rites. He took out his stole, kissed the embroidered cross and hung the stole around his neck. He took a second chair on the other side of the bed and folded his hands in prayer.

They sat in the silence of the room, listening to the gentle sounds of the tropical night that drifted in through the open window. Within the room, the only sound was the dying man's labored breathing.

Euan returned with Curran, both men slipping quietly into the room. Despite the lateness of the hour, Curran was in uniform, his helmet under his arm. Harriet wondered if he had still been at work.

They nodded to each other.

Lawson's eyes flickered open. "Is Curran here?"

"I am," Curran replied.

John Lawson licked his dry, cracked lips and his fingers tightened on Harriet's. "I don't have long," he said. "And I can't go to meet Annie without making a full confession."

Curran glanced at Julian.

"God has forgiven him. I think he means your sort of confession," Julian said, and relinquished his chair.

Curran took out his notebook and drew up the chair beside the bed. "Go on."

Lawson looked around the room that suddenly felt full of people. "Just Mrs. Gordon, her brother and the policeman," he said.

Mac nodded to the nurse and although she pursed her lips in disapproval, she followed him out of the room in a crackle of starched apron.

Lawson took a shuddering breath and began with a rambling justification of his involvement in the ruby-smuggling venture, adding nothing to what he had already told Harriet of his gambling addiction and Newbold's blackmail. Curran took notes, asking questions when he felt they were needed.

Lawson paused, struggling for breath, and Harriet raised his head, holding a beaker of water to his lips. The man took a few sips and fell back on the pillows.

"You make a good nurse, Mrs. Gordon," Curran said.

"Not my chosen profession," she replied, "but I learned a few things in my time in India."

A professional nurse would have stopped the conversation, claiming the patient was exhausted, but Harriet just placed her hand on Lawson's face, forcing him to look up at her. They had so little time.

"Go on, John, the inspector is waiting."

Lawson swallowed and turned his head to look at Curran. "Write this down, Inspector. I, John Alfred Lawson, hereby confess to the murder of Oswald Newbold." His breath came in ragged, uneven gasps. "I had a meeting with Newbold that night. I thought it was to pay me for the last shipment but when I arrived the man was in a rage. He was going on about treachery and betrayal. I had no idea what he was talking about but he made it clear he saw me as implicated and when I asked for my money he refused. I was desperate, I needed that money to pay the school fees, but he just laughed at me, called me a useless fool." He paused, his eyes closing as his throat worked with emotion and the effort of speaking. "I had my knife with me, the one I use to test the rubber trees. I didn't mean to kill him but he fought back and he wouldn't die . . . He got my knife off me." The man's voice choked and he raised his hand, covering his eyes as if he could still see Newbold lying on the carpet. "So, I picked up the knife he kept on the table in his study."

He struggled for breath, the onlookers waiting in horrified silence as he composed himself.

"I'd never killed a man before. It was horrible." He frowned, his face puckering in distress. "Then his servant appeared at the door. I knew he had recognized me so I chased him out into the kitchen and finished him there. He didn't deserve to die." His head turned on the pillow and his hand lifted toward Harriet. "It shouldn't have been you to find the body, Harriet. I'm so . . ."

"If you're going to apologize again, I will leave," Harriet retorted, but she took the hand he held out for her. "What a damnable mess, John," she said softly.

Lawson turned to look back at Curran. "I returned to the study. His safe was open so I took all the money I could find"—he paused—"and the sapphire. I knew where he kept it, in the base of the statue. That was my payment for everything I had done for that man. I didn't think anyone else knew about it. I was wrong. That's it, Inspector. The rest you know. I'm a thief, a gambler and an adulterer but until that night I'd never killed another man. I deserve to hang," Lawson said in a voice so soft that Harriet hardly made out the words.

The man's eyes closed and the shallow rise and fall of his chest stopped.

But even as Curran leaned forward, Lawson's eyes sprang open. "I can write a deathbed will, can't I?"

Curran looked first at Harriet and then at Julian. "I suppose so. You just need two witnesses."

Lawson took a deep shuddering breath and began to cough, blood bubbling at his lips. Harriet wiped the blood away.

"What do you need, John?"

"The doctor. I need him to be a witness. Curran can write it down and I'll sign it."

Harriet found the doctor waiting in the corridor and admitted him into the room.

Euan stood quietly as John Lawson said in a clear voice, "William needs a loving home. God knows I have been a poor parent for him. My sister-in-law has seven children and only agreed to take him on condition he spend his holidays in the school. That's no life for a child." He turned his head, seeking Harriet. "Harriet, Mrs. Gordon, I am asking you and your brother as good Christians, which I'm not, if you would become William's guardians."

Harriet gasped. "John, do you know what you are asking?"

His fingers tightened on hers. "I know he's not your son, Harriet. He can't replace your son but he likes you and you like him. I know you do. I owe you a debt of deepest gratitude for everything you did for him, when we were—" He closed his eyes as a spasm of pain contorted his face. "I know you would do for him what I have singularly failed. Give him a home with people who love him and will keep him from harm."

Harriet looked across at her brother, the question unspoken between them but perfectly understood. Julian nodded.

Harriet bent her head to hide the tears that sprang into her eyes. "We would be honored to have Will as our ward," she said.

Lawson's breathing had become rapid. He looked at Curran. "Write it in your notebook, as my last will I leave everything to William and appoint Reverend Edwards as trustee of my estate and he and Mrs. Gordon as guardians of my son."

Curran glanced at Harriet. "Do you know what you're agreeing to?" he whispered.

She nodded. "I do and I undertake it of my own free will."

"There's a little money but not much. Write that, Curran,"

Lawson said. His eyes were bright now and he anxiously plucked at the sheets with his hand. "It's a lot to ask . . ."

Harriet placed her hand over his, stilling it. "Rest easy, John. I shall care for William as if he were my Thomas."

Curran looked down at his notebook. "Mackenzie, I think you and I can witness this document."

Lawson barely had the strength to sign his name but the rough document was duly formalized.

"God knows what a court will make of it," Mac said.

Curran shook his head. "It's irregular but perfectly legal."

Lawson fell back on the pillows. "Thank you," he said in a voice that held no strength. His eyes closed. "I think I can go now. Reverend?"

Julian opened the Book of Common Prayer. The words for the ministration of the dying bringing a strange calm to the room, as everyone bowed their heads and Julian administered the last rites.

"*O Almighty God, with Whom do live the spirits of just men made perfect, after they are delivered from their earthly prisons; We humbly commend the soul of this Thy servant, our dear brother, into Thy hands, as into the hands of a faithful Creator, and most merciful Savior; most humbly beseeching Thee that it may be precious in Thy sight . . .*" Julian concluded and looked down at the man who lay still, his eyes closed, his face now untroubled by worldly care.

Mac crossed to the bedside and picked up the man's hand, checking for his pulse. He shook his head. "He's gone. Bad business, Curran."

Curran rose to his feet. "As he has just confessed to murder, better this way than at the end of a rope, Mac."

❧ FORTY-NINE

Friday, 18 March 1910

Curran had a visitor waiting for him in his office the following morning. Carruthers/Symes sat on the bench outside Curran's office, a neat bowler hat resting on his knee. He jumped to his feet as Curran unlocked the door to his office.

"You're very late, Inspector," the man complained.

Curran glared at him. "As I can count the number of hours' sleep I've had in the last forty-eight on the fingers of one hand, I would thank you not to provoke me, Mr. Symes. What can I do for you?"

Symes pushed into the office and set his hat down on the desk. "I've come to collect the rubies," he said. "The syndicate wishes to convey its thanks to you for their safe recovery."

Curran sat down behind his desk and, the fingers of his right hand tapping a soft tattoo on the blotter, he contemplated the agent. Curran had not forgotten, or forgiven, the man's obstruction. If Symes had confided in him at the start of the investigation, the result could have been quite different. Instead the pompous oaf had thought he could solve the mystery of the rubies by himself.

"Apart from the fact the rubies are evidence," he said, "I will be happy to hand them over to you on conclusive proof that they are the rightful property of the Burmese Ruby Syndicate."

Symes blinked at him. "But of course they are . . ."

"But can you prove it?"

"Yes . . . well, of course . . . I'm sure."

"I'll make it simple for you, Symes. These are stones that Newbold secreted away before they were catalogued or whatever it is you do to rubies. The syndicate may, quite justifiably, feel that the stones are their property but as far as I can see they can produce no direct proof that they were in fact mined from syndicate mines in Burma."

Symes straightened. "We can do chemical analysis . . ."

"Not sure that proves anything except they came from the same general area. No, Mr. Symes, the rubies remain in my custody until the trial and after that, in the absence of any evidence to the contrary, His Majesty's grateful government will put them to good use. I am sure the royal regalia requires a new jewel or two."

"This is outrageous," Symes snapped, jumping to his feet with such force the chair fell to the floor with a clatter.

Curran shrugged. "I've work to do. Good day to you, Mr. Symes."

Symes flounced out, slamming the door behind him. Curran smiled at the still-wavering door. Symes had not mentioned the sapphire. He might eventually get back the rubies but the sapphire would indeed go to the government and help replenish His Majesty's coffers.

Curran called for Singh to join him.

"Sergeant, the young police constable at Changi Village, Musa bin Osman. The boy has promise. I would like you to do the paperwork to have him brought to our branch, on a three-month trial."

Singh nodded. "He did well," he agreed. "If that is what he wishes then I concur, sir."

Singh saluted and turned sharply on his heel, almost colliding with Cuscaden. Curran sprang to his feet as the inspector general entered the office and shut the door behind him.

"Sir, what are you . . . can I get you a cup of tea?"

Cuscaden waved a hand, signaling for Curran to sit. "I won't stay. Just wanted to say that was a damned fine job on the rubies and the vases too. Well done."

"Thank you, sir."

Cuscaden's moustache twitched. "But if I read that illegible scrawl that passes for your report correctly, the matter of Sir Oswald Newbold's murder remains unresolved?"

Curran's hand closed over the notebook in the pocket of his jacket and he made a decision. "I do not believe Van Gelder or Foster was responsible for the death of Newbold and his servant. I am left with the conclusion that Newbold was murdered by an intruder." He heaved a sigh. "But I will, of course, continue to make enquiries."

Cuscaden tutted. "The coroner won't be pleased. A verdict of death by person or persons unknown is never satisfactory but at least we'll see someone swing for the murder of the young Dutch boy."

"Yes, sir."

"Carry on," Cuscaden said as he turned for the door.

"Sir, before you go . . . I have a proposal I wish to put to you."

Cuscaden listened to Curran's proposal. He harrumphed and tutted but in the end agreed and, shaking his head, left the room.

Curran waited until his superior had left the department before opening his notebook to Lawson's confession. He thought not of Newbold but of the innocent old man who had been in the wrong place. His murderer had died a ghastly death. Justice had been served. Nyan could rest in peace.

He tore the pages from his notebook and under the pretense of lighting his pipe, he set fire to the pages, dropping them into his rubbish bin.

The world did not need John Lawson's confession, particularly his son, who would live under its shadow for the rest of his life. He took a deep draught on the tobacco. Those who had been present to hear it would keep their peace, of that he could be certain.

↬ FIFTY

Harriet sat on the verandah of St. Thomas House, watching the rain fall on the leaves of the mango tree and letting her fingers play with the soft, sleeping head of the drowsing, purring kitten. The school gate squeaked and Julian, holding an umbrella large enough to cover both himself and William Lawson, came hurrying around the side of the house.

They dashed up the front steps and stopped in the shelter of the verandah. Julian shook out the umbrella and closed it, propping it against the rail.

"Are you wet, Will?" Harriet asked as the boy came forward and took the dozing Shashti from her lap.

The boy shook his head, snuggling the little cat up against his chin. Harriet looked up and caught Julian's eye. Julian shook his head in silent answer to her question. Harriet swallowed. As agreed, it fell to her to break the news to the boy.

"Do be a dear and see if you can rustle us up some tea," Harriet said to her brother.

"Are you sure . . . ?" Julian began uncertainly.

"Yes, quite sure."

Alone with the boy, she indicated the seat beside her. "Will," she began when he had sat down, "it's about your father . . ."

"He's dead, isn't he?" Will said in a small, flat voice.

"Yes, he died this morning."

Will cuddled Shashti tighter and the kitten let out a protesting mew.

"Reverend Edwards and I were with him," Harriet said. "There was nothing the doctors could do."

The boy bit his lip and his eyes welled with tears.

"It's all right to cry," Harriet said, wishing he would. "I don't believe in any of this stiff-upper-lip nonsense and it's only me and Shashti to see."

Will's rigid shoulders slumped and he looked up at her, the unshed tears brimming over and rolling down his cheeks. "Is it true what the other boys are saying? Was Papa a bad man?"

Of course, he would have to know one day but for now the fact that his father was a double murderer would be too much to bear. "Your father did some very foolish things, Will, but he did them out of love for you and your mother. He wanted what was best for you."

Will's head drooped and a large tear splashed onto Shashti's brindled coat. Harriet slipped her arm around the unresisting child and drew him in to her. He crumpled, burying his face in her lap. She stroked his head as his shoulders heaved.

"I s'pose," Will said at last in a voice muffled by Harriet's skirt, "I'll have to go to England now and live with Aunt Catherine."

"No," said Harriet. "That is, not unless you want to. How would it be if you came to live here with me and Reverend Edwards?"

Will raised his head and sat up. "Live at the school?"

"No, I mean live here at St. Thomas House with us and Shashti and Huo Jin and Lokman and Aziz . . . It's not quite the same as a normal family but we would like to have you, and"—she hesitated, gathering her courage—"it is what your papa wanted."

Will gave a hiccup and threw his arms around her waist, pressing his head against her stays.

"And I wouldn't ever have to go to England?"

There was no money to send him to school in England, Harriet thought grimly. As it was, Julian had already pleaded a case of dire necessity to the school governors to grant Will a scholarship to stay on at St. Thomas. Any schooling beyond the age of eleven would have to be done through another local school but they would cross that bridge when they came to it.

She heard Julian's footsteps. "Here I come with the tea," he said, rather too loudly.

Will sat up and Harriet passed him her clean handkerchief. He wiped his nose and eyes and by the time Julian stepped out onto the verandah, Will was sitting bolt upright, his face flushed and tearstained but otherwise calm.

Julian cast a quick glance at Harriet. "How do you like your tea, Will?"

"With sugar, please," the boy said. He looked up at Julian. "Is it true what Mrs. Gordon said? That I can live here with you?"

Julian nodded. "Yes, quite true, young man. I spoke with the school governors this morning and they have approved it. You'll be a day student."

Harriet saw the quick tightening of Julian's lips. John Lawson's estate would barely provide enough money to supplement the household costs. She would have to look for some paying clients, preferably ones who didn't get themselves killed within twenty-four hours of their acquaintance.

A now-familiar horse turned in through the gate and Harriet waved to Robert Curran as he dismounted. Aziz came running out to take the horse and Curran joined them on the verandah, dripping water around his boots as he took off his rain slicker and hat.

"I always seem to arrive in a rainstorm," he complained, running a hand through his hair.

"You do insist on arriving on horseback," Harriet pointed out.

Curran pulled a face. "I told you, I despise that motor vehicle."

Harriet smiled. "I rather like them. I must ask your Constable Tan how fast it goes. Huo Jin, another cup, please. Inspector Curran, you will join us for tea?"

Before she went on her errand, Huo Jin hesitated, her gaze on the boy.

"It true what the *tuan* says? Young master Will coming to live here? Long time since children in this house," she said.

Will looked up at Harriet.

"Huo Jin, why don't you take Will and show him his room?" Harriet suggested.

She waited until Huo Jin and Will had disappeared into the house, the unexpected sound of her normally surly servant's happy chatter fading away.

"Someone is pleased with the new arrangement," Julian said. "Who would have thought it?"

"Inspector Curran, tea to your preference, black, one sugar?" Harriet inquired, appropriating Julian's cup.

Curran smiled. "We've obviously spent far too much time in each other's company, Mrs. Gordon. Thank you, that is perfect." He took the cup. "Lawson's funeral will be tomorrow. You may like to know that I will be recommending to the coroner that Newbold's death and that of his servant were brought about by person or persons unknown."

Harriet stared at him. "But . . ."

Curran studiously stirred his tea. "Justice for Newbold and Nyan has been served. As far as I am concerned I heard nothing in that room except the feverish ravings of a dying man. Hardly evidential."

Julian glanced at his sister and cleared his throat. "If I were to be asked, Inspector, I would have to concur, and anything said by Lawson to me in his dying moments will have the seal of the confessional. Harriet?"

"The man was delirious, out of his mind with pain and grief," she said, adding, "How will you handle the newspapers?"

"Maddocks has the much bigger story about Kent and the VOC to keep him and his readers amused." Curran took a sip of the tea and hefted a sigh. "How did the boy take it?"

Harriet shrugged. "As you would expect, but he does seem rather pleased with the idea of living here, with us." She glanced at Julian.

"I wouldn't want to live with my headmaster," Julian said.

"Or me," agreed Curran. "Terrifying man. His name was Ivor Bulley."

"Really?" Harriet asked.

"On my honor," Curran said. "Do you mind me asking about the finances?"

Julian set his cup down. "I've been to see the lawyers. Clive Strong—do you know him? It's doubtful Lawson had much saved. There may be a bit of cash after the chattels at the plantation are sold up but nothing more. What he earned for his part in the ruby smuggling he gambled away in Chinatown."

Harriet glanced at her brother. "Julian and I are agreed that as we are Will's legal guardians it's our responsibility to give him the sort of life he deserves."

Julian reached out and put a hand on his sister's arm. "I'm afraid, dear Harriet, you may have to continue with your work as a shorthand typist."

Harriet rolled her eyes. "I shall just hope that my future clients won't prove quite as troublesome as Sir Oswald Newbold." Across the rim of her teacup, her gaze met that of Curran's. His eyebrow quirked.

"I suspect, my dear Mrs. Gordon, that a quiet life is not to your taste," he said, and cleared his throat. "I have a proposition for you. The Detective Branch is in sore need of a competent shorthand typist and I was wondering if you would be interested in such a position?"

Harriet's mouth fell open. "But . . . but . . . I'm a woman," she said.

"Yes, that was Cuscaden's reaction too, but I persuaded him that you were absolutely reliable, thoroughly discreet and not at all squeamish. Three days a week, paid. If that would suit you?"

"Suit me? Oh, Curran . . ." Harriet had to restrain herself from leaping across the tea table to give the man a hug. "You are the answer to a prayer. Three days means I can still put in two days at the school to earn my keep here."

"And no more villainous clients," Julian said. "What a relief!"

"Good. That's settled." Curran stood up. "Start Monday and you will need to provide your own typewriter for the moment, until I can secure a more suitable machine." He turned at the step and looked back at her. "And I warn you, I have atrocious handwriting."

AUTHOR'S NOTE

In 1910 the Straits Settlements comprised three British colonies: Singapore, Malacca and Penang. Four other states on what is now the Malay Peninsula (Selangor, Perak, Negeri Sembilan and Pahang) agreed to form a federation under the protection and administration of the British government. The remaining five Malay states (Johor, Kedah, Kelantan, Perlis, and Terengganu) were also nominally under British "protection" but did not share the common institutions of the federated states. It is a matter of history that independence came after a bitter struggle to Malaya, or Malaysia, as it is now called, in 1963. Singapore separated from Malaysia in 1965.

However, as far as my characters are concerned, that is all in the future and this story is set within the Straits Settlements—specifically the strategically important island of Singapore—in the years before the First World War.

Recreating a colonial Singapore, long since disappeared under a thoroughly modern city, was not possible without access to the National Archives of Singapore. I drew heavily on the digitized back editions of the *Straits Times*. It was in a 1905 edition of the *Straits Times* that I first saw the advertisement that inspired Harriet Gordon. These wonderful newspapers, filled with news of new arrivals, house auctions, sales, typewriter repairs and musical evenings at the Van Wijk Hotel, kept me occupied for hours. The opening of the Anderson Bridge on March 12, 1910, was the highlight of the year and I have used the newspaper account to record that particular scene.

The fun, as always, is blending fact and fiction and I'm happy to report that while the Hotel Van Wijk, famous for its tiffin curries and ice creams (and the Austrian Ladies' brass band), was a very real institution on Stamford Road, it was not, as far as I know, ever staffed by a murderous gang of jewel thieves.

At the time of the story the Straits Settlements Police Force was presided over by the very real Inspector General W. A. "Tim" Cuscaden, who was a great innovator in techniques of investigation. The magnificent Central Police Station on South Bridge Road and the law courts it faced, were, tragically, pulled down in the 1970s and exist only in photographs.

A Straits Settlements Police Force Detective Branch had been formed in the late nineteenth century. However, I confess to being an author and making things up! The Detective Branch as I envision it, including Curran and his staff, is entirely fictional.

Likewise St. Tom's school and staff are also fictional, although schools of this sort existed throughout the colonies with boys (and girls) packed off to boarding schools in England as soon as they turned eleven (or earlier) as I would have been, had my parents remained in Africa. It was unlikely they saw their parents again throughout their entire secondary schooling. In an odd coincidence, however, long after I had named and situated my fictional St. Thomas Church of England Preparatory School for English Boys on River Valley Road, I glanced at a map and there was a real street called St. Thomas Walk running off River Valley Road. It was meant to be.

I also invented the Explorers and Geographers Club but the Singapore Cricket Club, with its magnificent club house on the Padang, is still alive and well.

Batavia, which is mentioned several times, was the capital of the Dutch East Indies (modern Indonesia) and was roughly where modern-day Jakarta is situated. Like the British, Dutch colonization of the area did not end until after World War II.

I have drawn, consciously and unconsciously, on my own father's reminiscences. He served in the British army and was stationed in the Cameron Highlands in Malaysia (or Malaya, as it was then) for some time during the Malayan Emergency of the 1950s. "*Satu empat jalan*" (one for the road) was one of his favorite phrases. At one point in his schooling, Dad had a headmaster called Ivor Bulley. Sometimes truth is stranger than fiction, and poor Mr. Bulley (who was, by all accounts, a very nice man) has finally achieved immortality.

A. M. Stuart

ACKNOWLEDGMENTS

Singapore Sapphire could not have been written without the assistance and encouragement of a number of people, beginning with the ANZA Writers Group, which I belonged to during my three years in Singapore. I want to mention in particular Julie Vellacott, who beta read the final story and provided invaluable feedback.

I would also like to acknowledge my current writers group, the Saturday Ladies Bridge Club (particularly Ebony and Carol, who also beta read *Singapore Sapphire*). As a group they have walked the road with me and have been there to ply me with tea and sympathy during Harriet's long journey to publication.

Many friends have helped along the way, providing beta reads, information and general encouragement, and I would like to mention in particular Michelle, Kandy, Carla and Ryan.

A huge thank-you to my agent, Kevan Lyon, and my Berkley editor, Michelle Vega, who believed in Harriet!

Finally, and in no way least, my husband, David, to whom this book is dedicated. I am blessed to have a life partner who loves Harriet and Robert and is more than happy to go on research trips with me, critique with his red pen and brainstorm mad plot ideas.

Ready to find
your next great read?

Let us help.

Visit prh.com/nextread